THE SHADOWS ARE HERE

Sarah opened her eyes to the darkness of the ceiling in her bedroom. Gentle footfalls all around. Her mouth opened in a dry, soundless gasp of terror. The shadows whispered, silently, silently. She lifted her head and peeked down at the presence by her hip. The eyes stared back.

Sarah felt a pressure rise within her, a waterfall in deep woods, a wave about to crest, something dark and massive coming closer, shadows all around. By the door, more eyes stared back. Too big, too deep, too much of the night within them.

The shadows filled her bedroom. More eyes all around. The whisper of shadows and nightfall and darkness. She felt them move on the bed beside her. Felt them move against her hip. Tiny, delicate hands snaked out of darkness and she felt them flow around her, grasping her, lifting her up and up without movement as she stared into the eyes that swarmed around her and at last remembered and at last knew.

The shadows had come back. And this time, they had come for her.

NIGHTEYES

Garfield Reeves-Stevens

BANTAM BOOKS
NEW YORK · TORONTO · LONDON · SYDNEY · AUCKLAND

NIGHTEYES

A Bantam Spectra Book / published by arrangement with
Doubleday

PRINTING HISTORY
Doubleday edition published April 1989
Bantam edition / April 1990

FOR
BONNIE HEASLIP,
WHO WOULD PROBABLY BE
THE FIRST TO GO
IF THEY WOULD JUST ASK POLITELY

PART ONE

POPULATIONS

END QUATERNARY EVENT: T—52 DAYS

1

SUNDAY, JULY 8, 18:47 EDT

Sarah Gilmour opened the door of her microwave oven. Her baby was not inside. They had taken it. Again.

"Hold on." Sarah's voice echoed from the hard surfaces of her immaculate kitchen. Terra-cotta tiles on the floor and the work island. Matte-white Corian counters. Gleaming enamel surfaces on the side-by-side refrigerator and upright freezer. All returned her voice without comment.

Sarah laughed, quietly and briefly. She shut the microwave oven door. Of course there was nothing in it. She knew that. The glowing green digital numbers of its display showed the time was 6:47 P.M. The blue display on the solid-state ignition gas oven showed 18:47. The red display on the programmable coffee maker showed 6:47. The radio, 6:47. Steven hadn't been good for much in the last years of their marriage, but he knew how to set all the clocks to the same time.

She took her hand off the microwave door release latch. She hesitated. One more look? To be sure?

Something moved past her in the kitchen, or perhaps it was a flicker of the fluorescents hidden behind the frosted panels of the greenhouse ceiling or a shadow from the fan over the breakfast table. Sarah ignored it. Nothing, was the thought that came to her.

She pushed the white-enameled lever on the Moen faucet, and cold water splashed out onto the hard white surface of the mirror-stone sink. The roar of it sounded muffled and far away, like a waterfall hidden deep in dark, green woods. A shadow moved behind her. She thought she heard someone calling her name from far away in those woods. A shadow caressed her.

"Baby?" she whispered. Her perfectly modulated teacher's voice sounded fragile. Her third-graders would not have responded. But she was sure she had heard her name.

Sarah pushed down on the tap lever with a half-peeled potato in her left hand. Silence again. At least, no noises out of place or unexpected: a gurgle from the drain, a low hum from the refrigerator's compressor, soft footfalls dancing all around her on the terra-cotta tiles. The sound of shadows.

The potato was the size of a golf ball when the peeler slipped across its slippery surface and sliced into the pad of her left thumb. Sarah watched a thick swelling of dark blood grow, tremble, then slip down toward the sink to be lost in the white shavings of potato. How long have I been peeling this thing? she thought. Since they took my baby, she answered.

Sarah whirled. The peeler clattered against the tiles, sliding to a stop against the supporting cabinets of the work island. The ball of potato rolled along the white counter, stopping just before it would have nudged the coffee maker. The red display on the coffee maker showed 6:12. The radio showed, 6:14. The gas oven showed 18:18. The microwave, 6:22. Jumping like a broken movie.

"Who's there?" Not even Ms. Laskey's first-graders would have paid attention to her voice that time. But the shadows froze.

Sarah squinted as she stared at the door leading to the hallway. Everything seemed so far away. The cry of her baby. The silent shadow in the doorway. The last long golden light from the setting Connecticut sun shone directly in through the south-facing windows over the sink and through the sliding glass doors by the table. A fluorescent glare washed from the overhead fixtures, but she could barely see in the dim shadows.

"Smokey Joe?" she asked, or perhaps thought.

The cat blinked slowly as it returned her stare, moving its head as if nodding and agreeing.

"You stupid cat," Sarah said, voice back to normal. She

walked toward it, ignoring the drips of blood that fell from her thumb to splash gently on the tiles.

She bent down to ruffle the mottled gray fur on the cat's head. He walked away at the last moment, and her hand glanced fleetingly over his tail, soft as a shadow.

"There's no food out, you know," Sarah said, abruptly feeling as foolish speaking to Smokey Joe as she had felt when she caught herself searching in the microwave for her . . .

"Oh, God, no," Sarah cried in her kitchen. Skittering feet scraped against the tiles in surprise. Her fist slammed against the microwave oven release latch. The door sprang open. Empty.

"Don't take my baby," Sarah sobbed. Tears ran down her face, fell, and mixed with the few moist spots of her blood. "Not again." She ran out of the kitchen into the hallway, braced herself against the far wall and spun to look back into the kitchen.

Smokey Joe sat on the counter by the sink. His eyes were large and calm and unblinking. Just as they had been thirty years ago when he had been alive.

"Not again," Sarah sobbed, and this time no one would have responded.

Smokey Joe *smiled* at her.

She screamed and ran into the living room to start the search again.

"Mom?"

Wendy Gilmour stood in the entranceway to the living room, poised on the balls of her feet, ready to run. She felt awkward, somehow embarrassed at wearing nothing more than her bathing suit and seeing her mother hunched over that way.

"Mother!"

Surprise changed to concern as she stepped into the living room, letting her bare foot sink into the thick, springy tufts of the Sarough rug. Her swimsuit still felt inappropriate. Especially this one, the negligible two-piece she had been too chicken to wear at the aftergrad pool party, despite the teasing encouragement of her girlfriends. Why should I waste it on high school boys? Wendy had teased back, but the truth of it was, she had been nervous about the reaction her friends had said the suit would provoke in the boys, just as she was nervous about stepping into her mother's living room. She was only sixteen.

Wendy wished she had left the towel around her shoulders when she had come in from the pool, but the sunburn on her back was too painful even for the minimal pressure of soft terry. It was unlike her to fall asleep that way. She put her small bottle of Presun SPF 15 on the smoked-glass top of the brass-trimmed side table, then stepped carefully over the debris spread across the rug.

As she approached her mother, Wendy's concern slowly turned to anger. She saw fractured cobs of multicolored maize from the Thanksgiving centerpiece. The box of Christmas candles and holders had been emptied. Her mother had taken everything out of the antique pine blanket box and scattered it all over the room.

"How could you?" Sadness tempered the anger in her voice as she knelt beside her mother. The rug bristled against her bare knees. She reached out a hand to touch her mother's shoulder. Gently. Sarah Gilmour screamed as if she had been stabbed.

Wendy jerked back in surprise, falling against a misplaced sofa cushion balanced against the coffee table. Sarah rolled into a crouching position. Eye makeup had streaked down her right cheek. Her short black hair had sprayed out as it did when she slept on it. Her eyes were red and swollen. Her upper lip glistened from her running nose.

"Why, Mother?" Anger filled Wendy. Her mother had been so good for the past year. Not a drink. Not a drop. Their weekends together had almost become enjoyable.

"My baby," Sarah sobbed.

Wendy refused to play that game. "I'm not your baby anymore, Mother." She braced herself against the coffee table and stood up, snapping at her suit to pull it higher up her hips, abruptly changing her mind about her near nakedness, feeling defiant, saying to her mother that she was an adult now.

"They've taken my baby," Sarah said. Her voice was hollow, her skin dead pale.

Wendy opened her mouth to say something cruel, then stopped. This was not part of her mother's usual routine when she had been drinking before.

"What do you mean? What's been taken?"

Sarah erupted. "My baby, my baby, my baby!" She stumbled

against a box of Christmas ornaments as she frantically scrambled to her feet, sending small reflective globes spinning across the floor. Her voice was liquid with anguish. "I've looked *everywhere! Everywhere!*" Her trembling hands encompassed the living room. "In the sofa, the pine box, the hall cupboard, the rug, the oven, the—"

"Stop it!" Wendy could feel the tears starting in her own eyes. Not just anger now, but fear. "You don't *have* a baby!"

Sarah's face twisted in inarticulate rage. She stammered for a moment, hands flapping, reaching, trying to grasp a ghost, a shadow. "Then what's that!" she demanded. "Who keeps calling me?"

Wendy's voice climbed to match her mother's screams. "Nobody's calling you! What's what?"

Sarah's face went blank, rage exchanged for acquiescence. Her arms moved slowly to her sides. Wendy felt a sudden chill. How could she deal with this? Her mother was behaving like a switch had been thrown.

"Who's calling you, Mother?" Wendy asked, subdued.

Sarah's expression didn't change. Except for the look in her eyes: something within her was struggling to get out. She lifted a hand, slowly, languidly, and folded her fingers so that only one pointed away, past Wendy, into the hall.

"That," Sarah said, and Wendy heard the word as if it were peaceful and sad and distant all at the same time.

Wendy looked at her mother, looked at her mother's pointing finger, then slowly turned her head to follow its guidance, its warning, to see what waited in the hallway. And the shadows took her.

Sarah rocked on her knees in the living room, the faint melody of a childhood song rasping in her labored breathing. The Christmas ornaments were assembled before her on the rug. Red and gold and green and shiny. Sarah looked at them all, saw her own reflections multiplied within them, delicate miniatures, distorted within the curves of their surfaces, and sang to them. Row after row of her precious babies. The shadows moved through the other rooms and hallways of Sarah's house, leaving her to her task undisturbed. Even by Wendy's harrowing cries, which occasionally rose above the high-pitched hums and electric crackling that echoed off the hard tiles of the kitchen.

Sarah traced her fingers over the reflections in the Christmas balls. They were becoming dim. Almost night. Soft footfalls came down the hallway and into the living room. The reflections were gone from the ornaments. Sarah froze, stopped breathing and rocking as the footfalls approached behind her, disappearing as she sensed them move onto the soft, thick, silent rug. She turned.

Smokey Joe was back, staring at her silently.

Sarah gazed into the cat's eyes as she had so often when she had been a child, trying to understand what lay behind them, what thoughts they held.

"Time for dinner?" Sarah asked. She pulled herself awkwardly to her feet, feeling pins and needles as blood returned to her muscles and nerves.

"I'm getting old, Smokes," she explained to the cat as she leaned against the arm of the couch, wiggling her toes and tapping her feet as sensation returned. "I spend five minutes kneeling on the floor, and it feels like I've been there for hours."

She took a step forward and heard a thick crunching as she crushed an ornament into the rug. She blinked down in surprise. She could barely see it in the half-light remaining just after sunset. "Five minutes . . . ," she whispered, thinking that perhaps it had been longer.

Smokey Joe was in front of her, as clear and as distinct in the darkness as in the sun-filled days of her childhood when she had played with him in the fields behind her parents' house, catching butterflies, stalking crickets, lying peacefully in the sun as he told her stories. She paused again, feeling that a mistake had been made. What was the time on the microwave? she wondered.

Sarah stepped quickly into the hall. Smokey Joe moved away from her as gently as a breeze. She stopped in the hall, to the left the stairway leading upstairs, to the right the kitchen. Smokey Joe was beside her. She stared into his eyes. "Right," she agreed, "dinnertime." She turned to the kitchen.

The brilliant lights were on there, and a long shadow stretched down the hallway. Sarah followed the flow of it as she traced it back to the form that cast it. It was a girl. A very familiar-looking girl, standing upright in a tiny two-piece bathing suit.

Sarah studied the girl intently. The girl's eyes were opened wide. Her mouth moved to say a two-syllable word over and over, and one arm pulled free of all the hands that held her motionless and reached out to Sarah from the brilliance of the kitchen to the darkness of the hall.

"Speak up," Sarah said to the girl, but she was too far away and her voice didn't carry.

The girl's arm was withdrawn, and her form began to rotate sideways. Sarah peered to see how the trick was done, but the glaring light from the kitchen made the contrast too great and all the details indistinct. She knew there was a good reason for what she was seeing though, and so she felt calm and happy.

Smokey Joe called to her. She looked at him. "Of course," she said, calm and happy. "No dinner tonight. Bedtime."

Sarah turned to the left, stepped to the staircase, glanced back once at the kitchen door. The girl was gone, replaced by two tiny dark shadows that fluttered to the floor like falling leaves. Sarah studied them for a moment. A very tiny swimsuit, she decided, then looked away, calm and happy.

Smokey Joe stared at her from the top of the stairs. She followed him. Smokey Joe stared at her from the corner of her bedroom. She settled into bed, pulling the Bill Blass duvet over her clothes and tucking it around her face to protect her ears from the snapping, sparking, liquid sounds from the kitchen. And the screams.

She patted the bed beside her and called the cat. Smiled and was calm and happy as she felt him land upon the bed, knead the duvet, and settle in against her hip. The screams in the kitchen were becoming sobs. The shadows were almost finished.

Sarah peeked out from the comforting goose down nest around her head and saw Smokey Joe's large unblinking eyes staring back at her.

"Good boy," she whispered. Then laid back and closed her eyes.

Memories came to her then. Calm and happy memories: Smokey Joe's eyes as he intently tracked ants through the tall summer grass, hunted the string that Sarah draped across her toy box and pulled away just as he leaped. She had had a happy childhood. A calm childhood. Smokey Joe had been a good and loving companion. And she remembered how she had cried when her father had phoned her at university to tell her that good old Smokey Joe had finally and peacefully died at the ripe old age of seventeen, twenty years ago.

Sarah heard the scraping sound from her bedroom door as it swung slowly open. The cat coming in? she thought in confusion.

She felt Smokey Joe shift against her on the bed.

She heard Smokey Joe pad across the bedroom floor to stand beside her.

She remembered how she had cried when he had died twenty years ago.

Sarah opened her eyes to the darkness of the ceiling in her bedroom. Gentle footfalls all around. Her mouth opened in a dry, soundless gasp of terror. The shadows whispered, silently, silently. She lifted her head and peeked down at the presence by her hip. The eyes stared back.

Sarah felt a pressure rise within her, a waterfall in deep woods, a wave about to crest, something dark and massive coming closer, shadows all around. By the door, more eyes stared back. Too big, too deep, too much of the night within them.

The shadows filled her bedroom. More eyes all around. The whisper of shadows and nightfall and darkness. She felt them move on the bed beside her. Felt them move against her hip. Tiny, delicate hands snaked out of darkness and she felt them flow around her, grasping her, lifting her up and up without movement as she stared into the eyes that swarmed around her and at last remembered and at last knew.

The shadows had come back. And this time, they had come for her.

2

"Open up! FBI!"

The Malibu surf crashed in the night behind the beach house, but there was no answer from inside and Special Agent David Vincent felt panic build within him.

"Reese!" He shouted at the closed door, voice breaking in desperation. "Open the goddam door!" Vincent's hand trembled as he tried to bring his .38 to bear on the door's lock. What was happening to him? Where was his backup?

His gun went off, and Vincent jumped as though he hadn't been expecting it. A jagged hole appeared useless inches away from the door handle and lock.

Vincent shifted from one Adidas-clad foot to the other on the pressure-treated wood of the front deck. "Reese?" he called plaintively. Didn't he know there was no more time? Silence from the house.

Vincent slammed his foot against the door beneath the lock. The solid door didn't budge, but the frame cracked and Vincent saw his way in. He would have to work for forty years at his agent's salary to earn enough before taxes to buy a house like this, but the asshole who had renovated the place had upgraded the locks without replacing the original door frames.

Three more desperate kicks and the door, still securely

locked and dead-bolted, fell into the beach house amidst the splinters of its thirty-year-old beach-rotted frame.

Vincent stumbled over the door and crouched in the central foyer, using both hands to hold his gun stiff-armed before him as he scanned his surroundings. The house had been redone in an open plan, and he could see almost all of the ground floor from his position. A red-painted antique metal staircase went upstairs by the kitchen area. An arrangement of white leather furniture clustered around a black freestanding fireplace beside a back wall of floor-to-ceiling glass overlooking the Pacific. The glare of lights in the house prevented him from seeing anything on the deck beyond the windows, but where the shadows from a group of overgrown potted tropical plants cut the reflection, Vincent could make out the pale threads of breakers far at sea, glowing in the soft light of the full moon.

"FBI, goddam you!" he shouted. Still no answer. But Vincent knew he wasn't alone in the house. He knew . . . what?

Vincent moaned. He could feel his lungs aching. That terrible feeling that he couldn't exhale, that his lungs would fill and he would never be able to breathe again, came over him. More panic. More breathlessness. For a moment, as he stood ridiculously exposed in the foyer, he felt a sudden confusion, couldn't even remember who he was or what he was supposed to do next.

Something creaked above him on the second floor. He whirled toward the staircase and caught a sudden image of a man with a gun drawing on him from behind the white leather couch. Vincent's gun jerked in his hands as he fired to save his life and a floor-to-ceiling window explosively blossomed into a cascade of plate glass fragments, taking his reflection with it.

Vincent sobbed. It was a mistake a rookie would make. What was happening to him? The sea wind poured into the house, carrying the sound of the breakers. He felt the fresh air drying the sweat that trickled through his short, cropped red hair. He took a deep breath, concentrated on forcefully exhaling, and slowly, inexplicably felt reason returning.

His hands stopped trembling. Keeping his eyes locked on the point where the staircase disappeared into the ceiling, Vincent flipped his .38 open and snapped his wrist to knock the empty shells free. Before they had hit the pine floor, he had already scooped a speedloader clip from the pocket of his dark blue nylon windbreaker. He slid the six cartridges on the plastic ring into the open cylinder of his gun, then flicked off the holder to join the spent shells clattering on the pine floor.

In less than four seconds he had snapped the cylinder back into position. He crept toward the staircase and took another head-clearing breath of fresh air. The gun was steady and unmoving in his hand. He had overcome the panic. Then he remembered his backup.

Keeping his .38 aimed at the top of the staircase, Vincent thumbed the small microphone pinned to the inside of his windbreaker collar.

"Cy? You out there? Where's my goddam backup?" But even as he whispered those words into his collar, he had a flash of imperfect memory: his partner gasping and slumping in the back of the surveillance van, blank eyes staring, unconscious. Vincent's hand began to shake again as some undefined shape as black as the sea outside moved past the deck and the floor-to-ceiling windows.

Vincent froze as he felt the house vibrate with the shape's movement. He turned to stare out through the beach windows. His gun wavered from the staircase to the deck that overlooked the ocean.

The smell of the sea seemed to diminish, and he noticed with a start that he could no longer see the moonlit breakers out on the water. Clouds? he wondered. Then he realized that the shape he had seen from the corner of his eye had not passed by the deck and the windows. It was still there, blocking the view from the entire back of the house.

"Dear God," Vincent whispered as his eyes struggled to make out details past the glare of the interior lights. The vibration grew, passing through the floor, through him, and into his gun. His hand began to sweat and he felt his grip on the weapon loosening.

Something moved above him. He jerked his head to the top of the staircase. Nothing. But he heard the sound again. Above him.

Gooseflesh churning across his back and neck, Vincent looked *up*. Above him, to the ceiling.

Above the vibration of the darkness, above the crash of the waves, David Vincent's scream of horror erupted loud and pure and clear, and was itself drowned out only by the sound of two of the six bullets in his newly loaded gun firing straight up into the shadows. But they weren't enough.

In the brilliantly lit beach house, the shadows swarmed over him. Vincent jerked back and forth, waving and flailing against his attackers as if he had stumbled into a long, dark tunnel of spider webs. He screamed again and stumbled backward, falling across a heavy black glazed pot holding an eight-foot ficus. The shadows closed in. He tried to raise his gun but felt it burning in his hand, felt it slipping out of his grasp in a sudden flood of sweat.

The vibration filled him. He felt the gun expand and burn and disappear from his hand as the light in the house coalesced into a gleaming shaft that floated toward his eyes, narrowing and focusing and coming closer and closer until everything before him was swept up into its brilliance as it brushed his forehead.

He felt the light explode within him. Felt his skin pulled back from his twitching muscles. Felt himself tumble backward without limit, passing through the wall and floor and ground itself. He opened his mouth to scream one last time as death approached, but the sound he heard was the muffled explosion of ammunition. Four explosions.

The shaft of light instantly withdrew from him, and he felt himself pitch forward to collapse on the pine floor, skin and muscles and life intact.

He retched up the coffee and donuts he had had for dinner in the surveillance van. The searing acid taste almost obscured the smell of heat and charred wood and gunsmoke from somewhere nearby.

Vincent flopped on the floor, without the strength to lift himself. He slowly decided he was going to faint as his eyesight flickered from light to dark, shadow to brilliance, until he realized that the pattern was caused by someone passing between him and the lights. No, he thought, more than someone. There were several of them, carrying something, moving back and forth, down the stairs and out to the deck, the lights splashing through their running legs like sunlight strobing through trees on the side of a forest road.

Vincent tried to lift his head to identify the people in the house, but his body belonged to someone else. He lay still, cheek flattened against the cool pine floor beside his vomit, with no more strength left to open his eyes. Waiting patiently for the release of blackness, he perceived faint sounds through the smooth pine floor beneath his ear, a slow steady vibration mixed in with an irregular collection of gentle thumps and bumps like scampering footfalls, like the sounds of shadows, like the thing on the ceiling, he thought.

Swiftly the footfalls faded. Imperceptibly the vibration stole away. And as David Vincent finally surrendered to the air and light that had been used against him, he could hear the rising call of sirens above the crashing of the midnight moonlit surf and surprised himself by feeling calm and happy.

MONDAY, JULY 9, 02:47 PDT

"It's getting too complicated."

"I beg your pardon, sir?"

Special Agent in Charge Edmond Gardiner shook his head at the junior agent who stood beside him, and continued to watch the ordered commotion that surrounded the Malibu beach house where a week's worth of careful planning and surveillance had just been compromised. Six portable spotlights froze the house in eerie blue brilliance; and the two dozen agents who swarmed around in that pool of light, with their ID's bouncing from their necks like amusement-park necklaces and their foot-high reflective FBI letters on the back of their windbreakers smearing with the yellow glare of intense reflection, made Gardiner think of clowns in a circus. Hoover would be spinning in his grave.

"Never mind, son," Gardiner said wearily, though his voice still kept its distinctly clipped and precise tone. "Stay here and wait for Washington to check in." The young agent acknowledged the order and Gardiner walked away from his car by the house, past the ragged line of FBI vehicles, CHP cars with their roof lights flashing blue and white, and special service vehicles, toward the ambulance parked down the road by the now useless surveillance van.

The business of the FBI *was* getting too complicated, Gardiner thought as he marched along the road, moving with the bearing of a career military officer. The cool sea wind swirled sand over the asphalt, and the crunch of it beneath his perfectly polished black leather oxfords made him think of Korea, the long marches, and the same frustration of not being allowed to win. It was a sign of age, he warned himself, but he could not help feeling that he missed the old days.

Gardiner was three years away from retirement yet remained as lean and as fit as the day he had joined the bureau thirty years earlier. The fringe of hair he had left was white now, but still closely trimmed, and his suits were still dark and crisply pressed, his shirts still white, and his ties dignified and subdued. He watched three agents jog past him toward the house and shook his head in sadness for the passing of time. The new FBI uniforms seemed to be baseball caps, running shoes, and jeans. Next thing, Gardiner expected, the agents were going to want a union.

Special Agent David Vincent sat on the deck of the ambulance, slumped against an opened rear door and stared glumly at the shadow he cast on the pavement in the ambulance's interior lights. Beside him, an ambulance medic stood with a small aerosol canister connected to a large mouthpiece. Gardiner recognized it as an asthmatic's inhaler. The medic was offering it to Vincent, but the agent was not interested.

Behind Vincent, in the ambulance, a second medic took blood samples from a figure strapped to a stretcher: Special Agent Cyrus North, still unconscious after having been dragged out of his surveillance van.

Gardiner looked at Vincent with disgust. Even obscured in shadows, the red-haired agent looked like he was coming off a two-week bender. Vincent's head hung listlessly, and he made no acknowledgment of Gardiner's presence. His eyes were ringed, and his thin face haggard, making him look fifty instead of thirty-two. And his shirt was stained with vomit, for God's sake.

Gardiner wanted to strike the man. He was Vincent's commanding officer, yet after everything Vincent and his partner had done that night, Gardiner could only suspend them with pay, write a couple of 290 forms requesting a discipline hearing, and hope for the best.

A short, dark woman appeared beside Gardiner, wearing a standard-issue windbreaker and carrying a metal-covered clipboard. Gardiner jerked around at her sudden presence, then smiled as he recognized Dr. Maria Perez.

"Would you like to go over the preliminary statements?" Perez asked, then walked away along the middle of the road without waiting for a reply.

Gardiner followed the woman. The highway patrol had the beach road blocked a mile in both directions where it joined back to Highway 1, so there was no need to worry about traffic.

"Anything useful?" Gardiner asked, pointing to the clipboard. He was trying to determine what it was about Perez's appearance that seemed different tonight. He finally noticed that she was wearing makeup—something she didn't usually do at work—and decided that she looked even more attractive than usual. Gardiner counted himself lucky that he knew enough not to voice that old-fashioned opinion to a thirty-five-year-old woman like Perez. He would not enjoy losing her company.

"Nothing useful yet," Perez said. "But you looked like you wanted to rip off Vincent's head, so I thought the walk would do you good."

"You know me too well." Gardiner said, wondering if it might be true. Perez was a medical doctor attached to the Los Angeles Field Office and was not technically under his command. Because of that and because of her clinically efficient manner during the times they had worked together in the past, he had no trouble accepting her as an equal within the bureau, even though Hoover would have spun even faster at the thought of a nonwhite woman someday being a member of his elite group of agents.

"I know what you lost here tonight," Perez said with conviction. She looked past Gardiner, toward the beach house. "No sign of Reese, right?"

"Of course not," Gardiner said, trying to hide the anger he felt. He might raise his voice to his junior agents from time to time, but never with Perez. "Vincent went in through the front door without orders and without backup. My grandmother could have made it out past him."

"And you don't expect to find Reese with a sweep through the other houses?" Perez hugged the clipboard to herself, pulling her windbreaker closer to cut the cool wind from the sea. Beneath the jacket, Gardiner saw she was wearing an elegant shimmery blue evening dress. Sunday evenings were not her usual duty hours, he realized, and quite unprofessionally he wondered with whom she had been dining.

"Derek Reese has ten years' experience with the bureau," Gardiner said. "He knows every tactic we can use against him, and if he was staying in that beach house, you can be sure he had already worked out ways to escape."

Perez's eyes widened in interest. "*If* he was staying in the beach house? You don't know?"

"Thanks to Vincent and North, no. Whoever was there had time to clean the place out. Can't tell who was there, or even how many." Gardiner paused and looked back to the house. It was the last of a long, tight row of similar structures running to the south, with a wide stretch of public beach to the north. Supposedly, it was the seldom-used California home of a Hong Kong "investment counselor," though Documents hadn't come to the end of the paper trail that led to its real owners. Whoever's it was, a million-dollar-plus beachfront property was not the sort of place where Gardiner liked to think FBI agents spent their time while on suspension. If Special Agent Derek Reese was innocent, he had shown extremely poor judgment in staying there.

Gardiner stared up at the sky. It was rippled with pale blue ridges of moonlit clouds. Down the coast, he could see the searchlight from an FBI helicopter cut through the night, searching the beach for one lone man. By now, Gardiner knew it was a hopeless effort.

"Do you ever ask yourself what's the use anymore, Doctor?"

"All the time. Fortunately, medical science has a cure." Perez unexpectedly took a hand from her clipboard, reached out, and gently placed it on Gardiner's arm. "Do you dance, Ed?"

Gardiner looked at her in surprise. Her dark eyes smiled at him.

"You know," she went on. "Dinner, big band, dancing?"

Gardiner ran his left thumb along the callused indentation on his left ring finger. It felt hollow, empty. "Not for a long time . . . ," he said, distracted. Overhead, the thrumming of the helicopter increased as it swept back toward the beach house.

Perez looked away from Gardiner's eyes. "When I go dancing," she said softly, "that's when I don't ask myself what's the use anymore." She held her hand on his arm for a moment. "I could write you a prescription." She took her hand away to open the metal cover of her clipboard and reveal her report forms.

"The bottom line on Vincent," she said crisply as she glanced at the forms, angling them so she could read them in the light of an overhead streetlamp, "is that he doesn't remember anything."

Gardiner cleared his throat, wondering what had just happened. "At, ah . . . , at what point does Vincent's selective memory come into play?"

"Just after the check back at one-ten," Perez read from her form as though the entire time they had stood in the beach road, they had been discussing FBI business.

"And backup arrived ten minutes after Vincent and North missed the one-forty check back," Gardiner confirmed, wondering if the moment he thought he had felt had been real or just an old man's delusion.

"Giving us a forty-minute gap in the evening's proceedings," Perez concluded.

Gardiner watched the helicopter's searchlight probe farther north along the beach road. "In forty minutes, Reese could make it to LAX and be on his way anywhere by now."

"Or be hiding out at another beach house just outside the perimeter of the area he knew the backup team would search."

"Going after another agent is like playing chess with yourself," Gardiner said. "Impossible to hide a strategy." He stared at the house in the distance. Through its uncovered windows, he could see the blue flashes of the forensic photographer's camera.

"Looks like they found something worth photographing," he said to Perez. They started walking back toward the house.

When they came to the ambulance again, Gardiner saw that Vincent was no longer there. The attendant treating North inside the ambulance said that two police officers had escorted Vincent back to the beach house.

"Good," Gardiner said as he picked up the pace. "Then they really must have found something to ask him about." Perez had to take three steps to Gardiner's two to keep up.

Special Agent Terry Chandler met Gardiner and the doctor as they entered the house. Chandler's suit was rumpled and his tie hung loosely around his beefy neck. For the past year Gardiner had known that Chandler was one of those agents who was losing the battle. Within six months, Gardiner suspected, Chandler would announce he had taken a job with Westroc or Seldon or some other private security firm. It was a much easier life, Gardiner knew. Right and wrong had nothing to do with it. The company paid your check, so you did what was good for the company. A security officer's duty was always clear.

"We've got it pretty well reconstructed," Chandler said in his throaty smoker's rasp as he led Gardiner and Perez to the staircase. Two Day-Glo yellow strings stretched up from the floor, tracing the trajectories of two bullets that had been found in the ceiling.

Gardiner studied the angle of the strings. "Vincent shot directly above himself?" he asked.

"Looks like it," Chandler said with a shrug. "Maybe heard something upstairs."

Gardiner pointed to the empty window frame overlooking the beach. "And something out on the deck as well?" Three agents were on their knees there, gathering glass fragments.

"Hard to say," Chandler replied. "From the fracture pattern, I'd say four shots did that, and they definitely were fired from the inside out."

"So nobody was returning fire?" Perez asked, holding a pen above a form on her clipboard.

"Actually, Doctor," Chandler answered, "there's no sign that anyone was doing anything. I mean, no sign that anyone at all was here until Vincent broke in."

"All his bullets accounted for?" Gardiner asked.

"More or less. The guy's gun misfired."

"How do you know?" Gardiner asked.

Chandler directed Gardiner and Perez to a small section of the pine floor that had been sectioned off by forensic marker stakes and yellow police-line tape. Chandler pointed at the floor within the boundaries.

"What is that supposed to be?" Gardiner asked. It appeared to be a scorch mark in the same shape as a Smith & Wesson .38 Police Special. He crouched down and studied it closely. The center of the mark, corresponding to the cylinder of a gun, was indented into the floor and Gardiner could see that the wood there was actually charred. A halo of small blackened pits surrounded the gun shape, showing where a flurry of sparks had sprayed out from it.

Gardiner looked up at Chandler. "Did you recover Vincent's gun?" he asked. His voice was tight and controlled.

"Most of it," Chandler said. "That mark is exactly what it seems to be. A scorch mark from Vincent's .38. It got so hot, one round went off in the chamber, three in the cylinder."

Gardiner stood and looked around the room, trying to find some evidence of a gasoline-soaked rag which might have been wrapped around the gun. He looked over at the freestanding fireplace.

"Fireplace is cold," Chandler said when he saw where Gardiner was looking. "I'd say Vincent loaded his own rounds and his workmanship got sloppy. Spilled powder must have ignited when he fired his first shot." He pointed over to the taped outline of a body by a potted ficus tree. A second, smaller area was also marked off. "The gun started out by Vincent after Vincent passed out," Chandler explained. "There's a matching scorch mark over there, so that's probably where the cartridges started flaring up first. The gun obviously got hot enough that the round in the chamber ignited—see the entry hole marked on the baseboard over there?—and the recoil sent the gun over here, where it continued to heat up until the other rounds in the cylinder went off and blew the gun apart." Chandler laughed.

Gardiner stared at the outline of Vincent's body, then looked down at the charred image of the gun by his feet. "I want everyone out," he stated.

Chandler opened his mouth to say something, paused, then croaked, "Yes, sir." He walked off quickly to tell the other agents scattered throughout the house.

"What's wrong?" Perez asked Gardiner when Chandler was out of earshot.

Gardiner looked at her with a grim expression. It was a difficult decision for him. "This is no longer within FBI jurisdiction." His voice stuck on those words as if they were an admission of personal failure.

"Ed?" Perez's eyes creased in puzzlement. "Because a gun exploded?"

Gardiner watched while Chandler waved the three agents off the deck. He heard the waves crashing beyond and the far-off thrum of the searching helicopter.

"Would you like to go dancing with me some night, Doctor?" he asked.

Perez bit her lip and studied Gardiner in silence for a moment. "Maria," she said softly. "And yes, I would."

Gardiner nodded and turned away, and was thankful Maria knew enough not to ask any more questions.

Once the beach house was empty, Chandler directed the placement of police seals on every door and window, and a ring of barricades that would cut the house off from the road and beach. Gardiner watched for a few minutes to be sure the procedures were carried out correctly, then walked over to the four-foot-high wooden fence surrounding an unlit swimming pool. David Vincent leaned against the fence, staring into the dark depths of the smooth water. Two uniformed Highway Patrol officers assigned to watch him, both over six feet tall and straining their uniforms, stood ten feet away, stealing a smoke and observing Vincent cautiously.

Gardiner leaned on the fence beside Vincent.

"What happened in there, David?" It was the cold and calculated voice of a compassionate friend, a voice that had worked for Gardiner many times in the past.

"I don't remember," Vincent said quietly. His voice was slurred, unfocused.

"Do you remember what happened to your gun?"

Vincent shook his head.

"Did Reese ask you to come in?" Gardiner tried. "Did Reese ask you to come in and confuse things so he could get away?"

"Had to help him," Vincent said, struggling to say even that little.

Gardiner felt a sudden surge of excitement and anger. Was Vincent going to confess? "Why did you have to help Reese? Are you working for him? Did he pay you?"

"They got him."

Gardiner grabbed Vincent's shoulder and spun the man around to face him. "*Who* got him?"

Vincent's face was torn with anguish. "I . . . don't . . . remember." He was blubbering like a child.

Regulations or no regulations, Gardiner had hit his limit. He grabbed both of Vincent's shoulders and shook the man. It was like shaking a hysterical five-year-old. No resistance, no response other than wails of torment.

The two watching policemen dropped their cigarettes to the ground. But Perez beat them to Gardiner.

"He's still under the influence," she said to him with a hard, professional edge in her voice.

"Of what?" Gardiner asked angrily. He didn't take his hands off Vincent. "Cocaine? XTC?"

"I don't know," Perez admitted. "We've got blood and urine samples from both North and Vincent. In twenty-four hours we'll know exactly what they've been exposed to. But until then, you're not going to get anything out of him like that."

Gardiner took his hands off Vincent in disgust. "All right, tomorrow, we'll talk about it." He turned to Perez. "I'm sorry, Doctor." A fleeting smile crossed his face. "Maria."

"I'm not saying you're wrong," Perez replied in consolation. "Just that, for right now, it's counterproductive."

Gardiner looked over at the two oversized officers assigned to Vincent and snapped his fingers at them. They double-timed over to take Vincent back into their custody. Gardiner turned to Perez.

"Would you like him in a hospital or is central holding good enough?"

"Hospital for tonight," Perez said with a nod. "With North."

Gardiner gave his orders to the policemen. "Vincent goes into a secure ward. Dr. Perez will admit him. And I don't want him to have any contact with North until after interrogation."

The officers nodded and began to escort Vincent away, one on either side. Gardiner looked up and saw that the helicopter was sweeping back for another try, its searchlight now weaving across the rooftops and the road.

"Hey!" Gardiner suddenly shouted to the officers leading Vincent away. "I don't even want him in the same ambulance as North."

The policemen turned. One of them cupped his hand to his ear to indicate he hadn't heard the command. The helicopter was coming closer and the beat of its rotors grew.

Gardiner jogged forward to catch up with the men. He saw Vincent look up into the sky and start to struggle frantically.

"Hold him!" Gardiner called out, though his voice was lost in the roar of the helicopter. The man who only moments ago had no muscle tone or coordination was about to pull free from two burly police officers.

"What's the matter with you two?" Gardiner snapped as he joined the policemen and grabbed hold of Vincent.

Tried to grab hold of Vincent.

Angel dust, Gardiner thought as Vincent kicked him in the stomach and sent him flying away to land flat on his back on the road. That's the answer.

Gardiner looked up just as the searchlight swept onto him and Vincent and the police officers. He squeezed his eyes shut and twisted his head away in response to the sudden blinding brilliance. And he heard a horrible cry of heart-stopping fear cut through the thunder of the craft overhead.

Gardiner sat up instantly, holding his hands to shield his eyes from the searchlight's glare and see who or what was making the terrible sound.

It was David Vincent. He had gone rigid in the arms of the policemen. His head arched back, staring up to the helicopter, ghost-white in the brilliance except where the shadow of his upward-reaching hand fell across his face.

The scream still tore from his lips. Gardiner had never heard anything like it. Not even in Korea. He saw a stain spreading over the crotch of Vincent's pants. Gardiner looked up.

The helicopter flew on. The disk of its searchlight slipped across the road and disappeared onto the beach. The policemen lay Vincent carefully down on the asphalt. He convulsed into a fetal crouch, gasping and sobbing in hysterical fear.

Gardiner ran to the man. The policemen backed away, holding their hands up to deny responsibility.

Gardiner knelt by Vincent. Grabbed the man by his shoulders.

At Gardiner's touch, Vincent screamed again. Terrifying. Heartrending.

"No more!" he cried. "No more!"

"No more *what,* David?" Gardiner refused to let go. He twisted Vincent's head around, held him up so he see the man's face. "No more *what?*"

Vincent shuddered in Gardiner's arms. The trembling ceased. Far down the beach, the helicopter sped away and the night was again unbroken.

"I don't remember," Vincent whispered, and closed his eyes in peace.

3

MONDAY, JULY 9, 11:10 EDT

Sarah Gilmour sat in her kitchen, a three-week-old Sunday New York *Times* spread out before her, and lit another cigarette. Eight other cigarettes had burned out on the saucer of her coffee cup, forming perfect gray worms of unbroken ash. She set the ninth cigarette down among them, sipped her coffee, cold as breakfast juice, and stared at the front page of the Arts & Leisure section as she had for the past two hours. The time on the microwave oven display flashed EE:EE, EE:EE.

The telephone rang erratically, an electronic warble cut off, turned on, cut off again, like a wire sparking through old insulation. Sarah looked up at the time displays on the coffee maker, the oven, the radio. Red and green and blue, they flashed on and off to tell her that their power had been interrupted. She turned back to the newspaper. Something moved past the back window.

Sarah heard a sound. A foot scraping against the interlocking brick that swept out from the house and encircled the pool. A rich sand color that the landscaper had told her would play so well against the rich greens of the trees that ringed her property. Dark greens. Impenetrable greens. Sarah was all alone now. She knew that. She heard the sound again and did not look up.

A shape moved past the sliding glass doors, a sudden dark
flash between the floral strips of the vertical blinds. Sarah saw
the movement reflected on the polished oak tabletop that
showed between the sections of the newspaper spread across it.
She gripped the arms of the colonial style chair she sat in to
stop her hands from trembling. She broke a nail digging it into
the wood. Something hit the window. She closed her eyes. She
began to rock in time to the pounding on the glass. She was all
alone now and she knew it.

"No more, no more," she prayed to whatever would listen
beyond her closed eyes. "No more, no more, no—"

The glass broke.

Sarah stopped her rocking. Froze to become nothing more
than another piece of furniture, something to be passed over
and ignored. No more, she chanted in her mind as she heard
the lock slip off the sliding door, heard the door open and the
sudden shriek of the burglar alarm as it reacted to the broken
contact in the door frame.

Sarah didn't move. She heard heavy footsteps crunch across
the broken glass, click across the kitchen floor tiles, pause by
her, unmoving, then pass into the hallway. The alarm siren
stopped.

The furrows around Sarah's clenched eyes lessened just a bit.
She recognized that this was different. The footsteps returned.

A hand settled on her shoulder.

She screamed and with a violent twist collapsed onto the
tabletop, sending a spray of cigarette ash to mix with the sudden flood of cold coffee soaking into the newspaper.

"Mrs. Gilmour!" The shouting voice was deep and angry.

Like a computer being reset, Sarah's mind instantly cleared
to admit one complete, distinct, and unexpected thought: A
human voice?

She sat up in the chair, opened her eyes to see the black hand
on her shoulder, a thick gold ring set with diamonds larger
than any she had, a gold Rolex like the one Red Adair wore in
the *Times Magazine* on Sundays.

"Angel . . . ?" she asked, and looked up to see the anger,
the concern, and the relief on the familiar face above her.

Angel Good was six-four, three hundred pounds, and deeply,
proudly African black, and his hand on Sarah Gilmour's shoulder was gentle and caring.

"It's me, Mrs. Gilmour." For Sarah, his smile was like the sun shining. She wasn't alone now.

"Thank you," she told him.

Angel narrowed his eyes, not understanding. "How are you feeling, Mrs. Gilmour?"

Sarah sighed. She wasn't sure.

"Do you know where you are?"

Sarah looked around to confirm her suspicions. "The kitchen."

"Do you know what time it is?"

She looked at the microwave and its flashing time readout. For a moment she trembled. Had something *moved* inside the microwave? "The power must have gone off," she said.

"Do you know what day it is?"

Sarah couldn't see the calendar by the wall phone. She looked at the coffee-soaked paper before her. "Sunday," she said, but it sounded more like a question.

Angel patted Sarah's shoulder. "That's okay," he said kindly. "I'll cancel the alarm, and then we'll make some more coffee."

Sarah watched as Angel walked over to the wall phone. She liked the sound of his Italian-cut black leather jacket as it creaked with his movements. She liked the sheer bulk of his presence. The warmth, the security, the . . . thought came to her again. She didn't know why. He was *human*.

"Thank you," she said again.

Angel smiled and nodded as the dark mass of his hand engulfed the phone receiver. After a few moments of silence, Sarah heard him talk to someone on the phone, giving her name and address and her burglar alarm's system code. Angel identified himself and said he worked for Steven Gilmour and said his name was on the emergency sheet. The alarm was canceled.

"Is Steven with you?" Sarah asked when Angel had hung up. She turned away from him and watched as tiny, cold drops of coffee leaked off the tabletop and dripped onto her leg, soaking into her bathrobe, feeling like the cool prick of a needle. She was suddenly overcome with wanting Steven with her. It was almost sexual, and she was frightened by the strength of it.

"No, he's not," Angel said. She could hear his voice tense again as he watched her expressions and sensed her change of mood. "But I'm going to call him now. Did you know you were having trouble with your phone?"

Sarah rubbed her hand over her thigh, erasing the feeling of the needle prick, making it warm. She wanted Steven. "The power must have gone out," she said.

Angel nodded. "Actually, they're different systems." He put his hand on the wall phone again, almost completely hiding it. "Do you know where Wendy is, Mrs. Gilmour?"

Sarah narrowed her eyes. That was a familiar name. "Who?" she asked.

"Wendy, Mrs. Gilmour. Your daughter."

"My daughter?" That wasn't right.

"Your daughter." Angel's voice remained kind and patient. He had had these conversations before. "Sixteen years old. Lives with her father in the city. Spends every weekend in the summer up here with you."

"But I don't have a daughter."

"Sure you do, Mrs. Gilmour. She's your daughter and Steven's daughter."

"You don't understand," Sarah interrupted. How could she make Angel see what was so obvious? "I can't have a daughter. Not anymore."

"Why's that, Mrs. Gilmour?"

"Because all my babies are gone," she said, and as she voiced that truth, tears poured from her eyes with the unbearable sadness of it. "And I can't find them *anywhere.*"

Angel picked up the receiver and made his call.

MONDAY, JULY 9, 14:19 EDT

Steven Gilmour concentrated on the feel of the road through the sensitive steering wheel, so he wouldn't concentrate on his ex-wife.

The 911 Targa ate the highway between New York and Litchfield like a ravenous beast and the man gave himself to the stirring machinery of it. He had early on realized that there was something innately appealing to him about a car that had its tachometer dead-center in the instrument cluster while the unimportant trifles, like the speedometer, were placed to the side, half hidden behind the steering wheel's spokes. He liked the arrogance of that design decision, the priorities it spoke of in the car's manufacture and capabilities. He savored the precision machine and the control that it gave him. The control especially.

When Gilmour Package and Insert, Ltd. had its first five-hundred-thousand-dollar year-end, Steven Gilmour had his first Porsche. Eight years and three four-million-dollar year-ends later, he still had that Porsche and three others. Control. It was in his business, his cars, and his money. Where it broke down was in his ex-wife.

His illegal Escort chirped from its custom-installed hiding place in the dash, and Steven instantly braked the Porsche to sixty miles an hour. He crested a slight rise in the highway, and the detector squawked again as a patrolman's radar gun scanned him from the side of the road.

Steven kept his speed constant. They had never stopped him for sixty, and this time was no different. The patrolman didn't even turn his head as the black Targa rushed by. Instead, he kept his gun pointed at the top of the rise, waiting for the next unsuspecting car.

Steven drove on. He had driven each of his four Porsches over one hundred and twenty on public roads and still had never lost any points from his license. Control. Caution. They defined him.

He watched in the rearview mirror as the dot of the patrolman waved over a red Camaro which had been accelerating to catch up with the Targa. Steven found the scene satisfying. Not always to the swift, he thought, and for a moment caught his own eyes in the mirror before turning his attention back to the road.

There were a few too many wrinkles around those eyes for his liking. But at thirty-nine, he told himself, they were more a result of winters spent playing all-out tennis under the Hawaiian sun—before this ozone thing—than of age. He ran his fingers across his forehead, along the line of his fair brown hair, stealing another glimpse into the mirror. Still not too bad, he decided, but was glad he had made his appointment for the first transplant plugs in September, after the Italian trade show, when he wouldn't have to talk with clients for a few weeks. Maybe he should have his eyes done at the same time?

He crossed the Connecticut border and effortlessly took the car to ninety, smoothly slipping from one lane to the next to pass the sluggish Chryslers, Fords, and Buicks. Too many station wagons in Connecticut, he thought. His wife's type of car, not his.

Ex-wife, he corrected, feeling the Porsche respond to his slight tap on the accelerator, energetically springing from ninety to one hundred as quickly as it jumped from thirty to forty. Even after four years of divorce, he still had to remind himself. Ex-wife. *Ex*-wife.

He remembered a conversation they had once had. One of their early dates. They had sat side by side at the back of a candlelit restaurant after seeing something on Broadway, back in the bad old days, when he couldn't really afford evenings like that but wanted them like a man in the desert wanted water. He remembered her eyes in the candlelight that night. Sparkling, clear like the champagne they had had, back when she could have two glasses and not want more, not sneak a vodka on the way to the powder room.

She had called what he felt for her "imprinting." Like when those baby ducks followed after an orange balloon, thinking it to be their mother. Sarah had joked that she had just happened to be in the right place at the right time when Steven's hormones had told him it was time to fall hopelessly in love. He had laughed at her explanation for the strength of the bond they had felt then, but at the same time remembered wondering if, perhaps, he had been in the right place for her as well.

Over the years, into the days when he could afford evenings like that anywhere in the world and still felt trapped in the desert, he and Sarah had overwhelmed that first passion with anger and the contempt of familiarity. Sarah had also drowned it. But even after four years he had never recaptured that passion with any other woman. No matter how hard he had tried. The first few times its absence had surprised him.

Ex-wife, he repeated to himself. *Ex*-wife. Mother of my daughter . . . Wrong. He shook his head. Brought the car back to sixty. He never let himself drive above the limit when he was distracted. Caution. Control. Do not think of Wendy, he commanded himself. I can affect no change in the situation during the time it will take me to drive to Litchfield. I will not think of Wendy.

But, of course, he did. And at a steady sixty miles an hour, it took him much longer to arrive than he had planned.

* * *

Angel's silver Sovereign was parked off on the grass at the top of the unpaved driveway leaving Steven room to park closer to the house by Sarah's Volvo wagon. He could see that this year's fashion color for Connecticut houses must have changed since the last time he had visited. Christmas had it been? he wondered. The shutters and trim of the tall white house were now painted a dark green instead of the pale yellow he remembered. He found it odd that he didn't even remember signing the check. But so many of his memories of Sarah seemed to fade away like that.

Angel opened the front door, his face grim.

"Drinking?" Steven asked, stepping inside. His eyes automatically examined the parts of the house he could see, unemotionally assessing the mess of seasonal decorations scattered through the living room.

Angel shrugged. "Knew where she was. Didn't know the day, though." He followed Steven to the kitchen.

Steven had heard the hesitation in the private investigator's voice. "What else?"

Angel looked away, embarrassed. "She says she doesn't remember Wendy."

"That Wendy was here?" Ridiculous, Steven thought. The shared-custody arrangement was one of the few things about their divorce that had worked out.

"That, uh, that she has a daughter."

Steven stopped in the hallway. He put out his hand to the wall.

Angel continued. "She, uh, keeps saying that she can't have a daughter because all of her babies have been, uh, taken."

Steven was silent for a moment, letting all the pieces fall into place. "She had a miscarriage, you know." Angel shook his head. "First year we were married." Steven sighed, spoke quietly, sadly. "I remember sitting up with her in the emergency room. She was in pretty bad shape. They gave her Demerol or something. I don't know. Anyway, she was going on about it happening before. A fear or something. Losing her baby. It was the Demerol then." He was silent again.

Angel reached out his hand to Steven's shoulder. "For whatever it's worth, I can't find any bottles."

Steven shrugged it off. "Compulsive neatness," he said. "The kitchen?" Angel nodded.

Steven walked into the kitchen, pausing to look at two pieces of dark cloth on the floor. It took a moment for him to recognize it as a swimsuit. The band above one of the leg holes had been torn. The suit seemed too small. Not Sarah's style.

Sarah stood by the sink, her back to Steven, wearing a bathrobe, busy with something.

"Sarah?" he said to her.

She turned to face him, a happy smile on her lips. In her right hand she held a potato peeler. In her left, a small white fragment of potato. Her bathrobe was untied and hung open, and she was naked beneath it.

Steven felt his heart flutter like a knee-jerk reaction in the doctor's office as he saw the curve of her breasts and the dark shadow above her thighs. But the fluttering was gone just as quickly as the reality and severity of the situation returned to him.

He repeated her name bitterly, stormed up to her and pulled her robe tightly around her. She stumbled back to lean against the sink, staring in bewilderment as Steven angrily pulled at her undone tie cord, cutting into the flesh above her hips, firmly knotting the bathrobe closed.

Steven couldn't believe how his hands trembled when they brushed against the softness of her stomach. He snapped his hands back as if he had touched a live wire.

"Where is Wendy?" he demanded. He looked past her, out the window to the swimming pool, trying not to look at the abrupt swelling of her nipples where they pushed against her robe. Ex-wife, he told himself. Control.

"Gone," Sarah said. He could hear the throatiness in her tone. She was about to cry.

"Gone where?" He was desperate in his confusion of feelings. Unwanted desire. Sorrow for Sarah. Panic for Wendy. He heard Angel shift his position, waiting patiently in the hall. And humiliation, Steven thought, that Sarah had been seen like this by someone who wasn't family.

Sarah began to rock against the sink. She looked at the peeler and potato in her hand as though someone had just placed them there. She held them up for Steven to see.

"I have to get dinner on," she said. "Sunday-night dinner. The chicken's in—"

The peeler and potato flew from her hands as Steven grabbed her wrists and wrenched them together. *"Where is she?"*

Sarah watched the peeler slide across the floor. Closed her

eyes a moment, recalling something, then said uncertainly, "I thought she was with you."

Steven was about to shout at her again and stopped only with the sudden and inexplicably chilling revelation that as he stood so closely to her, as she spoke to him only inches from his face, her breath smelled of sleep and of cigarettes and of coffee, but not of liquor.

He was surprised how quickly the anger left him. He dropped her hands, turned to Angel.

"Did you try the neighbors? The Rothmans, I think. Their daughter's Maxine. And the Kellys?"

Angel took that as permission to enter the kitchen. "I called everyone on the list by the phone. She was over at the Rothman's for lunch on Sunday. But she went home at two and no one saw her after that."

Steven looked around the kitchen, freezing when he saw the glass on the floor.

"I did that," Angel said quickly, "when she wouldn't answer the door. It set off the burglar alarm and they got the signal at the monitoring station. It was working fine."

Sarah turned back to the sink.

"Kids run away," Angel said.

Steven shook his head. "She's got our place in the city to go back to if she didn't like it here. She could call Penny at the office and get the company limo if she wanted." He stopped talking. He couldn't take that chain of reasoning any further.

Angel could. "Then we've got to call the police, Steven."

Steven felt his chin begin to tremble. He struggled to stay detached, but a painful sob came from him unbidden.

"Not my little girl," he whispered. The monstrous thoughts that had dwelt in the shadows came upon him with full force, too long denied during the drive from the city.

Angel led Steven to a chair by the breakfast table. Steven watched as Angel went back to the phone. He watched as Sarah sang softly to herself, hands working busily in the sink. He saw the swimsuit on the floor again. The torn swimsuit. Not Sarah's style. A young woman's style. Wendy's style. He felt an anguished gasp escape from him.

Control, he told himself. Control.

But Steven Gilmour had lost it.

4

MONDAY, JULY 9, 15:00 PDT

"You know what I like about this bar?" David Vincent asked.

The bartender stopped on her way to the end of the counter, carefully holding two trays of clean draft glasses so water wouldn't drip onto her ruffled white dress shirt. She smiled at Vincent, politely waiting for him to continue. Vincent considered her smile for a moment, saw that it was a shade too formal, and realized that he was drunk.

His face became very serious. He hadn't intended to become drunk. At least not at three o'clock in the afternoon.

"The windows," he continued, concentrating too much on his diction. "Usually bars are too dark. Shadowy. Not enough sunlight." He looked over his shoulder at the row of wide picture windows that ran parallel to the zinc-covered bar. Citizens bustled by beyond them. Melrose shoppers mostly. "I like the windows," he said. I like the people being near, he thought.

"I like them, too," the bartender agreed congenially, then carried her trays away. Vincent was the only customer sitting at the bar, and the bartender was using the momentary break to set things up for happy hour.

Without intending to, Vincent stared at her as she passed by again, admiring her, wondering what her name was, whether she had tied her black bowtie herself. She stopped and smiled even more formally.

"Another?" she asked, glancing down at Vincent's ice-filled glass with its last mouthful of vodka, and the three red plastic swizzle sticks neatly laid out on the damp napkin beside his half-empty pack of Camels.

Vincent looked up over the backlit, glittering tiers of multicolored bottles behind the bar. Spuds MacKenzie, ringed in neon, smiled back from the clock face there. Merril would be arriving soon. She'd want something, and he owed her many times over.

"Club soda," he said.

"Lemon or lime?"

"Whatever." Vincent felt incapable of making any sort of decision. He felt numb. Empty. A dull echo of the way he had felt last night in the hospital.

The bartender headed for her soda pistols. Vincent lit another cigarette as he heard the clink of ice and the gush of the jet water. When the bartender returned, she put down his new glass and a small white plate, with two sections of lemon and two sections of lime, then held up his vodka glass and shook it so the ice rattled. "Finished?"

"Thanks," he said, dismissing it, then squeezed the lime into the soda. The juice stung where it ran onto his fingernails and under his cuticles. He dropped the flattened lime section on the bar and stared at his hands. How had they gotten so dry and cracked?

"Taking up palm reading, Ace?"

Vincent recognized the voice. "Yeah," he replied, examining his hands intently. "I see a long goddam forced vacation."

"In a federal institution by any chance?" Merril Fisher's laugh was light and fast. She hopped up onto the barstool beside Vincent's and dropped a flat red-leather carry case on the bar in front of her. She was short, solid without being fat, and always gave the impression of constant motion. Not the sort of woman to be weighted down by carrying a purse.

"North around?" she asked, leaning forward to see if another drink had been set up on the bar.

"Still in Memorial."

Fisher nodded, appearing to keep time to a private song. She fluttered her hands inside her carry case and brought out a stenographer's wirebound notepad and pen. The top sheets of the pad were attached to the cover with an elastic band so that when she flipped it open, the next empty page was ready for her notes.

"What's his condition?" she asked. Vincent watched her pen move quickly across the page, setting down the date, the time, and Cy North's name.

"Well, I'm just fine, thank you, Merril. It's a pleasure to see you too. Oh, no thanks, I just ordered a drink. But can I get one for you?" Vincent shook his head at her. "Goddam reporters."

Merril slouched back on her barstool and laid the pad and pen down before her.

"Sorry, Dave. Sorry." She reached across him to grab at his cigarettes. "How are *you*?"

"I don't know," Vincent admitted. "Better than Cy, anyway." He lit her cigarette, not from gallantry but because he had the lighter. The bartender appeared and Merril ordered a coffee.

"Look, Dave," Merril said after the coffee had appeared. "You can't blame me for being worked up over this. I mean, there *is* somewhat more to it than what you guys were originally talking about. Am I right?"

"I don't know," Vincent repeated. He sounded vague, even to himself.

Merril settled back, narrowing her eyes suspiciously. "Did they get to you?"

"Did who get to me?"

Merril shrugged and looked around for an ashtray. Since she didn't find one in two seconds, she flicked her ash on the floor.

"I'm missing something here," Vincent said. He could feel the anger and the apprehension in his voice. "*You* called *me*. Left a message on my machine. Said you'd heard about the suspension and wanted to meet with me here and now."

"Haven't missed anything yet, Ace."

"Why?"

"Why what?"

"Why do you goddam want to meet with me? So I can tell you what it's like to be a suspended FBI agent? What it's like to wait for a discipline board to be called? Would that make a good Sunday feature?"

"Flame off," Merril said with concern. "All I want is a few answers."

Vincent sighed. "About what?" he asked carefully.

Merril gestured palms up as though she were feeling for rain. "Well, how about who screwed the Feds over at the beach house last night?"

"The beach house?"

"What's the matter? English not your first language anymore?" Merril dropped her cigarette to the floor, crushed it, and flagged the bartender for a refill. "Look. I stayed hidden just like you told me, so I couldn't see everything, but I did—"

"Stayed hidden? Where?" Vincent was confused, and the terrible thing was that he knew he wasn't drunk enough to be confused. What was Merril trying to tell him? Why was she looking at him that way, eyes so intent and so watchful?

The reporter spoke very carefully. "I was eight houses down from the end unit where you said Reese was hiding out. I stayed under the wooden deck there, out of sight—"

Vincent couldn't fight the panic that suddenly rose within him. He reached out to grab her hand. "Why?" he asked urgently. "What were you doing there?"

Merril pulled her hand away. "You told me to be there, Ace." She peered at him. "A tip, you know? Like we've been doing for years? I give you information from my sources, you give me leads on FBI stories. How long have you been in this bar anyway?"

Vincent felt the bar spin. He put both hands out to its cool metal to steady himself.

"Are you okay, Dave?"

Vincent forced himself to say it. "I don't remember what happened last night." His throat felt so dry he was afraid he might choke, but he couldn't take his hand off the bar to reach for his glass. "And I don't remember telling you to be there." He turned to her. "*When?* When did I tell you that?"

Merril reached over for another cigarette. "Friday afternoon we had drinks at Tech Noir. You told me you and North had pulled weekend duty to run surveillance on Derek Reese, the agent suspected of taking payoffs from— Well, you tell me. Anyway, you told me to hang around on Sunday, Monday, and Tuesday nights because you thought Gardiner would make his move then and arrest Reese. I'd just happen to be there for the exclusive for the *Trib*." Merril took a long drag on her cigarette. "This ringing any bells?"

Vincent took deep breaths and spoke mostly to himself.

"Yeah. Yeah. Reese taking payoffs from some New York group smuggling restricted computer parts into the Eastern bloc. Right. He's on suspension after blowing a sting, and we're waiting to see if the group will contact him. Maybe give him a payoff." Vincent reached out for his glass of soda. His hand trembled violently. Merril swore under her breath.

"What else do you remember?" she asked. Vincent sensed the reservation in her tone, like the bartender's formal smile.

"We were in the surveillance van. Cy and me. Ten o'clock Sunday night." Vincent stared across the bar, but his eyes saw the confined space of the back of the van, op lights glowing from the tape recorders and the FM relays from the inductance pickups on the beach house's phone. The smell of coffee and donuts. The smell of . . . of someone's perfume? Cy's aftershave? He was feeling cramped, closed in. He could feel an attack coming on. He remembered reaching for his inhaler. Just in case. He told her everything.

"What else do you remember?"

"Nothing. I mean, that's a clear memory. *Nothing* happened. We could hear Reese walking around the place. I don't know. Making a drink. Some dinner. I . . . and then they were waking me up in the middle of the beach house. My gun was gone. And Cy was back in the van. Unconscious." He turned to look at Merril. It was so clear that his memory was gone. He *knew* that he had *forgotten,* and suddenly he felt helpless, as violated as a robbery victim.

"Those bastards."

"Who?" he asked, distracted. He wasn't paying attention to Merril anymore. Dear God, what had happened to him?

"I know what happened to you last night," Merril said, speaking softly.

Panic, *the* panic rushed up through Vincent like a tidal bore. His throat was locked. He couldn't speak. He only knew that something terrible was going to happen to him. Something—

"The DEA."

—it passed. That quickly.

"Drug Enforcement Agency?" he asked with a cough. He patted the side of his jacket and felt the reassuring presence of his inhaler. He didn't need it right now, but it was good to know it was available when the time came.

"Or," Merril added, shaking her head back and forth, balancing one explanation against the other, "considering it's a technology-transfer case, maybe the CIA. Wouldn't be the first time you guys tried to outmacho Langley."

"Back up a bit," Vincent said. "I don't follow this at all." He was surprised at how much more composed he felt. Nothing bad was going to happen. Why had he thought that?

"Okay, Ace, take a look." Merril dug into her carry case and snapped out six eight-by-ten black-and-white contact sheets. Each carried thirty-six tiny photographs, directly printed from a roll of 35mm film.

Vincent's reaction to the photographs was instantaneous. His hands shook as he took his inhaler from his pocket, held its mouthpiece two inches in front of his open mouth, sprayed and inhaled.

"Thought you had that beat," Merril said, looking up from the contact sheets.

"Not too often these days," Vincent said in a dry gasp as he forced air into his lungs, feeling the calming relief as the aerosol medication relaxed his swollen bronchioles, letting the oxygen flow back into his blood. "Doctor says I should outgrow it." He laughed, coughed, laughed again. "Adolescent asthma. I'm only thirty-two after all."

Vincent watched Merril's offhanded nod and guessed that she didn't really see what was striking him funny, so he decided he didn't really care. What was important was that he could breathe. The on-again, off-again panic had left for the moment. And, he discovered with surprise, he did want to see what she had photographed.

"Who's that?" he asked, slipping the inhaler back into his jacket pocket and pointing to the first pictures on the first sheet. They showed an attractive young woman holding a sheet of cardboard patterned with graduated strips of gray, running from black to white.

"Beth," Merril said simply, running her fingers along the edge numbers printed beneath each photo.

Vincent looked at the first photos more closely. He hadn't realized it was Beth. "She's really let her hair grow," he said. "Looks nice."

"Uh-huh," Merril muttered. Then, "Here it is. Look."

Vincent shifted closer to the reporter and looked at the miniature photograph just above her pointing finger. It was the beach house, shot from the south side of the row of other houses to which it was connected. The picture was dark, but

there was enough detail for Vincent to tell that the image had
been compressed by a telephoto lens. It showed the wide
kitchen window in the addition sticking out from the original
back wall of the house. He could see the silhouette of a man
against it.

"Reese?" he asked.

"Yep," Merril said. "The contrast is bad on these little guys,
but I'll probably be able to print them to bring out enough
detail to make him recognizable. He was clear enough through
the lens though. That's your boy."

Vincent looked at the rest of the photographs in the sequence. Reese at one window. Then gone. Then at another.

"What's he doing?"

"Waiting, I think," Merril answered. "He was really pacing
back and forth like he was nervous or impatient or . . ."

"Except for here." Vincent pointed to the final four shots on
the sheet. Reese was back in his original position in the kitchen
window in each one of them. Vincent took the first sheet off the
pile. The first strip of pictures on the next sheet were simply
white. Overexposed.

"That's when the helicopter came in," Merril explained. "I
was using that T-Max 3200 surveillance film. Sixty-four hundred EI. The searchlights burned out everything."

Vincent sat back for a moment. "The helicopter came in
after the backup team arrived, Merril." He felt a shiver pass
through him. "Don't you have any photos between the time
Reese was in the window until the time the backup—"

"Lots," Merril interrupted. "This is the *first* helicopter."

Vincent stared at her blankly.

"The one that took Reese out of there." She ignored his
confused reaction and went on to the next contact sheet. "New
roll," she said. "See? Here it is on the beach, behind the house.
Hard to make out the shape from the contacts, but wait till I
make some prints. Play with the contrast."

"I don't remember any helicopter," Vincent said.

"I'm not surprised," Merril answered with a snort. "You still
haven't figured it out yet, have you?"

Vincent shook his head.

She jabbed her finger against the photographs showing the
obscured helicopter on the beach. "This is what Reese was
waiting for. These are the guys who took him out." She revealed the next contact sheet and pointed to the sequence of

pictures where the helicopter's door opened and its passengers
came out, clearly outlined in the light from its cabin. Merril
took Vincent through the sequence. He could see the faint outlines of the helicopter crew as they walked across the beach to
the deck, as Reese stepped out on the deck to meet them.

"See?" Merril emphasized. "They're not grabbing at him.
There was no commotion. He was waiting for them, they came,
and he's out of there. Believe me, it was all set up ahead of
time."

Vincent stared at the pictures, and his mind was a void, as if
a switch had been thrown. He could think of nothing to say, no
questions to ask.

"You really don't remember, do you?"

He didn't even shake his head.

"About five minutes later, before the chopper took off, I
heard gunshots, a deck window shatter." She leaned over to
look at him closely. "Nothing?"

No response.

Merril gathered the contact sheets together. "Well, don't feel
too bad. Like I said, the Feds got screwed over, and since you
and North were on the scene, you're the guys who get hung out
to dry."

Vincent still couldn't force himself to say anything. His vocal
cords seemed paralyzed, no words left inside him. Merril
slipped the contact sheets back into her case. She took his hand.

"I don't know what they did to you in there, Dave, but it's
not your fault. The FBI got caught cutting someone else's
grass. DEA. CIA. Whatever. But you were on surveillance.
Heard the chopper come in. Went to stop your prisoner from
escaping. Ran into the house and got squirted with a hypnotic
drug. Diazaline. Methoprominol. Whatever's hot in D.C. this
week."

Vincent felt her squeeze his hand. He wanted to say something but was frozen, inert.

"It'll wear off, Dave. I've read about this shit. Two or three
days for your system to process it, and you'll be back to normal. Okay?"

There was something wrong in what Merril was saying, but
Vincent couldn't place it. It was so hard to concentrate on what
had happened the night before. But there *was* something.

"Why—" he coughed, startling Merril as much as himself,
"why do you think it was another government agency that

came after Reese? Why couldn't it have been the New York group? The smugglers?"

"Trust me, Ace. Number one, if it had been the bad guys in there when you broke up the party, you and North wouldn't be recovering from an encounter with an antipersonnel drug. You'd be cooling in the morgue. And number two, nobody but some grant-bloated government agency could afford a chopper with the whisper mode that thing had. And number three—"

"What do you mean by 'whisper mode'?"

Merril looked at him as though the question had nothing at all to do with what she was saying. "The thing was so quiet I couldn't hear it over the surf only eight houses down. Ten minutes later, the police choppers were rattling windows up and down the beach for a mile."

Vincent still didn't get it.

"The helicopter that took Reese out was state-of-the-art. And number three, you can't tell me that the Feds didn't have a Coast Guard cutter off the beach using radar for motorboats and aircraft. If the Coast Guard didn't blow the whistle on Reese's chopper, it's because they didn't see it. That's either billion-dollar Stealth technology or somebody got to the Coast Guard and had them conveniently look the other way. White-collar smugglers from the Big Apple don't have that kind of pull."

Merril took her hand away from Vincent and tapped her fingers against the bar, looking around at the new customers who had arrived, noticing them for the first time.

"It's so bloody obvious, Dave. The FBI has run up against another government agency. And if you and North are in trouble because of it, then you're being set up as the fall guys. When those drugs they nailed you with wear off, you'll see it too."

For Vincent, hearing the previous night put into those terms made it somehow easier to work with. The words came more easily.

"If it's a setup," he began, voice slow and thoughtful, "then we don't know if it's being run completely by the other agency or whether someone in the bureau is involved."

Merril smiled broadly. "That's the spirit. Proper FBI paranoia."

Vincent brought out his inhaler again. It was turning into a bad day.

"Can you print the blowups from those sheets?" he asked,

fighting the terrible constriction that threatened to close off his lungs.

"Twenty-four hours," Merril said. "And I'll go with the story only when you tell me me to. I owe you that much." She held out her hand halfway. "Deal?"

Vincent took her hand and shook it.

"I want to get the bastards who did this to me," he said with deadly conviction.

"We've got them right where we want them," Merril said. But as she patted her carry case with its photographic evidence inside, Vincent felt the nameless, formless panic rise up in him again.

Somehow, he knew, she was wrong.

5

MONDAY, JULY 9, 16:00 PDT

Like the innocuous door that had led to this safe office, far from
the Los Angeles Field Office of the FBI, the secretary who
guided Edmond Gardiner through the deserted corridors was
nameless. Her nondescript blouse was white, her shapeless skirt
was black, she would not be there when the meeting was over.

Gardiner had attended gatherings like this before, back in
New York in the sixties, when black-bag jobs to copy documents and place bugs in foreign embassies and corporations
seemed to be the FBI's normal trade. He even knew what the
conference room would look like before the secretary opened
the door.

It would be windowless, of course, so there could be no photographs, no transmission of sound by reflected lasers. The
meeting table would be long, with a covering of glass through
which the inexpensive wood grain of its veneer would show.
The table would be ringed by black plastic-covered chairs on
swivel rollers, because they were convenient to buy, hard to
trace, and cheap enough to be left behind in case of rapid de-
parture.

Before each chair would be a precise arrangement of one
water glass overturned on a paper coaster, two pencils, and a
single sheet of lined yellow foolscap. When the participants in

the meeting filled their pages, fresh sheets would be available from stacks lined up along the table's center axis. Given the nature of the things that would be discussed in such meetings, it would be important that no copies of any notes could be read from indentations that might be inadvertently left on a second sheet of a pad or a soft table surface.

The secretary opened the door. Gardiner stepped inside. It was just as he had pictured except for the person who waited for him—Special Agent Terry Chandler, still in the same rumpled suit he had worn the night before at the beach house. At least this time his tie was done up.

"Terry," Gardiner said, betraying no surprise, acknowledging the man with a nod as he chose a chair near the head of the table. Oddly, there were no chairs at either of the table's ends. Where would the unknown person who had arranged this meeting sit?

Chandler looked up and met Gardiner's eyes only for an instant, terribly nervous but not surprised. He had been told what to expect.

Gardiner pulled his chair closer to the table, fighting to preserve his outward appearance of composure. He had been correct in his suspicions that Chandler would be looking for new employment. Where he had been wrong was in the timing.

"How long?" Gardiner asked, refraining from adjusting the paper and pencils in front of him. They weren't exactly aligned.

"Sir?" Chandler cupped his hands on two long, beige file folders, one finger tapping errantly.

"Since my presence was requested here as a representative of the bureau, I'm assuming that you're here as a representative of . . . another organization." Despite his best attempts, an edge of anger came to Gardiner's voice. "How long have you been with them?"

Chandler looked down at the closed file folders. "Not too long," he said, embarrassed.

"Are you allowed to tell me who it is you're working for?" Gardiner tried.

Chandler glanced up at the closed door, hoping for deliverance from his awkward situation. He sighed. "It's . . . not up to me, sir."

Gardiner nodded calmly, mind racing with scenarios that all led to one conclusion: after this meeting, one or the other of them would not be returning to the FBI.

A minute passed in brittle silence. The doorknob moved. Chandler jerked his head up. Gardiner turned slowly, unconcerned on the outside. Until he saw the first man who entered. Then all his scenarios crumbled.

Roy Luck, Special Operations, Office of Combined Intelligence, appeared with the expressionless face of a corpse yet moved with the coiled, languid, living grace of a cat. Gardiner did not betray the loathing he felt for the man. He didn't have to. The OCI was everything Gardiner despised about the intelligence community and those planners who thought that jurisdictional fragmentation and the opportunity for review were signs of weakness rather than safeguards against the threat of unbridled power.

The OCI had the supreme authority to draw in products obtained by all government intelligence branches, from the departments of State, Justice, and Defense, to the CIA and the other, unnamed offices operating under the National Security Council. By presidential order, what the OCI did with that information and how it responded were unknown to all except its shadowy review council, believed to exist somewhere removed from the normal chain of command. But even the most stringent controls could not prevent rumors from flying in D.C. Rumors of absolute power. Rumors of absolute corruption. And some of those rumors Gardiner knew to be true.

The OCI agent scanned the room in what Gardiner took to be a reflex action born of paranoia, then slowly moved aside to allow the second man to enter.

Gardiner felt the tension build in his jaw as he heard the mechanical whine of a self-powered wheelchair. Even before he saw the second man's face, Gardiner knew who it was to be: Tucker Browne, Director, OCI.

The wheelchair was a new model Gardiner hadn't seen before. Two black rubber treads ripped along the floor beneath a triangular base. The chair section was attached to the base by a central column and had two armrests, on one an angled control panel with joystick and keypad. No metal parts showed. Everything was encased in a matte-white plastic shell with red fabric trim. Gardiner wondered what else could be hidden beneath that shell in addition to the motor.

Tucker Browne directed his chair to the near end of the table, and Gardiner realized why no office chair had been placed there. He held back a grim laugh. Here he had been concerned that he might be dealing with the Drug Enforcement Agency, the Bureau of Narcotics and Dangerous Drugs, or even the Secret Service. But the OCI could eat up all the other agencies operating out of D.C. and wouldn't even pause to spit out the bones.

Gardiner watched as Browne used the joystick to guide his small vehicle into a proper position, putting him within reach of his paper and pencils. The paraplegic's blue eyes bulged from beneath a fleshy ridge dusted with almost invisible blond eyebrows, a fat cherub with twisted legs. It was rare to see him outside of D.C., Gardiner knew. Like a spider, he concluded, Tucker Browne had left the hub of the OCI's electromagnetic web to take part in the kill.

Luck sat to Browne's right, on Chandler's side of the table, clearly establishing where the lines had been drawn. Then, with all present and respectfully silent, Browne pursed his full lips and rested his pudgy hands on the sphere of his stomach, incompletely hidden beneath the buckled cloth of his immaculate blue blazer. He began the meeting by coughing once and Luck responded instantly.

"We are concerned about the bureau's recent loss of surveillance on Derek Reese." Luck's voice was a slow monotone. It irritated Gardiner, made him want to finish the man's sentences for him.

"I thought that the conduct of an FBI agent was the concern of the FBI," Gardiner said evenly, wondering when they would bring up the matter of his early-morning report and recommendation based on what had happened to Vincent's gun. In the meantime, he chose a pencil and wrote down the date as the first of many notes, if only to make his adversaries nervous.

"Normally, that would be true," Browne replied. His voice was hesitant, uneven in rhythm, giving the impression of someone who was listening to a second conversation through an invisible earphone. "Whenever FBI agents have gone astray, as so often seems to happen these days, the bureau quite rightly should be the one to fight the fires, pick up the pieces, as it were." He held a small hand to his mouth and delicately coughed again. "But in the case of Derek Reese, I'm afraid that matters have spilled out, shall we say, over the normal boundaries of independent bureau concerns."

Gardiner wrote a quick note to himself: "Reese op conflict OCI op." "There are channels for reporting ongoing operations," Gardiner said as his pencil scratched across the sheet. "If Reese's investigation was impinging on another agency's operations, it wouldn't be the first time. For any of us. You should have come to me."

Luck's smile was like a nervous twitch. "Those channels aren't secure. Especially on the bureau's end. Mr. Chandler?"

Terry slid the topmost of his two file folders across the table to Gardiner.

Inside were four multicolored computer charts, printed out on a heavy card stock, perforated top and bottom for a plotting bed. Gardiner read the attribution on the printouts' legends: "TEU, 215 Pennsylvania Avenue, Washington D.C.": the Technical Evaluation Unit of the FBI lab. Two of the printouts were headed "North, Cyrus Malachi." The other two, "Vincent, Albert David."

"I'm impressed," Gardiner said, looking from Chandler to Browne, purposefully ignoring Luck. "These weren't to be delivered to Dr. Perez until five o'clock this afternoon." He spread the charts before him. "Which are blood and which are urine?"

Chandler told him where to look on the cards for the sample designation, and Gardiner used those tags to separate the computer analyses of all foreign substances that had been found in North and Vincent after they had broken surveillance.

At first glance, Gardiner was drawn to Vincent's blood chart. A series of squiggled colored lines had been plotted across the bottom of a graph, recording the computer's interpretation of the various testing methods used to break the blood into its component molecules. A dark green line was most prominent, shooting up the page away from the others like a seismic tracing from an earthquake, almost to the limit of the pale green grid printed behind it.

Gardiner squinted to read the annotation someone had printed in tiny letters beside the peak: "300 series, n/a." Meaningless.

"What was Vincent on last night?" Gardiner looked quickly at North's graph to see if he had shared whatever Vincent had ingested, but could see no extended green plot in the same region.

"The three hundred anomaly is not of concern," Browne said, dismissing Gardiner's query. "Mr. Vincent's employment file shows he suffers from recurring bouts of asthma. The line you noticed is consistent with a recently self-administered dose of Brophminol, a common prescription medication." Browne closed his eyes and appeared to read the information from the back of his eyelids. "Mr. Vincent's medical records also show he has a current prescription for Brophminol. Records at the All Star Pharmacy, near his apartment on Pico, show he purchased a repeat aerosol container of the drug three weeks ago." His eyes popped open. "Shall I continue?"

Gardiner turned back to the charts. "I don't see anything else marked off as significant," he said after a few moments.

"Did you expect to?" Browne asked.

"There was something wrong with them last night. I was prepared to accept that they might have been exposed to a hallucinogen. Maybe a hypnotic."

"Self-administered?" Browne asked, without indicating the answer he expected.

Gardiner tapped his pencil against the paper as he considered his response. He wrote, "TB fishing—negative what happened Vincent/North. How about gun?"

"If I understand the situation developing here," Gardiner said, taking care to choose exactly the right words, "you are . . . considering much the same scenario as I am."

"Go on," Browne encouraged, shifting in his wheelchair.

"Derek Reese was point man on a surveillance operation to apprehend a group suspected of shipping restricted computer components to the Eastern bloc. It was a straightforward setup. A plane lands in the Nevada desert. Material is transferred from truck to plane. Reese takes us in at the moment of transfer."

"But he didn't," Browne stated.

"Correct. Reese negated the operation. The suspects left the scene. Reese didn't have a satisfactory explanation."

"And the scenario you're considering?" Browne asked.

"Did Reese screw up from incompetence? Or was he bought off?" Gardiner printed Reese's name on his note sheet. "Reese was assigned from D.C., but as the local SAC, I pulled him from active duty. Told him to take some time off while we reevaluated the situation, and put him under surveillance to see if the smugglers would make further contact with him. D.C. concurred."

"And your surveillance team negated their assignment just like Reese," Luck sneered.

Browne ignored the OCI agent. "And your scenario for that incident, Ed?"

"Did Vincent and North screw up from incompetence? Or . . . were they bought off too?"

Browne waved a hand to silence another comment from Luck. "And any conclusions thus far?"

"I don't believe in coincidence," Gardiner answered. "But I don't have the evidence for a payoff either. Until this meeting, as far as I was concerned, it was fifty-fifty whether Vincent and North took a payoff and gave themselves a drug to cover up their loss of surveillance *or* whether they weren't bought off and were simply taken out with drugs administered by the people who helped Reese escape."

"But you feel Reese is guilty? That question has been resolved for you?"

"Reese was in the beach house when North and Vincent started their shift. He was gone when backup arrived. How he got out is not clear. But he did get out, and flight is a reliable indicator of guilt." Gardiner sat back, waiting to see where Browne and Luck would take his revelations.

"Shall we proceed to the endgame, Ed?" Browne pushed both hands down on the padded arms of his wheelchair and straightened his posture.

"The point being . . . ?"

"The point being that you are well aware that Reese stumbled upon an OCI operation."

Gardiner had expected almost anything except that. "Not until you rolled through that door, Tucker. No idea."

Another twitch of a smile from Luck. "You shut down the bureau's investigation last night, Ed. You said, it was no longer within FBI jurisdiction."

Gardiner looked blandly at Chandler. The agent didn't look back. At least I know why they haven't mentioned the gun, Gardiner thought. Now the question is, should I?

"It seems Terry is about as effective an OCI spy as he is an FBI agent," Gardiner said, hoping that Chandler would take offense.

"Whose jurisdiction would you place the matter under?" Browne asked. Gardiner could sense Browne's concern as the fat man felt control of the meeting slip away.

"I've already made my report to the appropriate agency," Gardiner answered. "I really don't think I should comment further until I've received clearance." He smiled briefly at Luck. The OCI didn't know about his morning report, so they didn't know about the gun. Chandler hadn't mentioned it. "At least some FBI channels are secure after all, wouldn't you say, Roy?"

No response. Not from Luck, Browne, or Chandler. Gardiner put his pencil down. He had them. He had information that they did not possess, and in this arena at least, information was power.

After a few moments of silence, Browne coughed again. Gardiner read the sound as meaning a decision had been made. Obviously, it had. Luck began to speak, and Gardiner relished the reluctance in the man's obnoxious voice.

"The suspects Reese was investigating are OCI operatives."

Gardiner turned to Browne, at last letting all the anger out in his voice. "This had better be damned good, Tucker. The suspects' names have been on the bureau's SPINTCOM watch list for three months. You know that the National Security Agency is required to inform all agencies involved in an operative overlap."

"In this case," Luck said, sounding surprisingly as if he didn't want to provoke Gardiner, "it was decided that FBI channels were not secure."

But Gardiner was provoked. Bitterly. "I'm taking this to Oversight."

Browne shook his head. "I think not, Ed. Roy has explained the OCI's involvement in Reese's investigation. The bottom line is that if Reese has sold out to . . . the other side—any other side—many of the covert agents he has been investigating are in danger of being identified. In any event, Oversight has been kept informed. They decided to allow the bureau to continue its investigation so that if the smugglers became aware of it, it would, shall we say, inject a certain note of verisimilitude."

Gardiner was confused. Given that situation, what was the conflict?

"Sorry, Tucker. I don't buy it. You're not telling me everything."

"Neither are you, my friend." Browne pursed his lips, a gambler deciding how many cards to draw. "Look at the blood analyses again. Both men."

Gardiner pulled the printout cards closer. "What am I looking for?"

"Red trace. Eight hundred series."

Gardiner ran his finger along the red line plotted on North's card. In the eight hundred bar, it slipped up slightly but abruptly. Beside the line's highest peak, the same tiny printing read, "47." It was followed by an exclamation mark. On Vincent's red line, the peak was marked as 32.

Gardiner shrugged. "I see it. What is it? Crack? Heroin?"

"Not a drug per se," Browne said. His voice had an odd flat quality. "Ribonucleic acid."

"Acid? A hallucinogen?"

"Among other things, it's the chemical basis of memory. That particular RNA compound should not be found anywhere in the body except in the brain. And even then, not anywhere near that concentration. The lab ran the test five times." Browne's expression became subdued to match his tone.

"What's the significance of the result?" Gardiner asked. He wasn't sure how to read the chart or the situation.

"It's called a neural-blocking compound," Browne said simply.

"For blocking pain?" Gardiner asked in clarification.

"For blocking memories," Browne replied. "It's sophisticated, Ed. In structure and in delivery system. It shouldn't even be able to exist outside the brain, let alone be able to cross over the brain-blood barrier."

"Make your point, Tucker."

"We don't have it," Browne said, frustration fueling every word. And the way he said "we," Gardiner knew he meant the United States.

"Biochemical warfare?" Gardiner asked.

"Absolutely," Browne said. "Spray a battlefield with it and no soldier could remember his orders. Spray an air-conditioning duct with it and no member of a military staff could remember his action codes, his initialization responses, perhaps even his allegiance."

Gardiner could see why the man was upset. "And 'we' don't have it?"

"We've got the theory. Not the manufacturing capability. And definitely not the delivery system," Browne said.

Gardiner was surprised at Browne's candidness. "You and I

are following the same scenario," he said, and told the OCI director about Vincent's superheated gun.

When Gardiner had finished, Browne glared at Chandler. "And you didn't see fit to pass that along to us in your report, Mr. Chandler?"

"The guy's gun misfired," Chandler protested, but was ignored by the other three.

"Did you draw any conclusions from the condition of the gun?" Browne asked Gardiner.

"In seventy-seven I was part of a group that was given a demonstration of the Laurel field," Gardiner explained. "I gather it was one of the few times that it actually worked the way the Israelis claimed it would. I couldn't pull the trigger on my weapon. Jammed completely."

"And you think a Laurel field might have been used against Vincent in the beach house?" Browne asked.

"Not like the one I saw demonstrated. The generator took up most of a tractor trailer, and the test room was wrapped in copper wire. It was impressive but impractical." Fifteen technicians and forty-seven-million-dollars' worth of equipment to stop someone from using a firearm in a room of fewer than eight hundred square feet. Two security guards and a fifteen-thousand-dollar metal detector would have had the same effect back in the days before plastic guns.

"But something similar?" Browne pressed.

"During the Laurel demonstration," Gardiner continued, "I remember that two of the participants had to leave the test room because their dental fillings started to hurt. The technicians confirmed that that was a problem. And after about ten minutes, I recall mentioning that my gun was starting to feel warm and they said something about the electromagnetic field having that effect also."

Gardiner assessed the expression on Browne's face. "Whether or not it's related to the Israeli generator, is a device similar to the one that might have destroyed Vincent's gun something that we have?"

Almost imperceptibly, Browne shook his head. Gardiner could see that the fat man's eyes were looking at things other than those in the room.

Abruptly, Browne's gaze returned to focus on Gardiner. "Who did you report this to, Ed? Whose jurisdiction?"

"Defense Intelligence Agency," Gardiner answered, no

thought of withholding information now. "That's who ran the Laurel demonstration."

Browne nodded. "I can handle the DIA." Gardiner had no doubt that Browne could. The fat man seemed almost relieved. "What course had you planned before coming to this meeting?"

"SOP," Gardiner said. "Put Reese on the Most Wanted and run surveillance on North and Vincent to see if they're contacted."

"And if they are?"

"Proof of guilt. We arrest them."

"And if they aren't?"

Gardiner smiled. It reminded him of his orals in the proficiency exams. "The situation at the beach house could have been an elaborate show to establish that they are not involved, but if they aren't contacted, that will not be proof of innocence."

"So you believe that it is possible that Vincent and North are guilty of complicity in Reese's escape?"

"Of course."

"Perhaps even of complicity in Reese's other activities?"

"What other activities?"

Browne's face was set, his voice cold. "In activities involving him with the people that our operation was designed to expose. People who might find value in identifying and eliminating our covert agents around the world. People who are a proximate threat to this nation's security."

Gardiner recognized the standard phrase. He had seen it used on withdrawal papers. Knew what it meant.

"Yes," he said gravely. Vincent and North were his agents after all. He was responsible for them. To a point. "Yes. There is that possibility."

"And you know the SOP when that possibility is confirmed?"

"Yes. Damn it." How had this happened? Gardiner had entered the meeting expecting a procedural battle with a sister agency and instead found himself drawn into an OCI operation involving advanced weapons and the possibility that three of his agents were proximate threats to the nation's security.

"I will arrange the briefing with the DIA," Browne said, holding his hand over the keypad on the arm of the wheelchair, a signal that the meeting was at its end. "You will begin surveillance of Vincent and North?"

"It's already in place," Gardiner confirmed.

Browne nodded once at Luck, pressed a finger on the keypad, and the chair backed away from the table. Then he paused.

"I will also prepare the withdrawal papers," the fat man said. It was that simple.

Gardiner nodded, his stomach twisting into a rock. The instant Vincent's and North's complicity was confirmed, they were to be "withdrawn." Like windowless meeting rooms and black-bag break-ins, withdrawal was another relic of those other days. A death sentence.

Chandler stood up hesitantly, watching Browne roll toward the door, Luck behind him.

"Mr. Luck?" Chandler asked, voice faltering.

Luck turned to smile at the nervous special agent. "Thank you, Mr. Chandler," he said smoothly. "But that will be all we'll be needing you for." He nodded to Gardiner, passing back the spoiled goods. "Good to be working with you again, Ed. Be sure to get the files from Mr. Chandler." He opened the door for Browne and followed the chair out.

Gardiner picked up his sheet of notes, folded it in perfect thirds, and slipped it into his inside jacket pocket. He looked at Chandler with contempt. At least in one of today's scenarios he had been correct: the meeting was over, and one of them would not be returning to the FBI.

Without a word, Gardiner took the files and left the former special agent in the windowless room, along with the rest of the temporary, replaceable furniture. And for one small moment, unexpected with its undercurrent of panic, Gardiner found himself wishing that he, and not Chandler, would be the one spared what was to come.

Whatever else these events would turn out to be, thirty years of experience told him they were going to be bad.

6

"You never liked this place, did you?"

Steven Gilmour turned away from the living room window to see Sarah standing in the hallway, cradling a blue coffee mug in both hands, watching him. He had the sudden realization that she might have been there many minutes before she had said anything. He didn't like that feeling. Never had. He turned back to stare out the window as the last long shadows of sunset stretched across the driveway and the deep front yard.

"No," he said. "Never."

"Why did we buy it, then?" Steven heard Sarah walk into the living room behind him. Her steps were slow, each one a struggle.

"You bought it," Steven said. "I just signed the check, remember?"

Sarah sat on the sofa and curled her feet up beneath her. Steven crossed over to the matching armchair. He thought he remembered that they had made love on that sofa once, near the end of their marriage. The Ethan Allen fabric that Sarah sat upon, a pattern of leaves all green and beige, seemed familiar. The same pattern was beneath his hands on the arms of the chair. He brushed his fingers against the smooth, slippery finish of it. Its texture was familiar too. He remembered it now. He had wanted to use a towel to protect it, but she wouldn't let him leave to get one. He remembered the passion. The desperation.

Sarah put her mug on the glass-topped table beside her and placed her hand over the sofa's arm, as if anchoring herself in a position from which she could never be moved.

"I found it," Sarah said. "You saw it. Then you signed the check." Her voice was flat. She recited a litany. "But *we* bought it."

Steven looked away. It was an argument in shorthand. Each of them knew where any given line would lead. All the paths had been exhausted years ago.

The house was almost completely quiet. Steven heard a tiny electrical hum, and it took a moment for him to realize it was the quartz clock on the second shelf of the brass bookcase. It showed the time to be eight twenty-five. Steven automatically checked his Rolex: eight thirty-two. Odd that a battery-operated clock should have gone out with the others. He fought the impulse to get up and adjust it.

Steven saw Sarah's mouth tighten as his eyes darted up from his watch. Old habits, he thought. Old paths.

"If this is keeping you from your precious office, why don't you head back?" she asked. "I mean, it must have been a real break in your schedule to actually come up here yourself to find your daughter instead of giving the job to Angel."

"She's been late before," Steven said without the strength for anger. "I thought the worst thing would be that she needed a ride—" He stopped.

They heard the tap gush on in the kitchen. A glass clinked as it fell into the sink.

Sarah and Steven caught each other's eye at the same moment, both grimacing with a trace of a grin. The moment was a spark, a soft, floating red spark from a slow fire, and Steven felt it.

"Can I get you anything?" Sarah called out.

"No, thank you," came back from the kitchen.

Sarah smiled. "At least the crystal's in the dining room."

Steven smiled too, but it felt wrong. He looked away again. The hum of the clock seemed loud.

"I never liked the country," he said.

"Connecticut?"

"Just country in general."

"Not enough phones," Sarah said with a wry smile. She reached out for her mug.

Steven thought about her explanation for a moment. "Maybe. Not just phones though." He looked out the window. Except for the coach lights on the posts framing the driveway entrance, he could see nothing in the darkness. He tried to remember what else it was he didn't like about the country. There *was* something else, he knew, but it seemed hidden, shadowy. "Not enough people," he finally said.

"Do you get lonely?"

"Sorry?"

"In the country?"

"Oh. No. Not lonely. Not missing people—just missing the nearness of people. I guess the 'hustle and bustle' you'd call it." Steven shook his head. He could explain why he didn't like a particular company or a particular process just by writing down a column of figures. But how to explain how he felt about the remoteness and the sense of dislocation he felt whenever he was in an area where the light from the streetlamps didn't overlap?

"Lonely," Sarah concluded.

"You don't feel that way?" Steven asked. After eighteen years, he was puzzled to think that he didn't know her answer would be.

Sarah looked out to the darkness past the window. "I like it here," she said as if no one else were in the room with her. "I belong here." She seemed to be watching something outside the window. Steven glanced, but there was only night and the two glowing white globes of the driveway lamps. "I'm nee—"

A glass shattered in the kitchen.

Before either could say anything, the voice called out, "Everything's fine. Sorry about that. It's fine."

They smiled at each other again.

"Better put out the plastic pool glasses tomorrow," Steven whispered, and the smiles fled. Dear God, he thought. Tomorrow.

Sarah shut her eyes in prayer. "Maybe we won't have to," she said. "I hope we won't have to."

Their eyes met again. There were tears in Sarah's. The gulf of the living room between them seemed to disappear. The leaves behind her head, beneath his hands, were a single sweep of fabric all green and beige, connecting them. He saw the memories in her eyes too. They had made love on that sofa. It brought them together. The passion. The desperation.

Steven parted his lips to speak. His throat was dry. The thudding of his heart eclipsed the hum of the clock.

The phone rang.

The leaves pulled back. Steven and Sarah were in their separate places, held apart by the rug and the coffee table and fourteen years of marriage. And four years of divorce.

The phone rang again.

Steven held his hand over the receiver of the old black set the police technician had installed.

"Now!" shouted the voice from the kitchen.

Steven snapped the receiver to his ear and mouth.

"Yes?" he said. His voice clear. Perfectly controlled.

"Angel here. I won't tie up the line." The private investigator was shouting into the receiver. Steven could hear muffled conversations, phones ringing, and the clatter of printers in the background.

"It's Angel," Steven said quickly and saw Sarah slump back into the sofa.

There was a click on the line. "That's all right, Mr. Good," the technician said. "We can take four incoming calls at the same time without putting out a busy signal."

"Anyway," Angel continued, "I just wanted to tell you that Wendy's picture is going out over the system now. It'll posted in virtually every police station across the country by midnight."

"Thank you," Steven said, his control no longer serving to hide the exhaustion in his voice.

"I'll be back up there in the morning. The TV crews will be by around nine-thirty, so . . . get some rest."

"We'll try."

Angel said goodbye and hung up.

"Mr. Gilmour? Still there?" The technician remained on the line.

"Yes, I am."

"Sorry about the glass, sir," the technician said.

"No problem," Steven replied. "Are you here for the night?"

"I'll be replaced at one, sir, but there will be someone with you and Mrs. Gilmour at all times. Just in case a call comes in."

"Thank you," Steven said and then, even though it he knew it was unnecessary, added, "Goodbye."

"Goodbye, sir." Steven could hear the smile in the technician's voice as he put the receiver down. From the kitchen, Steven heard the plastic clatter as the technician hung up his own extension.

"Angel's put Wendy's photo into the Child-Find Network. He knows his way around that kind of thing."

Sarah nodded slowly, twice. "I don't think I can stand to hear the phone ring again." She held up her hand. "Still shaking," she said. Her voice wavered like a child's.

Steven couldn't stop. Didn't try to. He got up and went to her, sat beside her, and wrapped his arms around her to shield her from the world and give himself a core from which to fight it.

He was startled that she still fit against him so perfectly. Her head pushed against his shoulder, her breasts against his chest. She burrowed against him. She stopped.

Steven turned his head, his nose filled with the scent of her hair. He could tell she had changed her shampoo from the time they had been together, but nothing could disguise the rich fragrance of sun and forest warmth that he knew was her.

Sarah was motionless against him.

"What's wrong?" he whispered gently, then instantly berated himself for asking such a senseless question. But with her in his arms, he realized, he had actually forgotten about Wendy. Inexplicably, the feeling was familiar and he felt ashamed. But Sarah did not react to the question.

Steven looked at her. Her face was rigid. Her eyes were locked on something behind him, over his shoulder.

"Sarah?" He turned awkwardly against her, craning his neck to see what she was looking at.

He saw his reflection in the window. He saw the darkness beyond. "What is it?" The driveway lights were out. He squinted. He couldn't even tell if the lights were still standing. Only then did he realize that there was something more in the window. As he stared out, another face stared in.

It was small and pale. Its eyes were large, hollow, haunted. Its delicate mouth opened silently, calling to him.

Steven Gilmour felt his heart shudder within him. Felt his lungs freeze as he recognized that face and those features.

"Wendy," he said, just as the face slipped down, leaving only the darkness and the two glowing white globes by the driveway.

MONDAY, JULY 9, 17:55 PDT

"We're being watched, you know."

David Vincent shifted his eyes to look into the rearview mirror of his black 200SX. He saw the four lanes of Highway 1 ribbon away behind him as the crowded beige band of the Santa Monica beach slipped by to the side. He found the car, afternoon sunlight blinding on its windshield.

"Brown Skylark? Six-one-two-four-eight Charlie?" Vincent asked. He had seen the car following them since he had picked up his partner at North's apartment in North Long Beach. He seemed to recall that he and North had once signed that car out of the motor pool on an assignment of their own.

Beside him, slouched in the black leather bucket seat, Cy North nodded. He reached out to adjust the right-hand mirror control switch to its original setting. "There's a green Nova too," he said. "This lane, four cars ahead. They keep shifting."

Vincent made the Nova. "Must have gone to the same school we did."

North slammed his hand against the dashboard. "This is serious, asshole! We're being tailed by our own guys!"

Vincent looked over at his partner. North still wore a bandage over his left eye because he had scratched his cornea when he had slumped onto the pot switches of the console in the surveillance van. The thick white square gave the older man's pale face a lopsided, belligerent look, as though he were constantly cocking his head to challenge whatever someone had said.

"I know it's serious, Cy. That's why we're out here, doing this." Vincent turned his eyes back to the road. An opening appeared to the left and he pulled into it, downshifting and accelerating away from the blaring horn behind him. He shifted back to fourth and pulled beside the green Nova. The car's driver didn't move his eyes as Vincent's Nissan held its position for a few seconds, then raced away.

Vincent checked the rearview again. He could see the Nova's driver speaking to himself, his VOX microphone obviously hidden in the collar of his shirt. Ten cars farther back, the brown Skylark pulled into the passing lane and began to gain. Vincent laughed.

"Are you enjoying this?" North demanded. Vincent's partner was forty-eight, but today he looked sixty.

"Not at all." Vincent laughed again. "They know where we're going. Why don't they just meet us there?"

North slumped back against the high headrest. "Because we're suspects. And they can't trust us." North held his hand over his bandage. "They don't know what we've done."

Vincent stopped laughing. "Neither do we, Cy." The entrance lane to the Getty Museum flashed by. "Ten more minutes," he added. "Maybe fifteen."

"If they let us anywhere near it."

"They have to. We're doing their job for them." Vincent checked the rearview mirror again. The Nova and the Skylark were both in the passing lane and gaining. Ten minutes later, they were still there when Vincent turned off onto a narrow beach road at Malibu.

The surveillance cars swerved onto the shoulder of the highway just past the cutoff, sending up two billows of sunbaked sand and dust. Vincent peered back through North's window as he slowly drove toward the beach road's guard shack. The drivers of the Nova and the Skylark stood by their cars, staring back. The Nova's driver held binoculars. They were no longer even trying to keep up the pretense of covert surveillance.

The guard was a woman with long dark hair tied back and eyes that constantly moved. The shield-shaped patch on her uniform's gray-blue sleeve said "Seldon Security Services," but Vincent knew that the woman's intent attitude was not that of a $12.50-an-hour agency guard. He looked at her closely as he brought his 200SX to a stop beside her and pressed his window button down, letting in the beach smell of summer sand and ocean water. He didn't recognize the woman from the Los Angeles Field Office. The investigation must have expanded, he thought.

"Can I help you, sir?" the guard asked, holding up a clipboard to check for an announced visitor's name. Vincent knew the challenge in her voice was not used by private guards when talking to guests who might hold the key to a thousand-dollar bill being placed in a thank-you card at Christmas.

"David Vincent, Cy North, FBI," Vincent announced. Why play games?

The guard blinked in what might have been surprise. Then she lowered her clipboard, stepped back, and waved Vincent through. Vincent smiled and nodded and closed his window as he drove off.

"She didn't even ask for a badge," North sighed.

"Why bother?" In the rearview mirror, Vincent saw the guard speaking into a walkie-talkie. "She knew we don't have badges anymore."

North twisted in his seat to look at back the guard. "San Francisco?" he asked.

"Or Highway Patrol," Vincent said. He leaned forward in his seat to look up at the solid row of houses they passed, each with a different style of design and finish, from blinding white twenty-first-century cubes to Cape Cod romanticism. It was like a street from Disneyland.

Vincent thumbed his window control, and another gust of hot air swirled into the car. He flicked off the air conditioner. Outside an actor he recognized lifted a small child, round with diapers and a floppy white sunbonnet, from a car seat in a sleek black Ferrari. The actor held the child protectively, watching closely as Vincent's 200SX rolled by. A striking woman with a mass of sunbright blond curls walked from a patio to stand beside the actor. She put a hand on his shoulder and also watched, hoping the force of both their stares would repel the intruders of their refuge.

"This is a bad idea." North played with the door handle.

"An hour ago, you didn't think so."

"So I was wrong, okay? Let's just turn around and get out of here."

Vincent accelerated the car. They passed a gap between the houses and for a moment glimpsed the sunlight flashing from the crashing waves.

"Almost there," Vincent said. They passed more houses. A gray-and-blue Pacific Bell van was parked by the side of the road. They passed it.

The next gap between the houses was coming up, marking a section of older houses, larger, more secluded from the highway that ran beyond the high cliffs to the east. Vincent slowed. An EPA consumer water test van was parked near a warped wooden telephone pole. "That one's ours," Vincent said. He parked his car a few lengths past the van and got out. North didn't move.

Vincent walked around to the passenger side and bent down to the open window. He could see North flipping the window button, but without the key in the ignition, the window remained motionless.

"You're getting out, Cy." It was an order. "We're going in there."

"Why?" It was a plea.

"Because we got screwed over Sunday night. And if Merril's right, we got screwed over by our team. If we leave the investigation to the bureau, they're going to say we sold out. Took payoffs." He pulled the door open. "Get out."

North emerged from the car and held onto the roof. "I'm dizzy, man."

Vincent took his partner's arm. They crossed the beach road.

In the few seconds it took them to reach the path that led past the small swimming pool to the front door of the last beach house in the row, Vincent could feel the heat of the asphalt through the soles of his sneakers.

"It was cool that night, wasn't it?" he asked North as they stood in front of the yellow plastic tape that closed off the path.

"I don't remember."

"Sure you do," Vincent encouraged. His voice sounded as grim as he felt. "We had coffee. We were in the back of the van, no air-conditioning, and we had coffee from the thermos. Quick! Where'd we get the coffee?" He snapped out his arm and tore the police tape from the fence.

"The Dunkin' Donuts back on the highway," North said without thinking. "We had donuts too." He put his fingers to his bandage as Vincent rolled the sticky tape into a ball and tossed it to the dry ground. "It was cool," North said.

"Okay, okay. We're cooking here," Vincent walked down the pathway, holding his right hand up beside his head, carrying an unseen gun at the ready. "That's what we're looking for here. The connections. The memories. C'mon." North followed uncertainly behind him.

Vincent jumped up to the front deck. He stood before the open front doorway. The door and its attached frame lay to the side on the deck. The plastic tape across the doorway read FBI LINE DO NOT CROSS. It fluttered in the hot breeze.

"Open up!" Vincent shouted into the open door, empty hand pointing an invisible gun to an invisible door lock. *"FBI!"*

No answer from inside. Vincent began to feel the first tendrils of doubt. He patted the small canister in his pocket. The panic wouldn't stop him. Not this time.

"I didn't come down here," North protested. "I never left the van."

"But you *heard* something inside," Vincent said, still peering at the missing door, seeing it as it looked that night. "We *both* must have heard something that made me leave you. Made me come here."

"There's nothing on the tapes."

"So they're going to say that you erased them."

"Don't go in, man. Please don't go in."

Vincent turned to his partner. North looked like he wanted to slip between the planks of the deck and vanish. Behind North, in the distance, beside the EPA van, Vincent saw a man standing, innocuously holding the small black shape of a walkie-talkie at his side. Vincent looked to the beach. Another man, another half-hidden walkie-talkie. He turned back to the open door and pointed his finger at it.

"Reese!" he shouted. "Open the goddam door!" He mimicked the sound of a gunshot, wheeled to North. His partner was as pale as the bandage over his eye.

"Did you *hear* that?" Vincent demanded. "Did you hear me shout on Sunday night? Hear the gunshot?"

North looked helpless. His mouth opened, his shoulders slumped, hands fluttering senselessly before him.

"I don't remember, man," he whispered finally. "I . . . I don't want to remember."

Vincent turned back to the doorway. He kicked at the tape, breaking it, sending the two ends of it fluttering to the floor. He ran inside, pulling North with him.

They stood in the central foyer. On the back wall, the empty frame of a floor-to-ceiling window was closed off with another piece of yellow tape. The rhythmic sound of waves and the rich, living smell of the ocean filled the house. Vincent no longer acted out his movements of Sunday night.

"They goddam cleaned the place out," he said.

Every piece of furniture, the custom kitchen cabinets, the potted plants, the fireplace, everything was gone.

"They even took the goddam floor," Vincent said, pointing

to two sections of the pine floor where square-yard pieces had been cut out and removed.

"RICO?" North asked.

"You decided to join the party?" Vincent replied, watching his partner closely. "The place is cleaned out, and all of a sudden it's okay to be in here?"

North took a deep breath. "I'm trying to help you."

Vincent's eyes narrowed. "Us, partner. Trying to help *us.*"

North didn't pay attention. "What did you do after you shot at the door?"

"Kicked out the doorframe," Vincent corrected. "I stood here, looked around, wondered where the goddam hell you and the backup were." He stopped. "No, take that back." He smiled as a clear memory surfaced. "I didn't wonder where *you* were. I knew you couldn't come to help."

"Why?"

"I don't know, I don't know," Vincent said. He stared at the floor. He saw the outline of his body by the staircase and walked over to it, then pointed toward the deck at the back, overlooking the beach. "I saw my reflection in the window. I blasted it."

"That'll cost you ten points on the test range," North said.

Vincent stared at him with surprise. "Why the change, Cy?"

"What change?"

"You cracked a joke. You almost smiled. Two minutes ago, I thought I was going to have to drag you inside here."

North shrugged. "I'm feeling better, that's all."

Vincent nodded but said nothing. He was beginning to see a pattern.

"So what else did you do?" North asked.

"Is this an interrogation, Cy?"

"What do you mean?"

"I mean that I know about the cars following us. I know about the replacement guard at the beach road entrance and the watchers in the EPA van and on the beach. But all of a sudden I don't know about you."

"They're all on the outside, David." Color came to North's cheeks. Vincent couldn't tell if it was anger at being falsely accused or embarrassment at having been caught.

"C'mon, Cy. In the time it took to clean this place out, they could have doubled the number of audio pickups." He waved his hand around the place. "Maybe even had time to finally put in the video camera they wanted to. See if one of us was going to say or do something to tell them what really happened."

"What did happen?" North asked. Vincent knew he shouldn't believe it, but thought he sensed the concern of a partner and a friend in that question, not the calculating inquiry of a snitch.

Vincent shouted out to all the microphones in the house, "I don't know what really happened! Can you hear me? *I don't goddam know!*" His voice echoed off the bare walls and floor above the thunder of the surf.

"Neither do I," North said quietly, for Vincent and not for the unknown listeners and watchers. "Neither do I."

Vincent wanted to believe. "I shot out the window," he continued, staring past the fluttering yellow tape across it. "There were lots of waves. Sounded just like this. I could see them. Full moon. I could see the whitecaps." Another memory flashed before him. He wheeled to North.

"And then I couldn't see them! I saw the whitecaps the first time I looked out. But the next time, they were gone. I saw something moving past the windows." He clapped his hands. "A helicopter! I saw it take off!" Then he dropped his hands to his side and stared back out the missing window. "Jesus," he said in awe. "It didn't make a goddam sound." He shivered.

North waited a moment. "Then what?" he prompted.

Vincent wrinkled his eyes. "I remember reloading. Two shots into the door. Four into the window." He looked around the bare walls and noticed a section of one had been cut out, too. Part of the baseboard. "I don't think I fired into the wall—"

"What would you have fired at?"

Vincent felt spiderwebs brush against his cheek and jumped back, brushing his hand across his face. "Spiders," he said. "There were spiders all around. Jesus." He stared at his hand. Nothing.

"You shot at spiders?" North asked.

Vincent thought about that. "No. Of course not. Just, I don't know. Probably I saw a spider just before I heard something."

"Heard what?"

"That's right," Vincent said. Another memory. The pieces were fitting together. "I did hear something. Not the helicopter. The . . . the . . ."

"Reese?"

"No, not Reese. Someone else." He snapped his fingers. "Is that what we heard? The guys from the helicopter?"

"No," North said, his voice flat and cold. "We didn't hear that."

"Then something like that," Vincent continued. "It's gotta be . . ." He stood in the center of the empty space, eyes closed, trying to bring it all back. He concentrated on seeing the house as it had been Sunday night: all the lights blazing, the floor shining, the whitecaps, the dark shape past the window. He concentrated on hearing the house as it had been Sunday night: the breakers, the gunshots, the footsteps, the noise upstairs. His eyes jumped open.

"Upstairs," he said, feeling the hair on the back of his neck ripple. He looked up to where the red metal staircase disappeared into the upper floor. Near it, a section of the ceiling had been carved out. What had happened to the ceiling? he wondered. He looked over to North. North stared up at the staircase too. His eyes were wide, sweat suddenly on his forehead.

"Cy?" Vincent asked urgently.

"There's someone upstairs," North whispered. "I heard something moving. Just then."

This time Vincent felt the hair *all* over his body ripple. He kept his eyes locked on the staircase as he squatted and pulled the velcro fastening tab off the leg holster wrapped around his left ankle, beneath his slacks. When he stood up again, he carried a Walther PP .380 automatic pistol. He thumbed off the safety and moved for the staircase.

Vincent paused at the first step and glanced behind. North followed silently, holding his thin Backpacker .44 Bulldog pistol to the side.

At that instant, as Vincent's eyes met North's one good one, partners in action again, they heard the sound from upstairs together. Vincent turned back and brought his second hand up to hold his weapon. Slowly, precisely, he climbed the stairs.

The second floor had also been stripped clean. Vincent could see gouges in the soft pine floor where furniture had been dragged away. He heard the sound again. It was something scraping or footsteps. He pointed down the short, wide hall, brilliant with the sun from two skylights. North nodded. He agreed. The sound had come from the farthest closed door.

They waited by that door. The sound came through again. Something creaking this time, like masts on tall ships. The partners held each other's eyes. Three nods and Vincent took the point, slamming into the flimsy interior door, smashing it open, and rushing inside, covering the room's right as North followed through to cover the left.

It was the master bedroom. It had a view of the ocean, another fireplace, and nothing else. Stripped clean and empty.

Vincent's eyes moved to the closet. Two sets of folding pine doors were closed. For an instant, a spark of light seemed to shine from the louvers, glinting from the large brass handles. Vincent heard the sound again. His heart raced.

Quietly, moving perfectly together with the experience of five years of putting their lives into each other's hands, North and Vincent took up their positions on either side of the closet. The sound again. Another spark.

Three nods. It was North's turn. He reached out his hand to the brass knob. Vincent held his gun ready. It was cool in his hand. Another memory began to come forward, but he ignored it, concentrating on the pine door about to be pulled open.

North's hand was two inches from the handle. The door exploded outward, pine slats flying across the room. North collapsed before the force of it, grunting as the body crashing through hit him dead-center and rolled to the floor.

Behind the explosion and the fallen figure, Vincent saw a second shape in the closet's shadows dart back behind the door on his side. Vincent tore open the door in front of him, thrust his gun into that side of the closet. Nothing.

Vincent looked up to the shelf. Nothing. He pounded at the side of the closet, the back wall. Solid. Nothing. He spun back toward the room. North struggled to pull himself out from beneath the splintered pine doors. It was a man who had crashed through them, now moaning, unconscious. Vincent saw blood from wood scrapes over the man's back and legs. He was naked.

"Oh, shit, man," Cy said, gasping for breath, scrabbling frantically to be away from the man and the shattered doors. "Oh, shit, man."

Vincent went to his partner. From downstairs he heard the running feet of the watchers and the listeners as they stormed down the path and into the house, responding to the sounds they must have heard.

Vincent pulled away a section of pine door. North was

moaning. Vincent grabbed the naked man's shoulder and rolled him away from North, onto his back.

The man stared up at Vincent in horror. Vincent pulled back with the force of the man's sudden, deafening cry of terror. His eyes were wide, unseeing. His body shook with convulsions. Vincent dropped his gun onto the floor.

The naked man was Special Agent Derek Reese, FBI.

7

TUESDAY, JULY 10, 10:30 EDT

"I've asked Wendy to wait outside," Dr. Kohl said.

Sarah Gilmour looked at her daughter sitting with perfect schoolgirl posture in one of the two chairs across from the doctor at his cluttered desk. Wendy's face was striped with the soft bands of shadow and light from the venetian blinds across the window. The pattern almost hid the numerous scratches that etched the right side of the girl's face like a child's clumsy attempt at cross-hatching.

The doctor's nurse held the door to the reception area open. Wendy got up from the chair and walked toward the door, slowly and carefully, every muscle in her body stiff. She looked up once, smiled weakly for her mother and father as she passed, then followed the nurse outside.

The door swung shut. Sarah heard the latch click like a bolt on a cell door in old movies. For a moment, the only sound in the office was the muffled drone of the traffic on Fifth Avenue, eight stories below.

Without looking up, Kohl gestured to the chairs in front of his desk. "Please," he said brusquely. Even seated, the doctor was tall and alarmingly thin, like a man of normal height and weight who had somehow been stretched into his present shape, losing in width what he had gained in height. His unkempt fringe of white hair reminded Sarah of the angel hair she used to drape on Christmas trees.

Kohl looked up from the chart on which he had been rapidly scribbling and caught Sarah studying him. He didn't acknowledge her. He turned to Steven instead. When he spoke, his voice carried the memory of an old German accent, perhaps from his boyhood and not quite lost during a lifetime in the States.

"There is nothing wrong with Wendy that is of immediate concern," Kohl began.

"Implying that there's something wrong of long-term concern," Steven said quickly. To anyone else, he would have sounded as even and as composed as if he were explaining a new production line for wrapping chocolate bars, but Sarah could pick up the faint tremors and hesitations that told her Steven was as nervous as she.

Kohl ignored Steven's comment. He looked at Sarah.

"The scratches on her face and along the right side of her body are superficial. Within six months they'll be gone completely." He glanced at the chart and made a quick mark, checking off an item on a list. "The sunburn on her back is the same. Superficial." Another check. He looked back to Steven. "And there is no sign of concussion or . . . any other signs of violence other than injuries consistent with the thorns and branches of the bushes she was found in by the window."

"What about the long term, Dr. Kohl?" To Sarah, Steven's voice was brittle, on edge.

Kohl looked from Steven to Sarah, judging them, Sarah felt. He tapped his pen against the chart.

"Can you tell me about Wendy's boyfriend?" the doctor asked.

"She doesn't have one," Sarah said, surprised. She turned to Steven. "At least, not in Litchfield. Steven . . . ?"

"Not in New York," Steven said.

Kohl looked tired. "Your daughter is sixteen years old. She is attractive, articulate. Even after all she's been through . . ." He left the question unspoken.

Steven shrugged. "Well, she does have a group of friends she goes out with. Boys and girls. But, it's always in a group."

Sarah thought she caught the doctor's intent. "You think she might have . . . run away, Dr. Kohl? With a boyfriend?"

"Do you consider that a possibility?" Kohl asked in return.

Before Sarah could reply, Steven cut in. "Why do you think it might have been with a *boyfriend*, Doctor?" His voice was hard, angry, no hint of control. "Do you think my daughter has been raped?"

Sarah felt her stomach double over inside her. That possibility had been there from the moment she realized that Wendy was gone, but by not talking about it, by not even thinking about it, somehow she had convinced herself it could never come to pass. Not her daughter. Not her baby. "No," was all she could say.

Kohl remained silent. His expression was the angry equal of Steven's.

"I want an answer, Doctor!"

"I don't have one, Mr. Gilmour," Kohl said, dropping his pen on the chart and leaning back in his chair. "Your daughter claims to have no memory of what happened to her from Sunday afternoon when she was lying by the swimming pool to the time you carried her in from the front garden, naked, late Monday night. Without memory, I cannot say whether or not she was raped."

"But are you saying that she . . . had . . . relations?" Sarah couldn't bring herself to say it any other way. Not for Wendy. She felt like vomiting.

"What?" Steven said, turning anxiously from Sarah to Kohl.

"At this time," Kohl said without inflection, "eighteen hours later, after she has bathed, all I can say is that there are no signs of violence, rape or otherwise. Your daughter is sixteen, Mrs. Gilmour. Anything else will have to come from her."

"What else? About what?" Steven demanded.

"About what happened to her during the time she was missing," Kohl said irritably. He glared at Sarah. "The long term is best left to a family psychologist, Mrs. Gilmour. And as soon as possible." Kohl made his medical advice sound like a threat.

"A psychologist, Doctor?" Sarah asked. She gripped the narrow wooden arms of her chair, trying to fight against all the forces conspiring to send her spinning from it.

"A *family* psychologist, Mrs. Gilmour." Kohl sounded like an actor who had said the same lines too many times. All spark and meaning was gone from them. "Your daughter was missing for thirty hours. Either she does not remember what happened during that time, or she chooses to tell us that she doesn't remember." He held up a hand to Steven. "Mr. Gilmour, please. I have been in practice thirty-three years. Let me finish.

"There are two possible diagnoses. In the absence of physical trauma, it is possible for her amnesia to be the result of hysteria. Perhaps something mentally traumatic did happen to her. A psychologist can help her deal with that. On the other hand, perhaps she ran away, for whatever reasons, correct or incorrect, and now doesn't wish to discuss it with her parents. A family psychologist can help the three of you overcome that feeling of distrust." Kohl sat forward again and picked up his pen. "But I urge you both, do it soon. Don't ignore this. Seek help and have the girl try to remember or at least admit to herself that she does remember, whether or not she chooses to share those memories." He pulled a prescription slip out of a small tray and began to write on it.

"A psychologist won't be necessary, Dr. Kohl," Steven said, his voice oddly back to normal.

Sarah felt a moment of shock—how could Steven think that? —but then, abruptly realized her ex-husband was right. "No, Doctor. We can manage on our own. It's not important for Wendy to remember if she doesn't want to."

Kohl's eyes widened. He held his pen above the paper, motionless. "I beg your pardon?"

Steven looked at Sarah. Sarah saw her own understanding of the situation mirrored in his eyes. There was no difference between them.

"Our daughter's not crazy, Doctor," Steven explained.

"That is not the question," Kohl said, voice trembling. "But your daughter might be traumatized. She *must* see a psychologist, or a psychiatrist if you'd rather, or some other medically trained specialist."

"No, Doctor," Sarah said calmly. She was surprised at how untroubled she felt, filled with the knowledge that everything was going to be all right now. "She's gone like this before and—"

"Before!" Kohl snapped. "Your daughter has had incidents like this before?"

Sarah blinked, confused. "Who said she's done this before?"

"You did, madam."

Sarah turned to Steven for confirmation.

"I . . . don't think so," Steven said uncertainly. "No, I'm sure. She hasn't."

Kohl's eyes burned with fury. He attacked the prescription note with his pen, then slapped the slip of paper down at the edge of his desk.

"This is the name of a psychologist specializing in family practice," Kohl said, his voice like steel, his German intonation becoming stronger. "*I* will phone her, and then *you* will phone her by the close of business today and make an *immediate* appointment for the three of you. Do you understand?"

Steven replied with matching intensity. "It isn't necessary."

"Oh yes, it is, Mr. Gilmour. Extremely necessary. Urgently necessary." His lips drew back from his teeth. "Because if I find out that you haven't made that appointment and if I find out that you haven't kept that appointment, I will be forced to suspect that you have some personal motive for keeping the truth of Wendy's disappearance hidden. I will be forced to report a case of child abuse, Mr. Gilmour. *Sexual* child abuse." He slapped the prescription note again. "The child welfare department will see to it that Wendy gets the care she deserves, and you—both of you—could be liable for criminal charges."

Steven sputtered. "I . . . I have lawyers . . ."

"So does this city, Mr. Gilmour. And the instant you tell me that you're foolish enough to want to take them on is the instant I know you're guilty of a despicable crime." The doctor thrust out his hand to the phone on his desk. "Shall we begin, Mr. Gilmour? Who shall it be? The psychologist . . . or the police?"

Steven's breath came in indignant gasps. Sarah felt the same sense of panic, the same sense of outrage that she heard in her ex-husband. Of course the doctor was right about Wendy needing care immediately. Of course the doctor was wrong that Steven had somehow hurt Wendy. But why couldn't she agree to the doctor's suggestion—now a demand—that they see a psychologist? What could possibly be wrong with that? What held her back? Held them both back?

"All right, Dr. Kohl," Steven said, his teeth clenched, mouth barely moving. "Call the psychologist. But it won't accomplish anything."

"For your sake, Mr. Gilmour, I pray it will." Kohl hit a button on the side of his phone and asked his nurse to make the call. "Believe me," he said, regaining his composure now that the right decision had been made, "it is always better to bring these things out into the open."

"No, it isn't," Steven whispered.

For the first time in four years of divorce, Sarah was surprised to find that there was finally something that both she and her ex agreed upon.

TUESDAY JULY 10, 09:38 PDT

The door to his office burst open, rattling the glass in the partition wall, but Gardiner looked up without surprise. He had been expecting it ever since he had made the call downstairs, ordering Reese's release from custody.

"You can't be serious!" David Vincent said. His tone was more one of amazement than insubordination.

"Could you shut the door, please, Cy?" Gardiner asked. Vincent's partner, hanging back in the open doorway, left arm in a new sling, quickly complied.

"You're really letting him go?" Vincent continued. He put his hands on Gardiner's desk and leaned over it. "Why, Ed?"

"Why not?" Gardiner countered. "Do you have any knowledge as to why the bureau would be empowered to continue holding Reese?" Gardiner could think of a few reasons on his own but doubted that either Vincent or North could. Neither looked recovered from whatever had happened Sunday night, and the stress of the most recent incident—finding Reese hiding in the beach house from which everyone had assumed he had escaped—only made them look more strained.

Vincent stepped back from Gardiner's desk, surprised by his SAC's question. "We should keep holding him for the same goddam reasons we put him under surveillance in the first place," he said.

"Which are?" Gardiner asked.

Vincent glanced at North, and Gardiner sensed the partners communicating something. Gardiner could see that North was more nervous and upset than Vincent, but both agents knew that Gardiner was acting inappropriately.

"Reese failed to act in a planned intercept of a suspected exchange of illegal goods," Vincent said. He watched Gardiner unwaveringly, eyes full of sudden suspicion.

"Off the record," Gardiner replied, "the suspected exchange

was part of an undercover operation run by another federal agency."

Vincent snorted, a sound of disgust. "Which one?" he asked. "Goddam DEA again?"

"Sorry," Gardiner said, dismissing the question. "Need to know, only."

"And Reese was in on it?" North asked, his voice weak, almost a whisper. Gardiner realized that North was in far worse shape than he had first thought.

"Let's just say that he is now."

"And that's it?" Vincent leaned against the wall and slammed his fist back against it. The partition glass rattled again, and Gardiner could see personnel in the central office area beyond it stop to look toward his office.

"That's it," Gardiner said. He found he did not have to try to keep himself from responding to Vincent's outrage. Vincent and North were good agents, well trained. He wondered how long it would take for one or the other to realize that Gardiner was setting them up just as they had helped to set up Reese.

"Nobody's interested in finding out what happened to Reese on Sunday?" Vincent asked.

"Reese claims he doesn't remember. And anyway, he was on his own time," Gardiner said with a practiced shrug. "If he figured out he was under surveillance and wanted to spend a day hiding in the attic, that's his business."

"C'mon, Ed!" Vincent paced like a caged lion. "The beach house was cleaned out. Forensics took pieces of the ceiling, walls, and floors, for God's sake. *Nobody* was in the attic. Or the basement. Or behind a false wall. Reese got out and got back in again while the whole place was *surrounded!*"

It was Gardiner's turn to lean forward. "And do you have proof that Reese actually left the beach house on Sunday night?"

Vincent stopped in midstep, eyes flicking toward North. Communication again, Gardiner saw, but about what? Did they have proof?

"No," Vincent said in a way that made Gardiner realize he was lying. "How could we? We were both taken out. Drugged or something. Remember?"

Gardiner took a beige file folder from his in-basket. It was the second folder that Chandler had brought to the meeting in the windowless room.

"Guess again," Gardiner said. "Here're your test results."

Vincent tore at the folder. He flipped it open. "There's nothing," he said, clearly not expecting that result.

"Shows you're conducting yourselves as bureau agents should," Gardiner said. "Hoover would be proud."

Vincent passed the charts to North. "So what about us?" he asked, the fire slowly sputtering out. "What about what happened to us Sunday?"

"David, the bitch of it is that it's not important anymore."

Vincent stared at Gardiner without comprehension.

"Between us," Gardiner continued, "still off the record, we all know you guys got screwed up Sunday night. *I'd* like to know what really happened. I know you'd like to know what really happened. But because Reese is no longer under surveillance, because Reese's investigation has been put on hold, the bureau doesn't have the need or the budget to figure out what went on." Gardiner stood up. The meeting was over. "Nobody cares what happened."

"We're not under surveillance anymore?" North asked.

Gardiner shook his head. "I apologize for that, but there was a mix-up in D.C. and we weren't informed that Reese was conflicting with the . . . other agency's operation. Some people in the bureau thought you and Reese might be working together."

"But they don't think that anymore?" Vincent asked.

"It's all been cleared up. You," Gardiner turned to North, "you, and Reese. All clear."

Vincent looked at the floor, deep in thought. "Are we back on duty then?"

Gardiner laughed for their benefit, tensely wondering when they were going to figure it out. "Look at yourselves. Why not take two weeks? Full pay. You've got it coming. You look like you can use it."

Vincent glanced up again. At last, Gardiner thought, he's got it. I can see it in his eyes.

"This is what you told Reese," Vincent asked, "isn't it?"

"That was different," Gardiner said, holding Vincent's stare. "It's over."

Vincent reached over to North and took the file folder with the blood and urine analyses. "Can I keep these?" he asked. It was a test.

"Sure," Gardiner said, waving his hand at the folder. "It's not an issue. There's no investigation."

"That other agency," Vincent said, "did they screw over Reese like this?" His words carried the quiet threat of the click of a safety being taken off a gun.

"No," Gardiner said, matching Vincent's smooth intensity. "Not like this."

Vincent held Gardiner's gaze for a moment, then nodded in understanding. "Thanks, Ed," he said at last, then turned to North. "C'mon partner, let's go fishin'."

Gardiner watched as the two agents walked away through the central area of the office. Tucker Browne would not agree, Gardiner knew, but he respected his men too much to try to mislead them completely, without giving them a chance. Eventually, Vincent and North would realize, if they hadn't already, that they had been cut loose just as Reese had been so they could be observed either confirming their guilt or proving their innocence.

Gardiner returned to his desk and picked up his phone, punching in a three-digit internal extension number, a number that had no connection to Reese, Vincent, or North. That avalanche was already in motion, he told himself, and nothing he could do now could stop it. Within the next two weeks, Vincent and North would be back at their desks, cleared of all suspicion, or they would be withdrawn. It was time not to think about it.

The extension was answered. Gardiner smiled. "Maria," he said into the phone, "I'd like to talk to you about a prescription."

TUESDAY, JULY 10, 10:14 PDT

"You know what the bottom line is, don't you?" Vincent looked over to his partner.

North was slumped in the bucket seat of Vincent's car, his right eye closed, his left eye still bandaged. He rubbed his heavily bandaged arm through the fabric of the sling. "I don't want to know," North said. "I just want to go away."

"We've been cut loose, Cy." Vincent turned his attention back to the front of the car, watching the up-and-down flow of citizens as they moved over the wide white marble stairs in front of the office tower housing the Los Angeles Field Office. "Just like Reese. It's so bloody obvious."

"What's so obvious?"

"What Merril said," Vincent explained. "Reese got involved in some other agency's action, and now the bureau doesn't know whether he's working for us, the other agency, or the bad guys. So they let him go so they could watch him and see who he'd go to first and he just goddam disappeared. And now we're next."

"For what?"

"For finding out who Reese is working for—if he's working for anyone. Who knows, maybe he just got drugged and used the way we were. But whichever way it went down, Gardiner's hands are tied, man. The other agency has stomped on him, made him pull our guys from the investigation. The only way he can find out what's going on is to send us on vacation and hope we've got the balls to break the case on our own, off the goddam record."

"Let's just leave it alone, Dave. Let's just take our vacation and leave it alone."

Vincent shifted his eyes over to North again. Tears were running from his partner's uncovered eye.

"If we do that, Cy, we're telling them that we don't have to solve the goddam mystery because we already know what it's about. That makes us guilty."

"What if we don't want to know?"

Vincent looked back to the crowds, scanning each face. "Then my guess is we do about twenty years for conspiracy."

"Conspiracy for what?"

"For whatever the hell they think Reese got himself mixed up—" Vincent threw open his door. "There he is!" Vincent shouted. A horn blasted and tires squealed as a passing car swerved to avoid Vincent as he emerged from the car by the curb. He ran over to the stairs.

"Reese!" Vincent called out as he ran up to the building, making only a token attempt to avoid the others in his way.

Alone among the shifting crowd of people, one figure stopped. He was tall, muscular, his body solid but his face sunken with fatigue and an expression that made Vincent think of North, slouched back in the car, still crying. Derek Reese's dark eyes, shadowed by heavy brows which gave him a perpetual expression of brooding inquiry, moved ceaselessly between the approaching Vincent and the other people passing by, waiting for an attack to be launched.

"David Vincent," Vincent said, reaching out a hand to Reese.

Reese didn't respond. That close, Vincent could see the bruises on the man's left cheek and down the thick cords of his neck.

"My partner and I were running surveillance on Sunday night."

Again Reese made no response other than to scan the steps again, eyes filled with suspicion.

"We found you in the closet."

Reese's eyes narrowed, his jaw clenched, powerful muscles working.

"Gardiner says you don't remember. That it isn't important. But we know you weren't in the house all that time."

Vincent still didn't know if he should suspect Reese of selling out, as the bureau first did, or try to enlist his help in finding out what happened Sunday night. But either way, he needed to open a line of communication with Reese.

Reese's eyes stayed cold, giving nothing. Vincent wondered what Reese's own blood tests would show, if they would give any clue as to what had happened in those thirty hours he had been gone. Vincent reached inside his jacket, then gasped as Reese's hand clamped around his forearm like a power vise.

"Jesus," Vincent breathed, struggling to pull back without success. He could actually feel the bones in his arm shift beneath Reese's grip. "I'm just going for a card, man. Take it easy."

Reese pulled his hand away, but his expression remained wary, like a hunted animal's.

Vincent produced a business card. He slipped it into Reese's shirt pocket.

"That's my address," Vincent explained. "I know how you got out of the house Sunday night." Reese's reaction, his instant flash of fear, was so strong Vincent stepped back in surprise. "I have photographs."

Reese put out his arm and pushed Vincent to the side. He began to move down the stairs, limping.

"Call me, Reese," Vincent said, moving beside the man. "If you want to find out what happened Sunday night, call me."

Reese stopped and turned to Vincent. His voice made Vincent feel the pressure around his forearm again, tight, strong, immovable.

"Maybe I don't want to know," Reese said, making it a threat. He turned back to move down the stairs again, and Vincent remained behind, for the first time wondering if he had made the right decision in confronting Reese directly. It was not the threat that made him feel that way; it was the echo of his partner's voice in what Reese had said, the echo of fear.

8

WEDNESDAY, JULY 11, 11:30 EDT

Twenty minutes into their first session, Sarah Gilmour made up her mind about Margot Jeffery. The family psychologist was an anchor to keep others from drifting, she decided. Her pale blue eyes were large and expressive, full of interest and enthusiasm, and despite the uncolored streaks of gray in her shoulder-length hair, those eyes were the bright eyes of a child and the delicate wrinkles that framed them really were smile lines. She made Sarah feel at ease, at home. It was a compelling reaction, a good one. Sarah made up her mind: she liked the psychologist.

"And I must tell you how delightful I find your daughter," Jeffery was saying. "Of course, the things that she and I talk about, like the things that you and I talk about"—she nodded her head to include Sarah and Steven—"remain confidential, but she is a remarkably composed young woman. Very steady. Extremely sure of herself." The psychologist's eyes sparkled, hers was the eager voice of a good friend. "You must be very proud of her."

After the uncertainty of the past few days, Sarah felt a welcome surge of relief pass through her. She was proud of her daughter, her baby. It was important to her that the psychologist had recognized those qualities in Wendy. It helped diminish the panic that had been growing since the appointment for this session had been made yesterday in Dr. Kohl's office. For the first time, she wondered if things were actually going to work out.

But Steven broke the moment. "I gather you're coming to a big 'but,' Dr. Jeffery."

The psychologist laughed, the sound like music. "A small one, perhaps. And please, call me Margot. Why don't we move over there?" she asked. "I think this desk of mine might get in the way."

"Over there" was a large sectional couch in the corner of her spacious sunlit office. The cushions were overstuffed, comfortable, and enveloping. Paintings of unicorns and Arthur Rackham prints hung on the walls, everything soft and magical, nothing upsetting or monstrous. Between the fanciful pictures, Sarah saw a scattering of official-looking certificates. The institution names printed on them included Johns Hopkins University, UCLA, the American Psychological Association, and the New York Psychoanalytic Society. There was also a small blue certificate with a familiar-looking spaceship printed faintly on it, framed with the same care and quality as the others, that identified Margot Jeffery as being a qualified crewman on the bridge of the USS *Enterprise*.

The psychologist caught Sarah blinking at the blue certificate and winked as she settled into her half of the couch, pushing a few brightly floral pillows to the side.

"Do either of you smoke?" Jeffery asked, leaning forward to a large ceramic ashtray on the square white coffee table framed by the couch.

Sarah saw a small orange Garfield doll wearing a No Smoking button sitting beside the ashtray. "No," she said.

Jeffery looked over to Steven, saw him shake his head also, then smiled as she pulled the ashtray off the table and slid it onto the sand-colored broadloom beneath it. All that remained on the table was the doll and a box of tissues, one white square already puffed out of the box like a flower, poised and ready.

"Now, about the little 'but,'" she said. "I'm not breaking any confidences or telling you anything you don't already know by saying that Wendy does have some problems in her life."

Sarah pulled a cushion onto her lap and held it there. Jeffery's tone was unconcerned, but the notion of Wendy having problems reminded Sarah that the panic hadn't gone; it was only waiting in the lower levels, ready to return at any second.

"What I find encouraging," the psychologist continued, "and refreshing, and which speaks well of Wendy and her relationship with her parents, is that she has discussed these problems with you in the past. In fact, it seems that she has a full and open relationship with you both."

"What sort of problems?" Steven asked. He was sitting stiffly, hands clasped between his knees, struggling between proper posture and the yielding stuffing of the couch. Sarah found his position unexpectedly endearing.

"For the most part, Wendy has all the problems of any teenage girl with her social, economic, and religious background." Jeffery leaned forward, sharing a secret. "High on the list is that she wishes some parts of her body were bigger and some parts were smaller."

Sarah laughed. Steven did too, though reluctantly.

"Also, she feels that she hates her music teacher, and she's worried that he might be her homeroom teacher next semester." Jeffery arched an eyebrow, underscoring how trivial these problems were in the large scheme of things. "A bit more seriously perhaps, Wendy also feels that she might bear some responsibility for your divorce."

"Oh no," Sarah interrupted.

"Not at all," Steven said.

Jeffery looked from one to the other, raising her hands to quiet them. "And I'm sure you're right. The truth is, many children of divorced parents share that feeling of guilt. Part of human nature is to try to find answers for everything. A child, who doesn't understand the character, the fragility of adult love, tries very hard to work out an explanation for why mommy and daddy no longer wish to live together. That explanation usually manifests itself as being linked to something within the child's control, something she or he can understand." Jeffery smiled. "Your daughter understands that. On her own, in a few years at most, I'm sure she'd come to feel it as well. With counseling, a few months at most. She is a very intelligent and aware child. And despite her minor suspicions of guilt, she loves you both very much."

"And we love her," Steven said, subdued.

"She knows that as well," Jeffery added. "A very fortunate child as well, I must say. In fact, I find it remarkable that in the midst of your divorce—four years, is it?—the parent-child relationship doesn't seem to have suffered in any way. Neither has Wendy's relationship with you tended to break off to favor one parent over the other. Tell me, Wendy didn't know the answer to this, but did you two by any chance have counseling when you decided to divorce? Did anyone help you develop strategies for making the process easier on Wendy?"

Sarah and Steven looked at each other. Sarah found herself feeling a ridiculous sense of pride. Talk about being a good parent, even their divorce deserved praise. "No, we didn't," Sarah said, trying to keep from smiling.

"It's funny," Steven added, "for all our differences, for all the reasons that led us to choose divorce, we, uh, never seemed to argue about Wendy. She was—is—the one thing in our lives that we usually find ourselves agreeing about."

Sarah nodded in answer to Jeffery's inquiring look. "Discipline, schools, the custody arrangement. Even her clothing allowance," she laughed. "We've been very fortunate." Sarah wanted to reach out and hold Steven's hand but restrained herself. Not appropriate, she kept reminding herself. So many things were not appropriate these days.

"Remarkable," the psychologist said, shaking her head in admiration. "More parents like you and I could be out of business."

"I hate to keep coming back to this," Steven tried again, "but you said that her problems were like other girls' 'for the most part.' What about the other part?"

Jeffery's face kept its kind expression, yet became more reserved. She was warning them that they had reached the serious part.

"I wanted to stress to you that Wendy is a normal teenager. The only thing that sets her off from other normal teenagers is what happened to her at the beginning of the week."

"What did happen?" Sarah asked urgently.

"That's just it," Jeffery replied. "I know Dr. Kohl suggested it was a possibility, but after my talk with Wendy, I do believe that she is not keeping anything from us. She does not remember what happened to her between Sunday afternoon and Monday evening, the time when her whereabouts were unknown."

"But that's a serious problem, isn't it?" Steven asked.

"Yes and no, Mr. Gilmour. I don't want to diminish the gravity of Wendy's . . . predicament, but it is absolutely essential that you realize how anomalous her behavior is. She does not exhibit any obsessive-compulsive tendencies. I detect no indications of other neuroses. There are children who can walk into my office and, after I talk to them for half an hour about their favorite TV shows, I know that selective memory loss will be part of their overall profile, for whatever reason. But that symptom is not one that I would expect in your daughter."

"But is that a good sign or a bad sign, Doctor, uh, Margot?" Steven was on edge. Sarah could recognize it. Steven didn't have the patience for a long discussion. He wanted answers. He needed something he could begin to act upon right away. She hated that about him. She—

"I don't know at this point," Jeffery said. "Dr. Kohl said she has no apparent injury that could provide a physical cause for memory loss."

"So it's got to be the result of a traumatic experience, right?" Steven said, an efficient manager trying to wrap up an office planning meeting.

"Not necessarily," Jeffery said slowly, and for the first time Sarah heard a hint of coldness come into her voice. "Psychological memory loss can occur because of traumatic events, that is true, but it can also be caused by less severe events, distinguished only because they are chronic. Your daughter might have developed selective memory because of something that happened to her on Sunday night. But the same symptom might have resulted because of something that happened to her much earlier and continued to happen." She stared at Steven. "Do you have any idea what that might be?"

"Now wait just a minute!" Steven exploded. "I wouldn't take that filth from Kohl, and I won't take it from you!" He fought against the cushions to jump to his feet, but the softness of the sofa robbed him of speed and grace.

"Why do you find it necessary to shout at me, Steven?"

"Don't you think I've heard this crap before? I get it from the doorman at my building. I get it from clients. Wendy's an attractive girl. She stays at my apartment. But for God's sake, she's my *daughter!* I didn't rape her! I—"

"No one said anything about rape, Steven. Please sit down."

Sarah pushed the cushion from her lap, stood up beside Steven, and this time didn't stop herself from taking his hands in hers. "What you're suggesting is impossible, Doctor. Steven is not capable of it. Wendy would not . . . it's impossible." She sat down beside Steven, still holding his hands.

"*Kohl* said rape was a possibility," Steven said. His voice was rough.

"A traumatic event such as a rape could induce memory loss," Jeffery agreed. "What else makes you think of rape?"

"Dr. Kohl thought that Wendy might have run off with a boyfriend," Sarah said softly. "He implied that she, uh, had, uh, a lover but, uh wouldn't get into it with us. He said that it was up to Wendy . . ."

"And so it should be," Jeffery pointed out gently. "Your daughter is old enough to be making certain decisions about her behavior on her own. You have certainly seen to it that she . . . will behave responsibly and sensibly in certain situations."

Sarah blinked at the psychologist. What were all these people trying to tell her about Wendy? "We told Dr. Kohl that Wendy didn't have a boyfriend. That she didn't have the time or inclination for a . . . an involvement like that," Sarah went on, trying to make Jeffery understand that they weren't just talking about any teenage girl: they were talking about her daughter.

Jeffery smiled. "Love is rarely a question of time or inclination, Sarah. Your daughter is a mature person."

Sarah shook her head. "But . . . but there's been no one. I mean, she lives in Manhattan. It's not as if Steven would let her run around with someone without knowing where she is. I certainly don't in Litch—"

"Sarah, it's all right. Parents often have a difficult time admitting that their children are growing up, maturing, becoming adults. Wendy and I didn't discuss any of this because it frankly wasn't necessary. In all the assessment tests I had her take yesterday—the Chicago Index, MMPI, the Vogel-Peterson Inventory—Wendy ranks in adult standings. Emotionally, at least, your daughter has experienced love; she does know what love is, as much as any of us do, that is."

Jeffery smiled like a teacher imparting great wisdom. "Please," she continued, "was there anything else that made you think that there might have been a sexual element to Wendy's disappearance?"

Steven remained silent, staring at the coffee table. Sarah could tell this development in the conversation was painful for him by the way he was now trying to avoid meeting the psychologist's eyes, trying to avoid the admission of failure.

"Her swimsuit was torn," he said finally. "The bottoms. They were ripped."

"What swimsuit?" Sarah asked. She felt a sudden chill pass through her. She hadn't heard anyone speak of a swimsuit.

"That bikini," Steven said. "It was on the kitchen floor. It was . . ." he waved his hand at her in anger. "You don't remember. Why would you?"

"Is that true, Sarah?" Jeffery asked with concern. "You don't remember Wendy's swimsuit being torn?"

Sarah felt her cheeks burn. She was furious with Steven. How could he bring that up now? How?

"No, Margot. I don't remember that." She took her hands away from Steven's and moved so that they were no longer pressed against one another.

Jeffery watched Sarah reposition herself. "I sense that something new has entered this conversation. Am I missing a subtext here?"

Sarah drew herself up and spoke precisely and clearly. "I am an alcoholic, Dr. Jeffery."

The psychologist nodded. "Wendy had mentioned that. May I ask how long you've been sober?"

"Eighteen months."

"That's what Wendy said. She's very proud of you for that accomplishment. I feel very happy for you myself." Jeffery turned to Steven.

"How are you feeling now, Steven?"

"Angry," Steven said. As if it wasn't obvious, Sarah thought.

"What is it that is making you feel angry?"

"That Sarah was there when Wendy disappeared and she didn't do anything. Couldn't do anything."

Sarah was surprised at how quickly Steven had answered, speaking without first considering his words and carefully selecting them for the best possible effect, the way he usually did. It was just an outpouring of rage.

"How does Steven's statement make you feel, Sarah?"

"I *couldn't* do anything because I wasn't there!" Sarah said to Steven. "And I wasn't drunk!"

Jeffery's eyes darted between the two. "Has Steven said that you were drunk, Sarah? Steven, is that what you believe?"

"He hasn't said it, but I can tell that's what he's thinking," Sarah snapped. She bit her lip.

"She blacked out!" Steven insisted. "She let her daughter disappear, and she didn't do a thing because she *blacked out!*"

"I did not!" Sarah sobbed. "I don't drink anymore!"

Jeffery slid the box of tissues to Sarah and watched Steven intently as she asked her next question. "Why do you think Sarah blacked out?"

"Because she doesn't remember *anything!*"

Sarah jumped. She had never heard Steven shout with such rage.

Jeffery turned back to Sarah. "Sarah, is that true? You don't remember when Wendy . . . disappeared?"

"No!" Sarah cried. "I don't remember anything because there's nothing to remember!" She grabbed a handful of tissues. "I was making dinner. It was Saturday night," she began.

"Sunday," Steven corrected testily.

"Sunday . . . ?" Sarah repeated, thinking it over. "But I was making dinner. We had chicken and potatoes and—"

"You never had dinner," Steven argued. "The chicken was still in the bloody refrigerator. You tore the house apart, but you didn't make dinner. You didn't eat dinner. You don't remember! Admit it! You *blacked out!*"

Sarah opened and closed her mouth like a fish out of water. It was so confusing. It was— "Angel!" she said suddenly. "He was there for dinner. He'll tell you."

"Angel?" Jeffery asked Steven.

"A private investigator," Steven explained. "My company's used him for years. Plant security. Loss control. Industrial espionage protection. He used to be a policeman. We're good friends."

"And did he have dinner with Sarah on Sunday night?"

"No, no, she's just confused. Wendy didn't come home Sunday night. I didn't think much about it because sometimes they go visiting and miss the last train. No big deal when there's no school. There was no answer at Litchfield, so I thought that's what happened again. When Wendy didn't call in the morning and when she didn't arrive at the time she would if she had made the morning train and there was still no answer, I asked Angel to drive out and see if Wendy needed a ride back or something. He called and said that . . . that Wendy was gone and that Sarah had had a blackout." He reached out to Sarah. "He found you at the kitchen table, Sarah. You were still out of it when I got up there."

"Sarah, is that true? Is that what you remember?" Jeffery's voice was gentle, hushed.

"I . . . I don't know," Sarah said, crying quietly. "I . . . don't remember."

"Tell me one thing, Sarah," Jeffery asked gently. "I know you've answered this before, but I have to ask again. And it's very important that you answer as best you can. Very important."

Sarah looked up at the psychologist and could barely focus through tear-flooded eyes. "W-what?" she asked.

"Were you drinking at all last weekend? Think carefully. Anything at all?"

"N-no. I told you that. I am *not* a drunk." Sarah bent her head to her knees. Why wouldn't they ever let her forget that? Why wouldn't they ever forgive her for that?

Sarah felt Jeffery's soothing hand on hers. "I'm sorry, Sarah. I really am."

"Was this necessary?" Steven asked bitterly. "Does this have anything to do with Wendy?" To Sarah, he sounded somehow ashamed, as he had those times before the divorce when their evenings could degenerate into shouting matches, words and accusations that were later taken back but never forgotten.

"I think it might," Jeffery said. The music had gone from her words, but the compassion remained.

"H-how?" Sarah asked. She wiped at her nose, having trouble catching her breath and talking without gulping for air.

"We talked about how memory loss could be triggered by a traumatic event, such as rape," Jeffery said, "and how something similarly traumatic might be an explanation for Wendy's situation."

"Yes," Steven prompted.

"It would appear, Steven, that Wendy is not the only person to have experienced selective memory loss in response to something traumatic that happened to her on Sunday night. Since Wendy was the one who disappeared, quite properly we have focused our concerns on her. However, it seems possible that Sarah was also involved in whatever happened on Sunday night and, like Wendy, has developed selective amnesia to protect herself from the memory of it."

Steven's voice was like ice. "Something happened to . . . both of them?"

"It is a possibility," Jeffery said.

"And," Sarah added, taking a deep breath, "we've both *forgotten* what it was?"

"A possibility," Jeffery repeated.

"But," Steven said, staring down at the table again, "if that's true, how can we ever find out what it was? How can we ever know what happened?"

Finally, Dr. Jeffery brought back her smile. She leaned forward and patted Sarah's knee. "Tell me, Sarah," she asked, "have you ever been hypnotized?"

WEDNESDAY, JULY 11, 08:47 PDT

Derek Reese slept, his body thrumming with the dreaming overload of heightened sensation, the sweat pouring from him like a blind, instinctive reflex to wash away the memories coursing through him, playing on his mind as lightning plays on the clouds. In his dream, he heard the thunder of that night . . .

. . . in the cloudless desert. Somewhere in Nevada. No name on the map. Too far from the test ranges and the cities to be important. Reese crouched behind two boulders, smelling the dry heat of them, still warm, even with the bloated red sun minutes from the horizon. Stars pierced the deepening blue of the sky poised above him. He looked away from the stars. He didn't want to know about the night. He wanted to know about the plane.

Reese brought the binoculars up to his eyes, pushed himself across the dirt beneath him, angling up over the protective screen of rocks to stare down the gully wall at the men hiding in the wide arroyo stretching away from his hiding place.

The men waited for the plane to land. The restricted computer components were packed in shipping crates on the back of their pickup, along with the portable landing beacons with which they would guide the plane to its landing.

The truck pulled out of the niche in the far gully wall in silence. A moment later, the purr of its motor reached Reese's ears. They were going to set out the landing lights, he decided. The plane must be approaching. Reese rolled on his side, took the walkie-talkie from his belt, and switched frequencies to an open CB channel. The best camouflage was no camouflage. He held the radio to his lips. "Breaker, breaker," he announced. "Pinball's coming home big momma. It's Miller time. Over."

Through the binoculars, Reese watched as the point man on the back of the pickup lifted his own walkie-talkie to his ear.

The coded answer came back from Reese's fellow agents gathered at the highway cutoff four miles away. "Yo, Pinball, c'mon down. We got 'em on ice, good buddy. Over."

All Reese had to do now was give the final "breaker, breaker" and fifteen agents would burst out of the desert. Everything was poised for Reese to give the final order.

He watched the dark shapes on the gully floor race to set out the lights for the airplane. They're fast, Reese thought. As if in a Charlie Chaplin movie, the smugglers streaked back and forth across the desert floor faster than Reese could follow. He blinked to clear his eyes, and that fast, it was night. Pitch-black.

A vibration filled the air, reaching him even through the ground beneath him. Almost here, he thought. But the beacons weren't lit. How will the plane land?

Something crunched on the dry desert ground nearby. Has it landed? Reese thought. Panic built up in him. The stars over the horizon seemed to jump erratically, then settle into a new position several minutes from their last.

He looked down into the wide gully. Indigo lights, almost invisible to all except the inbound pilot, who would be wearing filtered goggles, sparkled back. Reese looked from one beacon to another. Where were the men? Where was the truck?

The beacons winked out. "Oh, God," Reese moaned. *They knew.* They knew he was there, hiding in the desert. *They knew.*

The desert whispered to him. Reese stiffened in uncontrollable fear. It swept over him like layers of suffocating mud. The men from the truck knew! They had found him. Before he could give the go code, they were going to—

With a scream Reese rolled away from the boulders. The sky flashed above him. Empty of stars. Only the blackness of something descending, something that swallowed the sky, swallowed the stars, getting closer.

The men in the truck, he thought. They knew where to find him.

Another crunch behind him. Another whisper. He shivered against the floor of the desert. He drew his gun from his shoulder holster. They were coming closer, closer. He could feel the weight and the bulk and the black presence of them.

Of the men in the truck.

They were in front of him. They knew where he was hiding. It was too late. He rolled to meet them, and they made him drop his gun down into the desert. It fell for a mile before it hit. Reese sobbed in uncontrollable anguish, trapped by the smell of the dry desert rocks. They had found him again. And he knew they were not the men in the truck . . .

. . . who made him wake screaming in his hotel room.

Reese lay rigid on the bed, sheets soaked in sweat and twisted. He stared at the ceiling, brilliant in the glare from every light in the room. He stared cautiously at the window. It was still covered with the aluminum foil and the thick silver of the wide gaffer's tape he had used to seal it. He would be safe. But only for the moment. Sooner or later, he knew, they would come back.

Gingerly Reese rolled to the side of the bed and sat up. His body ached with the pain of strained muscles and the sting of the scrapes and bruises he had sustained when he had crashed out of the closet on top of the splintered pine doors.

Slowly Reese dressed. When he pulled on his shirt, he could see the card that David Vincent had given him still in the pocket. Good, he thought.

Reese carried his 92S Beretta at the ready as he approached the window and peeled back a corner of the foil. No one looked back in at him. Outside the sky was bright with morning, and he knew he would be safe for another day.

Three blocks away from the Sheraton, Reese found the type of phone booth he wanted, with curved acrylic sides that would smear any eavesdropping laser. He stood in front of the keypad and punched out the number from Vincent's card, keeping his body between the phone and any hidden watcher, any directional mike.

Vincent answered on the third ring.

"I want to see the photographs," Reese said. "I have to know."

He had no choice. Sooner or later, Reese knew, they would come back.

They always did.

9

THURSDAY, JULY 12, 15:00 EDT

Trailed by streams of Tink's fairy dust, Peter Pan led Wendy and her brothers over Big Ben, toward the second star to the right, then straight on till morning.

"Sarah?" Dr. Jeffery said.

Sarah looked away from the framed Disney poster hanging by the psychologist's desk. "I was trying to remember the names of her brothers," she explained, embarrassed at having been caught daydreaming.

Jeffery glanced over her shoulder to see which picture Sarah had been looking at. "John and Michael," she said. "Michael's the one with the top hat and umbrella."

Sarah smiled and nodded. "And who were the ones who couldn't go? It's been so long since I've seen it."

"Mr. and Mrs. Darling. And Nana, the St. Bernard. All the care-givers were left behind. A classic child's nightmare." Jeffery's voice was kind, unhurried, but she gave the subtle impression that she wanted to move on. "It really is a wonderful story. Many levels. Quite enjoyable."

"I'll have to read it," Sarah said, thinking how odd that after ten years of teaching, six before Wendy and now four more since the divorce, she never had.

The psychologist adjusted the tape recorder on her desk, a

black Sony microcassette about half the size of a paperback. "Nervous?" she asked.

Sarah nodded. "I've never done anything like this before."

"Sure you wouldn't be more comfortable over on the sofa?"

"Oh no. Here is fine." Sarah liked the authority and comfort of sitting in front of the doctor's desk. Like being at the principal's office, she thought. It made her feel better to know that someone with power was in charge.

"Wherever you're most comfortable," Jeffery agreed. She got up and walked to the corner of her office. Thick curtains moved with a hum to cover the last sprays of light managing to sneak through the Levolors. The fabric cut the sound in the office as well as the light. Sarah felt secure, protected. She had missed that feeling.

"Now, are there any questions about this procedure that I might not have answered for you?" Jeffery asked. "Anything I didn't cover when we practiced the induction exercises?"

There was one thing, but it was embarrassing.

"Anything at all?"

"I . . . I will be able to wake up, won't I?"

Jeffery didn't laugh. "Absolutely. In fact, you'll never really be asleep. I'm afraid that's all just movie talk." Now she smiled, disarming Sarah completely. She knew so much, Sarah thought.

"What we call hypnosis is more like a state of intense concentration than anything else. I find it similar to those times when I might wake up some Saturday morning with nothing urgent to do, and I can laze around in bed for a few minutes. Have you ever had days like that, Sarah?"

"Yes," Sarah said, wondering what Jeffery was getting at.

"And as I lie there, not thinking about anything in particular, sometimes I find that I start remembering something that's happened to me in the past, a dinner out, a party, a talk with a friend, and like a daydream, I see and hear and experience everything that happened before. Has that happened to you, Sarah?"

"Lots of daydreams," Sarah said, nodding.

"Well, then, you already know what hypnosis is like. You'll feel like you're daydreaming. And that means you can come out of it at any time you choose because nothing is holding you there other than your own concentration. The difference from daydreaming is that I can help you concentrate quickly and easily, and then I can direct you to those things we've agreed to discuss."

"Like daydreaming with a friend?" Sarah asked. There was something about the stillness of the room, the soothing tone in the doctor's voice that made her feel at peace.

"Exactly," Jeffery said. She reached out to a small crystal paperweight on the corner of her desk and gave it a shake. Hundreds of tiny silver stars swirled inside in a gentle snowstorm. "A friend gave me this," Jeffery explained. "I find it's like watching fish in an aquarium. Very calming. Do you find it calming, Sarah? Like fish in an aquarium?"

Sarah watched the stars fall and rise and wondered for just a moment what it was that kept them going. But, yes, they were compelling, floating like fish, serene and peaceful. The sort of gift a friend would give.

"Very much," Sarah said, whispering so she wouldn't disturb the library stillness. She heard the soft click of the tape recorder turning on.

"I want you to keep watching the stars, Sarah. Concentrate on the stars, and you will be able to concentrate on anything else you choose. Do you understand, Sarah?"

"Yes." It was so obvious, Sarah thought.

"Are you concentrating on the stars, Sarah?"

"Yes."

"Do you see them floating? Soft and slowly? As you concentrate, you will find yourself feeling that way too. Do you feel that way, Sarah? Do you feel calm and relaxed like waking up early in the morning with lots of time to laze around?"

"Yes," Sarah said and had to admit to herself that she did feel wonderful. The stars danced around like gentle morning breezes blowing open the sheers in her bedroom. She stretched and felt tension rush from her body. She had the whole day off.

"When I count to three, Sarah, you will be able to take all that concentration and direct it wherever you choose. Wherever you choose to direct it, you will stay calm and relaxed and feeling just as you feel now. Do you understand, Sarah?"

"Yes." She really is repetitive, Sarah thought. But she's the boss until she's hypnotized me.

". . . three. Sarah, I want you to think of that list of places and dates we talked about. The ones we agreed to discuss. Are you thinking of that now?"

"Yes."

"Think of the first place on the list, Sarah. Tell me where you are."

"The Sans Souci restaurant in Carmel." Sarah giggled. She was just about to put a breadstick into her mouth when Steven started to move his eyebrows up and down like a British night-club comic. "Stop that," she said, then snapped off the end of the breadstick and giggled again as Steven moaned in agony.

"Who's with you?" Jeffery asked.

"Steven, stop that!" Sarah giggled again. Somehow Steven had slipped off his shoe and he was doing something extremely bad with his toe. She felt her heart race and her cheeks flush. She slid her hips forward in the chair and hoped the tablecloth was long enough. "You're so bad," she whispered. She wet her lips and breathed softly through her mouth.

"What day is it, Sarah? What year?"

"April 29, 1971." She took a deep breath. How did Steven know her so well? How could he do these things to her, as though he knew everything there was to know about her?

"Why are you there?"

Sarah slowly rocked her hips. "Steven said we had to get out of the hotel so we could at least tell people we had seen Carmel. Oh . . ."

"Are you all right?" There was concern in the psychologist's voice.

"Ohh yes," Sarah said. "Oh!" She sat bolt upright in her chair and adjusted the napkin on her lap.

"What's wrong?"

"The waiter's coming." Sarah giggled again at Steven's whispered joke. "I was not," she said indignantly.

"Is Steven with you?"

"Yes."

"Tell me what he's wearing, please."

Sarah's eyes took in her new husband. God, he was handsome. His features filled gaps in her vision she never knew existed. "He's wearing his green polo shirt. And it looks so good on him. So tight on his shoulders and his chest. And he has slacks on . . . slacks I think the ones we got at Macy's. Yes, those ones. Great from the back. And—" Sarah paused. There were some things one didn't tell a friend, even in a dream.

"What else is he wearing, Sarah? Describe him."

Sarah spoke quietly, trying not to be overheard by the couples at the other tables. "When we were walking to the restaurant, he told me he wasn't . . . wearing any underwear. And you can tell."

"And what are you having for dinner, Sarah?" the psychologist asked quickly.

"The same that we had that first day we met. A Sebastiani chardonnay. Scallops. Perfectly cooked scallops. Oh, Steven, . . ." Her voice melted with love.

"What do you see?"

"Oh, my. He's bringing out a package from under the table and he unwraps it and it has an Oreo cookie in it." Her love for Steven exploded out of her, obliterating her in the process. She wanted nothing more in all of life than to be with him, to be part of him, and to bring forth life with him.

"Why an Oreo cookie?"

"That's what we had the first day we met. Our first dinner. I love you too. Oh, God, I love you too." Sarah felt her eyes fill with tears. He sat not three feet away from her, and still her need for him was so great, so overwhelming, so—"No," she whispered, "I don't want to wait for dessert either."

"Sarah, I want you to think of the second place on the list."

Sarah rubbed her hand over her face and squinted across at the alarm clock by her bed. She ran her tongue over her teeth and groaned.

"Is something wrong, Sarah?"

"Pizza hangover," Sarah said. She and Wendy had really done it last night. Triple anchovies. She looked down and saw her ankles had swollen. Double diuretics today, old girl, she thought.

"Where are you, Sarah?"

"In the bathroom off my bedroom."

"What day is it?"

"July 8."

"What day of the week?"

"Sunday."

"Who is with you today?"

"Nobody right now." Sarah looked at herself in the mirror. Sucked in her cheeks. Who would want to be with her? she thought. There had been lots of them after the divorce, when she had been drinking. They all blended into one blurry face and one blurry body. But since she'd been sober, no one. What was the point? Steven was the one she had been—

"Is anyone else in the house?"

"Wendy," Sarah said. "The little rat fink."

"Why do you call her that?"

"She's probably *lost* three pounds after all that pizza." Sarah shook her head at the unfairness of it. "The kid never gets sick and never has to diet. She's perfect, even if her parents aren't."

"Is it important that you feel perfect?"

"Oh no. I know I'm not. Neither is Steven. But parts of us are. Wendy is. I know that, too."

"What time is it?"

Sarah looked back at the clock by her bed. "Eight forty-eight," she said.

"Sarah, I want you to move ahead a few hours as we discussed. Where are you at noon?"

"I'm at Harper's. Have to get some vegetables for tonight."

"Is Wendy with you?"

"No, I dropped her off at Maxine's."

"What time did you drop Wendy off?"

"Eleven. Eleven-thirty. I'm going to pick her up at two so she can get in some time by the pool." She snapped her fingers. "Almost out of sunscreen. I think they keep it on the far aisle."

"Sarah, go ahead to two o'clock. Where are you?"

Sarah chewed the inside of her cheek. She didn't like to talk while she was driving. "Just driving up to Maxine's house. I can hear her silly dog barking."

"Is Wendy there?"

"Yes. Here she comes. No, wait. She has to turn and hug Maxine goodbye. I don't understand. She tells me she doesn't like Maxine, but then she always goes to visit her and then she complains about her for the rest of the weekend. Hi, honey. Yes, I got it."

"Is Wendy in the car?"

"Yes." Sarah laughed. "She's complaining about Maxine already."

"It's three o'clock, Sarah. Where are you?"

"In Wendy's bedroom." Sarah wrapped her arms around herself.

"Are you all right?"

"No," Sarah said. "No, I'm not."

"Where's Wendy?"

Sarah looked out of Wendy's bedroom window. "She's by the pool."

"What is she doing?"

"She's lying on her stomach on the green chaise, reading *Seventeen,* eating Ruffles, and drinking a diet Coke. What a kid. Potato chips and a diet Coke." Sarah shook her head, then pursed her lips at the sight of the tiny black strap that pretended to cover Wendy's backside. Only if you're in the backyard by yourself, young lady, she had said.

"Is she all right?"

"Oh yes. I rubbed the sunscreen all over her back. She won't burn."

"Why aren't you all right, Sarah?"

"The lock on Wendy's window isn't strong enough."

"Is it important for the lock to be strong?"

"Of course," Sarah said angrily. "You don't want people coming into your bedroom through the window."

"Do people come in to your bedroom through the window?"

The voice in Sarah's head answered. "No."

"It's three-fifteen, Sarah. Where are you?"

"Front hall. Damn!"

"What's wrong?"

"Steven didn't send the man to install the new dead bolt."

"Is the lock broken?"

"Which one?"

"How many do you have?"

"Where? Listen. There it is again."

"What did you hear?"

The voice answered, "Nothing."

"Where's Wendy, Sarah?"

Sarah stood in the hallway. Both dead bolts were thrown and the chain was on, but it wouldn't be good enough. It never was. She opened the closet and punched in the burglar alarm code on the Corby Keyless. The red light switched on beside the green light.

"Where's Wendy, Sarah?"

"Outside," Sarah said. She stared at the red light above the numbered buttons on the burglar alarm keypad. The system was armed. The system was useless. It didn't work last time either, she remembered.

"Where outside?"

"By the pool. Where they can get her."

"Where *who* can get her?"

"They have to be able to get her," Sarah said. "I can't keep explaining all this to you. I have to make dinner." She ran into the kitchen and clattered in the cupboard by the refrigerator, trying to knock around the Le Creuset pots.

"What are you doing, Sarah?"

"Trying to make noise."

"Why?"

"So I won't hear them."

"Hear who?"

"The door's opening. Oh, God. Oh, Jesus. I have to make dinner, but . . ."

"You locked the door, Sarah."

"*Locks don't work!* Don't you *know* that? They *never* work."

Something dark passed by her. She jumped back from the cupboard with a gasp. A casserole pot clattered noisily on the tiles.

"What's wrong? What happened?"

"I dropped a pot on the floor," Sarah said as she reached down and lifted it, checking the tiles underneath for cracks and chips, trying to keep looking straight ahead and not around.

"Does Wendy know they're in the house?"

"Who?"

"Wendy."

"I . . . don't know any Wendy. I have to make dinner."

"Why don't the locks work, Sarah?"

That was a relief. The voice didn't want her to say anything more about Sunday. But Sarah had often thought about the locks herself. "I think, and I don't know this for sure because they never told me for sure, but I think it's because they come in through the closets." She pulled the bag of potatoes out from under the sink.

"Who comes in through the closets, Sarah?"

"You know."

"I don't know. Who comes in through the closets?"

Sarah smiled. There was no more need to be frightened. There was the answer. "Smokey Joe."

"Who's Smokey Joe?"

"He's the bestest cat in the whole wide world. Aren't ya, Smokes?" Smokey Joe flipped right around on Sarah's little-girl lap and waved all four paws at her in a token effort of resistance to her tickling fingers. His purring was loud and sloppy. A little bubble of drool formed at the corner of his mouth.

"Is Smokey Joe your cat?"

"All mine, 'slong as I feed him an' change his box an' his water."

"Is Smokey Joe in the kitchen with you?"

She was back in the kitchen. The voice had taken everything away from her. Wendy, the babies, everything.

"No," Sarah said. "There's nothing in the kitchen with me."

"Where's Smokey Joe?"

Sarah kept her voice down. "He's in the hallway. He's staring at me."

"Why are you whispering?"

"I don't want them to know that you're here with me, otherwise . . . you'll have to go outside, too."

"Whom don't you want to know about me?"

"Smokey Joe. He hears everything."

"Is Smokey Joe watching you now?"

"Yesss."

"Tell me about him. What does he look like?"

Sarah looked around the doctor's office, shook her head.

"Sarah?" Jeffery asked with concern.

Sarah looked at the doctor and for a moment was shocked. The woman's hair was plastered on her forehead with sweat, her large, friendly eyes were round with apprehension.

"Margot? What is it?"

"You're out of it?" Jeffery asked.

"Out of what?"

"Do you remember what we talked about, Sarah?"

It rushed back to Sarah. "Was that it?" she asked, half smiling. She remembered being in the restaurant in Carmel, Steven sliding his foot along her thigh. She blushed. "Was I hypnotized?"

Jeffery nodded her head, nervously it seemed. "You were in what most people would call a hypnotic state. Do you remember what you were telling me?"

Had she told the doctor about what Steven had done to her? How she had almost responded? She sighed with relief. "Oh yes, I remember talking about the restaurant Steven and I went to on our honeymoon." She smiled. "I remember I could see everything quite clearly. I, ah, only answered a few questions that you asked me, but I could see a whole lot more. It really was like almost being back there again." Sarah stretched out in her chair. She felt wonderful.

"Do you remember telling me about last Sunday?"

Sarah blinked. "No, I— Wait a minute." It came back to her. She trembled violently. "Oh, dear God."

"You remember about the locks and Wendy being outside so that 'they' could get her? And how you didn't remember who Wendy was?"

Sarah crossed her arms over her chest and rocked in the doctor's chair. "Oh, dear God," she said. "I saw Smokey Joe."

"Your cat?" Jeffery asked anxiously.

Sarah felt she was in a raging windstorm. It was so hard to catch her breath.

"Used to be my cat," she managed to say. "Been dead for years." She looked at the doctor with all her fear spilling out from her, into her friend. "What did I see, Doctor? Dear God, what did I see?"

Jeffery reached for her crystal paperweight again. "That's what we're going to find out," she said. And the stars flew.

THURSDAY, JULY 12, 22:38 PDT

The tiny lights in the trees sparkled like fireflies, shifting in the soft evening breeze that lightly blew across the outdoor dance floor.

Edmond Gardiner looked down to the woman in his arms and saw those lights reflected in her dark eyes.

"Feeling better?" Maria Perez asked, wheeling about him with a lilting laugh and smile as the final notes of "Take the 'A' Train" faded to be lost amid the rustle of tree leaves and the murmur of the crowd.

"Much better," Gardiner said, joining in her laughter. "I feel like an old fool out here, but I feel much, much better."

She stopped her wheeling and held his arms, moved against him. "A fool, perhaps, but never old," she said.

Gardiner looked into her eyes and wondered how he could have worked so long with her without ever noticing how beautiful they were. "Thank you," he said.

They walked back to their table at the edge of the floor. White-jacketed waiters wove effortlessly among the other dancers returning to their own tables.

"Champagne?" Gardiner asked as a waiter stood by.

"How romantic," Perez answered. Gardiner placed the order

and marveled how the woman could say something like that and make it seem she were saying it for the first time. The empty space on his ring finger no longer felt so strange. He felt young.

Perez leaned forward and placed her chin on her hand, and he realized he had been caught up in his own thoughts for a moment.

"A good day at the office, dear?" Perez asked mischievously.

"We didn't win, but we didn't lose," Gardiner said, returning her smile. "So it was a good day."

"The Reese thing still getting to you?"

"Not under our jurisdiction anymore." Gardiner had wondered if they would be able to get through an entire evening without shoptalk, but strangely didn't find it upsetting to be discussing work with her. She knew all the players, all the problems. It was more like reporting than explaining.

"I wondered about that when my office didn't get the drug test results on Vincent and North." Perez frowned. "Everything's all right, isn't it?"

Gardiner considered her question carefully and knew that two hours into their first outing—at his age he couldn't bear to use the word "date"—he had reached a crossroads. If he told her everything he knew about the case, he would be letting her into his life with honesty and openness. If he tried to stonewall her, then she would be like all the other civilians out there, bureau agent or not.

Gardiner sighed. First and foremost, he was an officer of the law. Or tried to be.

"Everything's fine," he lied. "Just not in our hands anymore."

He watched Perez's eyes for a flicker of understanding, some indication that she realized the first brick between them had been put into place. Thankfully he didn't see it. Though that could mean she's able to hide her true reaction, he thought, meaning she's already put a brick in from her side too.

The champagne arrived, and the waiter opened it with great ceremony. Gardiner watched it as it frothed into the tall flute before him. It looked flat, its bubbles lifeless.

He toasted Perez with it. She smiled back at him, but the lights no longer danced in her eyes.

The evening deteriorated. As if he were donning a hair shirt, Gardiner began to talk about Maureen, their children, their cabin, her illness. Perez listened politely and more, but Gardiner kept himself from understanding where her courtesy sprang from.

"Do you still have the cabin?" she asked, speaking up over the band. She and Gardiner weren't dancing this set.

"The children have it. But I think they're going to sell it next year." He drained his champagne glass. "Things change."

"Not the important things."

"Their importance does. The cabin was there for twenty years. Maureen and I loved it. The cabin might keep standing for another hundred years, and during that time it won't be important to my children."

"Then maybe to your grandchildren, or the great-grandchildren of someone else will find it in the woods and fall in love with it all over again. It will be a hundred years old but brand new to them." Perez watched as she swirled a final sip of champagne in her glass. "At least, it happens that way with people sometimes." She drank it. An ending.

Gardiner stared at her as she fumbled for something in her tiny beaded evening bag. He had the terrible feeling that she had been speaking all night, saying profound things to him, and he hadn't listened to a word.

"Maria?" he began, leaning forward so she would hear him over the band. Perez looked up, her sudden smile vanishing, her eyes widening.

Gardiner felt the hand on his shoulder and twisted like a thirty-year veteran of undercover work and not a ballroom dancer.

"Take it easy, Ed. Take it easy."

But Gardiner couldn't. It was Roy Luck.

At least now the evening is perfect, Gardiner thought with disgust. He straightened his tux jacket, preparing to go through the motions of the game as though Perez were not a player.

"Maria, may I introduce—"

"Dover," Luck interrupted, stretching out his arm and grinning like a teenaged boy meeting a stripper. "Harry Dover. Pleased to meet you."

Perez shook his hand, but Luck held the grip too long, letting his hand slide away slowly. Gardiner half expected to see a trail of slime left behind.

"Ed?" Luck said, "got a minute?" He was acting like a bad salesman.

Gardiner looked to Perez. She smiled and told him she was going off to the powder room anyway.

"Reese has made a move," Luck said coldly, now that there was no audience.

"So?" Gardiner said. He wasn't going to stoop to asking Luck for information.

"He must have known he was under surveillance, but it didn't matter. He called your guy, Vincent, and we recorded the whole thing on his end. Reese said something about wanting the photographs. Ring a bell?"

Gardiner shook his head.

"Then Vincent said he'd arrange to get back in touch with Reese over a secure line. He's playing it cute, Ed. Must have had a good teacher."

"Is there a point to any of this, Roy?"

Luck scratched the side of his nose. His elbow jarred Gardiner's champagne glass, made it rock. "Only that they were going to set up a meeting to see the photos. Had to check with some guy called Merril."

Gardiner didn't blink. He knew about Vincent's friend, Merril. And that friend wasn't a guy. But he wouldn't tell Luck that. "So what, Roy? You wanted to go after Vincent and North because you thought they let Reese escape from surveillance. Then, surprise, Reese is back in the beach house under the noses of *your* people. Did you ever think that maybe Reese *didn't* leave the house? That maybe Vincent and North have been set up?"

"Reese left the house, Ed. There's no doubt. We took the place apart."

"Then how did he get back in?"

"That's what concerns us. Any organization that can circumvent our procedures so thoroughly is an organization to be feared. And if Reese is working for them, whoever *they* are, then every intelligence agent Reese has ever worked with, or knows of, is at risk of identification and assassination. We are not prepared to live with that risk."

"What *are* you prepared to do?"

"Tail them to the meeting. Take 'em down with the photos," Luck said, waving his finger back and forth like a stuttering machine gun. Standing on a suburban lawn, he could be talking about spraying the garden for weeds. Standing in jackboots, he could be talking about Bergen-Belsen and Dachau. Psychopath, Gardiner thought, and hated the man more than ever.

Luck looked away and saw Perez approaching. He stood up to go.

"Do you want the bureau in on this?" Gardiner asked.

"Third time's a jinx, Ed. Nobody in D.C. is going to trust your boys out here. But not to worry. We have it covered. You can come in to bag the pieces when the smoke clears."

Perez reached the table. Gardiner jumped to his feet, grabbed Luck by his shoulder and whispered forcefully into his ear. "Tell Tucker it doesn't have to be done that way. You don't have *proof*."

Luck pulled back, adjusted his jacket. "Sorry, Ed. But your boys are loose pistols, just like Reese. No one can risk Vincent and North giving away other agents' identities while we poke around for proof."

"But you don't know that they know anything for sure!"

Luck ignored Gardiner and turned to smile at Perez. "Goodnight, Doctor. I'll let you get back to your patient now."

Luck walked away in time to the music. Gardiner was shaking as he sat down. Perez changed her chair to sit beside him, put her hands on his.

"He's OCI, isn't he?" she asked.

Gardiner nodded, too upset to speak. The new generation of agents, he thought, that's what set them apart, that's what made what they did so insane—all they lived for was to act. And if they didn't have enough information, they made their best guess, no matter how many innocents might be caught up in their mistakes. He was sick of it. Sick of them.

"What's wrong, Ed?"

Gardiner turned to Perez. She was different. She would understand. After thirty years of discipline and duty, Gardiner realized that for once he was going to act according to his heart. Somewhere along the line, right and wrong had become separated from the rules and regulations. Gardiner realized that he might be having trouble adapting to the brave new world of Roy Luck and Tucker Browne, but right and wrong were things he had always understood.

"You're right," he said to Perez.

"About what?"

"The important things don't change."

"What important things are those?"

"Right and wrong." Gardiner nodded. He could see what he must do. He looked at Perez, into those eyes, with their welcoming light. He would begin by taking down the bricks.

"That man is going away to arrange the murder of two of my agents," he began. And then he told her everything, including his plan to save them.

10

Steven Gilmour sat on the sectional couch across from Dr. Jeffery. The only way he would sit with a desk between them was if it were *his* desk. He didn't like being with this woman. He felt she judged everything he said, analyzed every movement, every pause. Taking control from him.

"Are you comfortable?" the psychologist asked.

There she goes again, Steven thought. She knows I'm not. It's a technique to establish control.

"Actually," he said, "I find the cushions too soft."

"Oh, I could tell that," Jeffery said, smiling. "I was just wondering how you felt about being in a psychologist's office."

"I don't think that's important," Steven said blandly, though he seethed inside at this woman and her games. "What is important is that I find out what happened to my daughter."

Jeffery nodded her head. "Fair enough," she said. Then she picked up the black Sony recorder from beside the orange Garfield doll.

"Now, as I told you on the phone, Steven, what Sarah and I did yesterday was somewhat unusual."

Steven nodded calmly, thinking, What's on the bloody tape, for God's sake?

"Normally, in a case of hysterical memory loss such as exhibited by Wendy and Sarah, the pattern of . . . treatment . . . is conducted over many weeks, even months. However, there is a unique element to this case that I believe warrants the acceleration of traditional methods."

"That unique element being . . . ?"

"The fact that Wendy actually was missing. That, and certain things said by Sarah in our first hypnotic session, led me to suspect that a crime had been committed and that the authorities would need any information or leads as soon as—"

"What sort of crime?" Steven interrupted. Why wouldn't this woman get to the point?

Jeffery held her hands up in supplication. "A kidnapping, Steven. Please, this is a complex situation. Normally I wouldn't be playing these tapes for you, but I have Sarah's and Wendy's permission, and frankly, I can't think of any other way to proceed." She looked at the tape recorder. "Quite complex."

"Look, Doctor, I'm finding this very confusing. My daughter is kidnapped. The police are all over me. She comes back, and they say thank you very much, just another runaway. Dr. Kohl said she's okay, no signs of violence, but hints that she might have been raped and tells me to come to you for . . . psychological counseling. So I come to you, and you tell me that my daughter might have been kidnapped!" Steven clutched at air. "Can't anybody give me a straight answer?" He pointed to the tape recorder. "Does that give any answers?"

Jeffery returned the recorder to the table, beside a stack of three microcassette cases. Steven could see minuscule handwriting across the labels on them.

"I don't know if you'd call this an answer, Steven. I was hoping to get your opinion."

"Then play the thing."

"That's why I asked you here." She started the recorder and watched a digital readout, advancing the tape to the proper starting point.

"I'm going to begin halfway through our second session. Sarah is an excellent subject for hypnosis." She glanced up at Steven and gave him the feeling that she was reading his mind. "Which, I might add, is a sign of intelligence and a well-developed imagination. Admirable qualities." She turned her attention back to the recorder.

"Before the section I will play for you, I first led Sarah through some induction exercises that make establishing a hypnotic trance much easier. Then, once she was hypnotized, I had Sarah recall innocuous events. Wendy's last birthday party. Her school's Christmas assembly. A dinner you once had. Just to get her familiar with the technique and comfortable." She held her finger above the "play" button. "Now, I must caution you that some of what Sarah experiences in this session is upsetting to her. In the first session, she began to recall it and spontaneously came out of her hypnotic state."

"Was this dangerous for her?" Steven asked. Despite the divorce, he still cared enough for Sarah not to want her in the hands of a quack.

"Not at all. She's simply remembering. But to make the upsetting parts easier to handle, I helped her create the device of watching her memories on a television set. That way, if she sees something upsetting, she can stop the picture or look away. If she hears something upsetting, she can turn down the volume."

"Can she change channels?" Steven asked sarcastically.

"Yes, even that, if she chooses to, so she can switch over to other, pleasant memories." Jeffery sighed. "I sense your hostility to this technique, Steven, but the thing to remember is that it worked for Sarah."

"Just as long as you don't have her start wearing crystals and meeting with Shirley MacLaine when she's in a trance."

Jeffery looked at Steven with her large caring eyes and said nothing. She pressed the "play" button. "I believe you'll find that levity is not appropriate at this time," she said and sat back in the sofa as Sarah's voice filled the room.

"Now I'm looking behind the curtains. There's a space there. A shape . . . I don't know. I pull the curtains away, but there's nothing. I can still hear them crying . . . they're crying but . . . what? What?"

"What do you hear, Sarah?"

"Shhhh! Can't you hear? They're crying for me. I can hear them crying for me! But where are they? Where?"

"What's she going on about?" Steven asked. He was uncomfortable hearing Sarah talk like that. It reminded him of the times when they had been together and she had been drinking, out of control.

"She's looking for her babies," Jeffery said quickly. "She feels that she has lost some babies in the house or that they've been taken away from her."

"She had a miscarriage once," Steven said, confused. "Before Wendy was born."

"She told me," Jeffery said, leaning forward to rewind the tape. "Please, Steven, listen."

"Where are you looking now, Sarah?"

"The pine box . . . a blanket box . . . I can hear them in there . . ."

"Are you looking inside?"

"Yes . . . yes . . . but there's nothing there . . . nothing there . . ."

"Why is she crying?" Steven asked. This was completely wrong.

"She's responding in the same way that she felt at the time—Sunday afternoon, just before Wendy was taken."

Steven sat back in the sofa, cringing at the wild emotion in Sarah's voice. He thought of witch doctors and holy rollers in tents as he heard the anguish in Sarah's words. She described tearing apart the decorations in the pine box, looking in old shirt boxes for crying babies, for God's sake. Why?

Dr. Jeffery's voice came back on the tape.

"Where is Wendy now, Sarah? Is she still by the pool?"

"No, she's in here with me."

"In the living room?"

"Yes."

"What's she doing?"

"I . . . I don't know . . . it's like I don't recognize her . . . she's not one of my babies . . . she wants something . . ."

"What does she want?"

"She wants me to get up. That's it. I want to tell her to speak up, but it's . . . she's too far away . . ."

"Where is she?"

"In the living room . . . oh . . ."

"What happened?"

"They want her to go with them now. She has to go . . ."

"Who wants her to go? Where?"

"Ooops . . . it's okay . . . don't hurt her . . . you *don't* have to do that!"

"What did they do? Who's there, Sarah? Who?"

"Smokey Joe . . . hi there, Smokes . . ."

Steven let out a snort. "That's the cat she had when she was—"

"Shhh!" Jeffery said. Steven sat back, his knee bouncing up and down in impatience.

"What's Smokey Joe doing?"

"He's telling me that it's time to leave."

"Does he say that to you in words?"

"No . . . but I hear him . . . time to leave—right, Smokes?"

"Where are you now?"

"In the hallway . . . dinnertime, I think, but . . . oh . . . careful with her don't . . . *don't* . . ."

"Don't what? What do you see?"

"They're going to rip her swimsuit if they do that . . . I don't think they know what it is . . . it's . . . yes on her side, like that . . . I can show you if you want . . . *careful* . . . what? Oh, okay. No dinner. Bedtime, it is."

"Where are you?" Steven heard exhaustion in Jeffery's voice, maybe even fear. He began to have the terrible feeling that the psychologist somehow believed this fantasy, that she didn't have his own absolute knowledge that such things were impossible and never to be thought about.

"I'm going upstairs . . . Smokes says it's time for bed . . . up you get . . . want under the blankets, boy?" There was a long silence.

"Where are you now?"

"In bed . . ."

"What are you doing?"

"Sleeping . . ."

"Are you alone?"

"Smokey Joe is here."

"Can you see him?"

"I can feel him . . . he's on the bed . . ."

"Look at him, Sarah. Can you tell me what he looks like?"

"No." Steven resisted the impulse to ask Jeffery to run the tape back. That last answer hadn't sounded like Sarah.

"Why can't you look at him?"

"Don't want to. I'm afraid."

"Sarah, I want you to step back from the television set so the picture is very small, so small that you can just see everything but without a lot of detail. So small that nothing you can see can frighten you. Can you do that, Sarah? Can you put Smokey Joe on the screen?"

"Yesss . . ."

"Very slowly, I want you to step up to the screen. Very, very slowly, and tell me what you see. Describe Smokey Joe to me . . . Sarah, can you do that?"

Steven leaned forward again. He could hear the strain in Jeffery's recorded voice, the dread in Sarah's.

"He's white . . . pale white . . . dead white . . ."

"Is he big? Little? Thin? Fat? Tell me everything you see."

"Little . . . a little . . . I'm not sure . . . like a man . . . a little man . . . boy maybe . . . arms and legs are tiny . . . chest tiny . . . all wrinkled up like skin . . . like when I had Wendy and my stomach was so big and then wasn't . . . head is big though . . . big big head . . . big big eyes . . . oh no, oh no—"

"What's wrong?"

"He doesn't want me looking at his eyes . . . he says no . . . his eyes are so big . . . so black . . . so—" Sarah's scream ripped through the tiny speaker, and Steven jerked forward, slapping his hand on the coffee table to keep from falling from the sofa. He hadn't realized he had leaned over so far, drawn in by the voices on the tape.

"This is preposterous!" he shouted at Jeffery. "Listen to yourself on that tape! You believe it!" He pushed himself up to his feet and stormed away from the sofa. He didn't want to hear anymore. He *couldn't* hear anymore.

"I have to believe it," Jeffery said evenly. "And so must you."

"Believe what?" Steven exploded. "That some . . . some midget in a cat suit is climbing around my wife's bedroom in the middle of the night! Something with a big head is stealing my daughter when I'm not there to protect her? Give me a break, Doctor. Grant me some intelligence at least. How could anyone believe a pile of crap like that?"

Jeffery held the switched-off recorder under her chin, tapping it lightly against her neck. "I understand your anger, Steven, but I think that you're resisting an important realization here."

Steven flapped his arms at his side. "I'm listening, Doctor. I'm not resisting anything. Not anything important at least." He fought the unreasoning urge he felt to clamp his hands over Jeffery's mouth.

"The important point is that at the moment it is neither here nor there whether or not we accept that what Sarah is describing on this tape is the actual, physical reality of what happened in Litchfield on Sunday night. What is essential is that you realize that this is what Sarah *believes* happened. For some reason, Steven, Sarah honestly, truthfully believes that these are her memories of that night. No matter what you may say about the logic of those events, the likelihood of them, or whatever else, you cannot argue with the fact that this is what Sarah *says* happened."

Steven filled his lungs with air, held, and exhaled. He repeated the action until he was sure he could speak without hearing his own voice falter.

"Is Sarah crazy, Doctor?" he asked. And if she is, she'll never get within fifty miles of my daughter ever again, he thought.

Jeffery rolled her eyes at him. "Really, Steven. I think your whole family learned about psychology from 'General Hospital.' We don't use that word. And even if we did, Sarah wouldn't be. Now sit down. Stop expressing your anger by walking away. Confront me if you must, but be honest. Above all else, be honest with yourself and with me."

Reluctantly, Steven returned to the sofa. "Now what?" he asked. "Honest enough?"

"Lose the sarcasm too," Jeffery said, then shook her head. "Listen to me; I'm telling you what to do—the one thing I'm not supposed to. Guide, listen, inquire, but never proscribe." She smiled at Steven. "I was just as upset as you were the first time I heard this, you know. It really is incredible, I agree."

Steven studied her for a moment and for the first time felt that she wasn't sitting in professional judgment over him. That felt better. But he wasn't going to tell her that, give her that power over him. He looked at the recorder on the table and the stack of cassettes beside it. He wanted to forget everything he had heard. But he knew that Jeffery wasn't finished with him.

"Is there more?" he asked.

"Jesus, is there ever," Jeffery said softly. She wound the tape forward for a few seconds, then stopped it. "Up to this point," she explained, "it was like something was interfering with Sarah's recall. She kept mentioning that she couldn't see some things because they didn't seem close enough. Or that she couldn't hear some things because they were too far away. Or even that someone didn't want her to look or listen." She shrugged. "But starting at this next section, it seems that Sarah remembers taking a more active part in what was happening in the house and that the . . . people who—"

"People?" Steven asked. "More than one?" Please let there be limits to this, he thought.

"Several, apparently," Jeffery said. "Anyway, her description is a bit more clear in this next part." She pressed the "play" button again.

The thing that appeared before her as Smokey Joe prodded her hip lightly, and Sarah awoke.

She looked up at the ceiling and could see their shadows there, fluttering and quick, cast in the faint glow of the bedside clock and the hallway night-lights.

Her bed seemed to rush toward the ceiling, getting closer and growing smaller at the same time, so that no matter how fast she rose or how small she got, there would never be any impact. Only the terrible anticipation of something that would never be. It was a sign of their presence.

She looked around her room and saw them, as she knew she would. Somewhere, in some layer of her brain, a miniature Sarah shrieked in mindless fear, gibbering and drooling like a mad woman locked off in an asylum. But she herself remained silent and docile. Her fear had been compartmentalized, her mind sectioned off like a side of beef.

The part of Sarah that looked out at them now, the part that knew them and could stare unafraid into the glittering obsidian of their eyes, was under their control. There would be no resistance on her part tonight. And with that thought, she sensed that they relaxed, their movements slowed, the slender needles of focused light at their sides dissolved back into them. Things would go as they had been planned. Things would go as they always had before.

Sarah sighed as their tiny hands caressed her, wove their patterns around her, and floated her out the door and along the hall and down the stairs. It was at these times that she knew where her dreams of flying had come from. In her sleep, she had flown. In her dreams, she remembered times like these.

The kitchen was bright. Her eyes reacted slowly, as if waiting for the ophthalmologist's drops to wear off. But though her focus was blurred, she could see enough. The shadows that had corralled her earlier had shifted from black to white. They moved like mercury, like puffs of paper blown before a storm.

Busy, so busy. They reminded Sarah of her third-graders. And that thought made her remember something else.

She looked around the kitchen. Wendy floated over the breakfast table. Three of them worked over her with their wandlike probes. They seemed disappointed. But they were the drones, not the little mothers. She laughed. It was a funny name.

The one she was looking for stood beside her. He asked her if she were feeling well this evening. He had heard her laugh.

She tried to answer, but was unable to say anything. A spot of colored light floated across her face, and she felt her mouth released. "Will I be going up this time?" she asked, remembering to keep her voice soft, so they wouldn't be startled.

The one who stood beside her shook his head, the black lenses of his eyes almost sad. She could almost make out deep within them a faint iris, an even darker pupil. The delicate flaps of paper skin over his flat nostrils fluttered with his rapid breaths. The slit of his mouth remained open and unmoving. This close to him, the dry smell of sun and warm summer days faded and was replaced by the green scent of leaves and pine needles and growing forests. A fresh smell, a welcome smell. It was at these times that she knew from whence her love for these scents had come.

The one who stood beside her said that only Wendy would go this time but that Sarah shouldn't worry. Everything was going to be fine.

By now, Sarah could tell when they were lying.

From the corner of her eye, Sarah saw them float Wendy out through the kitchen door, or a space where the door used to be. She was naked of course; Sarah knew that that was necessary.

There were many other things that Sarah knew by this time, at times like these. Such as why they must be naked, such as why she avoided dark water, such as why she was still frightened by thunder as much as she had been when a child. But it was only at these times. Only with this part of her that they let loose to deal with them. At all the other times of her normal life, they kept her from remembering any of it.

The one who stood beside her lowered his silver probe to her forehead and told her not to be afraid. Sarah could feel the locked-up part of her pounding on the walls of its cage as the next procedure began, but she was not afraid. This part of her was not allowed to feel that way.

The forged light exploded.

When the sparks had faded away from her eyes, Sarah was sitting in her living room, naked, her nightgown, brought down from her closet and folded neatly by her side on the couch. One of them, another drone, knelt before her, between her legs. She wondered if they had finished, but those parts of her he worked on had not been released, so she couldn't tell.

They flew back and forth across the room in frantic motion, blowing like autumn leaves. Two scampered across the walls, and one across the ceiling. Her head was released. She looked around. Three scuttled through the hallway carrying what looked to be a dog. The dog stared dumbly back at Sarah for a brief second, then was gone from the doorway.

"Where's Wendy?" Sarah asked the drone before her.

The creature flew back in shock. She had forgotten. She apologized. The one who stood beside her was brought back. Part of Sarah wondered why she didn't recognize any of the others this time, as though a group different from all the others had come this time.

The one who stood beside her wherever she went, whatever they did to her, since the days of Smokey Joe, told her that Wendy would be fine, that everything would be fine. His eyes were so dark that they seemed to float before his face. Wouldn't be the first time, Sarah thought, that bodies had been deformed before her. And at times like these, she knew why there were some movies that she couldn't watch, whose makers had been here and unknowingly reproduced this, drawing from their own half-remembered dreams. Sarah did not want to see things like this when that locked-off part was free to react as it was driven to by its fear. Some movies she just avoided.

Sarah looked at the quartz clock on the second shelf of the brass bookcase. The minute hand vibrated back and forth. "Wendy should be back by now," she said.

They were rushing away, as if this time were over. The one who stood beside her patted her arm, ran his delicate white fingers gently across her cheek. Just like Steven used to, Sarah thought. With love.

The one who stood beside her said that Wendy would be back soon, that everything was fine. The same lie, Sarah thought. But before she heard another, she had been touched by a probe.

When the sparks faded, she sat at the kitchen table, all parts waking at different times, trying to link together. One part felt a hand touch her shoulder. She looked up. It was a human face. It had a human voice. It was Angel Good. It was over. For now.

Dr. Jeffery turned off the tape recorder after the final silence. She looked at Steven.

Steven felt her eyes upon him but refused to look at her. "Impossible," he said.

Jeffery said nothing.

"Insane," he whispered.

Nothing.

"There's no proof." It was his final defense. If there were such things, if such events could take place, then let her prove it to him or else send him home with his daughter and let him forget Sarah's madness. He knew he must forget.

Jeffery slipped another tape into the recorder, wound it forward, pressed the "play" button.

"Listen again, Steven. Listen carefully," she said to him.

Jeffery's voice was on the recorder. "Where are you now?" she asked. "Tell me what you see."

"The kitchen . . . I . . . floating . . . hard to see . . . the little one is there . . . I know . . . *don't* squeeze me like that . . ."

"What does the little one look like? Can you tell me?"

"His head is so big like those poor babies with that disease . . . and his eyes . . . so dark . . . go halfway around his head . . . but the rest of him is short . . . like a little boy . . . and white . . . like china . . . small and thin like the china people my mother has . . ."

"Dear God!" Steven said. His mouth dropped open. His chest froze as though an ice spike had been driven through him. "That's not Sarah . . ."

The voice on the tape recorder continued to describe the impossible and the insane.

"It's my daughter," Steven whispered. "Dear God, it's my daughter."

Jeffery reached over to touch Steven's hand. "And under hypnosis, she tells the exact same story as Sarah."

Steven stared blankly at the psychologist. Somewhere deep within him, a mad creature howled in its closed-off cell.

"They were both there," Jeffery said gently, chillingly. "They both saw and experienced the same thing."

"That's . . . that's . . . ," Steven stammered. He couldn't speak. Insane. Impossible. "That's . . ."

"Your proof."

PART TWO

CRITICAL GROUP

END QUATERNARY EVENT: T—46 DAYS

1

"Hey, Merril," Vincent shouted. "I think I finally realized something important about you." He turned from the life-sized poster on the wall in Beth's studio, showing a man in flames launching himself into the air.

"What's that, Ace?" Merril said from the studio door. She widened her eyes innocently as she brought a tray of coffee mugs into the room.

"Whenever I start running off at the mouth, you always tell me to 'flame off,' right?"

"So?" Merril put the tray down on a huge butcher-block table in the middle of the room, directly beneath a low-hanging light fixture that reminded Vincent of a pool-hall lamp. Every surface in the studio was covered with stacks of drawing paper and art boards, file boxes and more pens and pencils than Vincent had seen outside of an office-supply shop, but the central worktable was completely empty. Except for the pale gray ghosts of a dozen spilled ink bottles.

"It's this guy, right?" Vincent said, pointing to the figure in the poster, a muscular human shape covered in garish, comic-book streaks of black, red, and yellow rising into the air on a column of fire and, according to the word-balloon by his head, crying, "Flame on!" "So when he wants to cool down, I bet he says, 'Flame off.' Right again?"

"And I didn't think you could read," Merril said, screwing the top on a black thermos pitcher.

"So who is he?" Vincent asked, walking over to the table to see if he could help the reporter set things up. Vapor from the coffee in the pitcher drifted out in an almost invisible shifting curtain. Vincent inhaled. It smelled good. He guessed that Merril had decided this evening was not going to be a time for whiskey. He also noticed the absence of ashtrays and guessed that she also thought the evening would not last too long.

"He's the Human Torch," Beth said from the doorway. She came in and propped a large black-leather artist's portfolio against the table by Merril.

Vincent smiled when he saw Beth. It had been a long time since he had visited the women at their home.

"How are you, stranger?" Vincent said, giving and receiving a kiss on the cheek. "The hair looks good. Sorry there's no more purple in it though."

Beth laughed. She was about Merril's age, smaller, lighter. The smiling half of the theatrical masks, with Merril the tragic one. No, take that back, Vincent thought. Since Merril had bought this house with Beth and they had moved in together three years ago, Merril's intensity and drive had remained, but there was nothing more of tragedy about her. Merril had found her partner in life. Vincent considered her one of the lucky ones.

"So is the Human Torch one of yours?" Vincent asked.

Downstairs the doorbell rang. Merril said she'd get it and left.

"No," Beth said, slipping off her smock. "I don't do a lot of work for Marvel. This is what I'm up to now." She walked over to her drafting table and lifted up a crinkly sheet of tracing paper. Vincent examined the half-filled drawing board she had revealed taped to the table. It was neatly divided into a series of panels—he knew that much about comics, at least—and covered with intricate line drawings in blue pencil and black ink.

The action seemed to be taking place between some people in space suits and some other strange-looking people in robes. The backgrounds showed a skeletal ruined city half-buried in mounds of desert sand.

"Which one's the superhero?" Vincent asked.

"None of them," Beth said. Her distracted expression revealing how seriously she took her work. "It's a graphic novel. A comic book version of a regular book. This is for one of the stories in *The Martian Chronicles*. By Bradbury. I've probably read it twenty times."

Vincent shrugged. It didn't mean anything to him. He pointed to the people in robes. "These are supposed to be the Martians?" he asked.

"Uh-huh," Beth said. She reached into a cluttered red plastic tray attached to the right side of the drafting table, removed a small beige eraser from the tangled nest of drawing implements there, and attacked a smudge that Vincent hadn't noticed.

Vincent looked at the figures on the board. Beth was good. No doubt about it. He could almost see them move across the panel. Black ink lines against snow-white paper. Shadow and light. Almost flickering.

"They don't look like Martians," Vincent said in a quiet voice. He blinked. How would you know, asshole? he asked himself.

"Wait till I draw them without their masks," Beth said, concentrating on erasing just the right amount of smudge. "Big black eyes, the works . . ." The tip of her tongue was visible at the corner of her mouth.

"Everyone's here," Merril said as she came back into the studio.

Vincent and Beth turned to see North and Reese enter. Reese towered over everyone in the room. He looked carefully around, appearing to already be selecting escape routes. Unfortunately, there weren't many. Beth's studio took up the top corner of a small two-story house in Burbank. For quick exits there was either the door leading back to the upper loft-style landing, the bedroom, and the staircase, or there were two windows overlooking the suburban lawns and driveways of East Angeleno Avenue. The neighborhood was as neatly laid out and divided as a page of Beth's comic panels. Few avenues of flight.

"Glad you're here," Vincent said, approaching Reese.

Reese looked at Vincent's offered hand a moment before deciding to accept it.

"I had a long talk with North," Reese said. "We seem to be under the same thumb."

"Gardiner cut us loose. Just like you," Vincent agreed. "Cy

and I figure we have two weeks to find out which end is up. After that, the bureau's going to decide that whatever's going on is our fault and come after us."

"Any idea why?" Reese asked. His voice was dark, suspicious.

Vincent shook his head. "Gardiner claimed that your investigation of the people moving the restricted computer parts was suspended because it was an operation set up by another agency."

Reese snorted. "That's the same bullshit lie he handed me before he told me to take two weeks off."

"That's what we figured," Vincent said. "I'd guess that Gardiner is under pressure from the other agency, fighting claims that his agents have sold out. So he cut us loose to try and clear things up on our own, or to trip up somehow and prove that we really did sell out."

Reese walked over to a window and cautiously pulled back one of the vertical blinds covering it.

"Were you followed?" Vincent asked, suddenly nervous.

"Weren't you?" Reese asked in return.

"Of course," Vincent answered. "But I lost them."

"So did I." He turned back to Vincent. "You said something about photographs. Something that would show how I got out of the beach house on Sunday night."

"Yeah," Vincent said. "Merril's a reporter. Cy and I gave her a tip that you might be taken down on one of the nights we were running surveillance on you, so she hid out under a deck down the beach. She got your getaway on film."

"Let's see," Reese said simply.

"I'm going to head downstairs," Beth said, walking toward the door. She returned Reese's stare as she passed by him. "Nice to meet you, Mr. Reese," she said, then made a face at Merril and was gone.

Reese sat down. The wooden stool creaked under his mass. The others pulled stools to the table and joined him. Merril reached down to the black portfolio case Beth had left and brought out a sheaf of eleven-by-fourteen black-and-white prints. She stacked them on the table in front of her, sorted through them, pulled out one from near the top, and passed it into the middle of the brightly lit table.

"So who's that?" she asked.

The photo showed an extreme blowup of the back kitchen

window at the beach house. The figure in the window was a pointillistic study in random photographic grain, but the shoulders and the pattern of shadows on the face were easily identifiable, even if the precise features were a blur.

"It's Reese," Vincent said.

"Reese," North agreed. His voice sounded like he was recovering from a cold.

Reese picked up the photograph. "When was this taken?" he asked.

"Sunday night," Merril answered. "At the beach house. About one-thirty. Just before you were taken out."

"By what?"

Merril sighed and slid a second photo onto the table. "I was hoping you could sort of tell us."

"What's this supposed to be?" Vincent asked.

"The helicopter that took Reese out," Merril said. Vincent saw that she had a strange sort of smile on her lips. She was enjoying herself, even if the others weren't.

"That's not a helicopter," North said.

"Do you remember a helicopter, Reese?"

Reese took the second photo. He shook his head. "I don't remember anything about that night." His voice sounded tired.

"How about the night you were in the desert? When you were supposed to intercept the transfer from the truck to the plane?"

Reese shook his head again. "Nothing."

"That's not a helicopter," North insisted.

"How do you know?" Merril asked. "If it got by the Coast Guard radar, then maybe it's got Stealth capabilities. Could be a whole new generation. Look completely different."

North flattened the photo on the table. The image of the craft behind the beach house was barely discernible in the print. It was defined more by the slight change in contrast between the moonlit ocean in the background and the absolute black of the thing in the foreground than by any observable detail.

North traced the shape of it with his finger. Flat on the bottom. No hint of landing struts. A clean parabolic curve on top.

"If this is a helicopter," North complained, "then where's the rotor? Where's the rotor mount? This thing couldn't fly."

"I saw it land," Merril said. "I saw it take off. It flew. End of discussion." She turned to Reese. "What about it? Even if you don't remember the flight, you do remember that your buddies were coming for you, right?"

"No," Reese said, still staring at the photo of the thing.

"What were you doing in the house anyway, Reese?" Vincent asked. "Documents has it traced to some company in Hong Kong. Felt it was suspicious that an agent was taking vacation time in something that might be linked to drug money."

Reese tightened his mouth in irritation. "It's a safe house," he said. "It's owned by the government."

"Then why wasn't Documents able to track down ownership?" Vincent asked. That was ludicrous.

"If *they* could do it, then anyone else could do it." Reese rubbed his forehead. "I've worked counterespionage for a long time, Vincent. We've had so many budget cuts that almost all the real estate we pick up these days is taken from convicted drug dealers under the RICO provisions. We just don't bother to change the documentation, in case any of the targets in a sting operation do a title search on the place they come to meet us at. There're dozens of properties all over the city just like it, and every department keeps its own a secret. I was on vacation. That house was available. Everyone does it. What's the mystery?"

"The mystery is," Merril said, "if you're so squeaky clean, how come you ran away from surveillance?"

"I didn't run away."

"Look at the photos, big guy." Merril put three more onto the table. "You sure weren't putting up much of a fight."

The third photo showed the craft with its door open and light spilling onto the sand. Two crewmen had emerged and were walking toward the beach house; a third was just stepping through the door. All were backlit shadows, indistinct blurs of grain and low contrast.

The fourth photo showed the figures on the deck by the back door, Reese still waiting in the kitchen window.

The fifth photo showed Reese walking down the stairs from the deck, one figure on the deck behind him, two ahead of him on the beach.

Reese's hands trembled. He placed the photos on the table and sat back.

"Hard to tell for sure, but I'd say they were wearing uniforms," North said almost to himself. "See how the patterns of shadows are the same on all of them, like they're wearing the same clothes?"

Merril slid a photo back to herself and looked at the grainy images of the crewman. "Uniforms? Could be," she said. She still had a funny tone in her voice.

"Are you holding out on us?" Vincent asked.

"What do you mean, Ace?"

"I mean, you're acting like you know something we don't know. Like you're going to pull out one last picture that will show the Iranian Air Force symbol or something on the side of the helicopter."

"It's definitely not a helicopter," North muttered. "Probably a boat."

Merril glared at North. "I said I saw it *land* and I saw it *take off.*"

"Hydrofoil," North countered. "You saw it rise up and down on its wings."

"So what about it?" Vincent asked. "Is there another photo or what?"

Merril put the sixth photo on the table like an artist unveiling a masterpiece. It looked like all the others. The craft was on the beach. Reese was bending over to step through the door. Two figures waited behind him, almost invisible in the darkness.

"So?" Vincent said.

"Is there supposed to be something important here?" Reese asked.

Merril shook her head. "Pay attention, boys. What's Reese doing?"

"Getting into the helicopter."

"The boat."

Merril smiled at North. "Okay, *how* is he getting into Cy's boat?"

"Bending over . . . ," Vincent said, puzzled.

"And?" Merril asked, tapping a pointing finger on photo number three, showing the crewman emerging from the craft. "And? And? And?"

"The one in the doorway is not bending over," Reese said slowly, reluctantly.

"Let me see," Vincent said, snatching the last photo from in front of Reese.

It was true. The crewman fit the door perfectly. Reese had to almost fold himself in half to squeeze through.

"How tall are you?" Vincent asked Reese.

"Six-four."

"Then these guys aren't more than four feet tall," Vincent said softly. "Holy shit."

Several seconds of silence were broken by Merril's quick laugh. "Don't you guys get it?" she said wildly. "Don't you see what's on the goddam emulsion before your very eyes?"

The three suspended FBI agents turned those eyes to Merril and shook their heads. Vincent didn't know how the others felt, but he wanted to hold his hands over his ears. He no longer wanted to be in this pleasant studio in this nice suburban home in Burbank. He wanted to be somewhere away, anywhere where he wouldn't have to hear what Merril was going to say next. What Merril *had* to say next.

"Hey, boys. A lot of weird shit comes over the wire services this time of year, and I'm proud to say I read each and every screwball story that disgraces the paper it's printed on. And this is the best one I've ever seen."

No response.

Merril pointed to Reese. "It looks like your buddy here got picked up by a flying saucer, Ace." She laughed again.

Vincent shifted his eyes nervously back and forth between North and Reese. North stared down at the table. Not at the photographs, the table. Reese didn't take his eyes off Merril.

Vincent laughed to break the tension. The laugh was forced and sounded like it.

"So what's the real story, Merril?" Vincent asked, praying that the reporter would pull out another photo, any other photo.

"You're looking at it, Dave." She gestured to the photos. She was vibrating with excitement in her chair. "This is the real thing."

"It can't be," Vincent said. "I mean . . . no way. Those things aren't real."

Merril shook her head with an idiot's grin. This is why she was having such a hard time keeping a straight face all through the meeting, Vincent realized, feeling sick to his stomach. She actually believed this story was true.

"Listen to me, Dave," Merril began, talking quickly. "It's not that these things aren't real; it's that they have never been *proven* to exist. Lots of reports, lots of sightings, lots of claims of abductions even. But no hard evidence. No physical proof. No photographs until now." She slapped the table. Vincent jumped. North and Reese sat unmoving, staring blankly at the images before them.

"Those photos aren't *proof*," Vincent protested. "Look at them. They're too dark. Too grainy. You can't tell anything about what's going on in them."

"Not now," Merril agreed, still smiling, "but that's just what Beth could come up with in the darkroom downstairs. Think what we're going to get when we run the negatives through computer enhancement at NASA or someplace. Shit, Dave, we'll be able to count their antennae!"

North started to cry. Reese ignored him. He had grabbed a photo from the table and was staring at it. A photograph of himself standing in the window. Waiting.

"C'mon, Cy. It's just one of Merril's jokes. That's all." Vincent felt the panic announce itself inside, crawling slowly to the surface. He spoke quickly, loudly, to convince himself as much as to convince his crying partner. "There's never been any photos of flying saucers and goddam Martians because there's nothing to be photographed."

"No way," Merril said. "No photos because there's never been a trained photographer *in hiding* when they've been around." She didn't leave any confusion as to what she meant when she said "they." "I mean, they must have been coming for years, always picking out-of-the-way places, choosing just small groups of people, snatching a few like Reese, gassing witnesses like you and North, and they're off like bandits. But it finally happened. They finally screwed up."

"How do Martians screw up, for God's sake?" Vincent demanded. *"Shut up, Cy!"* he yelled.

"Last Sunday, Dave. They screwed up last Sunday. They came down, saw Reese all alone in a beach house, secluded. They decide to snatch him. Go for him. Ooops! At the last minute, they realize he's under FBI surveillance, so they zap you with a memory drug, figure the coast is clear, and take him away. *But they didn't know I was there waiting for something to happen to Reese.* It had to happen sooner or later that they made a mistake. They finally made one last Sunday!"

"It can't be!" Vincent shouted.

"It is, Dave! We've got them on film! Finally!"

"Noooo!" Reese bellowed, jumped up, and threw the table over. The photos swirled into the air, slid under counters and stools. North got caught by a table leg and fell to the floor. Vincent barely scrambled out of the way in time. Merril sat frozen, eyes wide, untouched. The hanging light swung crazily, shadows flickering back and forth.

"You're insane!" Reese shouted. "There's no such thing!"

"A bit of an overreaction, wouldn't you say, Dave?" Merril stated calmly. She slipped off her stool and walked slowly toward Reese, who stood his ground, his ragged breaths making his chest heave like a captured bull's. His face flushed deep scarlet. Vincent understood that rage. He had felt it himself. The rage of unthinking denial.

"Just listen to one more thing, Mr. Reese," Merril said calmly. "Just one more thing and I'll stop talking about it. If we assume that the things that grabbed you have the drug capability to blank out your memory of what happened—and those photographs, whatever else they show, *prove* that *something* happened to you that night that you *don't* remember—if we accept that they have that ability, can't we also accept that they have the ability to do *other* things to our minds? Program us to make us deny their existence or make us violently overreact to any discussion that they might be real? I was a skeptic until I saw those photos and figured out what they meant. I assume that you were a skeptic too. But I never got as angry as you are now when people talked about them. I never yelled or tossed—"

Downstairs Beth screamed.

The time for talking was over.

2

SATURDAY, JULY 14, 21:20 PDT

As Vincent dropped to take his Walther from his ankle, he saw Reese hold Merril back from the door as he silently opened it. With his right arm, Reese reached to the small of his back beneath his jacket and whipped out a 92S Beretta. Sixteen shots with one in the chamber, Vincent thought. Reese had been expecting something.

"Beth! Are you all right?" Reese shouted through the doorway, flattened against the wall to the left of the frame. Vincent ran to join him on the right. North slowly sat up from his sprawled position in the middle of the room, saw the guns, and reached for his own.

"Beth!" Merril called out frantically, but wisely stayed behind Reese. "Answer me, Beth!"

The voice that came back from the downstairs was just as frantic.

"It's O'Neill! Get down here! Get down here!"

Reese looked over at Vincent. "George?" he whispered.

Vincent shrugged. "George?" he called out. "Is that you?"

"It's me! Get down here! Get down here now!"

Reese held up his hand to keep Vincent by the door. "Where's the girl?" he called, then ducked through the doorway in a crouch. Vincent would not have believed the big man could be so graceful. The sudden action must have cut through Reese's unreasoning anger, he thought. The man seemed alert again. Focused.

Merril took Reese's place by the door. "Who's O'Neill?" she demanded.

Vincent watched as Reese cautiously peered over the railing on the loft landing, looking down into the living area. "L.A. office," Vincent said. "One of ours."

Reese suddenly sprang to full height, gun pointing down over the railing with both hands. "Let her go!" he bellowed. "Drop it now!"

"Goddam," Vincent said and rushed to Reese's side.

"You drop it!" O'Neill shouted back. "Now! Now!"

Vincent crouched by the railing, lifted his head over. Special Agent George O'Neill, wearing night-combat black fatigues, stood behind Beth, one hand over her mouth. The other held a gun to her head.

Vincent took a breath and jumped up, using both hands to draw a bead on O'Neill's head, inches from Beth's. "Two of us, George!" Vincent shouted.

O'Neill looked over to the counter that divided the living area from the kitchen. Vincent couldn't see what the agent was looking at. But he could hear a shotgun being pumped.

"More of us!" O'Neill said.

Vincent's heart raced. Adrenaline made him alert to every sound, every nuance. O'Neill was frightened. Vincent hoped the agent was more frightened than he was. He looked to Reese.

"What do you want, George?" Reese yelled. Everyone was stretched to the limit. Their voices echoed off the cathedral ceiling and the walls that stretched for the full two floors.

"We've got to get you out of here! Now!"

"Why?" Vincent demanded. He left Reese at the railing. Stepped back and headed down the broadloomed stairs to the front hall.

"Vincent's coming down!" O'Neill warned the man in the kitchen.

"Let the girl go!" Reese's voice had taken a different tone. Colder. He intended something.

Vincent stopped on the stairs, pressing against the wall, gun pointing down. He looked back to Reese. The man's finger was tightening on his trigger.

"Reese, don't!"

"Let her go!"

"Come down!"

Reese fired.

Merril ran screaming from the studio.

Vincent jumped down two steps, grabbed the banister, and vaulted over to the hallway, landing like a cat. He was under the loft landing, looking into the living area.

Beth was still standing. Sobbing. The right side of her face splattered with blood. She stared off to the left. Vincent realized the shotgun was still on her.

There was more screaming, more warnings, more demands. All of it confused and shouted together.

The shotgun. Vincent stepped back from the living area, moved silently through the front hall and into the dining room to approach the kitchen from the other side.

Another man in night fatigues crouched behind the counter that divided the kitchen from the living room. He aimed a shotgun at Beth. Vincent could see O'Neill slumped against the hearth, grasping his right shoulder, moaning senselessly.

"Drop it!" Vincent commanded.

The man with the shotgun wheeled. Vincent recognized him. Special Agent John Ying. San Francisco.

There was a crash from the living room. A grunt. Another scream from Beth.

Vincent squeezed the trigger on his Walther. "Drop it, John!" It was a plea. He didn't want to shoot another agent. But he would.

Ying hit his moment of truth. The shotgun wavered, came up.

"He said drop it!"

Reese appeared in the living room. The crash and grunt had been him jumping from the landing. Ying was surrounded. He passed over the shotgun. Vincent could hear Merril's footsteps thunder down the staircase.

"Listen, Dave," Ying began, putting his hands on his head. "We're here to fuckin' save you. Gardiner sent us to get you out."

Vincent grabbed Ying's left elbow and wheeled the man into the bent over, spread-eagle position against the refrigerator. "With guns, John? Gardiner sent you to save us with guns?"

He patted the agent down. A backup .45 automatic and a Shelton combat knife hit the floor.

"Save us from what?" Reese asked, back from the fireplace with O'Neill's guns and another knife. Vincent could hear Beth and Merril in the living room. Beth was still sobbing.

Ying turned and looked from one man to the other. "I . . . I don't know. He wouldn't tell us. Just that someone was out to get you and you had to be brought in before you were killed." He brought his hands halfway down to gesture to them. "You're in danger."

Vincent laughed. "Tell me about it, asshole."

"There's not much time," Ying pleaded.

"How do we get in touch with Gardiner?" Reese asked.

Ying turned to him. The kitchen window shattered. Ying's face disappeared in an explosion of blood. Vincent felt himself pushed against a counter as if an unseen wave had broken over him. He saw Reese firing his Beretta and O'Neill's .38 back through the window, one in each hand. The guns made no noise.

Reese stopped firing and rushed over to Vincent. Vincent realized that he had slid to the floor. Reese helped Vincent up and when he took his hands away, they were covered in blood.

"I'm shot?" Vincent said. He couldn't even hear his own voice.

Reese opened and closed his mouth, silently yelling at Vincent. He grabbed Vincent by the arm and pulled. Vincent's left arm felt molten, on fire. The Human Torch, he thought.

Reese pushed Vincent ahead into the living room. Vincent saw Merril and Beth standing together by the patio doors. North was beside them, still confused and dazed. Everyone's mouth moved, but no one made a noise.

He felt Reese's arm slam into him from behind. Vincent flew forward into the sofa, Reese beside him. Vincent's head twisted back. He saw the far living-room windows spray into the house like a broken hydrant, millions of glittering particles turning slowly as they floated through the air. Pretty, Vincent thought. They reminded him of the moonlit breakers on a beach he had seen once, a long time ago.

A line of little silent puffs of dust slowly blossomed across the fireplace brickwork. Vincent saw them change to red blooms when they reached the slumped figure of George O'Neill. O'Neill danced for a moment, then slumped again.

Vincent heard only the slow and regular pulse of his own heart-beat, keeping time with the strange burning pain of his arm. It was spreading.

Beside him, Reese leisurely flipped through the air to land behind the sofa. Vincent felt Reese's hands upon him one more time as he was dragged over the sofa too. Then he sat on the floor, looking at the crouching forms of Reese, North, Merril, and Beth. Why didn't they speak up?

Reese fired four more times over the sofa, back toward the far living-room window. Good silencers, Vincent thought. Still not a sound. No degradation at all. He tried to get up, to see what Reese was shooting at, but found his left arm didn't work. When he pushed his right hand down into the broadloom, he felt something wet and warm, like a trough of captured water on a sun-warmed beach.

Reese reached up and pulled the glass doors open. Vincent could see a small patio beyond, bounded by an eight-foot fence, outlined by potted hisbiscus. Reese motioned the others through as he kept a watch on the far wall.

Merril and Beth ran ahead. They pulled a wooden bench to the fence. North, still inside, jerked around to the right, staring back to the front hall. He raised his gun and fired. Fell back. Blood staining his left eye's white bandage.

"He's been shot," Vincent said, but for some reason, he felt nothing for his partner.

Vincent looked up in time to see Reese finish saying something to him. Vincent tried to shrug, but nothing happened. Odd, he thought.

Reese held his gaze for one long silent moment, then turned and rushed out to the patio.

Merril was on the other side of the fence, standing on something Vincent couldn't see and leaning over to help Beth. Beth went halfway up. Beth crumpled like a deflated balloon. Reese turned and fired. The patio doors erupted in front of Vincent. He tried to dodge the glass and wood but couldn't. He felt his luck was holding because all the bullets went over his head.

Merril screamed silently from the top of the fence, one hand straining to keep hold of Beth's. Beth hung limply. Reese care-fully lifted her down. Looked at her face. Laid her gently on the patio. He waved his hand at Merril's tear-streaked screaming face, turned and fired one more silent burst, then jumped on the bench and was over the fence and gone.

Vincent sat patiently by North, leaning against the back of the sofa, staring into the patio at Beth. His whole body seemed to be on fire. His flesh crackled when he tried to move. The things he saw shimmered in front of his eyes as if they were behind a veil of heat or vapor from Merril's coffee thermos.

"Flame off," Vincent whispered. "Flame off." It didn't work.

In a shard of glass still hanging from a door, he saw the reflection of a figure approaching from behind the sofa, dark and indistinct.

The Martians are here, Vincent thought, and immediately felt great relief. The Martian appeared beside him behind the sofa. Vincent struggled to lift his head up, to see what they looked like without their masks. He was disappointed to see that they were just like government agents in night fatigues. Oh well, he thought, at least they're real. At least they're here.

"Thanks for . . . coming back," Vincent whispered.

He squinted as the Martian lowered an alien artifact toward him. It looked just like a rifle barrel.

"I want . . . to get some . . . answers," Vincent managed to say to the Martian.

He never got them.

Gardiner felt the glass in the broadloom crunch beneath his gleaming black shoes. Like sand on a beach road, he thought. A hundred years ago.

He stood in the middle of Merril Fisher's living room as a forensics team disassembled it, layer by layer. Six grim, silent men and women in rubber gloves who moved through the house like beetles over a corpse, reducing it to empty bones. They were not an FBI team. They were not from the Burbank police force, still forbidden to enter the site. They were Tucker Browne's people, Gardiner realized, and like slugs, they probably only came out at night.

He blinked as a photographer took the last pictures of George O'Neill against the fireplace. The soft bump of the electronic flash, the high-pitched whine as it cycled up to fire again, all brought back the memory of the investigation in the house on the beach where Reese had disappeared the first time. And now he was gone again. But at least this time, Gardiner knew how Reese had made his escape.

He watched unemotionally as George was shifted into a glistening black body bag. John Ying had already been "collected" from the kitchen, as well as the two OCI agents who had been cut down by returned fire at the side of the house.

Another OCI agent appeared beside Gardiner as two technicians waddled out with George slung between them. "Mr. Luck would like to see you upstairs right away. Room on the right."

Gardiner nodded and stepped carefully over the living room carpet toward the staircase. He looked glumly at the unmoving body of David Vincent, cut off forever from the rest of the world by a border of white adhesive tape on the ground around him like a mystic hieroglyphic scrawled in an ancient cave.

Beside Vincent was the taped outline of Cy North's body. On the patio was an outline of an unidentified woman. Both North and the woman had been alive when the med team had removed them. But considering who was in charge of the operation, Gardiner didn't think it likely either would remain living for long. He shook his head. He went upstairs.

Luck was the only other person in the room on the right when Gardiner entered. He looked around briefly, recognizing some of the superheroes decorating the walls from the days when his children really were children, then joined Luck in the center of the room. Luck held a stack of flat, clear-plastic evidence bags. Within each one was a large black-and-white photograph. Luck held them as if they might explode at any second.

"You screwed up good, Ed," Luck said. If anything, Gardiner thought, the smell of blood and gunfire, the sight of dead and dying, had brought new color, new life to Luck's features.

"From the looks of things," Gardiner replied coldly, "it would seem as if my men were killed by your men. Not by Reese. Or Vincent. Or North. How did you know they were going to hold the meeting here?" It had been simple for Gardiner to track down Vincent's friend's house because her name had been mentioned in the taped phone call. But how had Luck managed to track her down?

The OCI agent stared hard at Gardiner, ignoring the question. "You shouldn't have come in when you did," Luck said. It wasn't an argument. It was a statement of fact.

"You shouldn't have followed us in. I could have gotten the photographs without bloodshed."

"You sent your people in armed, Ed. You were expecting resistance."

"Not from my agents, I wasn't."

Luck sighed, shifted the photos in his hand. Gardiner glanced at them but couldn't make out details.

"Reese's response proves my theory though," Luck said. "He's sold out, and we've got him on the run."

"Reese wouldn't be on the run if he had been offered a chance to come in on his own."

Unexpectedly, Luck laughed. "You know, Ed. We could stand here all night arguing with each other, but what's the point? You sure as hell aren't going to convince me that what I did was wrong. And I sure don't have the time to convince you that you were wrong. We both just want to minimize losses to our organizations." He shrugged. "Vincent's withdrawn, North's racked up. That's two out of three. And we both want Reese. What do we have to argue about?"

Gardiner considered his response for a moment. Luck was right. "Nothing," he agreed. They had gone beyond arguments. Their differences could only be settled in one way: defeat for one, victory for the other. Anything else was a waste of time. Gardiner shared Luck's cool laughter. "Nothing at all." And with that thought, the FBI agent imagined he could hear a clock begin to tick somewhere, counting down.

Down East Angeleno Avenue, where the Burbank police had blocked off the road at Fourth, a black van slipped by a police car and slowly drove toward Fisher's house.

"That him?" Gardiner asked.

Luck nodded. He stepped off the curb onto the street, the stack of bagged photos bulging under his arm. Three brown FBI Technical Evaluation Unit vans remained outside the house, but the ambulances and police cars had long since departed, leaving ample room for Tucker Browne's vehicle to park.

Gardiner watched with fascination as two solid mechanical sounds came from the stopped van. Its side door popped out three inches, then slid quickly to the back with an explosive puff of compressed air, leaving a wispy cloud of vapor spinning around the bottom of the doorway as Browne's self-powered wheelchair rolled into view.

Two red support legs puffed out of small panels in the van's side beneath the open door and ground quickly down to dig into the pavement. A metal tongue slid out from the door, bearing Browne in his chair. The van sighed and shifted, compensating for the change in the distribution of mass. The tongue hissed and dropped slowly, gently making contact with the ground.

Gardiner looked inside. Over Browne's pale bald head he saw the blinking lights and video screens of a Cobalt Halo communications console, walnut trim, leather upholstery, and a uniformed chauffeur. If the President needed a wheelchair, Gardiner thought, this would be the presidential limousine.

"Good evening, gentlemen," Browne said as though he had just happened upon Gardiner and Luck while on a late-night stroll. "Problems?"

"Reese got away again," Luck reported.

Gardiner waited for the OCI agent to say more, but he didn't. So Gardiner did.

"Vincent is dead. Two of my agents are dead. Two of your agents are dead. North is—"

Browne held up a silencing hand. "I asked for problems, Ed. Not a scorecard." He turned to Luck. "Anything other than Reese?"

"No."

"Wounded by any chance?" Browne asked hopefully.

"No. Left with a woman."

"Girlfriend?"

"Reporter." Luck held up the thick stack of photographs in their crinkly bags. "The one who took the photographs."

Browne's eyes lit up. "Ah, there *were* photographs. Splendid." He turned back to Gardiner and allowed his lower lip to protrude. "And who did you lose in addition to Vincent?"

"George O'Neill. John Ying."

Browne covered his mouth and cleared his throat. It sounded like a baby choking. "I recall that O'Neill was in your office," he said. "But I'm afraid I don't recollect a John Ying."

"San Francisco Field Office," Luck said.

"Oh, really," Browne replied. "Having trouble finding agents you can trust to take on . . . unsanctioned assignments, Ed?"

That was exactly it, but Gardiner was not going to admit it. Browne evidently didn't care to wait for a response. He reached out for the photos.

"Taken Sunday night?" Browne asked. "At the beach house?"

Luck nodded and passed them over. "These prints are for shit. The reporter set up a darkroom in one of the bathrooms."

Browne held the photos in his lap, smoothed the plastic down over the one on top, trying to make it out in the orange-yellow light from the streetlamps. "Any negatives?"

"Not yet. Either she took them with her or she's hidden them. Either way, it appears she knows what she got."

"And what's that, Roy?" Browne looked up from his chair. "I trust you were resourceful enough to at least glance at these before you sealed them?"

Luck nodded his head. "Looks like a helicopter extraction," he said. "Something big came down behind the house. Looks like Reese went without a struggle. Like he was expecting it."

"Something big?" Browne asked, flipping through the bags. "You *were* running radar that night, weren't you, Ed?"

"Of course," Gardiner said. "Coast Guard."

"Something big *and* clever, then," Browne said. "A Laurel field to electromagnetically disable firearms. Stealth capabilities to avoid radar. Very impressive. Any idea what the reporter was doing there in the first place?"

Gardiner and Luck shook their heads together.

Browne shrugged. "Obviously, someone knew that something was going to happen last Sunday night. And perhaps when we capture Derek Reese and his friend, one or the other of them will live long enough to let us know who it was and why."

"And then what?" Gardiner asked.

"And then, Ed," Browne smiled with fat pursed lips, "whoever they are, wherever they are, we go after *them*."

3

MONDAY, JULY 16, 14:42 EDT

"Skipper, if you keep talking like that you'll have to stay after school and you can't have any sand pies for recess!"

Wendy blew a strand of hair away from her face and said, "Phew," because she wasn't in the shade of the trees and it was so hot in the Saturday morning sun. Then she leaned over in her sandbox and adjusted Barbie's little sister so she wouldn't be sitting so closely to Midge because they always talked way too much and disrupted all the other kids.

"Settle down class," Wendy intoned with a frown because she was an adult now and adults always had to be serious to make kids afraid of them. "Barbie has to sit between Midge and Skipper, and Dino can sit in the front row."

Wendy changed the seating plan of her classroom by picking up her students and rearranging them, burying their legs in the sand because they didn't bend the right way. It was so hard to be a teacher. That's what her mommy said, and didn't Wendy know it was true. So many problems to deal with. Dino was her physically challenged student because he was a dinosaur and had only one eye left, so he always needed to sit at the front. But Midge and Barbie didn't like to sit by themselves, so they had to sit together in the back row. And Skipper was afraid that Dino might try to eat her, and so she had to sit back there too.

Wendy would have liked two more dolls to even out the rows and help make Skipper feel better, but Ken had to sit way over across the yard by the garage because he was the principal and he needed an office. Wendy wasn't exactly sure how it worked, but she did know that teachers, like her and Mommy, got to come home early, but offices were far away and the daddies who went to them couldn't get back until late at night.

She had had another boy doll once too. But he had been very bad one day and used the kinds of words that Mommy and Daddy sometimes used when they thought she was asleep, but then when they used them, they were so loud Wendy woke up anyway. So when she had heard Peter use those bad words, she had told him to shut up, shut up, shut up, and then had buried him in the garden.

When she went back a few days later to dig him up, she couldn't remember where she had put him, because the flowers all looked different and she knew that if she just touched Mommy's flowers, then Mommy would yell at her and maybe spank her. And even if Mommy would come into her room late at night when her breath would smell like medicine or something and tell Wendy that she was sorry and that she would never yell at Wendy again, Wendy always knew that Mommy would, and she never wanted Mommy to yell at her again, so she had never tried to dig up Peter. Which is why she didn't have enough dolls for her classroom.

After the class settled down, Wendy went back to making the sand pies for recess. She liked the way the small grains of sand stuck to her fingers like clumps of brown sugar. Every once in a while, she could almost convince herself that the sand pies should really truly taste good and she would try one at recess with the rest of her class. But they never did have any taste, though she did like the way she could bite down on a piece of sand and hear it crunch between her teeth.

Wendy patted the last of the sand pies and could see that it wasn't going to hold together all that well, so she leaned over even more, putting her head right between her legs the way she did when her mommy laughed and said that kid doesn't have any bones, and then she carefully drooled onto the last sand pie. She worked the little bubbles of spit into the surface, smoothing it carefully like her daddy polishing his car, and it was perfect. She would give that one to Dino she decided because his parents didn't love him and that made him feel sad and Wendy felt sorry for him. She sat up to announce recess.

"Hello, Wendy!"

Wendy didn't look away from her sandbox. She knew who it was.

"Hi, John-John."

He was her good friend. She liked him because he could talk just like Donald Duck, and Wendy thought Donald had the funniest voice in the world. John-John could talk like Donald all day and make Wendy laugh, even though she didn't always understand everything he said.

Once John-John had asked her if she would like it if he talked in another way, but Wendy said no, because talking like Donald was funny and the best part about Donald's voice was that when he got mad and jumped up and down and tried to get Huey, Dewey, and Louie, his voice was so funny that you knew he really wasn't mad, that it was all just pretend, and that he would never ever do anything to hurt anybody, instead of being like adults when they got mad and maybe broke things or spanked you.

"What are you doing?" John-John asked. Wendy heard the metal sides of the sandbox creak as John-John climbed in. She heard the sand crunch under his tiny feet as he settled on the seat across from her, a little green triangle of wood that fit over one of the sandbox's corners.

"This is my school," Wendy explained patiently. John-John was fun, but there was a lot of stuff he didn't know about. "And these are my pupils. And we're just about to have recess."

"Are you a teacher?" John-John asked.

"Yes," Wendy said as she jammed Midge a bit deeper into the sand and heard her hard plastic feet scrape along the metal bottom of the box.

"Just like your mommy?"

"Yes." Wendy took her hand away from Midge and sighed as the doll finally sat up by herself. John-John shifted his feet in the sand, and Wendy glanced over and saw that he was wearing his running shoes today. The ones with the three black stripes just like her daddy wore on Saturdays when he went off running but Wendy didn't know where.

Wendy picked up Dino and stuck him in the front row all by

himself. She could tell he was unhappy, so she patted his head. "Some day you'll understand," she said to the dinosaur because that's what adults told her all the time when she was feeling sad. She didn't really believe it because she was already seven years old and she still felt that she didn't understand what it was she was supposed to understand.

"Are we going to go away today?" Wendy asked as she scratched initials in the sand pies for her kids. She wondered if she should have made one for John-John, but she had actually gotten him to eat one once and thought it probably wasn't a good idea for him to eat another. Even though it was really funny when she told him it was chocolate-flavored and he acted like he believed her.

"Not today," John-John said.

"What do you want to do then?" Wendy glanced over at him again. He was wearing blue jeans and a bright yellow sweatshirt. Yellow was her favorite color. The leaves in the trees behind him were all different shades of green, dark and light, fluttering back and forth in the breeze, rustling with a far-off rushing sort of sound that made Wendy think of water and waves and being very sleepy.

"Hey!" Wendy said when she looked down again!

"What's wrong?" John-John asked.

"All my sand pies are broken." They were dry-white and cracked at the edges, as though she had left them in the sun for an hour.

"Do you think they might taste any better that way?"

Wendy laughed. He was so funny.

"We can't have recess now, so you can be our special visitor in class for show-and-tell, okay?" Wendy reached out and pushed the dry-white sand pies to the side, blending them together with the sand around them until they were gone forever. Then she wondered why she had done that.

"What's a special visitor?"

"That's like when Officer Friendly or when a fireman or somebody's daddy comes in and visits the class and tells them things."

"What sort of things do they tell the class?"

"I don't know."

"What sort of things do you want me to tell the class?"

"I don't know." Wendy thought about that. She could usually think of a lot of questions for people. So many questions

that her mommy would tell her to put a sock in it, and try and
save them for when she got home so she wouldn't bug other
people. Right now she wanted to know why her sand pies had
dried out so fast. She wanted to know where Peter was buried.
She wanted to know when Daddy would be back from running.
And why, when she had cut her toe yesterday and had eaten a
chocolate bar, the chocolate didn't come out her toe with the
blood. But she couldn't think of a single question to ask John-
John. Or to ask about John-John. As if the part of her that
asked questions didn't work where John-John was concerned.

"You could talk like Donald Duck," Wendy said.

"Ohboyohboyohboyohboy!" John-John quacked.

Wendy exploded with laughter.

"Framastataramastat!"

Wendy laughed so hard that all the muscles in her stomach
collapsed and she doubled over with tears in her eyes.

"Waughwaughwaughwaugh!"

He was so funny that Wendy couldn't breathe. She laughed
and laughed and oops. Wendy stopped laughing instantly. She
straightened up and looked down at the sand beneath her triangle seat. It was dark with moisture. Wendy felt embarrassed.
But it was sort of funny. She compromised by giggling. Then
she groaned because it did feel sort of uncomfortable and because she thought, Boy, am I going to get it.

John-John reached out suddenly, under her dress and up to
her underpants. She felt his hand on the inside of her leg right
near the top, rubbing something cool and rough against her,
like a cold washcloth.

"No!" she said, embarrassed and almost frightened. She sat
down, shoved John-John's hand away, and pushed her own
hands down against her dress, forcing the thin cotton between
her legs. "That's dirty!"

"I'm sorry," John-John said. Wendy saw him drop a silver
ball of fluff into a black circle. The fluff disappeared. He folded
the circle in half, and it disappeared too.

"You said we weren't going to go away today. You said we
weren't going to do that stuff again today," Wendy insisted.

"What stuff?" John-John asked as he reached under his
sweatshirt.

Wendy shivered. Her underpants felt yucky, and she was
mad at John-John for tricking her. "The dirty stuff," she said

accusingly. She hung her head down to stare at the sand and started to cry. She hated the dirty stuff.

"Don't cry, Wendy," John-John said. He didn't sound as much like a duck anymore. "See what I have for you?"

The sand beneath Wendy sparkled with brilliant light like a Roman candle had just been lit. Wendy looked up.

John-John had his wand.

Wendy watched in awe as John-John held the wand in front of his face, a long shimmering tube of light that was shiny like a mirror and pulled in and reflected all the bright sun, the blue sky, and the shifting shades of green leaves all around him, caught them in a swirl and shot them out in Fourth of July streamers straight into Wendy's eyes.

Wendy stopped crying. Instead, she listened. She watched. She smelled and tasted. And what was shown to her, she wanted more than she had wanted anything before in her entire life.

"WENDYYYY!"

Like the time she was stuck in bushes at the park, Wendy struggled to pull her head away from the light and look back toward the house. Back toward her mommy. Running at her. Screaming. Her mouth a small black circle that Wendy wished would fold in half and disappear.

"NOOO!"

Wendy looked at John-John. The colors ran back into his wand like dirty water down the bathtub drain. For a moment, even the leaves disappeared and Wendy saw her good friend's face.

Above the bright yellow sweatshirt was flesh like her hands when she swam too long, white and thick and wrinkled. His mouth was a crayon gash of black, his nose flat and marked only by two tiny black streaks. His head was too big, like the Great Gazoo, like a giant baby. And his eyes were bigger than her mommy's sunglasses, darker, as if the light in the wand had been stolen from eyes that big.

John-John blinked at her. Giant bug eyes, wet and moist like the sand beneath her, dark and empty like her closet at night. And the worst thing was, she knew she had seen those eyes before.

Wendy's screams joined those of her mother's.

John-John's wand exploded with a blinding glare.

Wendy watched as her mother and her sandbox and Dino,

the dinosaur whose parents didn't really love him, fell away from her far below the sky beneath her as she rose up and up and up and knew nothing more until Margot Jeffery's kind and loving voice told her that everything was all right and that she could wake up now.

Sarah Gilmour leaned forward and stubbed out her cigarette in the white ceramic ashtray beside the orange Garfield doll with his No Smoking button. Margot Jeffery didn't even bother to ask anymore. Smoking was suddenly far down the list of anybody's worries.

Jeffery turned off her microcassette recorder. It wasn't pleasant hearing Wendy cry. Especially with Wendy in the doctor's office with them.

Sarah sat back on the sectional couch and took her daughter's hand. Steven, on Wendy's other side, put his arm on her shoulder. Jeffery looked across at them, her placid blue eyes now darkly circled. Her right hand played with the unsealed flap of a large manila envelope beside her on the cushions.

"Comments?" the psychologist asked. Her voice was tired. "Shell-shocked" was the term that came to Sarah's mind.

"I remember Dino," Sarah said wistfully. "You found him on the beach at Cape Cod one summer. We promised you all sorts of new toys, but you wouldn't give him up for anything. I think he's still in one of the boxes in the basement."

Jeffery smiled patiently. "Do you remember anything about this John-John? Do you remember ever running out to find Wendy in the sandbox with another child or someone trying to . . . trying to reach under her dress?"

Sarah turned to Wendy, shook her head. "I remember that John-John was your imaginary playmate for a while. You never had that much to say about him though."

"When?" Jeffery asked. "Do you remember having a playmate called John-John, Wendy?"

Wendy sat with her arms wrapped around herself, lost in the folds of the oversized black sweater she wore over black jeans. Her hair hung limp and lifeless. Sarah's heart broke to see her daughter this way.

"I don't know," Wendy said quietly. "I'm confused. Maybe last week if you had asked me, I wouldn't have remembered. But now, after all this hypnosis stuff and all the remembering, it's hard to tell what I really remember and what you made me remember."

"Let's get our terms straight here," Jeffery cautioned. "I'm not 'making' you remember any of the incidents we recorded on the tape. In fact, that's one of the most important reasons for recording our sessions. Despite the common wisdom, people in a hypnotic state do not necessarily tell the truth, the whole truth, and nothing but. They can be very easily led to tell lies, create fantastic stories, if that's what they think the hypnotist wants to hear. Listen to my questions carefully the next time we play back a tape. I think I've gone out of my way to make sure that they don't lead you to answer in any particular way, don't 'make' you remember anything except those things you choose to tell me on your own."

"I remember John-John," Steven said.

"When?" Jeffery asked.

"About the time I opened up my first plant in New Jersey. Business almost quadrupled." Steven folded his hands in his lap and looked away. "Be about ten years ago."

Sarah swallowed hard. She squeezed Wendy's hand for support. For forgiveness. "That's about the time my drinking became . . . became problem drinking."

Jeffery nodded. "Most children do create imaginary playmates. Even those with what most people would call a perfect childhood. It's part of the socialization process. Helps children role-play in situations in which they can be in charge of others. Act out incidents from their own lives."

"The sandbox school," Sarah said. "I remember all the time Wendy spent out there with her dolls." She tried not to think of all the time Wendy might have spent out there with her "special visitor."

"In any event," Jeffery continued. "Even though most children have these playmates, it's also a typical response that when there's tension in the home or the loss of a parent or a sibling, say, the make-believe aspect of a child's play activities can become overwhelming. Again, it's a question, I believe, of the children having some control over their own lives. Choosing to forget or ignore the distressing reality that faces them."

"So with me being away and Sarah's . . . problem, you think that Wendy's memories of this John-John might just be a response to those tensions. That . . . whatever it was didn't really happen in the sandbox?" Steven leaned forward with interest. Sarah had noticed that he wasn't as keen to play power games with the psychologist today. Perhaps he was finally beginning to recognize her expertise and stop competing with her.

Jeffery sighed and stretched. "Steven, if I called in a colleague at this time and presented the case to her, I'm 99 percent sure that she—or he—would simply write the whole thing off as a sublimated stress reaction. All the classic triggers are there. The only thing unusual is that the specific stress response—fantasies of imaginary visitors—has continued for as long as it has."

"Is that unusual enough that your colleague might decide that these incidents are real?" Steven asked.

Jeffery shook her head again and rolled a corner of the envelope's flap between her thumb and finger. Sarah got the impression that the psychologist was trying to hold something back.

"Unfortunately, no," the psychologist said. "The red flag is that there's a strong current of sexuality underlying all these incidents."

Sarah concentrated on not moving her hand against Wendy's. She didn't want to call attention to her embarrassment at discussing sex in front of her daughter.

"On the ordinary side of the coin, we have Wendy engrossed in her sandbox school, inventing lives for her dolls, reenacting dialogue, emotions, and situations from her life. Then into this situation, already filled with talking dolls and an authoritative role for Wendy, comes John-John. He's wearing Wendy's favorite color, talks like Donald Duck, another favorite, and he becomes a special visitor to Wendy's classroom. Someone she can show off to her 'kids.' "

"I thought you said that was all normal," Steven interrupted.

"Quite normal," Jeffery said, showing her distaste for having to use that word. "As long as we're talking about a child," she qualified. "But remember what I said about play activities being a time to reenact incidents from the child's own life. I'm afraid the other side of the coin, the place where the 'normal' label doesn't apply, is when John-John . . . reaches under Wendy's dress."

Steven muttered something almost inaudible.

Jeffery shrugged. "I'm sorry, Steven, but most of my colleagues, upon hearing that an imaginary playmate had reached under a child's dress, would assume that in the child's real life that incident had already taken place. And I'm sure that I don't have to say what a strict Freudian would make of John-John's magic wand." She smiled, trying to lighten the conversation. "I mean, any object larger in one dimension than another can only be one thing as far as they're concerned."

"I'm getting sick of this crap," Steven said. Sarah winced at the cold rage in his voice.

"Daddy, don't," Wendy said.

"Margot, can't we just rule that out completely?" Sarah asked.

"Steven, I understand your anger. Sarah and Wendy, I understand your concern. I'd feel the same way myself. And if I haven't made it clear by now, I apologize. I do not believe that you, Steven, have in any way behaved other than as a kind and loving father to Wendy."

"Then why the hell keep bringing that crap up?" Steven said. The apology had had no effect.

"Because we're rapidly getting to the point where I can't handle this case alone anymore," Jeffery said. "And we have to be sure of exactly where we stand with *everything* before we decide to call in a consultant."

"So they can accuse me of . . . more of the same?" Steven said icily.

"You're not the point here, Steven," Jeffery said. It was as close as Sarah had heard the psychologist come to losing her temper. It *would* take Steven to do that, she thought.

"The point is that any other psychologist is going to review this case and immediately see it as a case of sexual child abuse. And even if they get around to ruling out the father of the child, as I have, nothing will change. They're just going to blame it on an uncle or a relative or a baby-sitter. Or a pederast who talked like Donald Duck and hid in the bushes by your house." Jeffery punctuated her outburst with a deep breath. "This is *not* about you, Steven. This is about Wendy. And Sarah. And I'm sorry I raised my voice like that. I'm feeling very frustrated."

"Yeah, well, I don't like this any more than the rest of us," Steven admitted. It was his way of accepting Jeffery's apology.

Sarah felt her cheeks burning with the mentions of sexual abuse. She wondered why Wendy had to be present for this kind of talk but knew that her daughter would get even more upset if she thought her mother wanted to treat her like a child.

Sarah held back and said nothing about having Wendy excused. But she had to ask one question at least.

"Margot, you keep saying that a colleague might believe all this to be, well, what you said it might be. But is that what you believe?"

"Not any more," Jeffery said, looking apologetically at Steven. "That's what I keep saying. I wish I could have additional black-and-white facts to put down in a report, but no, I think it's something much different."

"How could someone putting his hand under a little girl's dress be anything but abuse?" Steven asked, his voice still tight.

"Well, John-John didn't do that until he had made Wendy laugh so hard that she wet her pants." Jeffery smiled at Wendy. "Don't worry about it, Wendy. I did that all the time when I was seven too."

"I keep worrying that I'm still going to do it," Wendy said, returning the smile. Even though Sarah found talk about wetting one's pants still too private to be discussed in public, she could see that the psychologist and Wendy had developed a strong rapport and she felt a sudden pang of jealousy because of it. Sarah wondered if she and Wendy would ever share the same. Could ever share.

"What does that have to do with anything?" Steven asked.

"Instead of being seen as something sexual, we could look at it as an attempt to obtain a urine sample," Jeffery said. "Wendy recalled that John-John used something like a cold washcloth to touch her leg. Just after she told him to stop, she saw him put the object in a container. And . . . well, John-John told her they wouldn't be going to 'go away' that day. Perhaps to a place that would make it easier to take samples."

Sarah felt a shiver run through her. "Now you're saying that it might be true after all."

Jeffery's voice became hushed. "There are many points of agreement in both your and Wendy's account of what happened Sunday night. The rough sequence of events, the description of the, uh, visitors—almost identical to John-John—and the idea that you, Sarah, weren't going anyplace but that Wendy was. You saw Wendy taken out of the house through the kitchen door. One of the visitors held a tube of light in front of you— similar to John-John's wand—and you're unable to remember anything, even under hypnosis, until you came to in the living room with one of the things kneeling between your legs." Jeffery looked at each of the Gilmours in turn. "There's a pattern at work here. I don't know what it is. But it's not sexual abuse." She sighed. "Or at least not incest."

The realization of what Jeffery was implying made Sarah feel weak. "But then what can we do? What's left for us to do?"

"Consult an expert," Jeffery said simply.

"And go through all that Freudian crap?" Steven asked bitterly.

"No," Jeffery said. "Not a psychological expert."

Steven snorted. "What? There're experts on little white things that go around abusing children and kidnapping them?"

"I think there might be," Jeffery said in a quiet voice. She picked up the manila envelope on the couch beside her. Reached inside and withdrew a thick hardcover book. She put it on the table.

The cover showed a circle of colored lights swirling around over a group of people silhouetted by a swath of blue light coming from the sky. The book was titled *The Case for UFO Abductions*, by Charles Edward Starr.

"Oh, come off it," Steven said and looked away.

But Sarah and Wendy didn't look away. Sarah found there was something compelling about that beam of light, about the way the people were grouped. Had she seen something like that before?

"The author is, or was, a financial reporter for the *Wall Street Journal*," Jeffery said. "Apparently, about fifteen years ago two friends of his claimed to have been abducted by . . . well, aliens in a flying saucer, and Starr has been investigating UFOs ever since. This is his sixth book. Dealing specifically with people who claim to have been taken on board."

"This is just nuts," Steven protested.

"I'll admit there are flaws in the book. Some severe ones in a few of the cases. But Starr includes several descriptions of people's memories of being abducted, memories that apparently had been blocked before being rediscovered under hypnosis or by chance after a number of years." Jeffery lowered her voice. "What they describe and what Wendy and Sarah describe are very similar. Starr lives in New York, and his publishers are passing on a message from my office. I think we'd have better luck with him than with another psychologist. At this time at least."

Wendy reached out and picked up the book. Sarah watched

nervously as her daughter ran her fingertip around the circle of colored lights. Why did it look so puzzlingly familiar?

"This is what the wand colors look like," Wendy whispered. "It's like a photograph."

Sarah shivered again.

"This is *madness*," Steven said. His voice was louder, even more intense.

"It's part of my job to treat madness, Steven. And for hundreds of years, the types of disorders I treat used to be ascribed to the influences of demoniac possession. Today we say they're the result of maladaptive coping strategies or genetic defects or chemical imbalances. Who knows what we'll be calling them a hundred years from now?" Jeffery smiled. "Maybe UFOs are the next great step in our understanding of the universe."

Steven took the book from Wendy's hands and dropped it back onto the table.

"Or maybe you're the one who needs a psychiatrist," he said.

4

The explosive ripping noise of the unwinding gaffer's tape was like the thunder of a harpoon digging deep into the flesh of something half-seen at the water's surface. Reese could close his eyes and see the massive whale shape twist among black waves, heaving its guts to the currents, disintegrating as it sank to the ocean's floor and the all-embracing, featureless silt that waited there. He liked that image. That sound brought him comfort.

Reese bit off another length of the thick silver tape, feeling it tear easily as it was designed to do, and placed it over the last edge of the Reynolds Wrap on the last window of the bedroom. He was done. He was safe.

"What the hell are you supposed to be doing?"

Reese spun to face Merril Fisher. He fought the impulse to reach for his Beretta, now more comfortably resting in a low-slung shoulder holster.

"You don't want to sneak up on me like that," Reese said calmly to the reporter. "Not now."

Fisher chewed her bottom lip. Reese sensed that she was undergoing an interior struggle not to start arguing again. The past forty-eight hours had been tough enough for him. Fisher had gone through them too, he reminded himself, and she was only a civilian.

"I'm sorry," the reporter said. "I'll make more noise next time."

"Good."

"But what the hell *are* you supposed to be doing?" She gestured to the three small bedroom windows, each one neatly covered with aluminum foil and thick adhesive tape.

"I don't like the light," Reese said. "At night. It bothers me." Reese hoped his tone might keep the woman from asking anything more. Hoped she wouldn't ask how light could bother him when the house they were in comfortably backed onto a steep face of the Hollywood Hills, with no lights set up in the backyard and no neighbors' lights visible except from the front. Don't make me say what kind of light bothers me, Reese thought. Please don't make me even think about it.

Fisher studied the blocked-off windows one more time, started to say something, then thought better of it. "I've got to find out about Beth," she said. Reese could hear the pain in her voice. He had had to drag Fisher away from the patio that night. Beth had still been alive when he had carefully set her down on the ground, but he had no idea how well she would be treated or if she would be treated at all.

"If you did happen to find whatever hospital she was taken to," Reese explained, wrapping the loose end of tape back around the four-inch-wide roll, "as soon as you called to ask her condition, the nurse would say, 'Oh yes, of course, please hold.' In thirty seconds they'd have this phone number. In three minutes we'd be surrounded."

"I could phone a friend," Fisher protested. "I could have a friend phone around."

Reese walked over to the woman, towered above her. "Then they'd have your friend's number. In three minutes they'd be at your friend's house. In an hour they'd have something on your friend, dredged up from their computers or made up to do the most damage. Then, when you phoned your friend back, your friend would keep you on the line long enough that in three more minutes . . ." Reese shrugged. "Think what they did to Vincent and North. What they tried to do to us. Your friends wouldn't stand a chance."

Reese pulled the bedroom drapes over the covered windows

and picked up the blue-and-silver box of foil. "Let's go get a drink," he said, and walked out of the tiny bedroom.

He hesitated once in the narrow hallway of the bungalow, long enough to hear Fisher's footsteps coming after him, then continued on to the living room and wondered how long it would be before the woman tried something dangerous and he would have to deal with her decisively.

Reese entered the small, cluttered living room. He put the foil and tape down on an oversized stereo console dating from the fifties and covered with warped and cracked walnut veneer. Then he opened a smaller matching cabinet beside it and pulled out a bottle of Johnnie Walker.

"So how long are we safe here?" Fisher asked, after gulping down half her drink and sighing again. "This is another one of your safe houses, isn't it?"

Reese shook his head. "The people who live here are out of town. Won't be back for a few more weeks."

"Neighbors won't get suspicious?"

"They have a lot of visitors, especially when they're out of town."

Fisher sipped at her drink this time, looking over the rim of her glass at him. "So in other words it *is* a safe house and you don't want to tell me because you don't know how much you can trust me. Right?"

"If things don't work out, I think we'd both appreciate it if you didn't really have anything you could tell them."

"I won't tell those bastards a goddam thing," Fisher said.

"What makes you think they'll give you a choice?" There was no easy way to tell her the danger they faced. "They're not the sort of people to let you make a call to your lawyer."

Fisher walked over to the liquor cabinet. "Who the hell are they then? The FBI doesn't come in killing people like that."

"Sometimes they do. And if they don't, they're not the only game in town."

Fisher frowned and looked outside through the many-paned front windows. The streetlamps were coming on, illuminating the dark, shifting blanket of kudzu that enveloped the front garden.

"Why do you work for them?" she asked gently.

"Someone has to," Reese answered. "If none of us thought that one person could make a difference, then what would be the use of doing anything?"

"But they're maniacs," Fisher said. "Their world is garbage."

"It's our world too, Ms. Fisher. Maybe it is all garbage," he agreed. "But maybe it will get better."

"You honestly believe that?"

Reese was silent for long moments, searching inside himself, determined for some unknown reason to give this woman a truthful answer. Perhaps so he could know too.

"Yes," he finally said. "I do believe it will get better. How could anyone think it won't? And stay sane?"

Fisher shook her head. "Have you got somebody, Reese?" she asked.

"Sorry?"

"Have you got a girlfriend? Boyfriend? Lover? Wife?"

Reese shook his head. That was a question that couldn't be answered truthfully. A question that couldn't be thought about.

"Too bad," Fisher said. "You seem like the romantic type. Probably could use somebody close by."

"Who couldn't?" Reese said, holding his glass in salute to her.

"No way to find out anything about Beth?" Fisher asked again.

Reese stared out the front windows, watching the last of the daylight rush away. "Beth is a pawn now. She's of no value except to . . . us. So the people holding her are simply waiting to entertain offers."

"Like a trade?"

"Exactly. If we want to get Beth away from the people who came after us, whoever they turn out to be, we have to be able to give them something in return. Unfortunately, the only thing they want right now is me. And you by association."

"There are the flying saucer photos," Fisher said. "I mean, they show how you got out of the beach house. Establish your innocence. They've got to be worth something."

"Not to the people who want me." Reese squeezed his glass to keep his hand from shaking. He didn't want to think about those photos. He couldn't think about those photos.

"Then they're worth something to the media. If we make a big splash with them, we're in the news. We can tell what happened the day we got together to look at them. We'd be public. They couldn't touch us. And the media could track down

Beth." Fisher jumped up from her chair, walked over to Reese by the windows. "Whaddya say?"

Got to get out of this, Reese thought. "We don't have the photos anymore. We left them in the studio."

"I've got the negatives."

Reese's glass trembled. "Where?" he asked.

"Back at the house."

"It'll be torn apart by now. They'll already have them."

"Maybe not," Fisher said. "They were after *you*, right? Once they'd picked up the bullets and the bodies, why would they stick around to go through my stuff?"

"Where are they in the house?"

"Hidden."

"Where?" Reese demanded.

Fisher backed away. "If you can get me in there, I can get them." Her voice was flat and measured.

Reese studied her. Sighed. "Okay, Ms. Fisher. This is a safe house maintained by . . . a government agency responsible for ascertaining the motives of defectors from foreign diplomatic delegations. It's listed as belonging to a retired couple who are now doing ten years for acting as drug couriers. We'll be safe here at least four days, which means we'll head off in no more than two days. Any other questions? Any matters of trust?"

Fisher smiled. "Way to go, big guy. The negatives are in a little stash in the downstairs bathroom. That's the one Beth uses as a darkroom so it's a mess. Every place she's lived in, Beth always figures out a real safe hiding place for her jewelry and stuff. You have to unscrew the fan cover from the ceiling and then pull on an exposed wire to slide out the box. The trick is, if you've turned on the light to see what you're doing, then the wire is live."

"Very elaborate," Reese said. He decided Beth must have some extremely valuable jewelry.

"Too elaborate for whoever's going to tear the house apart?"

"Could be. Provided the photos on the studio floor don't make them think that you're somehow involved in all of this. I mean, by more than just accident."

Fisher held her glass up. "So, do we go for the gusto or what?"

Reese saw a way out. He could get Fisher in, get the negatives, destroy them, and then he would never have to think about them again. It would work. It would bring him peace. He smiled, clinked his glass against hers.

"I'll check out the level of surveillance they're giving your place tomorrow. As soon as they call it off, we can go in."

"No overreaction?" Fisher asked warily. "No urge to start tossing the furniture?"

"If what you say about those photos is true, then I should ignore any strong emotional response to let the truth come out, correct?" It was getting difficult to talk about this, Reese thought. He felt the rage and the anger and the fear rising up in him. Don't make me think about it.

"*Are* you feeling a strong emotional response to the idea of getting the negatives?" Fisher asked, suddenly concerned.

"Y-yes," Reese said. "Which is why I want to help you f-find them and make them p-public." Johnnie Walker sloshed over his shaking hand, dripped onto the sculptured rug.

"Shit," Fisher said, watching Reese battle his fear. "No wonder nobody ever found out about the guys in the saucers. They've conditioned you against even *thinking* about them."

Reese felt the blood rush from his face. He needed to smash out against something, make these thoughts go away. "P-please don't say anything more about it . . . about them . . . ," he said to her, voice quavering. "I . . . I can't . . ."

Fisher took the glass from Reese's hand, guided him to a brown sofa. Told him to sit and take deep breaths and not think about anything.

She saw his eyes stare panic-stricken out the front windows. The kudzu ground cover glinted under the streetlamps, swelling like a black tide moving toward the house. "Is there anything I can do, Reese. Anything?" she asked.

Reese nodded, forcing himself to swallow so his throat would work again to speak.

"The windows," he said. "Please . . . the windows."

Fisher looked at him a moment, uncomprehending, then followed his shaking finger as he pointed to the box of foil.

"You want me to tape them?" she asked. "Like the bedroom windows?" Reese nodded his head. "But why?"

"I don't like the light," Reese said. "It . . . it bothers me."

Fisher walked over to the stereo console and picked up the box of Reynolds Wrap and the roll of gaffer's tape and hefted them in her hands.

"Dear God," she said, whispering in awe, "what have they done to you? What have they done to you?"

"Whatever it is," Reese answered, choking despite feeling safety return with the power of the foil, "they're still doing it."

MONDAY, JULY 16, 23:35 EDT

Sparkling and radiant, New York City lay before Steven Gilmour like a galaxy of friendly stars. Thirty floors below him, the black of night was banished by the city's uncountable constellations, thousands of megawatts blazing in wild spectrums, protecting him with their brilliance from the darkness and the shadows and the absence of people. As long as those lights burned, Steven knew, he was safe. Even at night.

"Daddy?" Wendy said behind him.

Steven turned from the spectacular view looking south from Sixty-fourth and Madison and experienced a fleeting moment of dislocation. He was in his penthouse in the city, and yet his wife and daughter were there with him. A sense of satisfaction filled him, a feeling of warmth and completion, as though all his life's work was fulfilled in that one scene. The three of them. Together. The way it was supposed to be. Until . . . *ex*-wife he told himself. *Ex.*

"Hi, honey," he said to his daughter, smiling warmly at her. The realization of his present family situation was not enough to completely erase the emotion that had momentarily overcome him.

"I think I'll go to bed now," Wendy said.

Steven stepped forward to give his girl a kiss good-night, filled with wonder at how beautiful she looked, even with her hair wet and tied back and despite her ridiculous, brilliant red Roger Rabbit nightshirt.

Steven hugged her and knew that of everything in his life that was good and pure, Wendy stood out from them all, shining with a radiance of caring and unselfish love. Nothing bad must ever be allowed to happen to her. That thought was in him as if it had been engraved on his brain.

Steven kissed his daughter on her forehead and smelled the fresh scent of the soap she had used to scrub her face. It reminded him of the forest scents her mother had always used, and he closed his eyes and saw the dancing shadows of sun-dappled leaves on green grass.

"You okay?" he asked, stepping back, hands on her shoulders, looking into those young eyes that had seen too much worry in the past eight days.

"Yeah," Wendy said as if uncertain. But then she smiled, turned to Sarah, and said, "I'm glad Mom's here."

Wendy moved to the side to hug her mother. For a moment, a single step, Steven moved with her, just as he had so many years ago, for a family hug. But those days were gone, swallowed by endless factory production lines in four states, melted with the ice in countless glasses of vodka. He stepped back, held back, and let Wendy fill the void of those lost days, moving from her father's embrace to her mother's, the fragile cord that still joined them, the living memory that told them that once they had been bound.

He watched as Sarah held Wendy tightly, saw Sarah look up at him over her daughter's head, and found he couldn't read the thoughts or feelings that were in Sarah's eyes. Once he might have, he thought. And once she might have read his. But these were new days and that power was lost. Or just ignored.

Wendy kissed her mother on the cheek. "Night," she said, turned back to her father, said "Night" again, and stepped up the three stairs leading from the sunken living room to the hallway and was gone.

Steven sighed. He needed a drink but didn't want to have one in front of Sarah.

"If you want a drink," Sarah said, "go ahead. It won't bother me. Really."

Steven laughed. "That's just what I was wondering," he said. "I thought we couldn't do that anymore. Read each other's mind." He walked over to the door leading to the kitchen, paused. "You sure?" he asked.

"Go ahead," Sarah said. "But if you have a diet soda, I'll join you."

Steven went into the kitchen and poured a large tumbler of Wendy's diet Coke for Sarah, added a handful of ice, and chose an already opened and much-too-cold red wine for himself. Sarah had never liked red wine. Maybe it would make it easier for her, he thought.

When Steven returned to the living room, Sarah was standing by the glass wall, caught by the view. The recessed ceiling lights were turned down, producing only a warm orange glow, but the brighter lights from the minispots highlighting the paintings of his collection were enough to make reflections of parts of the living room against the glass and the lights of the city.

Steven paused for a moment, taking in the double exposure before him. Sarah, thoughtful and silent, the clear blue swimming-pool ripples of his Hockney floating beside her in its own pool of radiance like a sideways ocean over the light-strewn city. Steven loved this city. He loved that painting. And he stopped right there.

"There you go," Steven said, handing Sarah the tumbler. The ice clinked within it, floating among the coffee-colored froth of bubbles.

Sarah took the glass without turning, watching his reflection in the glass. "Not too shabby," she said, taking a sip. "Far cry from staring across the street into another building."

"I never minded that view all that much," Steven said, thinking of their old apartment off Columbus Avenue. He walked over to the farthest edge of the window, keeping what he thought was the appropriate distance.

Sarah smiled at Steven's reflection. "That's not what I remember. All you talked about was an apartment someplace that was so high up nobody could build in front of you."

"Someday they will. The buildings keep getting taller."

"You can just move to another. Keep moving up and up."

Steven left the window, went to his AV wall, changed his mind. He didn't think soothing music would be the thing to put on right now. He thought he really should turn up the lights.

"Have you got any music?" Sarah asked.

Steven didn't bother to laugh. He changed direction again and returned to the ten-foot-long black glass shelving unit, stacked with the latest solid-state marvels from Japan. He set up one of Wendy's CDs, a recent Paul Simon, well past his and Sarah's time and nothing to bring back memories.

"Are you laughing again?" Sarah asked, turning from the window.

"No," Steven said. He fumbled around the tightly packed bottom shelves, looking behind tapes and disks for the remote control. A few months ago he had worked out that the cost of all the tapes, disks, and records in his collection was more than he had made in his first two years working as a sales rep for

Kingsland Septipak. He had enjoyed discovering that. It gave him a hard and fast statistic with which to measure his life.

"Is it not working?" Sarah asked.

"Wendy's locked all the panel controls, so I can't change them except with the remote control," Steven said with a smile. "She says she finally got the balance perfect."

Sarah walked over to look at the stereo equipment and shook her head. "Sure you're not spoiling her?"

Steven stopped his search, looked up at Sarah. "This is *your* philosophy in action, remember? If she's going to be 'hanging around doing nothing' with her friends, might as well make sure that her friends will want to hang around at *her* place. Where we can make sure they really are only doing nothing."

They both laughed. Even when the money had been tight, Wendy had been the first kid on her block to get the latest toys and games. The memories of all those kids, Wendy's friends, playing in the house on the weekends when he was home brought back the same feeling of contentment that Steven had felt when he had seen Wendy and Sarah standing together in his home.

Sarah looked down at Steven, very thoughtful. "Why didn't we have more?" she asked.

Steven looked away. His mind blank. It was not a question to be considered. He peered into the last shelf. Stood up. "I don't know where she's hidden it," he said. "I'll go see if she's awake."

Sarah looked at him oddly, then said, "Let me."

Steven got up from his knees, thinking he should give her some sort of answer. But he couldn't remember the question. He looked at the tumbler of Coke in her hand.

"Your ice has melted," he said. He thought that the observation should be of some concern. Maybe something to do with the air-conditioning, he wondered. He sniffed the air and found it dry and dusty, like rocks baked in the sun.

Sarah looked at her tumbler, then handed it to Steven. "I'll go ask Wendy where the remote control is." She walked over to the hallway. A small sphere of light, no larger than a child's balloon, suddenly popped into being before her, spun madly with a low-pitched hum, then streaked down the hall, leaving a trail like a bright light strobing on a television screen.

Sarah stopped, turned to Steven. "Did . . . ," she began, faltered, shook her head.

"The remote control," Steven reminded her. "Sure, ask Wendy. See if she's up."

"Right," Sarah said with a nod. She turned back to the hall, hesitated, then continued on.

Steven watched her go, wondering if he should tell her to be careful. But of what? he wondered. There was nothing to be concerned about. Nothing to be frightened of. The part of him that knew fear was once again walled off. Everything was going to be fine.

Steven turned to stare at the stereo equipment, flat black metal boxes studded with rectangular glowing lights of red and green. For a moment, they seemed to shimmer like the constellations of the city. "It's got to be here someplace," he said to himself, looking for the panel lock button. This was important.

There was a frantic skittering sound in the hallway, as if two cats chased each other across the parquet floor. Steven turned around. Sarah was there.

"Is Wendy asleep?" he asked.

"No," Sarah said. She walked over to a chair, thick sheets of black leather hanging from chrome tubes, and sat down.

Steven finally found the panel lock button. He pressed it. "There we go," he said. Then he touched the operate button on the CD player and waited for the music to begin so he could adjust the volume.

"The apartment is looking nice," Sarah said. She sounded sleepy, dreamy.

A crackling, sparking sound echoed down the hallway. A muffled groan.

"Thanks," Steven said, trying to concentrate on the music.

"When did you redecorate?"

"Only painted."

The hall door opened. Closed.

"The dining room table is new. The sofa's recovered."

Something ran around the living room walls, just where they touched the ceiling. It jumped to the floor in the hallway and was gone. Steven brushed at his hair, trying to make sure there were no spiders in it.

"Just before Christmas," he said.

"Have any help?" Sarah asked.

"Penny," Steven said. He settled back on his knees. Something was finally coming out of the speakers. He held his finger on the silver triangle of the volume-down control. The glowing green numbers in the window above it counted down from Wendy's chest-thumping setting.

"Penny?" Sarah asked. "From the office, Penny?"

The volume was perfect. Steven stood up, turned around, blinked. The hallway was empty.

"Penny has good taste," Steven said, suddenly feeling defensive.

"Is she spending a lot of time here enjoying her handiwork?" Sarah's chair suddenly jerked an inch to the right. Her head wobbled. She looked straight at Steven.

"No," Steven said. He brushed at his hair again, looked around the room. "I . . . she just came around to give me some advice on colors and fabrics. You know I don't know about those things."

"You're not seeing her?"

"No," Steven said. He decided to sit down on the reupholstered couch, streaked with rich browns and greens like a forest floor, the one fabric he had chosen himself. He would be out of the way there. It was always important to be out of the way.

"How about you?" he asked. A second globe of light flickered above Sarah's head. Strands of her hair instantly bristled up as if a static-filled comb was above them. The light disappeared with a pop. Sarah absently brushed her hair down with her hand.

"I got a proposal this year," Sarah said.

"Really?"

"Jason Cooper." Sarah turned suddenly to look behind her. Nothing.

Steven looked outside. The city was blacked out. The galaxy swallowed by darkness. He turned back to Sarah. "What's this Jason do?" he asked.

"He wants to be a fireman," Sarah said.

"Wants to be?"

"He's only nine years old." Sarah began to laugh. "He's one of my third-graders." Sarah began to cry.

Steven jumped up to his feet, hands waving madly over his head. "Get this stupid bird out of here!" he yelled. "I can't stand it flying around like this."

Sarah looked up at him, tears in her eyes. "Wendy wasn't asleep, Steven. Wendy *wasn't* asleep."

Steven wrapped his arms around his stomach. He felt ill,

wanted to double over. Something was wrong. But what? What?

"The remote control . . . ?" he asked, face screwed up in concentration. "Wendy?"

Another face appeared beside him.

Floating in the air.

No shoulders. No arms. No body. Just a swollen gray-white egg with large black eyes full of the night that had swallowed the city.

The music stopped. The head floated in front of Steven, bobbing as if supported by an unseen surface of water. Steven felt his mouth open. Felt the spittle as it drooled down his chin. The eyes blinked, eyelids folding like flaps of dead skin from a blister. All the lights on the stereo faded out.

Sarah screamed. The head pulled back, vanishing as if disappearing between two curtains. Steven felt released. He spun to Sarah.

"They've come back," she moaned.

Steven looked over to the hallway. Two of them stood there, four feet tall, light-swallowing eyes, crouched over, waiting to . . .

"No!" Steven shouted. He ran for them.

One ripped a shimmering golden shaft from his leg, threw it at Steven. A javelin of light. Steven ran.

The creatures rotated as if on a turntable and slipped down the hall. Steven couldn't see their legs move. He ran.

In her bedroom, far down the hall, Wendy screamed.

Steven ran. He could feel his heart pounding, the painful impact of his feet on hard pavement, the acid burning of his stomach. He must stop, his body told him. I must save my little girl, his mind argued back. Lungs burning, he ran.

He saw Sarah beside him. How can she keep up with me? he wondered in his fog of pain. And then he realized she couldn't. He stared down at his unmoving body, shut his eyes, and felt himself running along sharp rocks and boulders. He opened his eyes. His body was motionless, still in his living room.

Sarah gasped. Steven followed her line of sight. One of them was on the wall, crouching upside down like a four-legged spider, its eyes watching them.

"You bastard!" Steven shouted.

The creature jerked back its head and seemed to slip *up* the wall a foot, as if it had lost its grip.

Steven wanted to charge at it, rip at it, but could only clench and unclench his hands over and over, uselessly.

The creature skittered back down the wall and placed one hand on the side of the AV shelves to steady itself. Steven looked at that hand. Saw that it was a tiny miniature of a real hand, every precise detail in place, wrinkled knuckles and delicate nails, like a baby's. But it only had three fingers.

The creature reached to its side and removed a thin strand of glowing metal. To Steven it seemed that the strand had been plucked from water, the creature only a shell with unlimited depth behind it.

The creature held its hand out, the strand pointing at Steven's face. Not a strand of light, Steven suddenly knew. A wand. John-John's wand.

Colors burst from it.

Steven heard a muffled explosion.

The creature squealed, fell back against the wall, slammed against the ceiling. The wand spiraled to the floor, glowing with a soft blue light. It hit without bouncing.

Steven heard more squeals behind him, more frantic scrabbling in the hallway. He looked up to see the creature flopping against the ceiling. He looked down to see the wand, pulsing with blue light on the floor.

Steven followed his instincts, ran for the wand. The creature screeched like fingernails on a chalkboard. Steven looked up to see it reach its hand into the ceiling. He saw the ceiling puddle back as if it were liquid. He heard an electric crackle and stared back at the floor. A tiny white hand emerged from a rippling surface of wooden parquet, grabbed the wand, and pulled back.

Steven lunged for the disappearing end of the wand. His hand slapped down on solid wood. He rolled. Looked up. The creature withdrew its hand from the ceiling. It held the wand.

Another muffled explosion. A distant shout of rage and pain.

The creature leapt down from the ceiling, into the air, stretched one arm forward, one arm back, and as if it had suddenly been grabbed by a giant and pulled in half, its body smeared and stretched ten feet in a twisted cord. And disappeared.

Sarah hit the floor, sobbing uncontrollably. Steven crawled over to her, aching and sweating and gasping for breath as if he had just finished a marathon. He looked to the hallway. Empty.

"I'll be right back," he gasped to Sarah. "I promise . . .

right back." Wendy had not been asleep. Steven forced himself to his feet, legs sore and rubbery, and staggered to the hallway, stumbled against the walls to Wendy's room, pushed the door open.

Empty.

"O Jesus," Steven moaned. "Not again, not again."

He ran to the foyer. Pain was a memory. Like an instinct from the dawn of time, his only motivation was to save his child, no matter what the cost.

He reached the corridor outside his penthouse. Ran toward the elevator he shared with the other apartment on the floor. Passed the elevator to the service door.

One flight of metal stairs led up to the roof. He flew up them four at a time. The stairs ended in a cinder-block room. A security camera watched from a corner across from the door to the roof. Its red light was out. The door was open. Steven burst out onto the roof.

A vibration took him. On the other side of the door there had been nothing. On the roof, the sound of thunder. Immense, overwhelming, as powerful as an avalanche. The gravel on the roof danced up in standing wave patterns. Steven was engulfed in heat. The air in his lungs pulsed with the beat of the rumbling noise. Something moved at the edge of his vision, and he turned to see the lights of the city come back, rippling like reflections in water, a giant black curtain of liquid slowly ascending, taking darkness and the harrowing thunder with it as it vanished. Steven stared up into the sky. Dark ripples there, looming above him. Pulsating, growing smaller and smaller until they were a black star in a black sky. A sky the color of eyes.

Then there was silence. Stillness. Only the distant rush and muffled horns of city traffic.

Steven leaned forward, hands on his knees, gasping for breath. He threw up. He had lost her. And he had lost—

"Steven?"

Steven wheeled. The voice had been weak, broken, and in pain. But Steven had recognized it.

"Angel?" he called out. "Where are you?"

"Over here," Angel said. He gave a cough like a retch.

Steven found the private investigator sitting against the side of a cinder-block wall that was part of the roof access structure.

"Oh, Angel," Steven said, seeing what had been done to his friend. The man's forehead was blistered with swollen red bub-

bles of skin. Some of the blisters had broken and a thin syrup of
pink liquid streaked his dark features.

"I . . . I got a couple of them," Angel said, coughing again.
He shifted his eyes to his left. Steven followed them. A smoking
piece of wood lay on the gravel beside Angel. It was attached to
a puddled mass of something that still glowed red like a heating
element. It took a moment for Steven to recognize the wood as
a gun stock. What was beside Angel was what was left of his
shotgun.

"And a couple more with . . . these," Angel said. He held
out his enormous hands. Steven felt his stomach twist as he saw
the torn flesh of his friend's fingers and palms. "Couldn't let go
. . . of the gun," Angel said. "Very . . . hot." He looked at
Steven, but his eyes didn't focus. The whites of them were
etched with red from a hundred broken capillaries. "Had to
sort of, uh, tear the gun away. Think I scared 'em though.
Think I got them . . ."

His hands flopped onto his legs. Steven stared at his friend
and saw, mixed in with the ruin of his wounds, thick smears of
pitch-black liquid, much darker than blood. He was afraid to
guess what it was.

Steven crouched down beside Angel. The man's head
slumped to his chest, came back up again, as he struggled not
to lose consciousness. "What happened to Wendy?" Steven
asked. "Did you see what—"

"The dish," Angel muttered. He waved a hand at the television satellite dish ten feet away. Steven looked over, saw the
dish on an angle. Saw a shape beneath it. He ran over.

It was Wendy. It was Wendy.

The ambulance for Angel arrived twenty minutes after the
building's security guard checked out the roof access door to
find out why the security camera had cut out. Steven had met
the guard as he had carried his daughter down the stairs, back
to his apartment. It hadn't taken much to convince the man
that the police weren't necessary. Steven's friend had chased
away a burglar who had managed to get past the building's
rooftop security systems. Why alarm the other occupants? Just
call an ambulance for the friend, repair the camera, and Steven
would be glad to keep the whole thing quiet. The incident was
handled in less than two minutes. The security guard had appeared relieved.

Steven carried Wendy into the living room then and placed her gently on the couch. She seemed dazed, muttering words that Steven couldn't make out. Except for one word, one name: John-John.

He went to the kitchen, chugged a mouthful of cold red wine for himself and got a wet cloth for her. When he pulled out another tumbler to fill with Coke, it finally hit him. He spun and ran back into the living room, calling Sarah's name. But there was no answer except the answer that he already knew. The answer he had always known.

She had been taken.

5

TUESDAY, JULY 17, 17:45 PDT

Gardiner sat at the drafting table in the studio of the house on East Angeleno and studied the half-finished drawing taped to it. He could hear the sounds of the forensics technician downstairs making his final run through the house before it was abandoned to simple drive-by surveillance by the Burbank police, waiting for Merril Fisher's return.

"This is going to make it difficult," Gardiner said, tapping his finger against the artwork. It looked like a scene from Bradbury's *Martian Chronicles*. Gardiner remembered being haunted by it as a boy. Told himself he should take another look at it someday.

Roy Luck looked over from the low pine storage cabinet where he stood with a phone receiver in his hand, evidently on hold. "How could it be more difficult?" he sneered, obviously not caring what Gardiner thought about anything.

"This woman," Gardiner said. "She's a comic book artist. People know her. She's not anonymous."

"And she's going to live," Luck said, sounding almost disappointed. "Which means as soon as Fisher tries to make contact, we've got her. Maybe even Reese." Luck turned away from Gardiner and pulled the receiver closer to his ear and mouth. "I'm here," he said, and began to write in a small notebook.

Gardiner leaned forward and shifted one of the vertical strips closing off the window beside him. The white LeBaron convertible with the flat tire was still down the street, exactly where it had rolled to a stop ten minutes ago. The passenger—a short man with a full moustache—was struggling with a jack handle, apparently having a hard time using it to remove the lug nuts. The driver hadn't bothered to get out and inspect the flat. Instead, he seemed to be napping behind his sunglasses. And Luck was running a make on the car. Ridiculous.

Gardiner dropped the blind back into position and spun on the drafting stool, running his gaze over the cartoon artwork on the walls without really seeing it. He realized he wanted to speak with Maria again. The other night at the dance club, when he had unburdened himself to her, that had been the night he had decided to take action. If his men had had five more minutes, he thought, just five more minutes Saturday night, they could have taken North and Vincent and Reese out of the house and into protective custody before Luck's murderers had arrived. Five more minutes and a comic-book artist would not be lying in the hospital with a tube draining her chest, three special agents would still be alive, North would be coherent, and a reporter—a reporter, for God's sake—would not be on the run with Reese. He thought of Maria and the decision to involve her in his work, to open himself to her. What might he have accomplished if he had done that five *years* ago?

Gardiner watched as Luck hung up the phone. The click seemed final.

"Tilden rental from LAX," Luck read from his notes. "Rented to a Barry Stroud. Matches description of driver. MasterCard number checks out to a San Diego address." He flipped the notebook closed.

"Feel better?" Gardiner asked.

"Yes," Luck answered, slipping the notebook back inside his jacket. "Because I leave nothing to chance."

"Because you leave nothing," Gardiner said.

Luck shrugged. "We still need you on this, Ed. So you tried to have an adventure on your own on Saturday night. Tried to bring in Reese, Vincent, and North by yourself." He angled his head forward. "But you didn't. So no big deal. No hard feelings."

"I know why you're keeping me on the investigation," Gardiner said. "You think I might have been trying to bring in Reese in order to cover up my involvement in . . . whatever it is you think Reese is involved in. You can't imagine that anybody might do anything because he has obligations to his people or because it's his duty or because it's right. You find it impossible to think that anybody does anything except for his own interests."

"Never leave anything to chance, Ed."

"Well fuck chance and fuck you!" Gardiner snapped. "You're so tangled up in paranoid scenarios that the only reason *you're* involved in this is because you're looking after *your* own interests. You're as bad as you're trying to make out my people to be! Worse!"

"I have no trouble admitting I'm looking after my own interests here, Ed. Except in my case, my interests are the OCI's interests."

"Fuck the OCI too. How about the country's interests? Aren't those what we're all sworn to defend and preserve?"

"That's what I'm sworn to. That's what I'm doing." Luck's voice was a cold, quiet drone. "If the OCI isn't strong, then the country isn't strong."

"And shooting goddam comic-book artists is supposed to keep the country strong, for God's sake?" Gardiner stood up from the stool.

"I don't care what anybody's cover is!" Luck stepped away from the counter.

"Some people don't have covers! Some people are just the ordinary citizens we're supposed to protect!"

"Like ordinary reporters that have been fed confidential FBI intelligence for the past four years?" Luck asked abruptly.

"What?" Gardiner was thrown off his rhythm. "What confidential information?"

"Nothing to chance, Ed. It's all in your files. *If* you check them out."

"For what?"

"For the connection between the reporter who lives in this house and your agents. Check Vincent and North's case files. Check Fisher's clipping file from the L.A. *Tribune.* What the data-processing boys call a near perfect one-to-one agreement."

"So?"

"So your agents have been passing information to an ordinary reporter for at least four years. Some of that information got her a headstart on a few stories."

"Christ, Roy, we all exchange information. We all trade sources."

"But what other information did they pass on during that time that didn't get put into a story? What other information got passed on to the criminals, to other organizations? Your office has been compromised, Ed. Just because a connection isn't apparent doesn't mean it isn't there."

"Listen to yourself!"

"No, you listen. Your agents are dirty, Ed. Your office is dirty. And that makes *you* dirty. Unless you help us break whatever ring is operating under your goddam nose."

The lights flickered and a cry of pain from the forensics technician came from downstairs.

In seconds, Gardiner and Luck found Eric Hodges lying outside the door to the downstairs bathroom. The young man held his right hand close to his chest, rubbing it vigorously. Luck looked around and holstered his Combat Magnum. Gardiner helped Eric sit up. The lights in that part of the house were out.

"I noticed some plaster or something in the chemical trays in there," Hodges explained, shaken by what had happened and nodding toward the bathroom that had been converted into a darkroom. "I thought it might have come from someone fiddling with the fan vent, so I unscrewed it, felt around. Found a box. Nearly electrocuted myself."

Luck smiled at Gardiner, then went into the bathroom, stood on the toilet, and shoved his hand into the open fan vent. He pulled out a thin strand of uninsulated copper wire. Attached to it was a small metal box which might have been used to store returned checks.

Luck brought the box out into the light, opened it, and pulled out a thick stack of glassine sleeves holding strips of black-and-white 35-mm negatives. Luck held the first strip of negatives to the living room light. His smile became wider. Feral.

"Another connection," Luck said to Gardiner. "By the way they were hidden, it's obvious that they thought these negatives were valuable. They've got to be connected to what's been going on."

"But what?" Gardiner said. He was sick of the man and his fantasies. "What's been going on?"

Luck carefully replaced the negatives in their box.

"That's what these are going to tell us," he said.

"Next time, you change the tire," Fisher muttered once they were out of the line of sight from her house. She pulled at the false mustache she wore and the latex adhesive gave way with a snap.

Reese drove back to the freeway from the house on East Angeleno, still keeping watch for following vehicles. He doubted there would be any though. Their disguises had worked, along with the false ID and credit card he had used to rent the LeBaron.

"Easier to make you taller than to make me shorter," he said sullenly, removing his dark glasses and his long, scraggly surfer-style wig.

"Still upset?" Fisher asked.

"It doesn't make any sense for Roy Luck to be involved."

"The guy who came out with your boss?" Fisher asked. "Carrying the negative box? I *thought* you recognized him."

"Roy Luck is with Special Operations in the OCI." Reese swerved the car onto the freeway entrance ramp. Still nobody following.

"I remember that the OCI is always involved in those defection cases, but what's Special Operations?"

"They're the OCI's 'animals.' A private army. Paramilitary operations." Reese's mind sifted all available facts, trying to find the thread of a connection that would link his case to Special Ops. There was nothing. Nothing.

"Why would the OCI's private army be involved with the FBI?"

"I have no idea. My investigation wasn't involved with anything military. Just commercially available computer components," Reese said as he guided the car back to the safe house in the Hollywood Hills, eyes tracking the river of headlights blazing behind him.

"Has the OCI ever worked with the FBI before?"

"Reluctantly," Reese said, moving the car back to the right to avoid the blinking red lights of a work crew blocking the lane up ahead. "The bureau's responsible for counterespionage operations inside the country, and the OCI coordinates all counterespionage operations outside. There's just no reason for any OCI agent to get involved in a domestic smuggling operation like the one I was tracking."

"How about if they just came on board to analyze the negatives?"

Reese shook his head. He was getting angrier. Felt his fingers dig into the yielding foam plastic of the steering wheel. "But how could they *know* about the negatives? They just found the photographs Saturday night. They wouldn't know what made them important."

"Then maybe the FBI wants the OCI to tell them if they *are* important."

Reese pulled the car off the freeway and immediately brought it to a stop at the side of the exit road, sliding against gravel. Nobody stopped behind them. He turned to Fisher.

"You don't understand how fragmented and uncooperative the intelligence community is. Nobody trusts anyone else. The FBI would never want to give any advantage to the OCI. It would be *impossible* for them to ask the OCI for help."

"Maybe the OCI didn't give the bureau a choice." Fisher looked around nervously. "And why have we stopped?"

Reese took a deep breath. He had been doing well for a while there, he told himself, but his anger and the darkness of the night were combining, bringing the old fears back. He pressed the rocker panel on the dash. "Just going to close the roof," he said. So they can't see me, he thought.

"Well, could the OCI force its way into an ongoing FBI operation?"

Reese looked up as the roof slowly ground over them, cutting off the sky. "It's possible. But with all the different reporting levels that those photos would have to go through in D.C., there's no way the OCI could become involved in only three days." He reached up and locked the roof on his side.

Fisher did the same with the toggle lock on her side. "Then think it through, Ace. The OCI must have come into the equation before the photographs were ever found. They're involved because of something you did earlier. Any suggestions?"

Reese waited for a break in the traffic, then gunned the car forward, spraying gravel behind. "What do you think?" he asked. "All this started when I didn't call in to stop the transfer of computer parts in the desert. I've been under investigation ever since."

"Why?" Fisher asked, but from the tone in her voice he realized she already knew the answer.

"To find out why I screwed up," Reese answered, voice trembling.

"And why did you screw up?" Fisher asked.

Reese jammed on the brakes again, swerved the car to the side of the road, ignored the horns blaring behind him, past him. He kept his hands locked onto the steering wheel, turned to Fisher, teeth clenched.

"Because *they* took me that night," he said in a whisper like a suffocating man. "Because they came down and took me and I wasn't there when the transfer took place."

Fisher reached out to Reese, touched his arm, as rigid as steel. "You knew what was on those photographs before you even saw them, didn't you?" Her voice was kind, gentle.

"Yes," Reese said, his own voice dry and cracking as the strain built up inside him. "No. I mean some of it. I mean . . ."

"How long have they been coming for you?"

Reese fought to hold back a sob. A plea for help. "Forever . . ."

"Do you know who they are? What they are?"

Reese held his hands to his face. "I can't remember all of it. They won't let me." He shook his head. "I'm going to be sick."

Fisher hurried out of the car and ran around to Reese's side, opened his door, helped him lean out just before he threw up. She had him get out of the car then, stand away from the side of the road, and fill his lungs with night air.

"Does this happen every time you think about them?" Fisher asked when his breathing had slowed. "Try to talk about them?"

Reese nodded, watching the cones of light that swept by as the cars on the road passed, headlights flashing once on the parked LeBaron as they entered the curve, and then darkness again.

"Why did you agree to go after the negatives then? Why go through this for me? Or for Beth?"

Reese walked back to the car to rest against it, turn his head from the flashing light and dark of the traffic.

"To destroy them," he said. "Have to destroy the negatives." He felt dizzy. If he closed his eyes, he could feel the car spin around beneath him.

Fisher put her hands on Reese's shoulders. There was compassion in her touch. "Did *they* tell you to destroy the negatives?"

Reese shook his head again. Didn't she understand how wrong this was? How painful?

"They don't . . . tell me anything," he whispered.

The reporter frowned. "They don't speak to you? Don't say anything at all to you?" Reese shook his head. "But then what do they do with you?"

Reese struggled more than he ever had in his life. Forcing the hidden words to come from deep within him, from the buried part of him, beneath the layers of suffocating mud.

"They . . . they give me . . ." He felt the headache hit as if he had been smashed with a pipe. His ears rang. He fought against it.

"They give you . . . ?" Fisher repeated, excitement and worry in every word. "What, Reese? What do they give you?"

Reese stared at the woman. Blackness rushed in from the side of his vision until he saw her through a tunnel of night. His head throbbed; his body resonated with pain.

"Love," he said. "They give me love."

And torn by that admission, tears rushing from his eyes, Reese collapsed against the woman and wept with the agony of it and the pain of it. And the hopelessness of it.

Love.

TUESDAY, JULY 17, 21:15 EDT

Wendy Gilmour took her father's hand and squeezed it as the elevator carried them to the fifteenth floor. Steven turned to his daughter, a look of pleasant surprise on his face. "What's that for?" he asked.

Wendy smiled at him. "You look like you could use it," she said. And she meant it.

Steven nodded, readjusted his grip on the beribboned bottle of Charles Heidsieck he carried, crinkling the clear plastic wrap protecting his ornate bouquet of red roses and baby's breath, then turned back to watch the green numbers advance on the panel above the doors.

Wendy studied her father in profile. He was handsome

enough, she knew. At least that's what her friends kept telling her. Too old by a long shot to be a hunk, but definitely not a geek. Even the Gilmour nose looked good on him, a strong feature on a strong face. Too bad it showed up on my face too, Wendy thought. A strong feature on a not-so-strong face. But she would live with it.

Wendy thought of her nose, which was way too big for her face, she had told Margot, in the same way that she thought of the gold pocket watch and fob that her father had given her when his father had died: as a mark of her family. Wendy had been twelve when Grampa had died, just before her parents split, and Wendy remembered that the old man's passing hadn't disrupted her home the way she had seen other deaths disrupt her friends' homes. Maybe her parents had seen it coming and hadn't told her. Maybe they had other things to worry about. But probably, Wendy had decided, her father simply had not allowed his own father's death to intrude on the careful compartments of his own life.

Except for the night he had come into her room and given her the watch and told her how proud Grampa had been of that watch. And how proud he, her father, had been of that watch. And now it was time for Wendy to have it. Maybe someday to pass it on to her child. Somehow, that night the watch had become more important than Grampa. He was a memory she held in her mind, and someday her mind would be gone too. But the watch was a memory she could hold in her hand. It would remain for others.

Now that watch rested in an old Tiffany jewelry box her mother had given her, and every once in a while, usually when she was feeling crampy and would rather just sit quietly in her room, Wendy would take that watch out of its box and hold it in her hand just as she pictured how her Grampa had held it, just as her father had held it. Then she would imagine all the other hands that might hold it, because unlike most of her other friends, Wendy had no trouble at all combining her future planned career as a doctor with a parallel career as a mother. She liked babies and she would have them. Living memories of things yet to be. She pictured the watch in soft, tiny hands, the hands of her baby. She jerked. The elevator had stopped.

"You okay?" her father asked.

"Uh-huh," Wendy said. She took a moment to place herself.

"Just tired." She moved the large gift-wrapped box she carried from one arm to the other. Cookies, her father had told her.

Steven put his hand on her shoulder as they stepped from the elevator, looking for the sign that would take them to apartment 1504.

"You sure we're not going to get in trouble for this?" Wendy asked.

"Just the doorman," Steven said, motioning to the left.

"And he's got a hundred-dollar bill," Wendy said. Just for "forgetting" to announce Mr. Starr's two dinner guests until they had time to surprise the writer at the door and wish him a happy birthday. Wendy had to concentrate on not laughing when she had watched the doorman carefully write down that today was Starr's birthday. Presumably he would send a card of his own and expect a bigger tip.

"Money's not worth anything until you spend it, kid," Steven said, stopping in front of the door marked 1504. He used the tone of voice that he saved for giving Wendy "a lesson on life."

Steven knocked on the door and Wendy tried not to think how totally humiliated she was going to feel if this didn't work out. If they had to walk past that doorman back in the lobby in the next few minutes and he knew they hadn't really come for Mr. Starr's birthday, she'd die.

The door opened and Wendy recognized Charles Edward Starr from the dust-jacket photo on his book. The writer had baby pink skin and his hair was surprisingly blond, and he was considerably taller than she had assumed, at least two inches taller than her father. But he did have a writer's look to him. Sort of bemused, Wendy thought.

"Yes?" Starr asked. His frown turned to an uncertain smile when he saw the champagne, the flowers, and the present.

"Mr. Starr," Steven said, quickly handing over the Heidsieck. "I'm Steven Gilmour. This is my daughter, Wendy."

Starr blinked, looked with delight at the dark green bottle, then tilted his head. "You left some messages at my publishers today," he said warily.

"Six," Steven said. "May we come in?" He started to step forward. Starr reflexively stepped back, caught himself, tried to say no but by that time it was too late. Steven and Wendy were in the front door. Wendy felt her cheeks burning. Her father was so good at embarrassing her.

"Now wait just a minute," Starr protested, eyes wide with alarm.

"Happy birthday," Steven said. He plunked the flowers in Starr's waving hand. Wendy had seen her father act like this before at a trade show he had taken her to downtown. He just smiled and blazed ahead, saying exactly what he had planned to say, as though he didn't hear the customer's protests. Keep it up long enough, he had told her in his special important voice, and you'll always close the deal. Wendy wished him luck, this time.

"It is not my birthday," Starr declared, trying to pass the champagne and flowers back to Steven.

Steven turned, took the wrapped present from Wendy, added that to the stack in Starr's hands. "It is now," he said happily.

Starr awkwardly dropped the items onto a scarred deacon's bench, already overflowing with books and newspapers. Wendy noticed that although he let the box and the flowers slide to the floor, he made sure the champagne was securely wedged into place between two stacks of old magazines.

"If you don't get out right now I'll call security!" Starr threatened.

"If you mean the doorman, I've already talked to him." Steven replied, smiling like a long-lost relative. Wendy shrank back against the wall, wondering when Starr was going to pull a gun. She looked around the apartment. Not as nice as her father's but okay. Modern but way too cluttered. Books everywhere. She tilted her head to peer into the living room. Someone peered back over the couch.

"You mean security *let* you through?" Starr stammered. "I pay three thousand a month and they let you through?" He reached for the intercom phone on the wall. Steven reached out for it too, held the writer's hand in place.

"Let's cut to the chase, Mr. Starr. Security let me through for a very good reason." He paused. So did Starr. Wendy had heard her father call that technique "the hook." Make them want to hear what you're going to say next. The person on the couch was getting up. Wendy looked away quickly when she saw it was a woman, doing up the top buttons on her sepia blouse.

"I'm a very wealthy man," Steven said. "I paid generously for the doorman's cooperation. I want to pay generously for yours." He looked around what he could see of the apartment, stopping when he saw the woman approaching from the living room. "Three thousand seems like a good price for all this," he continued after a moment. "What do you say to a month's rent for a few hours of consulting on your specialty?"

"I make a considerable amount from my book sales," Starr said haughtily.

"In cash," Steven said. "No receipt."

Starr stumbled for a comeback. Wendy's father had called this moment the "flinch factor." Even though Starr didn't know it, her father had just closed the deal.

Steven took his hand off Starr's. Starr took his hand away from the intercom phone.

"About my specialty?" the writer asked, bringing himself to the same conclusion Wendy had reached. "You mean . . . UFOs?"

"Abductions," Steven said.

"I was abducted," the woman in the doorway to the living room said. Wendy turned back to her. The woman's buttons were all done up now, but, Wendy decided, it didn't really change much. If she was wearing a bra, it was one of those sheer ones that Wendy wouldn't even try on, and her blouse was at least one size too small, making the bra's transparency brazenly apparent.

Starr returned to stammering. "Uh, Jocelyn, this is, uh, . . ."

"Steven Gilmour," Steven said. "And my daughter, Wendy." Steven shook hands with the woman. Wendy didn't offer. Considering what they might have been doing in there, Wendy didn't want to touch her.

"I'm going to be in Eddie's new book," Jocelyn said proudly.

"Really?" Steven said. Wendy could tell that her father was playing one of those adult conversational games. Nobody was saying what they really meant.

"Uh, yes," Starr said quickly. "We were just doing some research. Taping Jocelyn's memories of her abduction experiences." He turned to Wendy's father. "Really, Steven, it is a most awkward time to arrange for a consultation. Perhaps to—"

"Jocelyn is right here, Mr. Starr. My wife is gone."

Wife, Wendy thought. Not his ex. That was interesting.

"What do you mean by 'gone'?"

"Abducted."

"Really, Steven. She's probably just—"

"Wendy and I were there. We saw them."

"Them?" Starr swallowed.

"The creatures. Abductors. Whatever you want to call them. They came for Sarah and Wendy. My bodyguard fought some of them. Maybe shot one of them—"

"Can you describe them?" Starr asked.

"Of course. They were about—"

"*But* not in front of Jocelyn," Starr interrupted. "I don't like to have my subjects' memories confused until I've had a chance to record them." He glanced into the living room. "Uh, just give me a moment to straighten up," he said.

"What about my session, Eddie?" Jocelyn asked. Wendy made a face at the little girl sound of the woman's voice.

"Oh, we'll get right back to it," Starr promised, fluttering his hands as if some nail polish hadn't dried. "Just give me one second." He ran off into the living room.

"What do you remember of your abduction?" Steven asked the woman, finally dropping his salesman's approach.

"Abductions," Jocelyn emphasized. "They've taken me four times. That I remember."

Steven looked at Wendy. Wendy could see the desperation her father had been keeping inside come to the surface. She stepped over to him, wondering if it would be okay if she took his hand again.

"Do you have any idea why?" Steven asked. "Who they are? What they're trying to accomplish?"

Jocelyn shook her head. "I think they're trying to give me . . . a special message," she said. "But I'm not quite . . . ready for it yet."

"Ready? How?"

"Spiritually," Jocelyn said. "When I was on the moon and—"

"The *moon?*" Wendy interrupted. She knew her father was probably trying to be polite to the bimbo, but come on.

"They have their base there," Jocelyn patiently explained. "One of them at least. That's where they're preparing all these big sort of universities so they can teach us about living together with all the other beings in the galaxy." Her eyes took on a distant look. "It's going to be wonderful," she said in a hushed voice. "Eddie's helping me remember the pictures they've shown me, of how it's going to be by the year 2000.

Peace. And love." She smiled at Steven. "Sort of like on 'Star Trek.'"

Steven nodded in agreement, and Wendy prayed he really was only being polite. After all they had been through, this wasn't the time for her father to lose it.

Starr returned and asked Jocelyn to step back with him into the living room where they had a whispered conversation.

"'Star Trek'?" Wendy mouthed to her father, rolling her eyes.

"I think I might have just flushed three grand down the toilet," Steven sighed.

"Margot said she was impressed by some of this guy's work. I don't understand what he's doing with Jocelyn." Wendy gave her head an airhead shake when she pronounced the woman's name.

Steven smiled, patted his daughter on her head, but didn't say anything. That was when Wendy realized that she did understand what Starr was doing with Jocelyn. Adults, she thought, they went at it like animals.

A minute later when Starr called them into the living room, Jocelyn was gone.

"She's doing her relaxation exercises in the study," Starr explained.

"I'm sure she is," Steven said amiably, and Wendy saw Starr frown as they all sat down around the coffee table. Like every other surface in the apartment, it was covered with stacks of newspapers, magazines, loose sheets, and books. There was also a Sony tape recorder on the highest stack, silver and not as small as Dr. Jeffery's.

"So," Starr began, clapping his hands in front of his chest. "You say you've all been abducted by flying saucers."

"No," Steven snapped. "We haven't been to the moon with Jocelyn and we haven't seen any flying saucers."

"Then why are you here, Steven?"

Wendy's father sighed. "How about if we start at the beginning," he said, then filled in their story from the time he arrived at the Litchfield house to find Wendy gone and Sarah unable to remember what had happened. About two minutes into his story, Starr poked among the mess on the table and pulled out a pen and some paper and began to jot down a few notes. But he kept his questions to "And then what happened?" until Steven brought his story to the point where Margot Jeffery had suggested they meet with Starr.

"I'm not familiar with a Dr. Jeffery," Starr said.

"She had one of your books," Steven replied. "Thought some of the work you were doing might give you some kind of insight into what we're dealing with here."

"I see," Starr said. He looked at Wendy for a moment, silent, thoughtful. Wendy had seen lots of men look at her that way in her life in the city. Usually they did it when they thought she wouldn't notice. It made her feel creepy, then and now.

Starr turned back to her father. "And tell me, Steven, do you have any insight, even guess, of what it is you might be dealing with?"

Steven narrowed his eyes. "That's why I came *here,*" he said, obviously annoyed. "A psychologist tells me that my wife and daughter have been picked up by . . . something. I see the things in my own apartment. And my wife disappears. I don't have the *slightest* idea what I'm dealing with here!"

Starr blinked in surprise at the forcefulness of Steven's response. Wendy could tell the writer was going to start stammering again. She leaned forward and said, "Does what my father told you sound like the same things that have happened to other people? Like the people in your book?"

Starr glanced at her. "Have you read my book, young lady?"

"No, sir."

"How about books by other investigators? *Intruders, Communion, The Interrupted Journey*?" Wendy shook her head. Starr continued. "Seen *E.T.*? *Close Encounters of the Third Kind*?" Wendy nodded for those.

"What do movies have to do with anything?" Steven broke in. "This wasn't make believe. This was real."

Starr put his pen down, smiled at Wendy, and turned to Steven. "In this day and age, those books and movies have *everything* to do with what you've experienced. I hear about dozens of alleged abductions every week. Most of the details could have come from any one of a dozen books, a dozen movies, cartoon shows, comic books, even stage plays. Popular culture has become a polluter of the abduction experience. Anybody can say they've seen a ball of glowing lights land in their backyard and small, big-headed aliens emerge because they *have* seen it. Usually on television."

Wendy saw her father was mad now. His nostrils flared and he didn't open his mouth very wide when he talked.

"Let's just get one thing straight here, Mr. UFO expert. Do you or do you not believe that some people have been abducted by UFOs?"

"Of course I believe it!" Starr said. "It's become my—"

"Fine," Steven said, cutting the writer off. "Now how can you tell the difference between someone who gives you a rundown of last night's 'Twilight Zone' and someone who actually experienced it?"

Starr shrugged. "By listening carefully for those details that could not have come from a fictional source."

"What kind of details?"

"The kinds of details that two or five or fifteen people who have never seen or communicated with each other before independently put into their accounts of abduction, meaning that the only way their accounts could be similar is because they were all in a unique place undergoing a unique experience."

"So what are they?"

"What?"

"The details!"

Wendy shrank into her chair as her father nearly stood up from his.

"Steven, please!" Starr said like an angry teacher. "If I tell you something I've not allowed into print before, how do I know that you won't go away, tell a hundred other people who will all come to me over the next year, all claiming never to have met you, appear in my next book, and then a year from now 'Sixty Minutes' is after me for fraud?"

"So nobody knows what those magic details are?" Steven asked snidely, settling back into his chair. "Sounds convenient."

"Of course, all my research documents, including full transcripts and videotapes of all my subjects, are available for review by any bona fide researcher." Starr folded his arms over his chest.

"And who might a bona fide researcher be?" Steven asked. Wendy saw it was obvious that her father intended to go out and hire such a researcher to get access to Starr's files. Her father would stop at nothing to get what he wanted.

"Certainly not you, Mr. Gilmour," Starr said. "Fee or no fee, I think your consultation is at an end."

"Wait," Wendy said. "What if we told you more? My father just gave you an outline. Lots more stuff happened."

Starr pursed his lips in a self-satisfied smile and shook his head. "I'm sorry, young lady, but I don't think that would change my mind."

"Why not?" Steven snapped. "Our story's no good because we didn't beam up to the moon?"

Starr sighed. "Listen, your story is just about the same as any abduction story I've ever heard. But you people are not like any other abduction victims I've met."

"What makes us different?" Steven asked, and Wendy could see his anger was being replaced by the desperate need to know he struggled to keep hidden.

"Look at you!" Starr said, waving his hand to them both. "Your daughter was taken by inhuman creatures, Steven. Your wife has disappeared. Your mother, young lady. Yet you're both just sitting here as upset as if you'd been . . . delayed at the airport or something." Starr leaned forward, hands clasped like a preacher's. "The victims I've studied, the real ones I believe truly have been abducted, have sat right where you're sitting, quaking in their boots. They shake, they sob, they go into convulsions on occasion. But they don't sit around calmly and . . . and treat me with such disrespect!" The writer tossed his pen onto the stacks on the table and stood up.

"I cried in the sessions with Dr. Jeffery," Wendy said. He couldn't send them away now, she thought. Then it would seem that it had been her fault that Starr wouldn't listen to their story. What would her father say? What would he do?

"Well, good for you, young lady," Starr said with his same bitter smile.

"But I'm not frightened of them right now," Wendy continued. "I mean, sure, when I remembered all that stuff that happened, I remember that, at the time, I was scared and all. But only when they first come for me because I don't remember who they are or why they're there. But then . . ." She trailed off, staring at the writer expectantly.

"Then you do remember why they've come for you?" Starr asked, giving her a few second's reprieve.

Wendy shook her head. "I think I do. At least, it feels like I do . . . I haven't been able to remember everything yet. Neither has Mom."

"I see," Starr said quietly. "And how do you feel when you do think you remember why they've come for you?"

"Well, I feel okay then." Wendy was puzzled by the question and by her response. But the more she thought about it, the more she knew it was the right answer.

"Okay?" Starr repeated skeptically.

"Yeah, uh, yes," Wendy said, speaking slowly, trying to consider each word as her father had so often told her. "I mean, once they have me, it's like everything's going to be all right. I'm, uh, going to—Well, there's somebody there." Wendy looked down at the floor, confused. She almost felt as if she were back in Margot's office. Memories were calling out to her, but she couldn't quite get a grip on them.

"Somebody is where, young lady?"

"Wh-wherever it is they take me. I— Doesn't anyone else ever feel this way? That it's all right that they've taken them?" Wendy watched Starr shake his head slowly. "Nobody?" she asked again.

"Abductees usually feel terrified, tortured, violated—for reasons I won't go into. And other than . . . subjects such as Jocelyn"—Starr raised his eyebrows at Steven—"none has ever come away from a legitimate abduction experience feeling that it's 'all right.' "

Steven remained stubbornly sitting as Starr stepped around the coffee table. "So doesn't that make Wendy's experience worth studying?" he asked.

Starr sighed impatiently. "Tell me something more," he said. "Tell me something that I've heard before but that you couldn't have read in one of my books." Wendy looked at her father and expected to hear the 'Jeopardy' clock theme song.

Steven leaned forward, snapping his fingers together. "They . . . they used a type of . . . wand as a weapon. A long, thin piece of bright metal. Lots of colors. It—"

"They use that piece of equipment all the time," Starr interrupted. "Most abductees say the wands are called probes. It's in all the books. What else? What are their ships like?"

"They . . . they've never come after me," Steven said softly. Both men looked at Wendy.

She shrugged. "I've never remembered that far," she said.

Starr turned back to Steven. "Anything else?"

"One of them dropped its probe!" Steven said suddenly.

"Did you get it?" Starr asked, eyes widening.

"No. The probe hit the floor and then the thing reached . . . reached into the ceiling and . . . its hand came out of the floor, grabbed the probe, disappeared and then had it back on the ceiling again."

"On the ceiling?" Starr asked. Even Wendy stared at her father dubiously. She couldn't remember ever seeing any of the creatures on the ceiling.

"Yeah," Steven said. "It was walking around, crawling around, I guess, on the ceiling and the wall. Like the room was upside down or something. But Sarah and I stayed on the floor. And one of them, oh shit, one of them, his head just . . . appeared in front of me . . . just floating in front of me without a body." Steven wrapped his arms around himself and shivered as if he were cold.

Wendy saw Starr watching her father for long moments. Then the writer glanced over at her, and she saw something in his expression had changed. When he spoke, his voice had changed too.

"Steven, do you happen to have a card or a number for your Dr. Jeffery?" Starr asked.

Steven nodded, reached into his inside jacket pocket and passed over the doctor's card. Starr took it and slipped it into the breast pocket of his shirt.

"All right," Starr announced, "this is what I'd like to propose. You and your daughter go home tonight. Or check into a hotel if it makes you feel more comfortable. Near the ground floor turns out to be best. Makes it more difficult for them to spirit you away, I suppose. I would like to talk with Dr. Jeffery tomorrow and get her background notes, if you'll give your consent, so I won't be covering the same ground. And then next week we can set up some sessions. Look into your experiences in a bit more detail."

"Next week?" Steven asked.

"But what about my mother?" Wendy added.

Starr held his hands apologetically. "My new book's just come out and I'm doing publicity. I'll be out of town the next few days."

"Where?" Steven asked. "We can meet you."

Starr thought about that for a moment. "Los Angeles tomorrow until the weekend. Then Chicago on Sunday night. Detroit on—"

"The end of this week is fine," Steven said. "Los Angeles. When and where?"

Starr pulled a fat wallet from his back pocket, dug through it, and passed over another business card to Steven, telling him to call the woman on the card to get his itinerary and hotel and to set up dinner for Thursday evening.

Steven reached for his own wallet and fanned out a sheaf of bills.

"Not now," Starr said. "If things pan out, I'd like to sign an agreement sharing publication rights to your story. If things don't pan out, then you can make a donation to ongoing research." Wendy saw her father was surprised by the writer's change of heart.

"But what about my mother?" Wendy asked again.

"I wouldn't worry, young lady. Other than a few nicks and scratches, apparently for medical tests, there's never been a substantive case on record in which any abductee has been harmed by the creatures."

"But tell me," Steven broke in, "are there any cases on record in which any of the creatures has been harmed or shot by an abductee."

Starr looked thoughtful. "No," Starr said at last. "If your bodyguard *was* successful in injuring one of the creatures, then that would be something unprecedented. As far as we know."

"So you have no idea how the creatures might respond to an act of violence directed against them?" Steven asked.

"No, sir, I do not," Starr said. But his mouth was tight, Wendy saw, and he held her father's eyes too long. She had a sudden feeling that there was something the writer wasn't telling them. "But," Starr continued, "I would hope their response would be rational as befits intelligent beings anywhere."

"Rational," Steven laughed. "There doesn't seem to be a whole lot about this business that's rational."

"No," Starr agreed. "I'll be the first to admit that very little of it seems rational." And Wendy saw it in the writer's eyes again. She was sure of it.

Charles Edward Starr was lying.

6

Fisher stared at the pigsty that was Cy North's apartment, stared at North himself, slumped on the couch, mindlessly watching the television. Then she sniffed in disgust, even amazement, at the stench of old sweat and rotting food. "Why the hell did they let him out of the hospital?" she asked.

Reese quietly closed the apartment door behind them, replaced the chain lock he had just dislodged with a piece of fishing line and a tack, then slipped his lock picks back into his pocket. "They let him out because he's bait," Reese said. "For us. Isn't that right, Cy?"

North had not reacted to Reese's and Fisher's intrusion. He kept watching the eleven o'clock news, his one unbandaged eye glassy, his mouth open. Reese carefully stepped over the scattered newspapers on the floor and crossed the room to the set, an old RCA twenty-six-incher standing on its own wooden legs, with too much orange on the screen. He shut it off, and North at last acknowledged him.

"C'mon, man," he said, sitting up slowly on the couch, looking at the fading screen and not at Reese. "I gotta keep that on, okay?" He ran his right hand over the crumb-covered cushions of the sofa, underneath crumpled Taco Time bags and a balled-up dirty blue sheet.

"We've got to talk, Cy," Reese said, stepping forward to stand before the man, what was left of the man. "I want to find out what Gardiner is doing with Roy Luck and the OCI."

North moaned. He wouldn't look at Reese.

"And Beth," Fisher added. "That was part of our deal."

Reese glanced at the reporter and nodded. She deserved that much, as they had agreed. He squatted down in front of North.

"Do you remember the night we were at Merril's house, Cy? We looked at the photographs that night. Do you remember?"

Reese was right in front of the man, blocking the silent television. North hung his head down. His hand kept moving over the couch like a junkie looking for a lost gram.

"Come on, Cy!" Reese said, raising his voice. "David was there. I was there. Merril and Beth were there." He grabbed North by the jaw, forced his head up. "Look at me!"

North brought out a flat silver box from beneath a cushion, held it up to Reese's head. Instinctively Reese jerked to the side. North pressed a button on the box. The eleven o'clock news returned to the television.

"Jesus," Reese said, pushing himself back to his feet. "Give me that." He snatched the remote control from North's hand, aimed it at the screen. Someone in a tight red dress was saying that the weekend's weather was going to be h-h-hot.

"Want to keep watching, Cy?" Reese pressed a button and the set shut off.

North flailed his hand at Reese, trying to get the remote control back. "C'mon, man. I need that," he whined. "I *need* that."

"Why?" Reese asked. This was the first real sign of life North had shown since he and Fisher had broken into the man's apartment.

For the first time, North met Reese's eyes. "For the light, man. I need it for the light." He tried to stand up, almost made it, then collapsed, holding the thick bandage around his upper right thigh. "You know about the light. I *know* you know about the light. The way they talk to you. The way they make you look at them." He stared up at Reese in agony. "Give me the goddam control box!"

Reese felt North's words cut through him. He did know about the light. He did know about the pit that North's pleas sprang from. But he had to know more.

"Will you talk to us?" Reese asked, aiming the remote control at the set like a terrorist holding a gun to a hostage's head.

"Aw, yes," North sobbed. "Anything you want. Just don't make me *look.*"

Reese heard Fisher mutter to herself. She had guts, he knew, but North's anguish was so strong, so painful, he wasn't surprised that it would affect her in some way. He looked over at her to offer encouragement. But she wasn't watching him. She was over by a balcony window, peering carefully behind the drawn drapes.

"Watch it!" Reese warned. Why did she think they had spent twenty minutes crawling through the utility tunnel connecting the underground parking lots of the five apartment buildings on this block? "We saw four agents out on the street. He's being watched."

"Not by the FBI, he isn't," Fisher said, pulling one panel of drapes open. "Not through this."

Reese felt his stomach tighten. The balcony window was covered with aluminum foil.

Reese turned back to North, switched the set back on, but adjusted the volume down so he could speak over it. "Let's talk, Cy. You keep talking and I'll keep the set on, okay?"

North kept his eye focused on the set. Screen after screen of baseball scores flipped by. He nodded in time to the announcer's cadence.

"What happened to Beth? The woman who was taken in with you. The woman who was shot when you were shot."

"David's dead," North sighed.

"I know he's dead," Reese said gently. "I saw him get shot. I saw the blood. Nobody lives through something like that. But what about the woman, Cy? What about Beth?"

"They're keeping her." He nodded in time to basketball scores. He stared vacantly at Lakers highlights.

"Where are they keeping her? In the hospital?" North nodded. "Is she alive?" He nodded again. "Is she going to make it?" North groaned as though he hadn't slept for days. Probably hasn't, Reese thought.

"I think so," North said. "I don't know. They want to keep her."

"Why do they want to keep her?"

"To get Merril. To get Merril to call." He nodded his head to a beer-commercial tune. "Then they'll get her."

Fisher walked over from the covered windows to stand by Reese. "Looks like you win the Secret Square," she said. "Thanks for not letting me call."

Reese kept after North. "Why is Gardiner working with Roy Luck? What's the OCI's involvement, Cy?"

North's lips were wet, open. He stared vacantly at the set. "Your fault," he said. "Your smugglers were OCI. You were trying to break an OCI sting."

"It was more than an OCI sting," Reese said coldly. "It has to be. Was the OCI at the beach house the night I was . . . got out while you and Vincent were running surveillance?"

"What?" North asked dreamily after a moment. More commercials, more head-nodding.

Reese grabbed the man's jaw again. "Talk to me or I'll kick in your television set. Then you'll *have* to look at them when they come for you, Cy. You'll have to listen when they come for you."

North twisted away from Reese and fell into a corner of the couch, burying his head into the blue sheet, sobbing.

"Take it easy," Fisher said, putting her hand on Reese's shoulder. "David told me all about the night at the beach house. They were drugged. The things that took you must have sprayed a hypnotic drug. Prevents short-term memories from being stored in the brain. I guess the aftereffects leave you pretty confused. Cy's still experiencing them. He's still drugged."

"Nooo," North moaned into the sheet.

Reese forced himself not to yank North off the couch, not to throw him across the room. "What do you mean, no?" he asked, trying to keep his voice unthreatening, without success.

"Not drugged," North said. He turned his head so his face was no longer pressed into the sheet. "We weren't drugged. We weren't drugged. There was nothing wrong with us," he chanted.

"But David described the symptoms," Fisher protested. "I've read reports of drugs like that. You must have been drugged."

"No, no, no, no," North said, rocking his body.

"How do you know you weren't drugged?" Reese tried to get North upright again by pulling on his arm.

"Gardiner gave us the test results," North said wearily, like a child kept up too long. "We were clean." He pointed to a chair piled with dirty clothes. "Look at them. We were clean." He sat up again, wiped at his running nose with his hand, wiped his hand on his sling. He stared at the television. The news anchors were discussing their plans for the next day.

"Look at what?" Reese asked, staring at the stack of laundry.

"The results," North said. "Gardiner gave us the results. We were clean. We were conducting ourselves properly, Gardiner said." He reached out for the balled-up sheet and hugged it to his chest.

Fisher went over to the chair North had indicated and cautiously pushed some of the clothes to the floor. She found a beige file folder, opened it up, brought it to Reese.

"Blood and urine test results," she said. "From the FBI lab in D.C., according to the labels."

Reese looked at the multicolored computer graphs. All the plot lines fluctuated along the bottom of the grid. He checked the names and dates printed on the sheets. "Nothing," he said. "There's nothing here."

"We were clean," North repeated, rocking to another commercial, never taking his eyes from the screen.

"Hold on," Fisher said. "Give me David's blood test results." Reese handed the sheet over. "This is all wrong," she said, frowning.

"We were clean," North whispered.

"What's wrong?" Reese asked.

"David has asthma." Fisher exhaled sharply. "Had asthma. He told me that it had been acting up recently." She looked at Reese. "He told me he used his inhaler that night."

"So?" Reese asked.

"So nothing shows up on his test results. I mean, the stuff in an inhaler is a drug. It's absorbed by the lungs, dilates the air passageways. Some of it goes into the bloodstream and in broad-spectrum drug testing, asthmatics can score false positives. But there's no indication that anything at all was found in David's blood."

Reese took the printout back. "So, this isn't David's test result."

"And these probably aren't Cy's," Fisher added, holding them up.

"But why give them false results?" Reese asked.

"We were clean," North breathed. "Your fault, not our fault." He rocked in time to the "Tonight Show" theme.

Fisher ignored him. She patted the back of her hand on the printouts. "Because the original tests showed that they *were* drugged. Probably with something exotic. And the FBI and the OCI didn't want David and Cy to follow up on anything."

"And when they did try to follow up," Reese said slowly as the awful realization grew, "somebody tried to kill them."

"Tried to kill us too," Fisher added.

The sound of laughter came from the television. North rocked silently, obliviously.

"That means they know, Reese," Fisher said. "Somebody knows what's going on. The FBI, the OCI. Somebody. And they're trying to cover all the loose ends."

"But *what* do they know?" Reese asked. "That's what doesn't make sense."

"Maybe it does," Fisher suggested. "The UFO fringe groups have always been going on about a government conspiracy to withhold the truth about flying saucers. Maybe there's something to it after all."

Reese shook his head angrily, then abruptly stopped. "My immediate reaction there was to . . . tell you you were wrong. I felt the anger rise up again. Maybe that's just because I'm tired, I'm frustrated. Maybe it's part of my . . . conditioning. Maybe it's part of what's happening to North to make him behave this way. I can't be sure." He took a deep breath and spoke slowly. "But, thinking rationally, not emotionally, I really don't think that is a valid conclusion."

The audience laughed again.

"And why not?" Fisher asked.

"I know the people in D.C.," Reese said. "Nothing that big could ever stay a secret. Maybe for a few months, maybe a year. But D.C. runs on stupidity, greed, and the desire for power. Eventually someone would make a mistake, sell out to the media, or expose someone else's involvement for revenge."

"The military are good at keeping secrets, aren't they?" Fisher asked. "The Stealth fighter was operational for seven years before the Air Force admitted they had it. One even crashed in a national park and the plane was still kept secret for three years."

"The military is good at keeping their secrets because the only other people who want to know those secrets are other military groups. The average person doesn't care about a new laser-guided missile or exact measurements of a submarine propeller blade. But keeping something secret about flying saucers would affect too many people. It wouldn't just be a military secret. It would be too big, spread too far. The mechanism for secrecy would break down." Reese shook his head, discounting Fisher's suggestion. "Nixon couldn't keep Watergate secret. Reagan couldn't keep the arms-for-hostages deal quiet. Nobody could keep the truth about flying saucers quiet. D.C. doesn't know anything."

"Then maybe they're finding out right now," Fisher said quickly. "Maybe the FBI ran some kind of investigation to find out why you didn't call in your people when you were supposed to intercept the smuggler's plane. Maybe they found out you were taken then and set up surveillance on you to see if you'd be taken again."

Reese clenched his fists. "I— It's so hard to talk about this, Merril." He grimaced like a weight lifter. "If . . . if that were the case, then I would have been covered by a lot more than a couple of microphones and Cy and David on Sunday night. They were just watching to see if the smugglers would make contact with me. That's all."

"Then it was Sunday night," Fisher concluded. "Sunday night was when they found out about the things taking you."

"This is only ten days later," Reese said. "No agency could move that fast. The assessment reports alone would take two weeks to prepare. Analyses a week. Position papers another week. Then go through the whole process again for presentation to the National Security Council and Oversight." He smiled, the first time that evening. "The Martians could take half the population back home with them before anybody in D.C. had even put together a budget proposal to fund a study proposal. I guarantee the secret wouldn't last that long."

The audience applauded. North watched on.

"Well, whatever else it was we stumbled into," Fisher said, defeated, "they've got the photos and they've got the negatives, so they'll know all about what happened to you eventually."

Reese stood up and stared glumly at North. "And in the meantime, we're a target, and unless we can figure out what kind of an operation we got caught in, we've run out of places to go."

"Know any good safe houses in Mexico?" Fisher asked.

Reese shook his head, gestured to North. "We'll talk about that when we're out of here." He handed the remote control back to North, patted the man on his shoulder. "Thanks, Cy. I hope it works out for you."

North stopped rocking and lovingly examined the silver box.

"For whatever it's worth," Reese continued, "I think they only came after you because you were close by when they came after me. I . . . I don't think they'll be back . . . for you."

"I don't want to look at them," North said. "I don't want to hear them when they call." He aimed the remote at the television. Johnny Carson's voice rose in volume.

Reese reached out and touched Fisher's arm. "Let's go. Get some rest."

Fisher patted his hand. "Will I ever see Beth again?"

Reese shrugged. "I don't have any more answers," he said. Wherever they went, he thought, it would have to be a lot farther away and safer than Mexico. And with that thought, he realized that he had admitted defeat. He was beaten.

Reese and Fisher walked back to the door, leaving North to his reveries. Reese reached for the door handle. Johnny Carson spoke again, echoing off the apartment's walls. Reese froze.

He and Fisher turned back to the television as one.

". . . been on the show many times before, and I guess you could consider him an expert in his field," Carson said. "But tonight he's here to talk about his new book . . ." Carson held the new book up. Reese made a sound as though he had been hit. The ring of colors. He recognized the ring of colors on the cover.

"The Case for UFO Abductions," Carson continued. He turned the book around, flipped through it. "Now, I've read this book. There's fascinating material in here. It's scary. But I suppose the big question is, is it true? Well, I guess that's what we might find out. Please welcome the author, Charles Edward Starr."

The audience applauded.

Exhausted, defeated, and running for their lives, Reese and Fisher sat down in North's apartment and watched TV.

7

"Smokey Joe would appear to be what is called an 'inappropriate animal,' " Charles Edward Starr said, then placed another forkful of salmon into his mouth. "And the creature whom Wendy named John-John would be another variant manifestation," he continued as he chewed, the salmon making his right cheek bulge.

Steven Gilmour leaned forward over the white-linen-covered table, straining to catch every word Starr spoke. Trump's restaurant was a candlelit oasis of calm, the soft hum of background conversation from other tables made a soothing white noise, but Steven was unaware of all except the man across the table from him and Wendy beside him.

"What's their purpose?" Steven asked as Starr washed down his salmon with the last of the second bottle of chardonnay. "A disguise?"

"Apparently," Starr agreed. "Even though this young lady," —he smiled at Wendy—"does not appear to remain frightened for very long when in their presence, she herself maintains she was quite startled when she saw John-John's face for the first time."

Steven looked at Wendy. She was also leaning forward in her seat, trying to hear everything Starr spoke. We're like the faithful at a religious revival, Steven thought, waiting for the messenger to give us a message from the skies. Maybe that accounted for the success of people like Starr: the promise of secret knowledge.

"Abductees have reported seeing wonderful deer, beautiful owls, cute rabbits, mesmerizing cats, almost all animals known for having large or unusual eyes. It's as if the aliens scan our minds for an image that is both familiar to us and that takes into account their own appearance, blending the two to prevent shock. At least initial shock." Starr carefully scraped away the last shreds of flesh from the salmon bones on his plate. "Or," he added, "the human mind is simply creating a false message to preserve our sanity. 'A screen memory,' Freud called it. Either way, the aliens often appear disguised."

Steven sipped at his wine, his own meal only half-eaten. Wendy, he noticed, had cleaned her plate of everything except the ubiquitous leaves of cilantro.

"How long has this been going on?" Steven asked.

"When did it begin?" Starr asked himself, looking up to the ceiling and licking at the fingers that had handled the bones. "Well, the original case that was brought to public attention was the abduction of Betty and Barney Hill on the night of, um, September 19, 1961. They were returning from a vacation in Canada, driving along an empty highway in New Hampshire, saw a UFO, were frightened. Then the next thing they knew, it was two hours later and they were seventeen miles down the road."

"What happened to them?" Steven asked.

"For a long time, not much. They reported their UFO sighting to the Air Force—the Air Force had an ongoing investigation at the time—and that was that. But they continued to be puzzled about those missing two hours. And they began to have anxiety attacks that started to interfere with their lives."

"Anxiety connected to the UFO?"

"As it turned out," Starr said, "yes. Barney, in particular, began to exhibit signs of severe psychological stress, and just over two years later they both went to a psychiatrist who decided to use hypnosis to try and see what was causing their amnesia. Well, he recorded their sessions separately, and both Betty and Barney told pretty much the same story: during those missing two hours, they had been taken on board a UFO, subjected to medical examinations, and released."

"By little white aliens?"

"Gray in their case, I believe," Starr said, smiling. "Lighting conditions change. Maybe their skin is like chameleons'."

The waiter appeared at the table, pulled the wine bottle from its ice-filled bucket, saw it was empty, and asked Steven if he would like another. Steven nodded, knowing Starr would keep talking as long as there was wine on the table.

"Now, where was I?" the writer asked after his plate had been taken away.

"Betty and Barney Hill," Wendy prompted. She had been quiet through the whole dinner, and Steven sensed that she didn't like the writer. He also knew that she was going to be very uncomfortable around Starr if he actually did make his way through a third bottle of wine, a sensitivity left over from her mother's drinking.

"Ah, yes." Starr removed the last pencil-thin breadstick from the basket and dipped it into what he had left in the little dish of whipped butter. "News leaked out of what they discovered about their sighting under hypnosis. *Look* magazine ran a feature story on them. Then John Fuller wrote *The Interrupted Journey.* Published it in 1966. It's the classic abduction story."

"What sort of details were in that book?" Steven asked, still wondering where the dividing line was drawn between delusional abductions and the ones that people such as Starr would investigate.

"The usual. That's why it's a classic. The almost hypnotic effect of the aliens' eyes. The medical exam inside the UFO. Betty recounted a rather long conversation she had had with the alien she thought of as the 'leader.' He showed her a star map of some sort which depicted trading routes between different stars, exploratory expeditions. Even showed her a book— she couldn't read it of course, alien language—and offered to let her take it with her as proof."

"A book?" Wendy asked, suddenly excited. "What happened to it?"

"Sadly, just as Betty was leaving the ship, the aliens took it back. The leader explained that the others objected to her taking it. They didn't want there to be any proof."

"How convenient," Steven muttered.

"How puzzling," Starr countered. "From some accounts it almost seems as if there are a wide variety of aliens dropping in on us, some with differing motives."

"From all the abductions you've studied," Steven said, "have you been able to put together any idea about what any of their motives are?"

Starr glanced at Wendy for a moment, looked back to Steven, hesitation in his eyes. "The common motive appears to be some form of genetic sampling of humans," he said. "The medical examination Betty Hill remembered does seem to be part of most abductions. She reported having a large needle stuck into her navel. The aliens said it was a 'pregnancy test.' Other abductees have reported similar experiences—causing those intense feelings of violation that I mentioned—very much like procedures we use to harvest eggs from women for *in vitro* fertilization procedures."

"Why?" Steven asked. Now the topic was becoming truly grotesque.

"We can only guess, Steven, but it appears that men have been subjected to a parallel procedure." Again Starr glanced at Wendy, sitting in rapt attention, candlelight sparking in her wide eyes. "Male abductees often report that . . . um, mechanical means are used to obtain sperm samples. Intriguingly, in the 1966 book, Barney Hill said the aliens had placed a circular device over his groin as part of his examination. And that was all. Years later, when other men came forward with details about their own abductions and told how they had been made to ejaculate by having their genitals somehow stimulated by a device that fit over them, the book's author confirmed that the same had happened to Barney but that the information had been withheld from the book because it was considered too sensational at the time."

Starr leaned forward and gestured at Steven with the last two inches of breadstick. "That's what I mean about the value of withholding some details from publication. The fact that Barney's sperm was taken but not reported means that the next abductee who said his sperm had been taken could not have been merely repeating what he had read in the book. Either both men made up identical stories or else both had undergone the same experience." He shifted his eyes once more to Wendy, then crunched the breadstick to establish that his point had been made.

"What are they doing with the sperm and egg cells?" Wendy asked, evidently fascinated by the topic and not showing the slightest bit of embarrassment. Steven smiled at the earnestness

of her expression. He wished Sarah could see it. He wished he
had answers. But he found it difficult to even think of the questions for any length of time.

"Well, young lady," Starr began, "since you've obviously
studied biology in school, what do you suppose they would do
with sperm and egg cells? What is their purpose?"

"Making babies?" Wendy said.

Starr nodded imperiously. "Just so. But not just any babies.
Crossbred babies. Hybrids of aliens and humans."

"Oh, now you're going too far," Steven complained. He sat
back in his chair, shaking his head. "That's—"

"Too far?" Starr interrupted. "As if aliens from another star
are not a concept that is too far out? As if UFOs being real is
not too far out?" He leaned forward and jabbed a finger against
the linen cloth. "Once you've opened the door of unlimited
possibilities, Steven, nothing is too far out."

Steven shook his head again. "Has anyone ever seen a hybrid
baby?" he asked, and his tone showed what he expected the
answer to be.

"All the time," Starr said. "That's one of the most common
details included in abduction accounts."

"How?" Steven sputtered. Then laughed. "How, I ask. As if
I'm taking this seriously."

"Daddy, shh!" Wendy said. "Tell us more about the babies,
Mr. Starr."

"Some men who have not had sperm samples taken mechani-
cally, with some device, describe episodes in which they have
had sex with alien females."

"Fantasies," Steven said.

"Oh, certainly," Starr agreed, "if the men tell how they were
given in passion to beautiful six-foot-tall women in silver underwear, right out of the pulp science-fiction magazine covers of
the fifties. But the point is, the men don't tell that kind of story.
They talk about being being subjected to a gas that makes them
vomit, being strapped to a table, and then being mounted by a
different variety of creature, female in general form, who is
gray-skinned, hairless, and with large dark eyes. That is not a
fantasy of mine, I assure you."

The three of them then turned slowly to stare at the waiter
who stood beside their table, bottle of wine and corkscrew in
hand and who had overheard Starr's last statement.

"Yes?" Steven inquired.

The waiter blinked and held the chardonnay's label out for inspection. Steven nodded and the waiter began opening the bottle.

"And does the same ever happen to . . . women?" Wendy asked, her voice subdued, turning back to Starr.

"Not in legitimate abduction experiences," the writer said, ignoring the waiter's stare. "And that in itself is intriguing. If abduction reports were all fantasies, then surely the far more common nightmare of rape would appear more often to join with the common dreams of flying or being rendered paralyzed, say, that most people have, abductees or not, and that also often appear as part of the abduction experience. The fact that rape is not reported indicates to me that what abducted women experience is real and not a nightmare."

Wendy jumped when the waiter yanked the cork out of the bottle with a loud pop. Starr smiled, and Steven told the waiter to just pour.

"And what about the babies?" Wendy asked when the waiter had left. "You said people see them?"

Starr slurped at his wine, rolled it around his mouth, swallowed, and smiled. "Once the abductee is taken aboard the ship, a standard abduction experience follows a five-part scenario. How the abductee gets on board can range from being floated out of a bedroom, parking his or her car at what seems to be an all-night supermarket with lots of lights and strange, short clerks, being lifted up with some sort of antigravity beam while inside a traveling car, or simply answering the doorbell late at night and finding an alien waiting in the shadows, ready to escort you to the local park."

Wendy shivered. "Ooo," she said, "that's creepy."

Starr smiled at her. "You should know, my dear." He held his wineglass by the stem and examined it against the flickering candle. Steven saw a star-shaped highlight fall across the writer's smooth pink skin, just below his left eye. No doubt about it, Steven thought, he can tell a good story.

"You said an abduction follows a five-part scenario," Steven prompted as Starr sipped his wine.

"Ah, yes," Starr said, blinking as if he had just wakened. "One, the medical examination, with fingernails clipped, hair taken, bits of flesh scooped out of legs—leaving distinctive and documented scars, I might add. Sometimes the exams involve the insertion or removal of small artifacts, about the size of a

BB pellet, into the victim's nose or ear. Alas, they are too small to be resolved by a CAT scan and apparently transparent to standard medical X rays."

"What are they for?" Steven asked.

"The current thinking is that the pellets act as a type of radio transponder, enabling the aliens to track down their subjects anywhere, at any time. Just as we tag moose and bears in the wild, then track them with satellites and helicopters." Starr leaned forward again and his elbow slipped off the table. "Remember, Steven, abduction is not a onetime event. Most abductees are first taken at age five and then regularly past that point, sometimes more than a dozen times until their forties, even fifties."

Steven reached out and took Wendy's hand. He had wanted Starr to tell them that there could be an end to this nightmare, not that it might continue for another thirty years.

Starr looked at Steven's hand on Wendy's, frowned for a moment, then continued. "So, after the examination comes step two, which is usually the egg or sperm collection. And then, young lady, usually comes the baby presentations. A wonderful room, like a nursery, filled with unusual incubators and tiny infants. Half-human, half-nonhuman."

"W-why?" Wendy asked. She didn't take her hand away from her father's.

Starr stuck out his bottom lip. "The babies are generally presented to the abductee as being somehow theirs—conceived from their sperm or from their eggs. The aliens seem to want the humans to touch the babies, stroke them, teach others about how to care for them."

"That's really creepy," Wendy said.

"On the contrary, dear, some women report this part of their abduction experience to be a great relief. Very fulfilling."

Steven grimaced. "Why, for God's sake?"

"Because they feel they're being shown their lost babies," Starr said. He reached out for the wine bottle in its bucket and much too carefully filled his glass again. Steven allowed his to be topped up. Wendy still had her diet soda.

"You mean like what my mother was looking for?" Wendy asked. "Actual lost babies?"

Starr nodded his head with exaggerated motion. "Labeled a brand-new neurotic condition," he said. "First women feel they are pregnant, even if there is no chance that they could be.

Then the pregnancy ends, usually coinciding with an abduction. And then, nine months later or thereabouts, whoosh! Back they go to the ship and see their little dickens."

"But if they know all that," Steven asked, "why do they think their babies are lost in the first place?"

"Because it appears the aliens are trying to keep their work here a secret. They cloud men's minds." Starr laughed. "Excuse me. They can affect our memories. All a woman knows is that somewhere she has a child—or children—that are not with her. For some women, this turns into a compulsion to find those lost babies. But once they've remembered their abduction experiences and discovered the cause of their neuroses, poof— the obsessive-compulsive behavior is gone! More proof!"

Steven sat very still and controlled his voice, reacting to Starr's growing animation by becoming more reserved himself. "How does that qualify as more proof?" he asked. He knew there could be no proof for any of this.

Starr arched an eyebrow. "Most abductees exhibit some form of neurotic behavior. Common wisdom states that a neurosis is cured only when the underlying cause of the internal conflict is identified and then either it is resolved or an appropriate defense strategy is adopted. Since the lost-baby syndrome—a neurotic condition if ever there was one—is alleviated once repressed memories of abductions are brought to the surface, by conventional psychological theory the abduction experience is the trigger event, and therefore real. Q.E.D."

The waiter arrived, approaching cautiously. He presented the dessert menu, and Starr entered into a long conversation with him about the merits of the various cakes, at last deciding on something the waiter claimed had too much chocolate. Steven smiled when Wendy conscientiously ordered the fruit salad.

When the waiter left, carrying the menus and the empty breadbasket, Wendy brought the writer's attention back to the conversation.

"That's four parts of an abduction you've told us about," Wendy said. "What's the fifth?"

"The fifth part is a puzzler, young lady. Sometimes it's like a movie, sometimes a lecture; sometimes abductees are shown a book like the one Betty Hill tried to take from her ship."

"Is there a point to the movie, the lecture, the book?" Steven asked.

"Something to do with the babies," Starr said, shrugging

elaborately. "Apparently the abductees are shown, or told about, a different way of life. Usually peaceful, beautiful. We could see it as an attempt by the aliens to reassure the humans that the children created with their seed will end up living in a good place. We could see it as an attempt to educate humans as to how we are supposed to conduct ourselves in the future." Starr sighed. "We just don't have enough information."

"And you say that these abduction experiences generally last only a few hours?" Steven clarified.

"Two to four hours," Starr said, rocking his hand back and forth to indicate more or less. "There are a few cases of someone disappearing overnight or for twenty-four hours, but some of the lost hours appear to be spent sleeping back at home, recovering from the ordeal. Indeed, there is some indication that the aliens feel it is not healthy for humans to spend too much time aboard their ships."

"Sarah's been gone three days," Steven said softly, the hidden desperation in his voice apparent even to him.

Starr leaned back in his chair. His eyes seemed to clear for a moment, as though he had just remembered something important. "That is one of the many details that trouble me about your alleged abduction events," he said.

"Alleged?" Wendy repeated in surprise.

"You've been talking as if you accepted what we've been saying," Steven protested.

"No, no," Starr said, waving a hand. "You misunderstood me. I accept the abduction experience as something that has happened to other people, yes. But I'm not yet willing to . . . put you into my next book, shall we say?"

"What's the problem, Mr. Starr?" Steven said coldly. "My wife is gone and you're the only one it seems we can talk to about her. If you can't help us, what are we supposed to do? Go to the police? I can just see us sitting down with the police artist and coming up with a composite of E.T."

Starr's expression remained frozen, delivering a message, Steven thought.

"The problem, Steven, is that while you have accurately described some details of alien abduction that have not been publicly reported, to the best of my knowledge, there are other details concerning your case that cause me a great deal of doubt. Such as Sarah's extended disappearance. An absence of more than two days for someone who would be bound to be missed would be a completely unprecedented abduction. However, a two-day disappearance could also be a disgruntled ex-wife off on a vacation. Or, and it troubles me to say this, an alcoholic off on a binge."

"My mother doesn't drink anymore," Wendy said, eyes flashing.

Steven patted Wendy's hand. "Just a minute, here. We never said anything about Sarah being an alcoholic. How did you know that?" Steven had a sudden feeling that he had stepped into a darkened elevator and not felt the floor of it beneath his descending foot.

Starr rubbed his face and looked apologetic. "I contacted your Dr. Jeffery," he explained.

"And . . . ?"

"Quite impressed with her," Starr said, and Steven saw the writer was happy to be given control of the conversation again. "A cognitive behaviorist, my favorite kind. We're going to get together when I return to New York. She's quite interested in my work and how it might apply in the case of Sarah and Wendy."

"And she told you about Sarah?" Steven asked.

"I had your consent to be fully informed, remember? She told me a great many things."

"Did she tell you some things that made you doubt our story?" Steven persisted.

"Frankly, yes," Starr said. "But I don't think this is the time or the place to discuss them. Actually, I would like to work with you over the next few months, in collaboration with Dr. Jeffery, and see if we can't find a more . . . mundane explanation for what your family has been experiencing. I hasten to add that your kind offer of a consulting fee is not necessary for me, though I would expect that Dr. Jeffery's time would be covered at her professional rates."

Steven leaned forward over the table and spoke in the voice he used for his employees on the line. "This is the time to discuss it, Charles. I need answers. And I need them now."

Starr sat up and straightened his suit jacket. He held Steven's commanding stare for a moment, then turned to Wendy.

"Young lady," he began, "I apologize at the beginning if what I am going to say next causes you any embarrassment, but it would appear to be your father's wish and perhaps, the best thing to get all of this out in the open."

Wendy blinked. "All of what?"

"Initially I was troubled about your story for two reasons. First, that you didn't retain any residual fear for the aliens. Quite extraordinary in the annals of abduction, I assure you. And second, because you couldn't remember anything about being taken on board a ship. Again, that's generally the key event. People often don't remember everything about their incarceration, but they do remember some of it—the rooms, the lighting, symbols on the wall, the number of aliens, the types of aliens, all sorts of important detail that you at first appeared to be lacking."

"Appeared to be?" Steven repeated.

"Do you know what I'm talking about, young lady?"

"About my memories of being . . . on board," Wendy said quietly.

Starr nodded as Steven squeezed Wendy's hand. "Do you remember something about that?" Steven asked. He turned back to Starr. "I didn't hear anything about that on Margot's tapes."

"She said she hadn't had time to play them all for you. Only the most clear. And the least upsetting. As far as being parents, that is."

"What do you mean?" Steven turned back to Wendy. "What does he mean?"

Wendy kept her head tilted to the linen cloth and rolled her eyes up to her father. "Well, it's not exactly clear. I mean, not like remembering John-John in the sandbox or anything. But I sort of do remember some of what I think went on in the . . . well, ship or whatever." Her voice had dropped almost to a whisper.

"What was it, honey?" Steven asked. He felt his stomach begin to twist. Dear Lord, what was he going to hear this time?

"Well," Wendy said, turning her eyes back to the table, "sort of like what Mr. Starr was talking about before. About, well the baby stuff."

"You saw the crossbreed babies?"

"Not that," Wendy said. Her hand felt cold and clammy in Steven's.

"Well, what then? A medical exam?" Steven's stomach was like a rock. What warped delusions had Starr brought into his daughter's mind?

"The . . . the sex part," Wendy said. She drew her hand

away from Steven and took her napkin from her lap, wiped her lips, folded it. All nervous gestures.

Steven opened his mouth to yell at Starr, then closed it as he remembered his surroundings. The waiter arrived with dessert. Starr ordered a double Rémy Napoléon. By the time the waiter left, Steven was able to keep his voice in a normal range.

"You have memories of having had sex with one of the aliens?" It was harder to say those words than it had been when he had told Sarah he wanted a divorce. Wendy shook her head, a brief flutter of denial. "Then what, honey? Come on, look at me. I'm not mad. I'm not upset. I'm just worried about you and your mother."

Wendy looked up. Her cheeks were flushed, even in the dim light of the restaurant. "I, uh, I remember—I *think* I remember —having . . . making love . . . with another person. A man. Not one of *them*. A human."

Steven closed his eyes and exhaled softly. He reached for Wendy's hand again. "That's okay, honey. Now, was it like a . . . a dream? Like a fantasy dream maybe? We all have them." He tried to smile but felt like his face had locked into position.

"Yeah," Wendy said, shaking her head, meeting Steven's eyes for an instant, "I know about those kinds of dreams. But . . . this seemed different. More, uh, more real."

The sensation in Steven's stomach was overtaken by the fluttering of his heart. If he let go of Wendy's hand, he knew his own would tremble uncontrollably. "I, uh, I know that I have no right to ask this question, but, do you . . . you said it was more real—Well, have you made love before?" Steven grimaced as he felt the tension in Wendy's hand, the stiffening of her posture.

"No," she whispered, and Steven could see tears come to her eyes. "Except in . . . my dreams. Except when they take me."

"It's okay, Wendy. Shhh. It's okay," Steven soothed. He glared at Starr, but the writer didn't respond in kind, returning Steven's look with indifference.

"And was it like Mr. Starr said?" Steven asked, forcing himself to go on. "Were you . . . tied down? Forced?" Sickening, Steven thought. Completely sickening. And what if it were true?

"N-no," Wendy said, suddenly looking up. "Not like that at all. It was . . . I, uh, . . . it was something good." She looked down at the table again. "I wanted to. Like I was in love . . ." Her words were almost inaudible.

The waiter arrived with Starr's cognac, eyes wide at the current state of the table. "That's fine," Steven snapped at the man as he lingered by the table too long. "We'll let you know when we need you." The waiter hurried away.

Starr broke the silence. "As I said, young lady, I apologize, but perhaps it's for the best."

"What's for the goddam best?" Steven demanded, hands gripping the edge of the table as if he were going to push it over onto Starr.

"That we start the examination of Wendy's experiences with an upfront analysis of all the factors. Even the disturbing ones that make me think that this might not be a cut-and-dried abduction."

"Why does what Wendy said make you doubt she was abducted?"

"You haven't listened, Steven. I've related all the pertinent facts and you haven't paid attention."

"To what?" Steven felt several pairs of eyes upon him, heard a corresponding lull in the surrounding conversations. He lowered his voice. "Enlighten me, Charles."

Starr tapped his fingers on the table. "Budd Hopkins once had a group of abductees he was working with undergo a complete battery of psychological tests. To see if they shared some common psychological problem that might account for them making up such fantastic stories. The results? They were sane. They were normal. The only things that they shared, the only things they had in common, were increased levels of anxiety and a sense of violation. The testers, who hadn't been told about the nature of the group, assessed the test results and assumed that the group members were all victims of a traumatic incident, most probably rape."

"I don't understand," Steven said slowly. He wanted to hurt Starr if the man didn't start making sense soon.

"Think of the inappropriate animals, Steven. The screen memories. The human mind makes up explanations for bizarre, hurtful events that it doesn't want to acknowledge." Starr sounded like he was pleading with Steven.

"Are you saying that abduction experiences are all *made up*? You said you believed in them."

"I believe that some people are abducted, yes. But I also

believe that with all the publicity surrounding the phenomenon, other people make themselves believe they have been abducted. Either for fame and attention, or to provide a comforting mask to obscure an even more traumatic event."

"Abductions comforting?" Steven was barely able to speak.

"Compared to other, more serious intrusions into one's life, yes."

"Such as?"

"Steven, please. Think this through. This is why I want to work with you and Wendy. And Sarah when she turns up. Your daughter's abduction doesn't ring true. It's deficient in one important detail."

"What?"

"All the reports of sexual activity on board the alien ships have been reported between humans and aliens. Wendy's is the first I've ever heard or heard about that reports sex between two humans." Everyone in their room at Trump's had turned to look at the table where Starr waved his hands at the red-faced teenage girl and the man who trembled, about to erupt.

"And," Starr continued, "Wendy reports that the sex wasn't forced. It was with a man. For whom she has feelings of love. Yet, she has clouded her memories of their lovemaking with a screen memory of traumatic abduction."

"What are you saying?" Steven didn't care who heard him now.

"Daddy, please," Wendy said.

"That Wendy might be caught in a unique chain of circumstances. Some of her memories seem legitimate. Perhaps she was a witness to her mother's real abduction at some point in her childhood. But her other memories, of her own abduction, her own sexual experiences, are simply an attempt by her mind to cover up a more terrible event."

"What?" Steven pushed his chair back from the table. He heard the hurried clatter of feet approaching on the tiled floor. Someone gasped.

"Incest, Steven!" Starr said angrily, rising from his own chair. "Your daughter loves you and you have abused her and the conflict has resulted in her—"

The table flew out of the way as Steven lunged at the man. All thought had stopped. He only wanted to stop the lies in the most direct way he knew how.

"Daddy!" Wendy screamed, scrambling out of her chair.

The thrashing forms of Steven and Starr were rescued only by the strong grips of the waiter and the maître d', who each grabbed arms and shoulders before the altercation could upset another table.

Steven felt his head throbbing with pain as he was led past the small crowded lounge and bar to the entrance. Starr struggled with the waiter who escorted him. Wendy walked beside, head hanging so low she seemed to be melting.

The maître d' inquired who was going to pay for the meal, and Steven pulled out his wallet and with trembling hands passed over three hundreds.

Starr pulled away from the waiter, tugged down on his jacket. "I shall be on my way then," he announced. "Good evening, Mr. Gilmour. Young lady."

"Just a minute!" Steven called after him. He pulled away from the maître d'.

"A moment, sir. Your change," the maître d' said.

"Forget it." Steven pulled away from the man. He grabbed his daughter's arm and said, "Let's go."

Steven and Wendy rushed out to the front lot. Two Excaliburs were parked beside a white Rolls. A handful of BMWs and Porsches filled the rest of the display parking spaces. A parking valet approached Steven, asking if he wanted his car. Steven ignored him, scanning the immediate area. He saw Starr walking down the side street beside the restaurant, away from the lights of Melrose.

"Come on," he said again, pulling Wendy after him. "He's not going to get away with that."

"No, please don't, Daddy," Wendy said. Her voice was broken by sobs. "He's wrong. I know he's wrong. Let him go."

They stormed from the parking lot. Steven called out Starr's name. Ten yards down the street, Starr walked on without looking back. A set of car keys jangled in his hand.

Steven began to run, not letting go of his daughter. A black van sped by, and the girl faltered, startled by the sweep of its headlights, the roar of its engine. Steven slowed for an instant, caught between keeping his grip on Wendy and keeping up with Starr.

The van squealed to a stop beside Starr. The writer paused to look at it.

"Let's go!" Steven shouted at Wendy. He half dragged her as he shot down the street, the hard soles of his shoes slipping on the sidewalk pavement, clattering in the night silence away from the traffic.

The back door of the van slid open with a metallic clang. Something moved inside. Steven was ten feet away.

A short dark figure emerged, holding something in its hand, pointing it at Starr. Steven heard the writer protest. He heard something click.

The dark figure swung around at Steven and Wendy's approach.

"He's got a gun!" Starr warned.

The figure looked back and forth between Starr and Steven. Steven heard a call from behind him, up the street. He turned and saw two valets and the maître d' from Trump's peering down the side street.

The driver's door of the van slammed open. A deep voice called out harshly. "Don't leave witnesses. Take 'em all. Let's go!"

"In the van!" the figure barked, waving the gun. "Now! Now! Now!"

Wendy jumped at the van, stumbled, fell in. Steven felt the gun barrel dig into his back as the figure pushed him and Starr in on top of Wendy. He heard the clattering of running feet coming closer. Shouts growing in volume.

The dark figure jumped in behind them. "Go!" it shouted. "Go! Go! Go!"

The van lurched forward, wheels spinning. Steven smelled the tires burning. Heard his daughter sobbing. Saw the maître d' ten feet from the van as the figure moved its arm and the door swung shut again, cutting off all light.

So this is what it's like, Steven thought. And swallowed by the night, the black van took them all away.

8

THURSDAY, JULY 19, 23:30 PDT

A flurry of green numbers sprayed across one of the computer screens in front of Gardiner, but he dismissed the display as meaningless. Instead, he tapped his fingers against the arm of his chair and checked his watch again, squinting to read its fine numbers in the control room's dim light. He was not impatient because Roy Luck and Tucker Browne were keeping him from bureau work but because Maria was waiting for him at her apartment. Gardiner knew that no matter how things turned out in the Reese investigation, Luck's report would label him "tainted" and he would never work for the bureau again. The knowledge that that part of his life was over made Gardiner's decisions for the future much easier to make. By confining him, controlling him, and taking him away from his position as Special Agent in Charge, Luck and Browne had made Gardiner into the most dangerous of adversaries, the one all professionals knew enough to fear—a man with nothing to lose.

Gardiner crossed his legs again, more to take up time than to find a comfortable position, absently pulling on his gray trousers to prevent creasing. He found the video control room too dark for this time of night, too quiet. Its light came from a bank of twelve video monitors mounted in the wall before him and ten computer displays and three small desk lamps on the console in front of the monitors where the young and intense picture technician adjusted innumerable knobs and switches like a shaman arranging his bones and beads.

"Getting restless, Ed?" Luck asked. Gardiner could see that the OCI agent, sitting beside him, hoped it was so.

"Not much longer," Browne said. The bald paraplegic had sat in his chair behind Luck and Gardiner, unmoving for almost the full hour they had waited for the data to be downloaded from the OCI's computers in D.C. A little Buddha, Gardiner thought of Browne, with Luck as his temple dog.

Three computer screens suddenly cleared at the same time. A line of type scrolled across the top of each one, flashing.

"Here it comes," the technician said.

Eight of the twelve video monitors suddenly switched from a dull gray display to a blue field with yellow letters and numbers. The technician rolled back and forth between keyboards on his wheeled chair. "Okay, we've got it," he finally announced. "You want the raw data or the significant frames first?" He lifted his head as he spoke, but did not turn around, making his words an incantation to unseen gods.

"Significant frames, I believe," Browne said. "To give us an overview."

"Sorting," the technician responded, fingers dancing across one of three keyboards on the console. "Main screen."

The central monitor had a three-foot screen with a picture as sharp and as steady as a projected slide. The image of a resolute eagle clutching an ancient key, a thunderbolt, and a parchment scroll in its talons appeared: the seal of the OCI. Six other, smaller screens on the wall echoed the image.

"Begin?" the technician asked.

"If you please," Browne answered.

The eagle was replaced with a black-and-white image of a young woman holding a piece of cardboard banded with a graduated series of gray bars.

"That's the woman from the hospital," Gardiner said, surprised to see her. That image hadn't been among the photographs they had found in the studio at the Fisher's house.

"The reporter's constant companion," Luck sneered. "Though we still haven't detected any inquiries about her status. Guess it wasn't true love."

"Or she's listening to Derek Reese when he tells her not to

make those inquiries." Gardiner turned to look at Luck. "How much longer can you keep her in custody?"

"As long as it takes," Luck said. "She's not under arrest, so she has no precious rights to infringe."

"You're holding her without cause," Gardiner said. "That's a breach of the Sixth Amendment."

"We're holding her in the hospital for important care which she is not mentally competent to request voluntarily." Luck smiled. "And we have the doctors' signatures to prove it."

Browne held his hand over his mouth and gently cleared his throat. "Gentlemen?"

Gardiner turned back to the screen. "Why is this considered a significant frame?" he asked.

"The girl's holding a photographer's gray scale," the technician explained. His hand lightly moved across a control surface near a keyboard, and on the screen, a large white crosshair pattern moved in response. "It's a calibration technique. We know what the reflectance characteristics of each of those bands is, so we can adjust for variations in the development of the film to establish a precise relationship between the actual shade of an object and the way the film responded to it. Whoever the photographer was, he was professional about his work."

" 'She,' " Gardiner said. "The photographer was a woman."

"Whatever." The technician typed something on his central keyboard. "Here's the next one."

The screen shifted. Gardiner recognized the next black-and-white image as showing the back of the Malibu beach house at night. He saw the moon in the upper right corner; the kitchen window ablaze with light, silhouetting someone inside; a dark shape behind the house, on the beach.

"That's about as clear as the photograph we saw," Gardiner said. "I thought these were supposed to be enhanced."

"The data are being calculated for this display system," the technician muttered. "Just a minute."

The white crosshairs danced over the screen, the technician's keyboards clacked noisily, and section by section, shape by shape, the image became clearer. After three minutes, it might have been a shot taken on a bright, foggy day.

"What is it?" Gardiner asked. The object behind the beach house was obviously a craft of some kind. Its ventral outline was almost as smooth and as clean as the upper half of an aircraft wing, though its dorsal surface appeared to be completely flat, meaning that its overall shape would generate virtually no lift. "Some kind of helicopter?" It was the only thing he could think of.

"Apparently not," Browne answered. He seemed almost amused. "There appear to be no rotors."

"Could be an aerodyne," Luck suggested. "Internal turbines blasting air over skin-mounted control surfaces. A fourth generation Bell, maybe, or just an extremely thin composite rotor pointed directly at the camera."

"They sent a wireframe breakdown," the technician announced. "They combined different angles of it and created a three-dimensional model. You want it?"

"Yes, please," Browne said.

A pattern of thin green lines grew over the craft's shape on the screen. In ten seconds, every contour had been traced, and the line pattern they formed suddenly appeared on the four blank monitors on the wall. A series of other similar patterns, much larger, appeared one after the other, shrinking down to the size of the green line image and then disappearing. When all the screen activity had stopped, the technician asked if they would like it rotated. Browne politely answered, "Yes."

The three-dimensional reconstruction of the craft revolved from its original, side-on profile to a three-quarter view from the bottom, returned to its profile position, and shifted to the left to present the rear section. Then the image went through variations of combined rotations.

"Want some detail?" the technician asked after eight pattern repetitions.

"Please just give us everything they sent on this," Browne replied. His courtesy was becoming exhausted.

The wireframe drawing replaced the photograph in the large central monitor. Slabs of solid gray appeared on it, like armor plate being bolted to a tank frame. The craft suddenly became solid. Then the straight edges between the plates dissolved as the image became more detailed. A small arrow appeared in the upper right-hand corner of the screen and the craft immediately became shadowed as if the sun were shining from that direction. Gardiner saw that it was not a smoothly rounded design as he had first thought. An irregularly contoured section jutted out from its right front side.

Then a series of circular indentations appeared on the craft's side, in three regular patterns of eight. "Windows?" Gardiner asked.

"Or intake openings for an internal rotor?" Luck said.

The technician pushed himself over to another part of his console and read something on a computer display there. "The data says those are slight depressions in the side, not openings."

A larger indentation, a round-cornered rectangle, appeared low on the side of the craft. It flickered on and off.

"And that must be a door," the technician explained. "In some shots it's open; in others it's closed."

"Tell me," Browne asked, "can you rotate it all the way around?"

"Don't have any shots from the top or far side," the technician answered.

"Yes, yes. I understand that. But can't the computer fill in? I've seen images of airplanes done this way. Even if the fuselage is imaged from only one side, the computer can deduce the complete shape."

The technician pushed back to the central keyboard and typed again. "Sorry," he said after reading the computer's response. "The craft does not exhibit symmetry. The computer can't extrapolate."

"Like trying to guess what the far side of a rock looks like after seeing only the near side," Gardiner said. He turned to face Browne. "So, is this thing the answer you expected, Tucker?" Gardiner hoped the man was as confused as himself.

"Most of it," Browne said unexpectedly. "Strikingly close to what we expected for our worst-case scenario. Especially given the results of North's and Vincent's drug tests and the destruction of Vincent's gun."

"You're joking," Gardiner said.

Browne smiled sweetly. "Often," he said. "But, unfortunately, not this time."

"Time to call the White House?" Luck asked, obviously far more aware of what the photographs signified than was Gardiner.

"I think not," Browne answered, tapping one pudgy forefinger against his upper lip.

"Tucker," Luck argued, "if these photos confirm our scenario, we don't have much time for second-guessing."

"I'm not thinking of second-guessing, Roy. I'm thinking of a more detailed analysis." Browne tapped the keypad on his chair and the device immediately moved its treads in opposite directions, turning him smoothly on the spot. "It pains me to say this, but I believe it is time to pass these photos on to our friends at the NRO." Browne guided his chair to the four stairs leading up to the control room door. The treads slowly climbed up as the chair seat whirred and angled forward, keeping Browne vertical at all times.

Gardiner sat still, staring at the computer simulation of the craft and felt what he could only call shock. The National Reconnaissance Office was the ultimate "black" agency in D.C. It appeared on no budget sheets, it had never been acknowledged to exist, and even its name was still considered classified almost thirty years after it had been formed. And Tucker Browne was giving up his autonomy to it, just as Gardiner had decided to relinquish the Reese investigation when he had seen what had happened to Vincent's gun. Gardiner didn't know what surprised him more: that Browne was admitting he needed help or that Browne, too, might operate according to some sense of duty, a loyalty to his country that transcended his loyalty to himself.

"Excuse me," the technician said. "There are twelve more photographs in the significant file to be displayed."

"I'm sure there are," Browne said over his shoulder, sitting calmly as his chair crested the staircase and assumed its normal configuration. "And better eyes than ours will no doubt study them in far greater detail." He coughed, and Luck rose to his feet. "We've been wrong about this type of thing before," the fat man said serenely. "It would not be advantageous to be seen to be calling wolf again. Come along, Roy, Ed."

Gardiner got to his feet, glancing one more time at the strange craft moving slowly through its range of rotations.

Wrong about this *before?* he wondered, eyes searching the screens for an explanation. But, like the numbers flashing across the computer displays, the only answers he could see were meaningless.

THURSDAY, JULY 19, 23:55 PDT

After bumping jarringly against the ribbed metal floor and the unpadded wall braces for ten minutes of fast turns and sudden braking, the van finally settled into an even motion, and Wendy assumed they were now on a freeway.

They tried to protest, Starr especially, as the van took off, but the figure with the gun shouted at them from the darkness to shut up. When the driver slowed after an initial burst of wild speeding, the figure slid open a small partition at the front of the van and Wendy saw streetlamps flashing by through the driver's windshield. Unfortunately, before she was able to recognize any street signs or buildings or billboards, the figure blocked most of the partition by leaning forward and holding a whispered conversation with the driver.

But at least she saw streetlamps, Wendy thought, and not stars. At least they really were in a van, and not in . . . something else. If she had been alone, she knew she would be crying at this point, probably hysterically. But her father was with her, and she held his hand in the darkness. Part of her strength right now, her emotional control, came from her need to please him —Wendy knew he wouldn't want her to be hysterical—but part also came from the protection he offered. Her father would never let anything bad happen to her. That knowledge sustained her.

"People are going to miss me," Starr suddenly said, his voice a trembling mixture of anger and fear. No trace of the wine.

Their abductor smashed something heavy against the floor of the van with a deafening clang. Wendy jumped in alarm.

"Shut up!" the harsh voice growled.

Starr said nothing more. The van droned on. Wendy stared into the darkness and thought about her father's love. And the other love. The different love that she felt when she remembered her times away. Away from what, Wendy wasn't sure. But at some point between the shock of being taken away and the relief of being returned, there was a period of warmth and love and fulfillment. Wendy had barely been able to talk about those times in Margot's office; they had seemed so dreamlike. And she had felt ashamed when Starr had mentioned them in front of her father. But however hazy her memories remained, the feelings that sprang from them were real, both the passion that filled her heart and the purely physical sensations that made her body a miraculous new channel of pleasure. Just as her father gave her the courage to face whatever it was that was happening now, it was those feelings that let her face John-John and the others like him when they came for her. She found it odd that in both situations, only the threat of terror and loss made her truly appreciate the love that she held within her.

The van slowed. It followed a gentle curve, angled as if going uphill, turned sharply but without speed, then stopped. The motor cut out. Wendy listened carefully but could hear no other sounds of traffic. The words "secluded spot" came to mind, and she fought to keep herself calm. On the news, too many terrible things happened in secluded spots.

The partition slid open again, and this time Wendy couldn't see anything through the van's windshield except a fluorescent light fixture hanging from a low concrete ceiling. She immediately knew they were in a parking garage. At least, with the partition open we can see what's going on. Which wasn't much, she thought.

Beside her, arm protectively around her, Wendy's father wore the set, expressionless look he got when he was furious and refused to show it. Wendy had learned to be wary of that expression and was glad it was directed toward the people who had kidnapped them. Starr huddled by himself in the opposite back corner of the van, arms wrapped around his knees. He reminded her of Maxine's dog cowering under a table during a thunderstorm. Trapped without understanding. Wendy was surprised when she discovered she was happy to see the writer in that condition. He deserves it, she thought, for the ugly things he had said to her father.

She was surprised even more when the person who had forced them into the van spoke for the first time with a normal voice. She was a woman.

"Believe it or not," the woman in the black ski mask said to Wendy and Steven, "but the first thing we want to do is apologize. We just couldn't risk leaving you two behind to tell those people from the restaurant what we did."

"Does that mean we can go?" Steven asked. Wendy shivered when she heard her father speak. She knew the rage he was hiding when he spoke in such a cold and rational way.

"Soon," the woman said. "And provided you don't try to leave before we say you can, nothing bad will happen." She gestured to Starr. "Do you know this man?" she asked Steven.

Steven stared at the woman without speaking. She shrugged, then looked at Starr. "How about it, Mr. Starr? These people friends of yours?"

Starr shivered when he heard the woman address him by

name. "W-what do you want?" Wendy smiled tightly when she heard the fear in his voice.

The woman, however, seemed exasperated. "What we don't want is to cause trouble," she said. "Now, who are your friends here?"

"They aren't friends of mine," Starr said. "Take them. Let me go."

"Unfortunately, Mr. Starr, you're the one we want to talk with." Starr moaned. "Just talk," she repeated impatiently. "Calm down."

"We'll all calm down if you put the gun away," Steven said.

"You had your chance to talk before, asshole." The woman pointed the gun at Steven and Wendy's side of the van. "The sooner we finish with Mr. Starr here, the sooner we all go home. So shut up." Wendy felt the slightest of tremors in her father's hand.

"What do you want with me?" Starr whined. "I don't have any money. My book just came out. I'm already—"

"Shut up!" the woman commanded. "I'm going to ask a few questions, and you're going to answer them and that's all. Then you can go. Understand?"

"Questions about w-what?"

The woman shook her head. "A couple of things Johnny Carson didn't get to last night, all right?" Starr's face screwed up in total confusion. The woman continued. "So from your books, we know you've been investigating UFOs for at least fifteen years. Is that right?"

Starr shook his head slowly, mouth open, eyes glazed with shock.

"So how long have you been investigating UFO abductions full time?"

"Seven or eight . . . ," Starr said cautiously. "Who are you people? Why don't you take off your mask?"

"Aw, think it through, Mr. Starr. If I take off my mask then you could give my description to the police."

Wendy felt a sudden realization of relief. The woman meant to let them go. Then she had a sudden sensation of fear. *If* she was a woman.

"Okay," the woman began again, "UFO abductions, Mr. Starr. We need some information. First of all, have you ever been aware of any government interest in your investigations or in UFO abduction cases in general?"

"W-well," the writer stammered, "well, yes. And no. Um, there's always been government interest in UFOs, beginning back with the Air Force investigations started after World War II, but—"

"Modern-day, Mr. Starr. What's the government's involvement now? Today?"

Starr took a deep breath, and when he began to speak again, he was calmer, more in control. "Officially, the government maintains that UFOs don't exist. In the sense that they are technological devices or otherwise a manifestation of nonhuman intelligence."

"And unofficially? I mean, have you ever been approached by a classified government agency that appears to have taken an interest in your work?"

"Unofficially?" Starr repeated to himself, obviously considering the question carefully. Wendy thought he had recovered well from his initial fright. It was almost like watching him on the "Tonight Show" again.

"This is going to depend on what you might mean by unofficial," Starr said. "If you ask me have I ever been approached by a government employee who has identified himself to me as such, I would have to say no. But I do believe that some of the inquiries I have received might have come from government sources."

"What was the nature of those inquiries?" the woman asked quickly. Wendy got the impression that she was someone who was used to asking a lot of questions.

"I was on a lecture tour last year and in Germany, Frankfurt as I recall, I had many American soldiers in the audience. Well, I always send audiences off with a few questions to consider—things like, what's your most remarkable dream or what's the strangest experience you ever had—questions that can sometimes trigger a memory of a missing-time incident or a UFO sighting. Anyway, as always, a group of people, mostly soldiers, stayed around after the lecture to talk informally, and I could tell that there were a number of them who were reacting in a way consistent with people who are just beginning to suspect that they might have had a suppressed abduction experience."

"What way is that?" the woman asked. "Reacting in what way?"

"There's a particular nervousness I've come to see," Starr explained, as though he were back at dinner with someone who wasn't wearing a ski mask and carrying a gun. "It's not absolutely reliable, but I've come to develop a feel for it. For people who are not involved, have never been involved, UFO abductions elicit an intellectual response. Either one of fascination or one of indifferent dismissal. But some people have an immediate emotional response. Either of uneasiness or, oddly enough, of pronounced disagreement. People who can't read more than a few pages of one of my books because they find the stories in them vaguely upsetting in some way or people who vehemently deny that such things could ever happen, without trying to construct a rational argument. Well, these are people who often have something buried in their pasts. And there were a few soldiers there, in the Frankfurt audience, who were acting in that way."

"So what did you do?" The woman glanced over at Steven and Wendy. "Hope we're not boring you." Her gun was still pointed in their direction.

"Same as I always do. I gave out my business address. Asked them to write me with the answers to the questions I had asked."

"And?"

"I received nothing from that group."

"Is that unusual?"

"Very much so. I always get a written response to my lectures. Fifty letters to a couple of hundred, but there's always something, especially from the people who stay around afterward to talk."

"Do you have an explanation?"

"I think they were told not to write to me by a commanding officer. Or else, when they did write, the letters were intercepted."

"Why would that have happened, do you think?" The woman used her free hand to scratch her cheek through the mouth hole of her mask. Wendy felt her father tense, and she hoped he wouldn't try anything. There was still the driver in the front of the van to worry about.

"Two reasons that I can think of. The first being that people who claim to have been abducted are subjected to ridicule and the Army wouldn't want its soldiers open to those charges. The second being that the Army has its own investigation going and wanted the letters for itself."

"Do you think that's likely?" The woman adjusted her position on the floor. Steven moved as she did. The woman didn't notice. Wendy pushed down on her father's hand to try to tell him to stay put, but very slowly, he drew his hand away. No, Wendy thought. But didn't know what to do.

"Very likely," Starr said. "Do you mind?" he asked, then adjusted his own position to a half crouch. Steven shifted again. "Anyway, shortly after I returned home, I received a letter from a professor at Stanford who was specifically interested in examining abduction stories related by members of the armed services. I connected that inquiry with the lack of response from Frankfurt and concluded that I had somehow inspired a military investigation. I mean, I think it probable that the military would want to conduct their own investigation, if only for the purpose of gathering psychological information about their soldiers. If anyone in the military takes the idea seriously, then there would also be information to be gathered concerning how the aliens avoid setting off alarm systems, how they get into locked buildings, how their ships are invisible to radar. I'm sure the Army would be interested in knowing about the technology that could land a counterterrorist group inside a besieged embassy without risking hostages' lives. It's probably foolish to think that they wouldn't be investigating in some way, considering the other claptrap they throw our money away on."

"But have you ever detected any direct evidence of a military investigation into abductions?"

"Circumstantial only. Statistically, I receive far fewer letters from members of the military than I would expect, indicating that their reports are somehow being siphoned off to a separate investigation, especially given that I have interviewed abductees from virtually every area of endeavor." He narrowed his eyes at her. "Except, perhaps, kidnappers."

The woman laughed. Wendy felt her father start to move forward, tensing, ready to strike.

"It's happened to me!" Wendy said suddenly. It was the only way she could think to stop her father.

The woman instantly turned to Wendy. Steven slipped back against the wall after having traveled no more than four inches.

"So that's why you were with him," the woman said. "When were you taken? How often?"

Wendy avoided looking at her father. She knew what she would see. "Lots of times," she said. "Last week was the latest. My mother was taken on—ohh!"

A dark face had appeared in the partition, and Wendy was startled into silence. The driver, she told herself, it's only the driver. She felt the hidden eyes beneath the featureless ski mask burning into her. It was more than the driver. But what?

The face disappeared. Wendy heard the driver's door open, felt the van rock as the driver stepped out. The woman was peering through the partition, turning her head back and forth between the back of the van and the driver's compartment.

The van's back door clanged. Wendy gasped again. The door burst open as if it had been ripped from its hinges. The driver was there, in black, but now unmasked.

Wendy saw his face.

Wendy recognized his face.

"Derek," she said, a moan, a gasp, a tearing out of her heart and soul. She pulled away from her father, pushed herself off the floor of the van, went to him, floating, running, rushing, to feel her arms wrap around him, press her face against his broad chest, feel his arms crush her to him, arms that had held her so many times in the past.

Far away, Wendy heard her father cry out her name. She didn't care. She was almost oblivious to Starr as he clawed past her, out of the van. But she didn't care. She heard the thud as the woman struggled to chase after Starr, heard his footsteps on the concrete as he rushed away, heard her father as he fought the woman, took her weapon. Heard the clicking of an empty, unthreatening gun.

But Wendy didn't care.

She kissed Derek. Deeply, completely, with more passion than even her memories had told her was possible. Her tongue moved over his, drinking him in, swallowing the taste and the scent and the heat of him. She heard the rushing thunder of her heart as it raced within her, making her body resonate with the frantic need to feel him pressed against her, slipping into her, filling her with love and life and hope.

Every other part of her existence fell away from her as sound and light and all awareness collapsed into a narrow tunnel of sensation focused only on the man in her arms, the man who held her, her friend, her lover, her mate in all ways. Just as it had happened so many times in the past. And would again, so many times in the future.

When they came to take them away for good.

9

FRIDAY, JULY 20, 13:45 PDT

"They tell me that Reese and the reporter came to see you on Wednesday night," Ed Gardiner said calmly, trying his best to sound friendly.

Across his desk from him, sitting with shoulders rounded in defeat and one staring, haunted eye, Cy North nodded but said nothing.

Gardiner turned to look at Roy Luck. The OCI agent leaned against the partition wall of Gardiner's office, arms crossed, face contorted in a smile. Gloating, Gardiner knew, because he had answered none of Gardiner's questions after Gardiner had read the preliminary report now sitting on his desk.

"Did he give you any indication when he would be back?" Gardiner asked, looking back at North. Cy was the only way left to reach Reese, and Reese had to be reached soon.

"No," North said weakly. He rubbed at his eye patch and kept glancing at the window over Gardiner's shoulder. The agents who had brought North in this afternoon had first taken him to the infirmary in the basement to have the dressings changed on the bullet wounds in his right leg, switch the eye bandage for a patch, and replace the filthy sling with a crisp new one. The agents had even had North shaved. But the man's clothes were grimy, and his good eye reminded Gardiner of a hunted animal.

"What did you talk about with Reese, Cy?"

"Television," North answered.

Gardiner sighed. "This isn't going to work, Roy."

"I watched you read that," Luck said with a shrug. He pointed to the report on Gardiner's desk, bound in a bright red cover, marked MOST SECRET and carrying three paragraphs of fine print describing fines of not less than twenty-five thousand dollars and imprisonment of not less than fifteen years for unauthorized possession of the document contained within. "It has to work, doesn't it, Cy?"

North stared out the window.

"Cy!" Gardiner said sharply, bringing the man's attention back to the room. "Listen carefully because this is extremely important. Do you understand?"

"Do . . . you want me to do something for you?" North asked.

"Yes, Cy. The bureau needs you. Your country needs you."

"Will you do . . . something for me?" All of a sudden, North's eye did not appear as unfocused. Gardiner was intrigued. It appeared there was still something left in the man that could think.

"Try me. What would you like us to do?"

"Protect me," North said. "Keep me safe."

"From what, Cy?" Luck asked, stepping away from the wall, making the glass rattle as he did so.

"From the light."

Gardiner glanced up at the window. "Do you want me to close the blinds?"

"No, no," North said, almost angry. "The daytime's okay. But at night, I can't . . . think. I . . . you have to protect me from the light."

Gardiner and Luck exchanged a glance. "How can we do that?" Luck asked.

"Keep me someplace safe," North answered. "With guards."

Luck smiled at Gardiner. He never intended to let North out of his sight in any case. "We can do that, Cy. No problem at all. Where would you like to be kept? A nice hotel someplace?"

North looked panic-stricken. "No! Not a hotel. A prison." His eye widened. "Holding! Keep me in holding downstairs. No windows."

"Anything you want," Luck said, patted the man on his good shoulder, then went back and leaned against the wall, grinning like a death's head.

"Anything else?" Gardiner asked.

"A television set," North said, nodding. "A big one."

"It's yours. Is that all?"

"If it works," North said, "that's all."

"All right, then," Gardiner began, "this is what we'd like you to do for us."

"Go ahead," North said and for the first time, he appeared capable of sustained conversation. Gardiner was surprised the promise of protection from the light had somehow taken an edge off North's sense of panic, because the report said North's reaction was a side effect of the drug he had been exposed to at the beach house. A psychotic drug reaction shouldn't be lessened by a promise to offer protection, Gardiner knew. It was almost as if North wasn't under the influence of drugs but was actually concerned about a physical threat. Gardiner decided he would have to ask for Maria's advice—if he could ever lose his OCI escort and make his way to her apartment.

Gardiner folded his hands precisely and spoke. "Recently the OCI was involved in an operation to uncover an espionage ring believed to be operating out of New York and Los Angeles."

"The group that Reese was investigating?" North asked.

A remarkable recovery, Gardiner thought, then replied, "Not exactly. When counterespionage detected signs that an organization might be shipping restricted computer components to the Eastern bloc, Reese was assigned to the investigation. However, the organization he targeted was the same group that the OCI was investigating at the European end." He paused as North nodded in acknowledgment.

"So, the OCI set up a false shipment of restricted computer parts," North concluded, "and that was the transaction that Reese was set to bust. Good thing he didn't."

"Two ways to look at that one, Cy," Luck said. "If Reese had done his duty and intercepted the plane transfer in the desert, the OCI operation would have been exposed. However, Reese *didn't* do his duty, and there has to be a reason. He was working for someone else. Someone who wanted the transfer to go through."

North turned in his chair to look at the OCI agent. "Do you know who was paying him?" Gardiner couldn't get over the transformation in the man. How could this be the result of drugs?

Luck came back to Gardiner's desk and picked up the MOST SECRET report. "We do now," he said. "The reporter you and Vincent set up at the beach house took a series of photos showing how Reese got away. You saw them the night there was . . . a mix-up at the reporter's house."

"So you don't think David and I were paid off along with Reese?"

"We know you weren't," Luck said. "You were drugged that night."

"But the tests showed we were clean."

Luck smiled evilly. "We had a second set printed with a standard no-response just so you wouldn't think we were on to you. That is, if you had been involved with Reese."

"And you say that report clears us? Completely? Because of photographs?"

Luck tapped the report against his open hand. "The reporter was a good photographer. The OCI enhanced the negatives, and then the NRO had a go at them."

"The NRO?"

"They're the ones that take pictures of Soviet army uniform insignia from one hundred and eighty miles up," Luck said, holding out the report to North. "You can count the stitches on their division badges."

"So what do the photos show?" North asked, hefting the report in his hand. Gardiner thought he detected a note of reluctance in North. Either he didn't want to be cleared or didn't want to read the report.

"Let's just say it wasn't anything the NRO hasn't seen before," Luck replied. "Go ahead, read it. See for yourself. Then you'll understand why it's so important that you help us track Reese down." Luck patted North's shoulder again. "The man is a threat, Cy. To the entire country. He's got to be stopped." Gardiner was amazed that North did not respond to Luck's obvious insincerity.

North placed the report on his lap and opened the cover. He looked up suddenly, glanced at the window, turned back to Luck. "And you will protect me?" he asked.

"From the light?" Luck said kindly. "Of course, of course. Bodyguards, no windows, a big television. Anything you need."

North smiled and turned back to the report as Luck returned

to lean against the wall. Gardiner sat behind his desk, using all his military discipline to appear patient as he watched the scene in his office and realized that he was at the mercy of a madman and an imbecile.

But then, he thought, when has that ever been different?

FRIDAY, JULY 20, 15:20 PDT

Steven Gilmour closed his eyes and concentrated on the feel of the smooth, cool glass as it pressed against his fingers. He took a long, deep breath and slowly exhaled, feeling the tremors leave his hand and arm. Control, he told himself, focus and control. He brought the glass to his lips, listened to the sound of ice hitting glass, took in the complex scent of the Scotch beneath his nose, and swallowed half the drink in one long draw.

The liquor scorched through him. With the warmth, he told himself, comes calm. I will be calm. He sighed. He opened his eyes. He saw Derek Reese and he wanted to kill.

"More?" Fisher asked, holding the yellow-labeled Cutty Sark bottle by his glass.

Steven nodded and Fisher poured. She had an odd look in her eyes, Steven saw, almost of sympathy. He took another swallow of the Scotch, then looked away, his heart hammering savagely within him.

Reese had called the place they were in a safe house. Steven wanted to know what was so safe about it. It looked just like any other low-rent bungalow, the kind his parents had lived in in New Jersey and the kind he had sworn he would never live in again. It made Steven's bottom line easy to quantify: he didn't like being here—wherever "here" was, since Reese thought it best if they didn't know the location of the house— and he most certainly didn't like Wendy being here with Reese. He sipped the Scotch again and tried not to think of murder.

Steven heard the toilet flush down the hallway leading to the bedrooms, and a few moments later Wendy returned to the living room, face glowing from a brisk scrub, hair tied back, and a new light in her eyes, a light that Steven felt did not belong in the eyes of a child.

Wendy smiled at her father as she entered the room, but

smiled even more when she looked over and saw Reese sitting on the too-small tan sofa, hunched over the shiny green lacquered coffee table, flipping through one of the newspapers Fisher had returned with from her shopping expedition. Wendy went to Reese, sat down beside him, entwined one slender arm around his thickly muscled one, and leaned against him. Steven felt rage overtake him. He couldn't help himself.

"Wendy," he said sternly, as if she were six years old again and pulling a kitten's tail, "sit over on the chair." He pointed to a small beige-and-tan-striped armchair in the corner.

Wendy looked at her father with challenge in her eyes. She frowned, preparing to protest. But Reese turned to her, laid his solid hand on her arm, and said, "That's probably a good idea." There was no challenge in her eyes for Reese, Steven saw. Wendy stood up, defiantly bent over to kiss the top of Reese's head, then walked over to the armchair and threw herself in it, drawing her legs up to her chest and wrapping her arms tightly around them.

Reese looked at Steven apologetically. "We're going to have to talk about this," he said.

Before Steven could reply, Fisher interrupted. "But not right now. I think we all need some time to decompress. The stuff we were talking about in the van is pretty hairy, and we all have to be able to come to grips with it before we go on."

"What's to come to grips with?" Steven asked bitterly. "It's in the *National Enquirer* all the time. Space aliens have been taking my little girl to their spaceship so she can . . ." He couldn't bring himself to say it. He had seen the way Wendy had kissed Reese. That had been no sixteen-year-old-girl kiss, the kind kids learned in the back row of a movie theater or at a party with the lights turned down low. That had been a lover's kiss. The way Steven remembered kissing Sarah. It had only taken him an instant to realize what that meant. Reese and his daughter— Steven had felt ill in the back of the van, before he had managed to break them apart. The feeling still hadn't left him.

"Daddy, don't, all right?" Wendy said. She tilted her head forward until it rested on her knees. "I think Merril's right. We need time."

"For what?" Steven asked. He gulped at his drink again. He could feel the alcohol getting to him. He wanted it to get to him. So nothing else could. There were some things he knew he wasn't supposed to think about.

"To understand what it is we're up against," Fisher said. "There's a pattern here. Some purpose. Derek has been abducted by the same creatures that have taken your daughter and her mother. Both Derek and Wendy disappeared last Sunday night for almost twenty-four hours. They remember being together then. They remember being together dozens of times before then too. I know it must be painful for you to learn something like that, Steven, but we can't deny that it has happened."

"It can't have happened," Steven said. He felt himself choke. He wanted to cry but wouldn't let himself.

"It happened, Daddy," Wendy said. "I know it happened." She turned to Reese. Steven felt his heart twist when he saw the look that came to her eyes, the expression of love, the hunger of wanting that man. "*We* know it happened."

"It's sure as hell not going to happen again," Steven said suddenly. Reese was at least six inches taller and solid muscle, but Steven was fortified by Cutty Sark. He wanted to tear the heart out of the man who had raped his daughter because that was the only way he could think of it—in the vilest, foulest, most violent way possible.

"I think that's why we need time," Fisher said. "Here, take one of these, why don't you? It's an asthma inhaler." She handed him one. "I think you should keep it with you at all times."

"I don't have asthma," Steven said, wondering how it would feel to throw the canister at Reese. "And neither does Wendy."

"Doesn't matter," the reporter said. "It might come in handy the next time the creatures come."

"How?" Steven asked.

Fisher looked over at Reese, who studied the canister carefully. "Should I tell them the rest of it?" she asked him.

"Why not," Reese said. "It's not as if we have anything to lose."

And Fisher told them the story of the night at the beach house.

"And you think the medication in the asthma inhaler somehow blocks the effects of whatever drug the creatures saturate an area with before they appear?" Steven asked when the story was over.

"It fits the facts," the reporter said. "Especially when you add in details from the books of Charles Edward Starr." She patted a stack of those books on the table beside her. His latest one was on top. "A common account is that just before the creatures arrive, victims feel uneasy, smell strange odors, sense that something is wrong. That's consistent with the beginning effects of being exposed to an aerosol drug. A drug that will rob people of their short-term memories, as well as make them unable to resist the creatures as they get poked and prodded."

"And remember when Mr. Starr was on the 'Tonight Show,' " Wendy added, "and he said that a lot of people report seeing a mist or a fog around the ships? Or appearing just before the creatures do? Could that be the drug? Like being sprayed into the air?"

"Possible," Fisher agreed.

"But some people don't just feel uneasy," Reese said. "Some people just feel . . . mindless terror. Panic."

"Different people have different reactions to the same drugs all the time," Fisher said. "But even when you lump the different emotional experiences reported by abductees together, they're all internally consistent with the more developed parts of the human brain being repressed so the abductees are unable to take action against the creatures."

"What more developed parts?" Wendy asked.

"The outer parts of the brain," Fisher explained. "The sections of the brain responsible for higher reasoning, logic, self-motivation. Those structures are unique to humans. Well, at least to the higher primates and cetaceans. Beneath those layers are the more ancient brain structures, the ones that evolved early on, like the limbic system, the rhinencephalon, the parts that relate directly to emotional response and the sense of smell."

"Why smell?"

Fisher shrugged. "I guess because it was one of the earliest senses ever developed by living creatures—a form of chemical awareness of the immediate environment. It's logical that the first sense had to do with distinguishing between things that were good to eat and things that were bad to eat. Past that, the sense became more refined, more capable of multiple distinctions between classes of substances. But it's right at the heart of our brain, so to speak. Take away all the higher functions and we're left with gibbering monkey brains from the dawn of time." Fisher laughed at the image. "Naked, raw emotion—mindless terror. It all fits."

"But," Steven complained, "Starr also said that there's evidence that the control the creatures exert might be telepathic. Mind-to-mind communication."

"If that were the case," Fisher answered, "then why wasn't David knocked out like North? It's a perfect controlled experiment. The only difference between the two men was that David used an asthma inhaler that night. How does that make a difference? Well, David chemically altered the surface of his lungs. Perhaps the asthma drug blocks the action of the creatures' drugs. Doesn't let them enter the bloodstream. David was still affected, but he managed to get out of the surveillance van, break into the house, maybe even fire his gun at one of them. North was just flattened."

"And the drug tests were altered," Reese added. "Maybe that means that whatever drug the creatures used *did* turn up in the blood and urine tests and the FBI wanted to withhold that information. So they substituted standard clear results without bothering to add back the readings from Vincent's asthma drug. It fits."

"So what are we supposed to do with these?" Steven asked, holding the asthma inhaler before him.

"Keep it with you," Fisher said. "And the next time you start to feel anxious or uneasy or building toward a feeling of panic, use it. Maybe it will counteract or block the drug the creatures use."

"If it is a drug," Steven said, reading the instructional pamphlet attached to the inhaler.

"If they ever come back," Fisher said.

"Oh, they will," Wendy said, then looked up in surprise as if she hadn't meant to say anything at all.

"What makes you say that?" Fisher asked.

"I don't know," Wendy replied. "I just get this feeling that, like, they're not finished with us yet."

"So do I," Reese said. "So do I."

Reese had waited as long as he could, but half an hour before sunset he knew that he couldn't resist anymore and was forced to tell the others what he had to do. He was thankful that they asked no questions, made no jokes. Instead, they helped him cover the windows with the aluminum foil Merril had bought at the Safeway.

Even Wendy's father was making an effort, Reese knew. Steven had gone to sleep around four, letting the Scotch work its way out of his system, and now he was at least trying to be civil, going as far as holding double-folded sheets of foil in place as Reese plastered them with masking tape. For his part, Reese was trying to stay a respectful distance from Wendy, despite the ache that was in him. She was the love the creatures had brought to him, and in her presence he only wanted to experience her, without thought. In their present situation, Reese knew how dangerous that could be.

"I think that's the last one," Steven said as he took his hands from the final panel of foil and stepped back to scan the rest of the windows in the tiny dining room off the kitchen.

"Thank you," Reese said, and hoped it sounded as if he meant it, which he did. He examined the window and placed two more lengths of masking tape along a seam where one foil panel didn't quite touch a second. Now he knew he would be able to sleep this evening. As long as he didn't think about Wendy being so close and so inaccessible at the same time.

"I can't remember how many times I've seen foil in apartment windows, house windows," Steven said, rolling extra lengths of foil around an empty cardboard tube. "I always thought it was to cut out the light or the heat."

"It's to cut out the light," Reese said, walking back into the kitchen as Steven followed. It was easier to talk about his experiences now that the initial resistance had been overcome. But it was still odd that he could say such things and that people would believe him. How long had he known? How long had he lived with this secret? He couldn't remember. It had become his life.

"I meant sunlight," Steven said, putting the extra roll of foil away in a kitchen drawer. "I mean, if you see foil on five windows or so in one apartment building and you multiply that by the number of apartment buildings in the country, then— Well, surely they can't be taking that many people, can they?"

"This Starr fellow seems to think so," Fisher said from the living room. She walked into the kitchen to join them, carrying a copy of *The Case for UFO Abductions*. "He says the total number of abductions could number in the tens of thousands."

"But they'd need thousands of ships for that," Steven said. "Far too many people would have stumbled on something by accident by now. A chance witness like Vincent. Some old guy getting a heart attack when they came for him. Something would have gone wrong before now."

"Maybe not," Fisher said. She opened the refrigerator, took out a Budweiser, and as she juggled the book and the bottle to get at the twist-off cap, Reese reached out and opened it for her. "Thanks," she said and added, "Anyway, when you go through a bunch of these books all at the same time, there does seem to be a pattern developing."

"So how come you're the first to notice it?" Reese asked. He had developed great admiration for Merril. She was smart and tougher than she had any right to be, considering she was a civilian. Every once in a while, he would catch her staring at a wall, face mirroring an inner pain that Reese knew had to be her longing for Beth. But Merril didn't let it stop her and so far hadn't let it compromise their safety, no matter what the personal cost. And Reese knew it had to be high.

"I'm probably able to see the pattern because I'm coming to the material free of the biggest stumbling block anyone else would have to face," Fisher said.

"What's that?" Steven asked, opening a beer for himself.

"I know the phenomenon is real. That knowledge makes the information a whole lot easier to deal with."

"So what pattern do you see?"

"A sampling program for sure," Fisher said, leaning against a counter. "But not a survey. I mean, the abductions don't appear to fall into some sort of zoological study of our planet. It's more like the creatures are looking for something."

"Like what?" Reese asked.

"Babies?" Steven suggested. "Starr was telling us all these strange stories about genetic sampling, sperm and egg cells being taken. Crossbred babies." His eyes opened in alarm. "Where's Wendy?"

"On the couch," Fisher said, pointing out to the living room past the swinging kitchen door she had propped open with a folded *Time* magazine. Wendy's head could be seen on the arm of the sofa. "Sleeping."

"Good," Reese said with relief.

"Anyway, all the genetic fumbling about seems to have picked up recently," Fisher continued. "Around World War II seems to be the trigger period. Late thirties, then forties, and on to the present."

"I thought flying saucers had been reported for hundreds of years," Steven said. He had positioned himself against a second counter where he could easily look out at his daughter.

"Oh yeah, sightings have been," Fisher said. "But I'm talking about abductions. I mean, it seems likely that some type of abduction has been going on for centuries maybe. You know, a person here, a person there. Could have started a lot of legends about visiting the caves of goblins and dwarfs. Going to Fairyland, that sort of thing. But there was never a lot of it. However, since the late thirties, early forties, the abductions really seem to have picked up steam. Especially now."

"Or maybe there are just as many as there have ever been, but more people are remembering them now," Steven suggested.

"Well, might be," Fisher reluctantly agreed. "But why would we be any better at remembering these things today than people were a hundred, two hundred years ago? I mean, Derek, you weren't ever hypnotized or anything to get your memories of your abductions back, were you?"

"No, no hypnosis," Reese said. "There was one time they came for me, about six years ago, that when I woke up, I remembered just about the whole thing. Something must have happened. Whatever they do to make people forget didn't happen. Or maybe didn't work. And another funny thing is that the more I talk about it, the easier it gets. Like once the barriers are broken, they don't reform."

"That shows they aren't perfect," Merril said. "So let's assume that maybe one out of a thousand times, something goes wrong with their memory-blocking process and somebody remembers. Well, two hundred years ago when they were only taking a handful of people, if that is what was going on, then it didn't matter if the odd person remembered something. After all, who was she going to tell?"

"Certainly not a priest," Steven said.

"Exactly," Merril agreed. "Throw another witch on the fire, boys. But these days, with so many more people being abducted for one reason or another, the standard error rate on their memory-blocking suddenly yields a much larger number of people, like Derek, who spontaneously remember what took place. Some of those people talk about it, write books about it, get on the Carson show, and that spurs the memories of a bunch of borderline people who wouldn't have remembered anything unless something else reminded them of it. So it's like a snowball. The more people talk, the greater number of people start to realize that it's happened to them too."

"Or a lot of people claim that it happened to them when it didn't," Reese said. "At the bureau, some people always called to confess to the latest crime reported on the news. They see a big story going on and they want to be part of it."

"Sure, there will always be out-and-out liars," Merril said. "And people who aren't lying because they really have deluded themselves into thinking it's happened when it hasn't. But they're just noise in the signal. As we all know, abduction is a real phenomenon."

"But how do you explain the thousands of ships they'd need?" Steven asked.

"I don't think they'd need that many," Merril said. "Remember what I said about how instead of a survey, it seems to be a search?" Steven and Reese nodded. "Well, think of this. The creatures are searching for something, so they come down and abduct huge numbers of people. And judging from the books, they're abducting most of them for the first time as children. Think about that the next time your kid says she saw something in the closet.

"Now, what I think might be happening is that most of those people are not what the creatures are looking for, so they, well, throw the children back. But some of them are whatever it is the creatures want, and those kids are somehow tagged and monitored and picked up regularly, according to the books, from about age five up to their forties. So it seems to make sense that the ones who are most likely to break the memory block are those to whom the experience has happened a number of times. Maybe it becomes familiar in some ways. Perhaps not quite as upsetting. Or maybe there's just a limit to how much terror our minds can keep hidden from us. Anyway, those people start blabbing about it, and soon it filters down to the people who may have been abducted only once." Fisher finished her beer and put the bottle on the counter beside her. "And the next thing you know, you've got soaring sales of aluminum foil because tens of thousands of people are lining their windows with it, trying to keep the light out. Brrr."

While Merril shivered with the thought that so many people

might have been abducted, Reese was pleasantly surprised to realize that he liked that idea. Somehow it took part of the loneliness out of the terror. He wasn't alone. It was a good feeling.

"If that's the pattern behind the abductions," Steven asked, "what's the purpose behind them?"

Merril laughed. "That's the one thing these books don't tell you. They tell you who, what, where, and when. But they don't tell you how or why."

"Did no one ever ask them why they're doing it?" Steven asked.

"It's not that easy," Reese said awkwardly, and he saw the odd look that came over Steven and Merril as they realized he was speaking from experience. "You're not totally in control when you're among them. My . . . experiences always begin with a feeling of absolute terror. It affects the way I think and feel. And then . . . then they come for me and take me to their ship and . . . well, it's like I'm in a badly cut movie. Things jump around so much."

"Have you ever talked with them?" Steven asked.

"Sure, lots of times. But strange things."

"Like what?"

Reese stared down at the floor. "It's so hard to say. I can see it. Hear it. But it's as if I can't remember how to describe it."

"It's okay, Derek," Merril said. "Don't force it. You're doing a lot better now. You'll be doing even better next week. Don't worry."

"I explain books to them," Reese said abruptly, looking up. That was an easier one to talk about.

"What kind of books?" Steven asked, keeping his eyes riveted on Wendy as she slept.

"Our books. Earth books," Reese said. "I remember it took them a long time to realize that our books are written in different languages. Some of the first books they showed me were in languages I couldn't read: French, German. So now they just show me English books." But Reese had no recollection of what kinds of books they were.

"Are they putting together a library?" Steven asked.

"That might make a bit of sense," Fisher said. "There's a strong feeling of apocalypse running through a lot of the abductees' stories of talking with the creatures. You know, the world is facing imminent destruction, the abductees are the chosen ones, that sort of thing."

"You don't sound very convinced," Steven said.

Fisher screwed up her eyes in consideration. "Well, that kind of talk picks up naturally as we get closer to the turn of the century. Nostradamus gets reinterpreted for the millionth time. Someone makes a new measurement on the Great Pyramid. The problem is that the abductees don't report as much consistent detail in their discussions with the creatures as they do in their physical descriptions. The creatures are all pretty much the same. About four different types—"

"Four or five," Reese agreed, counting their images in his memory.

"And their ships and equipment are all generally the same," Fisher continued. "But not their conversations. Either the memory blocks work to some extent on everyone, or different people are being told different stories."

"Why?" Steven asked.

Fisher shrugged. "Maybe there's more than one set of them. You know, like the British, Italians, and Portuguese all arriving in the New World at once, each trying to con the natives in a different way." She turned to Reese. "They ever say anything to you about what they're doing?"

"I never asked." He laughed and they joined him.

"Dad?" Wendy suddenly called from the living room.

Reese held back and let Steven precede him out of the kitchen to Wendy's side. "Right here, honey. What's wrong?"

Wendy pushed herself up from the sofa. Her hair stuck up on one side where she had been lying on it and her eyes were half open, blinking drowsily. "Nothing," she said thickly. "I just heard laughing." She looked up at Reese, her eyes opening as her mouth made a sleepy, happy smile. "You're still here," she said, her voice soft with sleep.

Reese couldn't hold back any longer, despite Steven. He held out his hand to her, touched the back of his fingers to her sleep-warmed cheek. She took his hand in hers, pushing it harder against her, rubbing her face against it. Kissing him.

Reese pulled back, and it was like a physical pain. He wanted her. A rational part of him told him it was insane. The girl was only sixteen. He could be her father. She was only a child. But at his core, Reese knew he wanted the girl because they had both had each other before. He knew the feel of her, the shapes of her, how she moved and called out to him. He felt bound to her in all ways but in no way that he could describe or even imagine. He pulled back his hand so he wouldn't pick her up and run away with her—today. So he would not run away with her today, he thought, as if it were a given that he *would* run away with her at another time, in another place. He pulled back his hand and the contact was broken. But not the ache and the longing.

"Oh my," Wendy sighed, reluctantly releasing his hand. She stretched. "What time is it?"

"Just about nine," Merril said. "How about some dinner?"

Wendy looked at her father. "Are we safe here? Is this going to be okay?"

Steven gestured at Reese. "It's your safe house."

"We'll be fine," Reese said, smiling. "We're—"

The doorbell rang.

They froze like deer trapped in the glaring headlights of an oncoming car. Reese held up his hand for silence. Merril reached for her inhaler, held it in front of her open mouth, and pressed down. The canister hissed, and she fought to keep from coughing.

Reese pulled his Beretta from his shoulder holster and held it up beside his head. He crept silently to the door, peered through the security viewer. Then lowered his gun and opened the door.

"Looks like we have a visitor," he said.

It was Charles Edward Starr.

10

Reese pulled Starr in through the door, dragged him into the living room, and shoved him down into the armchair. Then he told Merril to go out on the small porch and check the street. She was back in thirty seconds.

"Just a burgundy T-Bird with a Hertz sticker in the driveway," she reported.

Starr jangled a set of keys. "I'm quite alone, I assure you."

Reese towered over the writer. "Then you better have a good explanation for how you found us."

Starr pocketed his keys. Reese felt uneasy as he sensed the writer wasn't as nervous as he should be, stepping back into the lair of his kidnappers.

"I used to be a full-time reporter," Starr said. "I still have my sources."

"Name them," Reese said. He had made a point of not holstering his gun.

"First, there was the licence plate on the van. I hid outside the parking garage this morning until you came out."

"It's not registered to this address." Reese turned to Merril. "Keep watching through the peephole." To Steven and Wendy, "Check the back door."

"The van is registered to Tilden," Starr said. He read from a scrap of notepaper he had taken from his back pocket. "Renter's name is Barry Stroud, San Diego. Want his MasterCard number? Or is it still in your wallet?"

"That's tough information to get, Mr. Starr."

"For me, maybe," the writer agreed. "But not for three news service stringers eager to do an old friend a few favors on a slow summer day for hard cash. All this information is in computers, Mr. Stroud. All it takes is getting the right people to press the right keys."

So he thinks I'm Stroud, Reese thought. Meaning Starr really did track him down through legitimate means or, if he was working as a blind for the bureau or the OCI, he was playing it very cool. He doubted the writer could be that disciplined.

"You still haven't told me how you found this address."

"First, a few police friends were happy to put out an APB on your van—I told them an old friend I happened to get a glimpse of was having a birthday, if that sounds familiar, Steven, and they were kind enough to find it for me four blocks over in the Safeway parking lot. That gave me a general area to look through."

"Go on."

"Mr. Stroud, please," Starr said sincerely. "This is the only house in the neighborhood with *all* of its windows covered with aluminum foil. I know what I'm looking for. I've done it before."

Reese stepped away from the writer, hesitated a moment, then slipped his Beretta into his shoulder holster. "Why did you come back?" he asked, more immediate concerns now dealt with.

"Kidnapping me was the act of a desperate man, Mr. Stroud. I understand where that desperation comes from. I want to help."

"How?"

"You and Wendy Gilmour are special people, Mr. Stroud. You've been chosen by forces beyond most people's comprehension for purposes which few people understand. In the course of my work, I've met many like you. I can help you understand what's happened. Help you cope. Even help you come to accept it."

"I've read your books, Mr. Starr," Merril said from her post at the front door. "You offer no explanations. No descriptions of forces or purposes."

"I don't put everything I know into my books."

"Why not?" Reese asked.

"We're dealing with a breakthrough here of unprecedented proportions," Starr explained, conviction solid in his tone and delivery. "The most staggering occurrence in the history of humanity. Of the world."

"And what might that be?" Fisher asked again, her condescension rising to match Starr's confidence.

"We are not alone, Ms. Fisher." He stated it as the most sublime, self-evident truth ever uttered.

"Surely that's the point of your books, isn't it?" Steven asked. "And they certainly haven't changed the world."

"Because my books offer no proof," Starr explained. "They present none of the absolutely incontrovertible hard facts."

"Are you saying there are such facts?" Fisher asked, an odd catch in her throat. "Facts that would convince people who hadn't been through the experience themselves?"

"Most assuredly."

"Then why aren't they in your books?" Wendy asked. "Why hold back?"

"You have to understand that the purpose of my books was never to convince the skeptics," Starr said, eyes wide and intent.

"Then why did you write them?" Fisher's expression showed her confusion.

"To help the chosen ones," Starr said. "So the ones who have been taken away and remember some of what happened to them will not be troubled by those memories. So they can find solace in knowing that neither are they crazy nor are they alone."

"I think you might be crazy," Fisher said.

"And I think you have never been abducted," Starr replied.

"What does that have to do with anything?" Fisher got out of her chair and approached Starr. "I photographed their spaceship or whatever it was. I already believe Wendy's story. I just don't believe that you know any more about what the creatures are up to than any of us know."

"Ah, but I do."

"Then why not tell the world?"

"Because it is not yet time. There is an order. A timetable. The time is drawing near—"

"Hallelujah, brother!" Fisher exclaimed.

"And soon all of the people of the earth will know everything they need to know," Starr concluded angrily.

"And Charles Edward Starr will be the one to enlighten the world? Is that it, Mr. Starr?"

"No, Ms. Fisher, that is not it." Starr's eyes became shadowed beneath his wrinkled brow. "The creatures will make that announcement themselves."

"Oh, really?" Fisher said. "And when might that glorious day be? Wait. Don't tell me. 'Soon,' right? Or is it, 'Real soon?' "

Starr shook his head in annoyance at Fisher's scorn and turned away from her.

"What will they say, Mr. Starr?" Wendy asked gently. Reese saw no amusement in her eyes, no derision. Just worry.

"One way or another, we've all been there," Steven added. "I've seen them. Merril photographed them. Can you tell us anything? So we might know why Sarah is gone?"

Starr smiled at Wendy, nodded at Steven. "Very well," he said. "You do deserve to know." He turned back to Fisher. "And please don't feel forced to listen.

"There is a galactic civilization in our Milky Way," Starr began.

"Oh, spare me," Fisher said and flopped back into her armchair, hand over her eyes.

Starr ignored her. "Thousands upon thousands of years old. It consists of more than *eighteen hundred* separate intelligent races, all bound together in an interstellar organization dedicated to the preservation of life and the pursuit of knowledge."

Fisher blew a raspberry, and Wendy shushed her.

"Millennia ago," Starr continued, his back to Fisher, "scout ships from this galactic civilization made contact with our planet and saw that an intelligent race was arising upon it. We were then placed under a type of protection." He smiled. "Like a game preserve. So we could develop at our own rate and in our own way."

"How long is that going to last?" Wendy asked.

"Wendy, come on!" Fisher complained.

"Not much longer, my dear," Starr said. "The time has almost come for the race of earthlings to take our place in the galaxy, no longer planet-bound creatures but called to a greater, more magnificent destiny among the stars. Do you know what this means?" the writer asked Wendy, arms outstretched to her, tears in his eyes. Wendy shook her head, enraptured.

"Your mama dropped you on your head as a child?" Fisher asked politely.

"It means that there are *answers* waiting for us!" Starr exclaimed. "It means that someday soon there will be no darkness, no ignorance, no sickness or war or hunger. Other races have been along those paths before us. They will be our teachers. Our brothers and sisters." He waved his arms around the room.

"And it means this little, puny planet is not all there is for us. There's more to existence than being born here, dying here, never to see the stars. It means there is purpose for us." He turned to Fisher. "It means we are not alone."

Fisher shook her head sadly, biting her bottom lip.

"But what about the babies?" Wendy asked.

Starr's eyes lit up. He brushed at the tears in them. "It's all true, my dear. All of it. Right now there are children—half-human, half-alien—living in orbiting space stations above us. And when they are grown to adulthood, they shall be our ambassadors to the great galactic assembly."

"Why can't we go?" Wendy asked.

Starr shrugged. "Something to do with the propulsion system they use to go faster than light," he said offhandedly. "Apparently it's very stressful. Humans are not able to withstand moving into a higher dimension, so the aliens are creating a modified form of us which can."

"So we'll never actually get to go to the great galactic assembly or whatever?" Steven asked.

"Oh, certainly," Starr replied. "In sleeper ships. They're hollowing out asteroids between Mars and Jupiter right now. Volunteers will be frozen and make the voyage in them. Of course, it will take centuries that way."

"I think someone's brain has been frozen," Fisher muttered.

"Why doesn't anyone else know this?" Reese asked. He didn't share Wendy's enthusiasm for what Starr was saying, but neither did he share Fisher's cynicism. If he could accept the abduction experience itself, what was wrong with accepting Starr's explanation as well?

"Fear of panic mostly," Starr said, glad to have someone on the other side of the room who wanted to talk with him. "The aliens feel the general population isn't ready to accept their presence yet, so they've begun a long-term consciousness-raising project. Implanting positive ideas in people's minds. Having them filtered into the public's awareness through movies, television, even books like mine. Getting us used to the idea of them."

Fisher sputtered again. "So like, are you telling us that a bunch of these creatures are hanging out at Steven Spielberg's place, doing script rewrites for him?"

"Except for Ms. Fisher," Starr said, addressing the others, "you've all seen the aliens. You know there is no way they could come down here and interact with humans. That's why they have to resort to . . . such drastic means to arrange for the new generation of galactic ambassadors."

Fisher exploded out of her chair. "You're so full of shit!" she shouted at Starr.

"Leave him alone!" Wendy yelled back. "Let him finish!" Steven pulled her back to the couch.

Reese stepped into the living room. He didn't like the way things were going. He put his hand tentatively on his gun. "What's wrong?" he asked, looking nervously around.

Fisher stood in the middle of the living room, fists clenched, mouth twisted with scorn. "If they can't interact with us, then how come they know so much about us? How do they manage to affect our television and movies?"

"Because they have *emissaries*, Ms. Fisher!" Starr went head-to-head with her. "Humans who are smarter than you are. Humans more sensitive, more aware. Humans that do the aliens' work for them here on earth to save us all!"

"Humans like you I suppose?" Fisher seemed ready to strike the writer. Reese moved toward her. Something was wrong here. But what?

"Yes!" Starr shouted. "People just like me!"

"Jesus," Reese moaned as he figured it out. He grabbed at Fisher, reached into her jeans pocket as she struggled away from him, striking him with her fists.

Reese heard Wendy screaming at him to let Merril go. He heard Steven shouting at Wendy. Heard Starr ranting about the chosen. But there was only one thing Reese cared about. He found it.

Reese jumped back from Fisher, held the inhaler to his lips, sprayed the medication into his mouth, and inhaled. He coughed and tried to spray again, but the canister had a delay built into it. He fought to remember how it worked. Tilt, spray, inhale. He tried it again.

"That won't work anymore," Starr said to him. "The dosage has been recalibrated to compensate for any lung surfactants."

Fisher stared in horror at the inhaler in Reese's hand. She lunged for it and Reese let her have it.

"How do you know what they've done to the dosage?" Reese asked. His lungs felt cold and tender, as if he had just run a long-distance winter sprint.

"You're right," Starr laughed. "Why should you have to take my word for it?" He walked over to the kitchen door. Put his hand on it. "When you can take *theirs!*" He pushed the door open. It swung into the kitchen with a bang.

And there they were.

The creatures poured out from the kitchen like scampering ghosts. Reese stumbled backward as they swarmed past him. These were the smallest ones, he remembered, the drones in their loose blue coverings. But with the same round, hairless gray-white heads. The same light-swallowing eyes, though rounder, less slanted. He spun around to see where they ran.

Wendy. They were on her like piranhas in a feeding frenzy. Their tiny three-fingered hands clutched her hair, her arms, her legs. One carried a large black device that looked like the pincer end of a wrench. The creature struggled to attach it to Wendy's shoulder as the others pulled her down.

"*NO!*" Reese shouted and he lunged at her.

Wendy screamed mindlessly. Steven was sprawled on the couch, trembling hands straining to reach for his daughter.

Reese tore through the creatures like they were dry grass, scattering them as he ran for Wendy.

The creatures squealed. Two scampered up a wall and cowered at the corner of it and the ceiling.

"Stop fighting them, *Reese!*" Starr shouted from the front door, safely out of the way. "They just want you and the girl."

Reese pulled Wendy to his side. The drug had taken effect, and she slumped against him. The creature with the pincer device stood in front of Reese, out of arm's reach, bobbing and weaving before him. Beside the creature, a second one faced Reese, matching the first's movements exactly, sway for sway, arm movement for arm movement, like a double exposure.

Reese followed the eerie dance of the two, expecting an attack from one or the other. He stared into their ebony eyes but could see no emotion there, no motive, no intellect.

"Reese! Behind you!"

Reese whirled at Fisher's warning, saw her backed against the wall, inhaler in hand. Behind him was a second type of creature, an operator, taller than the drones and garbed in a tan-colored coverall stretched tightly over unnatural joints and muscles. And it held a long, thin probe pointed at Reese.

Reese's hand flew to his Beretta. Quite clearly, a voice which appeared in the middle of his head said, *Please don't do that, Derek*. But without drugs to back it up, the suggestion was useless.

The ring of colors grew at the probe's sparkling tip. They reflected from the dull blue finish of Reese's gun barrel as he aimed at the creature, automatically going for the largest part of his target.

For an instant, Reese thought he might have seen those black eyes widen. For an instant, he might have sensed something like surprise. But whatever it had been, it didn't last. Reese pulled the trigger.

The creature's head disintegrated like a balloon. Reese blinked in astonishment. There was a spray of liquid, but no splattering of bone and flesh. As if its head had been empty.

The drones squealed like pigs in a slaughterhouse as an over-powering stench of sour cheese filled the room. Starr's screams rose above them all.

All around Reese, the drones flopped and twitched errati-cally. The two on the wall collapsed upward to lie flat against the ceiling. Four more slid sideways to smash against a wall as though they had been drawn there by a magnet.

Convulsed with sobs, Starr pushed the shuddering drones out of his way as he ran to the body of the operator. He cradled the headless corpse, a thick black syrup emerging from its shat-tered neck to cover the writer's hands. Starr reached for the probe, still loosely grasped in the dead creature's hand. He touched it. The light within faded to nothing, and the probe became an ordinary rod of dull copper metal.

"Do you know what you've done?" Starr sobbed, turning his face to Reese.

From the corner of his eyes, Reese saw Merril going to help Steven up from the sofa. Reese held Wendy's almost limp body closer to him. He kept his gun trained on Starr amidst the confused dances of the drones.

Starr held out one black, dripping hand to Reese. "Look at it!" he shrieked. *"Look at it!"* He hugged the inhuman body to him. Behind the kitchen door, Reese heard an electric crackling. Blue flashes of brilliant light leaked out around the door's edges.

Starr turned to look at the display.

"Interstellar war," he said to Reese. "You've brought the end of everything."

"What is it?" Reese shouted as the crackling increased in volume and the flashing light around the door intensified.

Abruptly, all around the living room, the drones stopped moving and came to attention, even the ones on the ceiling and the walls. Like toy soldiers propelled by magnets, they slid into an ordered position, legs and feet unmoving.

The crackling in the kitchen stopped. The blue light was unwavering.

"What is it?" Reese shouted again.

"The soldiers are here," Starr said sadly. "The soldiers."

Reese held his gun on the kitchen door. There were drones, he knew. And operators. Slights, connections, and engineers. The names all came to him as he needed them. But he had never seen soldiers.

"Merril," he shouted. "Get Wendy out. I'll get Steven."

Reese stepped backward, dragging Wendy with him, eyes fixed on the kitchen door, waiting for it to open.

Starr stayed kneeling in the line of fire, crying over the dead operator. Reese checked quickly behind him. Fisher had Steven standing up, his arm over her shoulder. "We'll all go for the front door together," she said. "Let's move it."

The kitchen door didn't open. It puddled. Dissolved like a frame of melting film. A soldier stepped through the transparent distortion.

Reese felt fear arc through him like electricity. The soldier resembled a slight. Almost six feet tall, impossibly thin, arms and legs too long and jointed like insect limbs. Its face was narrow, its chin pointed like a turtle's beak, and its smoke-gray uniform was threaded with rippling strands of silver light, pulsing over its body as if ball lightning were within it and trying to escape.

The soldier's probe was larger than the others', three feet

long and ten inches across. Four joined hollow tubes of sparking, glowing metal dropping thick white vapor that pooled around the soldier's feet. The soldier's eyes slanted at twice the angle of the other slights, almost vertical. Reese felt them lock onto him. Saw the soldier's probe move smoothly to aim at him.

Reese fired his gun.

A brilliant flash of silver light appeared on the soldier's shoulder, then flared out. The creature didn't even absorb the impact of the bullet. It brought its probe to bear.

Starr looked over at Reese. "Satisfied now?" the writer asked, and began to laugh hysterically.

Reese looked over and saw Fisher dragging Steven through the front door. He fired at the creature again. Another flash of silver light, and it was as if the bullet had not existed.

The probe produced its own ring of light, but this time, all of the colors were blue.

Reese squeezed Wendy against him. Fired his gun one final time. Aimed at the probe itself.

The probe jerked in the creature's hand just as it discharged. A blinding, thunderous bolt of ragged blue lightning tore through the air, catching Starr in his midsection and blasting him across the room.

The writer hit the wall, and Reese saw the plasterboard collapse behind him. For a moment, Starr hung there, blue fire dancing on his chest, then the energy raced away along his arms and legs, swirling in vortices of incandescent blue arcs until Starr held his flaming hands before his shocked face and slumped, still imbedded in the wall.

Reese turned back to the soldier. It turned back from Starr. Reese fired twice more, both shots jarring the thick weapon in the soldier's hands. It stepped to the side like a slow-motion man on stilts. Through the rippling hole in the door, Reese could see another soldier. And another. Coming through the white mist.

Reese ran for the front door, dragging Wendy with him, her limp feet dragging across the floor between the motionless drones.

And then they were out on the porch and running to the street where Fisher struggled with Steven. The man was coming around.

"Keep going!" Reese shouted.

He glanced behind and could see blue light spraying from the bungalow's open front door. Pencil-thin lines of blue light shot out from the cracks in the foil on the windows. He swung Wendy's legs up and carried her like a child. Beside him, Fisher and Steven ran.

They pounded down the street, past people who watched them from their front yards, holding hoses and sprinklers, dogs on leashes, kids with skateboards and bicycles. A peaceful summer evening broken only by the speeding footfalls of three terrified people and their frantic gasps for undoctored air.

They stopped four blocks away, turned and looked at the house. Steven bent over with hands on his knees. Fisher clasped her hands on her head. Wendy's eyes slowly looked around without awareness.

Down the street, they saw a long line of interested neighbors staring first at them, then back toward the bungalow. The blue light was fading. A final flurry of blue beams played through the windows. And then there was only darkness.

Reese closed his eyes. For the moment they were safe. Then he felt a sudden wave of heat on his face and opened his eyes just as an oddly subdued thunderclap reached him and he saw the bungalow swallowed by an enormous blue fireball.

A solid shaft of cobalt flame blazed straight up from the fireball, twisted like a tornado, then disappeared like vapor sucked through a vent. Debris rained down on the street. A real fire started among the ruins of the house.

The four of them watched in awed silence.

Then Fisher gasped, "We better keep moving," still struggling to catch her breath.

"It won't matter," Reese said, pulling Wendy's precious head against his chest. "Starr knew who I was. They knew where we were." He looked at Steven. "And they can find us anytime they want," he said. "Anytime."

11

△△∠ ▽∠∠ △△△ △∠

Sarah Gilmour sat patiently while the *pa* creaked and shifted restlessly around her. The distant rumbles and shudders of transference and placement echoed through the unending corridors outside her room as if an immense underground train system ran in deep tunnels beneath her. In a sense, she thought, that's what it is. And by now, she was used to it.

Her room, when she was in it by herself, was comforting. It was peaceful and simple, a twenty-foot squat bubble, ribbed and paneled with a pleasant dusty rose-colored material. They weren't able to tell her exactly what that material was, but it was soothing in the soft daylight glow that shone down from the crystal-faceted light source at the very highest point of the domed ceiling.

A narrow bench ran around three-quarters of the room. Its surface was pastel blue, and it was made of another untranslatable material, soft and yielding to slow and gentle pressure yet hard and resistant to any sudden, powerful impact. Part of the bench was wider than the rest and that's where she slept. When they let her be tired. Which wasn't often.

Sarah knew little of the *pa* except for the brief stretches of tube-shaped corridor that weaved through its bulk between her room and the *kohanga reo*. But what she did know was that the whole of this place was filled with a sense of urgency that she had never felt before. Whatever its purpose, there was not much time left. And no time for sleep.

With a gentle sound like falling rain, the light source rotated above her. One of them is coming, Sarah thought. That is why they sent me to my room to wait without sleeping. One of them is coming here. I wonder if it will be— But she found she could not remember the names or the faces of anyone else she might expect to join her.

Slowly, subtly, the light changed. The room grew dimmer, the pale rose of the walls changing to an indistinct brown, the pastel blue of the bed and bench becoming a dull gray. This light was better for them, Sarah knew. One of them would be there soon.

She looked to the door, centered between the ends of the bench. It was circular, almost large enough for her to step through without bending over. Built for the slights, she thought, though none had ever visited her here. None, at least, that they had let her remember.

Sarah felt the soft tickle of the silent voice. She prepared to listen.

A thing will happen, were the words spoken into her mind. *Show us how you do this thing so they will know.*

Sarah prepared herself for the light that teaches. She had fleeting memories of another brood—her third-graders, she called them. They would have enjoyed the light that teaches. She closed her eyes, settled into the bench, and prepared to act out whatever they required her to put into the light.

It didn't come.

Instead, her room became chilled, as if a freezer door had been opened on a hot summer night and the cold had spilled to the floor in a glacial torrent of air. Sarah opened her eyes and looked into the center of her room, at the circular fluid surface of the portal, pooled in the floor's central depression. There was to be a transference.

The surface of the portal rippled and a low bed emerged, gray and brown in the altered light. There was a large figure on it, swaddled in gray cloth. Sarah walked to the edge of the rippling portal and peered at the bed to see what kind of creature was on it. Almost large enough to be a slight, she thought. Or a soldier.

The portal closed. Sarah stepped out onto its now-solid surface and went to the bed. The figure was human. It had no forearms or hands. It was going to die.

Show us how you do this thing so they will know, the silent voice repeated.

"Give me a cloth," she said. "Dip it in cool water."

She stepped back from the portal. After a moment it rippled again and a large clear bowl emerged. In it was a white cloth.

The portal closed. Sarah retrieved the bowl and placed it on the side of the bed. The cloth was a terry facecloth. The label on it showed it was made by Fieldcrest and told her how to wash it. The cloth was cool and moist.

She pulled the cover from the figure and saw it was a man, covered in soot, his hair stubbly where it had been singed away. The stumps of his forearms were crudely wrapped in more gray fabric. Sarah wiped at the man's face with her washcloth. Some of the soot would not come off because it was burned into his skin. She rubbed at one small fleck at the corner of his mouth and a gleaming red crack appeared and began to bleed.

"Who is he?" Sarah asked.

Listen to us, said the silent voice, and Sarah's mind filled with knowledge of the man.

"He will die," Sarah said, seeing that the man's burns were even worse on his chest.

A thing will happen, the silent voice agreed. *Show us.*

So that was it, Sarah thought. Another lesson, but this time for real.

"Can you wake him?" she asked.

After a moment, the man's eyes fluttered open. The left was filled with dark red blood. The right looked around, twitched each time the sounds of distant thunder rumbled through the room, and at last came to rest on Sarah.

"You're . . . Sarah," the man gasped. His voice was dry. His lips cracked. Sarah dipped her facecloth into the water in the glass bowl—a salad bowl from Sears, she saw—and dripped water onto the dying man's lips.

"That's right," she said gently, smiling at the man. "And you're Charles Edward Starr."

The man smiled as best he could. He looked around the room. "Am I . . . am I *on board?*" he whispered.

"Yes," Sarah said, bathing his forehead. "You are on board."

Starr began to cry from his one good eye. "I've waited so long. Worked so hard. Nearly gave up hope . . ."

"I know," Sarah said. "And they know too."

"Are they here?" Starr asked.

Sarah nodded. "Right outside the door."

Starr tried to raise his head to see the door. He pulled his arms back to support himself, groaned in pain, and fell back. He held his stumps up.

"Will . . . will they give me new arms?"

Sarah saw he was approaching shock. If not for the silent voice in Starr's own mind, he probably would be gone already.

"Yes," she said.

"My reward?"

"That's right. Your reward."

Starr closed his eyes, nodded slowly. "That's right. I've . . . been so good for them. When they make a mistake . . . I can investigate . . . confuse things . . . make it easy for people to discount them . . ." His eyes sprang open. "I spoiled those soil samples for them, you know. Last year, when they set down in the wrong place and the sheriff scooped up those samples from the landing rings. If he hadn't have given them to me to test . . . everybody would have known. But I switched them—" He began to cough. White foam appeared at his mouth. "I switched them . . ."

"Shhh," Sarah said. "They know how hard you've worked. They know how much you've done."

Starr sighed. "When do I get new arms?" he asked. His voice was drifting away.

"The shuttle will take you to Ceres in just a few minutes."

"Ceres?"

"The first asteroid to become a sleeper ship. They'll grow new arms for you while you're in suspension."

"Then I'm going?" Starr asked.

"To the great galactic assembly," Sarah said.

He smiled then. Oh, how he smiled. "How long?" he coughed. "How long will it take?"

"Five hundred years," Sarah answered. "You will sleep for five hundred years, and when you awaken, you will be a hero of the assembly. Five centuries of earth children will learn your name as the first and greatest of the first-chosen. And you will be there to address the assembly yourself."

"I'm going," Starr said.

Then he died.

Sarah dabbed a final bubble of foam from the man's silent

lips, then folded the cloth and placed it back inside the glass bowl. She sighed and turned back to the bench.

The one who stood beside her was there in his own form, and not that of Smokey Joe. Sarah hadn't heard the door spin open. But she wasn't surprised. That was one thing she had definitely noticed about being in the *pa:* she was never surprised and never frightened. Why is that? she sometimes wondered. But then she would feel calm and happy, and the questioning thoughts would fade away.

The one who stood beside her was an operator, almost four feet tall, gray-skinned in the altered light and as fine-boned and as graceful as a humanoid bird. His coverall was a darker brown than the room's color, and his symbol was an open triangle, shifted to the right, worn on the left edge of his collar. Today the triangle was missing its bottom bar. Sarah knew the triangles were used to record time on the *pa,* but she didn't know how to read them.

"A thing has happened," Sarah told him.

The one who stood beside her blinked. His lids flicked down as his black eyes pulled back.

"You are feeling . . . ?" he asked. His spoken voice was high like a child's, whispery like that of an old woman awakened from sleep.

Sarah looked back at the bed with Starr's body as it was placed back through the portal. A mild tremor passed through the room when the bed was gone and the empty portal solidified and closed.

"I am feeling sad that he has ended," Sarah said. "I am feeling sad that I had to lie to him."

The one who stood beside her blinked again. "But Charles Edward Starr was . . . happy that you lied to him."

"Only because he didn't know I was lying," Sarah explained.

The one who stood beside her made a reflexive gesture of thought, pulling his left arm in to his side, elbow down, his left fist touching his shoulder with its thumb. He stretched his right arm over his chest to wrap his right hand over his left fist. He remained in that position for several seconds, like a standing fetus.

"Thirty-five years with you," he finally said, "and still no . . ." He shook his head and Sarah smiled. That was one of the few things she *had* taught him in the thirty-five years he had stood beside her.

"What would make you not feel sad? Feel happy?" the creature asked.

"If I could have told Charles Edward the truth," Sarah said.

"Ah, Sarah, what makes you think your truth is any more than Charles Edward Starr's truth is?" The creature shook his head briefly. "Was?" he corrected uncertainly.

"It's your truth, isn't it?" Sarah asked.

"There are many truths within the *pa*. That is why we must hide some of what we do from the devices that do things." The one who stood beside her stepped toward the closed door. "What makes you think that my truth is the truth that will bring victory?"

"I know the truth," Sarah said bluntly. "I've seen it. Held it in my arms."

The one who stood beside her turned by the door. His eyes held only the deep black of glistening space. Sometimes, Sarah thought, sometimes I look into those eyes and can almost really see them. A hint of pupil, a suspicion of iris. But now, across her room, there was nothing in them but endless night.

The creature drew in a breath, and the thin flaps of skin that ringed his mouth fluttered in, becoming a smile. Another of Sarah's lessons.

"So you have," the creature said. "So you have."

He held out one thin, bony hand to Sarah. *"Kohanga reo,"* he said. With the other hand he twisted the spherical black handle in the center of the door, and the door unwound itself like a watch mainspring, disappearing around the edges of the doorframe until only the handle was left jutting from halfway up the left side.

Sarah walked over to the one who had stood beside her for thirty-five years, and took his hand, pleased for the intimacy he offered her. It was a rare thing here, she knew. They seldom seemed to need it or even understand it. She looked out into the corridor, lit with the same unusual light as her room, and watched the passageway twist like a rope bridge over an impossibly high chasm. The thunder and shifting of the *pa* was louder with the door opened, and each sound, like the creaking of ship masts at sea, sent a new movement rippling along the ridged tan surface of the tunnel. But Sarah was used to that too, and she followed the operator out into it.

Walking in the corridor was easier than it had first seemed to her so many years ago. The center ridge was more solid than the others, and though the apparently stable surrounding walls might suddenly produce a rushing billow as if a wave had hit them, the vibration along the center ridge was minor. Sarah no longer had to be floated through the corridors. And she no longer fell.

A drone team passed by them, smaller beings in blue coveralls, with rounder eyes than the other creatures, moving together under the influence of a single operator. They traveled along their own wall-mounted ridge in the corridor, smoothly sliding along without moving their feet, relying on the snaking conduits of transference and placement that ran beneath the corridor's skin.

They came to the first intersection, and the one who stood beside her turned to the left, following the pictograph that Sarah called an ankh. Like the ancient Egyptian symbol, it was a circle mounted on a bar, with a long tail beneath it. The tail on the ankh Sarah remembered had a single cross piece, but in the *pa*, the ankhs had two, one at a slight angle to the other. The ankh was the symbol for the *kohanga reo*, and though Sarah always wondered if she could find her way back to her room alone, she knew she could always follow the ankh to someplace familiar and important.

They walked in silence for another few minutes. A second drone team passed by, moving in perfect lockstep this time, running on automatic. Two slights, arms intertwined, moved gracefully out of the way as Sarah passed by, after they had reached down to touch thumbs with the one who stood beside her. Sarah was not able to hear their silent voices and so did not know what had been exchanged.

At the final intersection of six corridors, the one who stood beside her held out his arm to Sarah. The silent voice said, *Stop, please,* and Sarah and he waited while two dachshunds, barking in terror, flew along one of the corridor sections, pursued by one of the smaller creatures called a connection wearing what Sarah thought was supposed to be a military uniform of some type. It had been a long time since any of the connections had come to question her about clothes, as if they had finally realized they would never get them right and had given up.

As they waited, listening to the howling of the running dogs, Sarah wondered how far the animals might get. Once, she remembered she had asked one of the engineers how many corri-

dors there were in the *pa*. She had been told there was only one
but that it went everywhere.

After the chase had passed, the one who stood beside her led
the way again, and they began to walk down the final stretch.
They paused by the last door, a flattened circle this time, as two
visitors were guided past them, back to placement. One was a
middle-aged woman in a flowered dress. She floated peacefully
on her back as the drones aimed her down the corridor. Her
eyes were closed, she wore an angelic smile, and she softly sang
a child's lullaby. Behind her floated a man in his early twenties.
He wore a hiking outfit and struggled against the drones who
floated him, with both his hands clutched over his genitals. He
looked up at Sarah as he went by, and Sarah could see the
unbridled terror in his eyes. But he had not been released, so
there was nothing he could say or do. Sarah looked away.
There were many things here she was used to.

The one who stood beside her touched the door handle and
stood back as the door panel spiraled open and the brighter
light of the *kohanga reo* spilled out into the corridor. Sarah
entered the large room, and the light that teaches immediately
enveloped her as it did every time she arrived there.

Each of her actions in this room was valuable. Every gesture,
every motion, would be recorded and played back a thousand
times. By the entrance to the long passage of incubator stalls, a
drone team stood waiting for her, ready to be slaved to an
operator and play back Sarah's actions the moment she left.
Sarah had always thought of these drones as the little mothers,
a name from her childhood. Two more slights waited by the
crèche entrance ramp, resplendent in iridescent purple coveralls and wearing breastplates depicting a winged serpentlike
creature. Their costume and symbols marked them as coming
from another section of the *pa,* a section where they did not
know what the one who stood beside Sarah was planning. Both
slights drew in their breath and held their kind's more pronounced lip flaps into a smile. Sarah smiled back. The door
spiraled closed behind her.

"Are there new ones today?" she asked the connection who
stood by a feeding portal which was safely mounted high up the
wall, away from curious fingers. Sarah's voice was lost in this
room. The domed ceiling was more than forty feet high, the
row of incubators more than one hundred feet long.

"Yes, Sarah," the connection said. She wore a doctor's white outfit. It was much too big for her four-foot frame, but it did say "Mount Sinai" on the back of the scrub shirt, which meant it had been stolen, not made.

Sarah walked over to the first incubator stall. Behind her, she could sense that all the other creatures in the *kohanga reo* had stopped their tasks so that they might observe her. Sarah didn't mind at all. Why should she?

Because before her were five more new ones. Each one like a tiny doll, encased behind a clear curved window in a gleaming pewter-colored cylinder, stamped with the modified ankh. At the top of each incubator cylinder, where the ornately engraved control surfaces were, three small blue open triangles, the third one missing its bottom bar and shifted to the right, glowed with blue brilliance. The mark of this day, Sarah thought. Newborns.

Touch them, said the silent voice, and Sarah held out her arms as the drones and the connection came and opened the first cylinder and let her hold the child. It was so small, Sarah thought, but she knew it would survive. She checked beneath the swaddling. A boy. With translucent gray skin over almost human features. A thin halo of fine white hair. And eyes that could swallow the night.

Sarah turned to the creatures who crowded around her, watching with expressionless black eyes as they noted every move, every gesture, every touch. Waiting expectantly.

"Charles Edward," Sarah announced to them, holding the child to her chest and wrapping him in the warmth of her arms, the love of her heart. "His name shall be Charles Edward. And he shall know the truth." And it was so noted.

She stayed in the *kohanga reo* for an hour this time, each child given his or her time in Sarah's arms. Each child named and dedicated, and each name and dedication noted. And when she was finished and the incubator cylinders sealed again, Sarah looked out over them. She smiled at their small gray faces, their tiny dark eyes combining the two worlds that had brought them into being. Her heart felt calm that they were safely protected beneath their curved and gleaming clear coverings. And she found herself thinking of Christmas, of reflections within ornaments, of love.

She felt a gentle tug on her slacks and looked down. One of the toddlers from the crèche, a little girl in a long tan dress with locks of star white hair, had escaped from a drone and was asking to be picked up. Sarah laughed and swept the child into her arms. The child returned the laugh, and Sarah saw that the toddler hadn't escaped—she had been brought. There were twenty children gathering around her at the incubator stall. Twenty pairs of fathomless black eyes, twenty pairs of gray reaching hands, hungry for sensation and attention.

Sarah smiled as she looked out at them. She glanced at the drones, the connection, and the slights. She saw the one who stood beside her. All the creatures waited well back from her. All the creatures sucked in their lip flaps and held them in a smile.

Sarah laughed again, and the children laughed with her, reaching for her, touching her, calling for her with both sound and silence. She radiated her love to the light that teaches. She gathered the children to her with the love that nurtures. And never in her entire life had she felt such peace and such calm and such happiness.

All her precious babies had been found.

12

SATURDAY, JULY 21, 01:10 PDT

"I said I'd never eat another one of these things for the rest of my life," Fisher sighed, then sank her teeth into a Big Mac.

Reese smiled and snapped the lid off his coffee, leaning to the right as Steven sat down in the attached chair beside him. Wendy slipped in beside Fisher on the green banquette. Her hair was still standing up on the side where she had been sleeping on it just before Charles Edward Starr had arrived at the safe house. Reese blew across the surface of his coffee, sending away the tiny whorl of white vapor. No house was safe any longer, but for now, the restaurant was brilliantly lit and packed with diners. For now, the four of them could relax.

"Is this open all night?" Wendy asked. She popped the clear plastic cover from a container and then proceeded to cover her low-calorie salad with two packets of thick dressing.

Fisher said, "Yes," around a mouthful of fries, and Steven added, "But she said it shouldn't take that long."

"Good," Reese said. He looked over by the main doors where a table of teenagers pushed all their litter onto one tray and stood up to leave. He wondered what the restaurant would look like at two in the morning. At three.

"How many witnesses are too many?" Fisher asked, studying Reese as he watched the customers leave.

Reese shook his head. "If the OCI comes after us again, there won't be any witnesses."

"Isn't that encouraging," Steven muttered.

"But I can't see them taking out a restaurant. At least, not in their own country," Reese concluded.

"And Starr's pals will probably wait until we're alone again," Fisher said. She slurped on a milk shake.

"You really think they can track us anywhere?" Wendy asked. She toyed with her salad with a white plastic fork and kept glancing at Reese.

"That's what the books said," Fisher answered. "A lot of the abductees report having something implanted in their nostrils or in their ears or directly into their brains. Could be some sort of locating beacon, I suppose. Or a communications device. Though I don't know how many of Starr's conclusions we can accept now, knowing who he was working for."

"OCI or Starr's aliens," Reese said, "both groups have secrets. As long as we stay close to a lot of people, we'll be safe."

Steven looked around the restaurant. "They all have to go home sometime." They ate the rest of their meal in silence.

An hour later, there were only twelve other people in the restaurant. Reese was on his third coffee, Wendy on her fourth diet soda, and Fisher on her second Big Mac. Reese thought it somehow amusing that their continued freedom might depend on how stringently the management was prepared to enforce the twenty-minutes-per-table regulation posted on signs on three walls.

A white van pulled up outside the restaurant, stopping in front of the main doors instead of moving through to the parking lot or the pickup window. Reese put his coffee down. "Is this it?" he asked Steven.

Steven shifted to look past an obstructing pillar. "She didn't say."

Reese studied the vehicle. It was a large, blocky Vandura with no side windows. On its front door was a line of type which Reese couldn't read at that distance and a small symbol which he didn't recognize. They were the van's only markings. But on the roof, a white pod five feet long and three feet high had been added. It was smoothly contoured and gave no clue as to its purpose. Reese didn't like the look of it. He sat up straight in his chair and placed his right hand on the table, close to his holster beneath his jacket.

The driver of the van came into the restaurant. He was a young man, perhaps twenty, with wildly scattered brown hair, loud knee-length shorts, and a T-shirt that showed two blue whales swimming in front of a mushroom cloud. The shirt read "Nuke the Whales." Reese moved his hand away from his gun. The young man's clothes were worthy of an OCI operation—give witnesses too many details to focus on and they'd neglect to see an assassin's face—but the driver was too young to be a domestic operative. Though Reese did start to wonder at what age Starr had been recruited by the aliens.

The young man stood to the side of the main doors and looked over the people still in the restaurant. When his eyes met Reese's, the man smiled, gave a gangly wave, and walked over to the table with long strides and a pronounced bounce to his steps.

"You've got to be Derek Reese," the young man said, smiling widely, extending his hand. "I'm Miles Hirschhorn." Miles took in everyone's tight expressions and Reese's penetrating stare. "Ah, Margot sent me?" he tried.

"Why?" Steven asked.

Miles looked around at the others in the restaurant and grimaced. Then he held up his hand as though giving a stop signal and spread his fingers, two to a side. "Nanu nanu?" he said.

Reese stood up and told the others to follow. If there was one thing Charles Edward Starr hadn't had, it had been a sense of humor.

Wendy rocked back and forth in the van's passenger compartment as Reese, out of sight and out of touch, drove the vehicle. Miles had complained about the university's insurance regulations, but Reese hadn't even argued. He asked where Miles wanted to take them and then drove in the opposite direction like a race-car driver along a circuitous route. Twice in two days he's taken me for a ride like this, Wendy thought. But at least this time the lights are on and nobody has a gun. Except for Reese.

Wendy and her father sat on a narrow bench which ran down one side of the compartment. Across from them was a counter topped by an empty series of different-sized wooden cubbyholes.

Fisher and Miles sat at the front of the compartment in backward-facing jump seats. Wendy watched as the reporter ran her hand over the material with which the compartment was lined. It was soft and spongy but definitely made of metal. Like a coarse fabric or a fine screen, Wendy thought, covering everything from ceiling to floor to doors. Here and there where the overhead lights reflected against it, she could see something like silver foil gleaming beneath the layers of mesh.

"What is this stuff?" Merril asked.

Miles reached into his back pocket and pulled out a small yellow pocket radio tangled up in earphone wire. He unwound the wire, held the earphones out to Merril, and gave her the radio. "Try to get a station," he said.

Merril put the earphones on and fiddled with the radio tuning control for a minute, then shook her head. "There's not even very much static," she said.

"And all that static is produced by the radio itself," Miles said with pride. He swept his arms around him. "This is a Tempest cage. Completely impenetrable to virtually all electromagnetic radiation."

"Why?" Fisher asked.

"The Tempest projects," Miles said as though he were explaining which way was up. "Almost everything that uses electricity produces an electromagnetic signal. Like radio waves. And if you're using your computer, then somebody down the street can use a sensitive antenna to pick up the signal produced by your internal circuitry as it operates and by your display screen as it presents information."

"So?" Fisher said.

"So what if you're using your computer in the Pentagon?" Miles said, eyes wide. "Espionage. Computer theft. Spies wouldn't have to connect anything physical to a computer system to break in; they could just eavesdrop from a distance."

"I get it," Merril concluded. "Unless the computer is used in a Tempest cage."

"Well, no," Miles said with a frown. "That gets hugely expensive. So what you do is just build a small, cheap Tempest shield into the computers themselves. Then you can carry them around, use them anywhere, and you're safe from prying antennae."

"Then why do you have such a big one?" Merril asked, suddenly grabbing on to Miles as the van made a ninety-degree turn without slowing down.

"You know about the big one?" he asked, disappointed.

"We're sitting in it, aren't we?"

"Oh, this one," Miles said, happy again. "Naw, this was built for an experiment that didn't work out."

"For the Pentagon?" Merril asked.

"Give me a break," Miles protested. "Do I look like Dr. Strangelove?"

Merril looked at Wendy and crossed her eyes. She turned back to Miles. "Let's try this again. What do you use this van for?"

"You mean, what do we use the van for while it's Tempest-shielded?"

"Close enough," Merril agreed, nodding her head patiently.

"ESP experiments," Miles said. "Remote viewing. That sort of thing."

"Our tax dollars at work," Steven muttered.

"Oh, the experiments didn't work," Miles said happily. "After all, there's no such thing as ESP. But the experiments sure made last summer a lot more interesting than this summer."

Merril smiled at Miles. "You sound reasonably sane for a university student. So tell me, did Dr. Jeffery explain why it was we needed to be picked up in a MacDonald's at two o'clock in the morning?"

Miles laughed. "Of course she did. That's why I brought the van."

"Humor me," Merril said. "What exactly did Dr. Jeffery tell you?"

"That Wendy here might have been abducted by nonhumans in something that might have been a UFO and that she or Derek up front might have been implanted with some sort of transponder that gives away their location and makes them vulnerable to being found and picked up again." His tone was so neutral that he might just as well have been reciting the instructions for changing a light bulb.

"So," Merril said, "you discount ESP, yet you're willing to accept a UFO abductee story. How come?"

Miles laughed again. Wendy thought it was nice to see someone enjoying himself, even though she didn't know what to make of him exactly.

"Let me put it this way, ah, Merril, right?" Miles said, and

Fisher nodded. "It's summertime. I'm a student. And the prof who hired me to mince up frozen rat brains in an industrial-strength food processor for six bucks an hour says I can still get paid for helping out his friend and mine—Margot Jeffery—in her little thought experiment for a week or two." He put his hand meaningfully on Merril's arm. "Do you have any idea what it's like to spend an entire summer chopping up frozen rat brains?"

"As a matter of fact," Merril said, "I think I had a job like that once."

"Summer jobs notwithstanding," Wendy's father interrupted, "the idea behind this Tempest thing is that if Wendy does have one of those transponders in her, then she won't be transmitting anything through the van walls, right?"

"Essentially," Miles replied. "Though given the size that Margot said the device might be, it's unlikely that they contain a power supply that would let them generate any kind of signal on their own. It's probably more likely that the UFOs send out something like a radar signal and wait for a reflection. Either way, you know, in or out, no signal is likely to get through the mesh and screens and counterphase signals the generator up top puts out."

"How about Derek?" Steven asked. "Is he protected?"

"No," Miles said. "I told him that, but he insisted on driving so he could watch out for following cars. Like, I'm not going to arm-wrestle the guy, you know?"

"So they could still know where we are?" Steven said.

"Well, Derek said he'd drive around for an hour or so to make sure we weren't being followed, then he'd get back here and let me drive us back to campus."

Wendy saw her father relax. Then Miles added, "And you know, that's another reason I told Margot I'd help her out. I mean, it does seem pretty silly that UFOs would be tracking you guys down by having someone follow you in *cars.*" Miles smiled. "I know you're probably not allowed to tell me or anything, but whatever it is you guys are mixed up in, I bet it's a lot more interesting than any flaky stuff like UFO abductions."

Merril laughed. She howled. And Wendy and her father didn't let her laugh alone.

SATURDAY, JULY 21, 06:45 PDT

Ed Gardiner and Roy Luck waited well back from the shattered ruins of the tiny bungalow in Pasadena. A Strategic and Tactical Nuclear Arms Pursuit Network team from Edwards Air Force Base moved through its charred timbers. Encased in formless white environmental suits, the team members' faces were invisible behind the silvered faceplates of their helmets. As they waved about their slender detectors and sensors amid the tendrils of smoke drifting up from the still-smouldering debris, they cast solid shadows in the blood-red sunrise.

After half an hour, the four members of the team worked to clear a small area near the center of the destruction and placed a long yellow pole in the ground. Three members then proceeded to attach blue cords to the pole and string them to other areas corresponding to the outer limits of the house when it had been whole. Gardiner watched them work in silence, all their comments transmitted by their suits' radios.

Eventually, when it appeared that a blue spider's web had been spun across the wreckage, the team leader, identifiable by the red stripes on his arms, legs, and life-support backpack, left the house and walked over to Luck and Gardiner. As he approached, he pulled two tabs on his helmet and removed it. The team leader's hair was almost nonexistent, ravaged by a precise military trim, and his face was too young, Gardiner thought, too earnest.

The leader turned to Luck. "The site is clear, sir. Totally SNAP white."

Luck gestured at the three white-suited men still moving in the ruins. "If there's no radiation, Lieutenant, then why are your people still in their helmets?"

"Smoke, sir," the lieutenant said.

Luck pointed to the man's chemical sniffer, a long metal tube with a small fan housing near the top, connected to a thick black box with telltale lights strapped to his forearm. "So what's the signature? TNT, nitro, plastique?"

"There is no signature, sir," the young man said. Some of the military edge had gone from his voice.

Luck smiled, tight-lipped. "The house just blew up by itself?"

"No, sir," the lieutenant said. "We located the blast point. It was a device, sir."

"But not nuclear?"

"No, sir."

"And not chemical?"

"No, sir."

Luck spoke very slowly. "What else is left, Lieutenant?"

"Mechanical stress, sir. Explosive decompression. Earthquake. Meteor strike—"

"I'm not interested in having you recite the manual!" Luck leaned into the young man's face. "You said it was a *device*. I want to know what *kind* of device it was, understand?"

"Yes, sir," the lieutenant said crisply.

"Then let's start at the beginning. What was the shape of the device, Lieutenant?"

"Blast pattern indicates a spherical charge, sir."

"And what was the size of the device?" Luck smiled again. "Approximately."

"Physical dimensions or explosive force, sir?"

"Both," Luck said.

The lieutenant looked at Gardiner as if he wanted to ask for help. "The approximate physical dimensions of the device cannot be estimated because it is below the recording threshold"— he swallowed—"sir."

Luck exhaled in surprise. "What is the recording threshold these days, Lieutenant?" He wasn't as harsh with this question.

"Volume of approximately two hundred milliliters, sir."

Luck looked over at what was left of the house. "A baseball," he said softly. "You're telling me that whatever blew that house to kindling, sent a blue fireball five hundred feet into the air, was the size of a *baseball?*"

"N-not necessarily, sir," the lieutenant stammered. "It could have been smaller." He looked away from the shocked expression on Luck's face.

"Okay, okay," Luck said to the lieutenant, "it's not your fault. Any estimate on the explosive force?" He kicked at a roof shingle lying next to his foot. "That *has* to be over the recording threshold, right?"

The lieutenant looked like he had been suddenly stricken with stomach flu.

"You *have* calculated the force required to destroy this structure, haven't you?" Luck demanded. "You can look it up in your goddam SNAP manual, can't you?"

The lieutenant shook his head. Luck was ready to explode himself.

"What seems to be the problem, son?" Gardiner asked, interceding.

The lieutenant turned to Gardiner gratefully. "The blast effects are not consistent, sir," he said. "The structure is completely destroyed, indicating a force-five detonation. However, we estimate that half the mass of the house structure itself has come down outside a half-mile radius of the blast, indicating a force-eight detonation." He took a deep breath and glanced back to Luck. "But, sirs, there is *no* apparent blast damage outside of a one-hundred-foot radius of the blast point. The neighboring houses' windows aren't even blown out. That makes it less than a force-point-one detonation. I've never heard of a charge being that directed. I didn't think it was possible except in a vacuum."

Luck stared blankly at the young Air Force officer, then waved his hand in dismissal and stormed away.

"Continue making your measurements," Gardiner told the lieutenant. "Whatever ones you can make." Then he followed Luck down the evacuated street.

"This shit goes way past the Laurel field that melted Vincent's gun," Luck said when Gardiner had reached him. The OCI agent stopped in the middle of the deserted street and examined the house next to the remains of the bungalow. "Not one goddam window gone," he said.

Gardiner looked down the street and saw the barricade the police had erected. A crowd of people waited, most of them the owners of the evacuated homes. Overhead in the distance, three helicopters kept the area sealed off to air traffic as well.

"Too bad Reese wasn't in it when it went," Luck sighed. "Make it all a lot easier."

"At least the eyewitnesses who saw Reese running down the road agreed that he was with two more people in addition to the reporter. Harder to hide four people than one," Gardiner said. "Maybe the two new ones are involved."

"We've got to push North harder," Luck said.

"Have conditions changed that much?" Gardiner asked.

"Look at the goddam house, Ed." Luck pointed angrily

down the road. "Something the size of a baseball did that! Something that left no chemical signature. That puts it beyond the capabilities of our bomb detectors and chemical sniffers." He turned to Gardiner with something close to fear in his eyes. Gardiner liked the look of it.

"What happens if Reese is involved in a *two-way* smuggling operation? It's one thing if he's sending restricted computer parts out, but what if he's helping get this kind of shit *in?* What would happen if terrorists put it into aircraft? Public buildings? We couldn't find bombs made with this stuff. It's a nightmare."

"How much harder *can* you push North?" Gardiner asked. He just didn't believe that a method couldn't be developed to detect the explosive that had destroyed Reese's safe house. No matter who the MOST SECRET report had said he was working for. "He's cooperating with us down the line. He just doesn't know anything."

"Or just *thinks* he doesn't know anything." Luck watched as a gas-company leak-detection van rolled slowly down the street. Gardiner realized the cover story had already been decided upon. "Chemical interrogation," Luck said. "It's time we pulled out everything."

"Cy deserves better than that," Gardiner said.

"I'll put it in your hands, then," Luck said unexpectedly. "Use the bureau's own staff. Who's that doctor—Perez?"

"Maria Perez," Gardiner said. He kept his expression blank, hiding the alarm he felt at the way Luck had said Maria's name. The OCI agent knew her name as well as Gardiner did. So why had he made a point of groping for it?

"That's her," Luck agreed. "Put her in charge. Use the standard protocols. Concentrate on what happened the night Reese and the reporter crawled through the parking garage utility tunnel and went visiting in North's apartment. If you have to, go back to the night at the beach house too."

"Why are you so eager to trust the bureau again, Roy?" Gardiner didn't like it.

"Hey, Ed. We're on the same side, remember? North's one of your people, and you could probably delay things if you made me go through channels for chemical interrogation. So, do your stuff. Take control so you know nothing bad will happen to the guy."

Gardiner felt even more alarmed at Luck's offer of control.

What was behind it? Luck put his hand on Gardiner's shoulder.

"Look, Ed. You know I don't like you, and I know you don't like me. But we both saw that house. We both saw the photographs. And we both read the report from the NRO." He met Gardiner's eyes, no smile now. "We both know what we have to do."

"Okay," Gardiner said, stepping back so his shoulder would be out of reach. "But I'm in it until the end, and I want a written guarantee from the director stating that I will continue in my present position with the bureau when the investigation is closed." Gardiner wondered if Luck would see that demand for the test that it was. After being tainted by being suspected of being in collusion with Vincent, North, and Reese, Gardiner knew there was no possible way the bureau would let him remain as a Special Agent in Charge.

But Roy Luck smiled. "Sure," he said. "I can arrange that. Whatever you want, Ed. Whatever you want."

Gardiner nodded his thanks and walked away, back to his car and OCI driver. *Whatever you want*, he thought, just what Luck had said to North when he had promised the man everything in exchange for cooperation. And now Luck was preparing to disassemble North's mind with drugs. Whatever you want, Gardiner thought, the same promise for cooperation now made to him.

Gardiner picked up his pace. There wasn't much time left.

13

MONDAY, JULY 23, 14:00 PDT

Technically, it was called the Experimental Facility for the Testing of Remote Viewing in the Absence of Detectable Electromagnetic Radiation. In practice, the staff referred to it as "the Darth Vader Honeymoon Suite." But whichever name was used, after only three days of living in the facility, Wendy hated it. It was as horrible as she imagined a prison cell would be. And she had never known that people could be so . . . well, smelly.

The facility was located in the second basement of the auxiliary psyche building on the UCLA campus. Miles had been able to drive the Tempest van down a ramp beneath the building and back up directly against a shielded canopy. The canopy was the entrance to a low-ceilinged narrow passageway which was lined with mesh and foil and which twisted back and forth eight times before opening onto the suite. Miles had called the passage "a wave baffle."

When Wendy had stepped out of the passageway into the main suite, she had immediately understood how it got its funny name. Against the far wall was a big bed—she had felt a momentary rush of excitement when she thought that maybe just she and Derek would be staying there—and beside it two columns of electronic equipment the size of large filing cabinets from which snaked two thick black cables ending in all sorts of multicolored wires. Someone had carefully draped the cables across the bed's pillows like sprays of high-tech flowers.

Above the bed was a wooden track which had a video camera mounted on it, pointed down. There were a number of old wooden chairs, two battered wooden desks, and a portable blackboard pushed off to the side, and the walls, the entire ceiling, and the floor were covered in layers of the Tempest mesh. At the time, Wendy had thought it looked depressingly grim, but when she had realized that the odd jog in the corner farthest from the bed hid a chemical toilet, she had known she was not going to enjoy the next few days. And she hadn't.

That first night, Miles had helped them split the big bed into mattress and box springs. Late the next afternoon, he had returned with camp cots and food and a few boxes of items he claimed to have "borrowed" from some offices closed for the summer. Wendy had been especially grateful for the cassette player and kept it going almost all the time, next to the awful toilet.

Early Saturday evening, a short bald man with a black-and-white beard had come to visit. He wore a short-sleeved white shirt with a dark blue tie, neatly pressed blue trousers, and a pair of beat-up leather sandals that Wendy thought could be twenty years old. The man, whom Miles had introduced as Professor Earl Lurie, had brought that day's newspapers. They all carried the story of the house exploding in Pasadena the night before. A gas explosion, the newspapers had called it.

Professor Lurie said he had driven by the house that afternoon with a Dr. Rachel Zeifman from the physics department, and everyone was in agreement: it was time to take Margot's thought experiment a little more seriously.

Margot finally arrived Monday afternoon. "My God," she said as she emerged from the wave baffle and looked around the Tempest facility, "I used to go to a summer camp that looked like this."

Wendy had been reading a newspaper on her cot when she heard the psychologist's voice. Immediately she jumped up, ran over to the woman, and hugged her.

"It's been kind of tough, hasn't it, Wendy?" Jeffery said, putting down her small brown canvas satchel. Then Jeffery stepped back and shook Steven's hand as he introduced Reese and

Fisher. Lurie followed with introductions to Miles and Dr. Zeifman.

"Call me Rachel," the young physicist said, lifting the paper plate stacked with celery and carrot sticks from her lap as she stood to take Jeffery's hand. Her brown eyes crinkled with such a warm and friendly smile that Wendy thought that the two women might have been sisters. Except that Margot's hair was straight and light brown and Rachel's hung around her face and shoulders in a thick halo of dark curls.

Then Jeffery looked over to read what had been written on the chalkboard in Dr. Zeifman's small, precise printing. "Interesting," she concluded. "Is this as far as you've gotten?"

Professor Lurie chuckled. "That's a substantial amount of work considering that if anyone finds out what we're doing down here I might have my tenure revoked. May I fix you a sandwich?"

Jeffery went back to the cluttered desk and lifted some lids from the anonymous plastic containers mixed in among plastic bags full of bagels, pretzels, and jelly beans, a crusty jar of brilliantly yellow mustard, some exploded bags of potato chips, and a messy stack of paper plates, napkins, and plastic forks and knives. "I think I had something like this on the plane, Earl. But thanks anyway," she said. "Any coffee?"

Miles filled a plastic Disneyland mug with coffee from a laboratory Dewar flask and passed it over to Jeffery as she went back to the blackboard. "You really think you'd get into trouble for this?" she asked.

Lurie went to stand beside her. "As long as we keep it informal, probably not," he conceded. "Though right now my department head thinks that we're dabbling in some more ESP experiments on our own time."

Jeffery turned to the biologist. "So you haven't told anyone what this is really about?

"We're following the rules you set up for us exactly," Zeifman said happily, gesturing with her stick of celery. "The basic assumptions are that the nonhuman visitors are real, the abductions are real, and some humans are in league with them. Based on those givens, and without further data concerning how the collaborating humans are selected, we concluded that no one can be trusted. Therefore, Miles and Earl have spread the story that we're conducting more ESP tests."

"Can't trust anyone, hmm?" Jeffery nodded. "I hadn't taken it that far. Good thought."

Fisher walked over to Jeffery then, and Wendy knew what the reporter was going to say. She had been saying it four times a day since they all had arrived. "Here's another thing they've taken too far," Fisher said, scowling. "Steven and I have never been abducted, so we could never have been tagged with one of those transponders, but your pals still won't let us out of this room."

Jeffery turned to Lurie. "What's the point in that, Earl? We're only supposed to be shielding Wendy and Derek."

Lurie shrugged. "Well, we're trying to play by the rules after all. Since you told us that abductions are hidden from the abductees by giving them screen memories, just because Merril and Steven don't recall being abducted is no reason to accept that they haven't been, especially since we've been told to accept that the nonhumans have invaded Steven's home several times in the past and that Merril has been present when they've been present. Logically, we must assume that they also might have been tagged."

"But by that reasoning," Jeffery complained, "I might have been tagged, or any of you."

"Certainly a possibility under the conditions you laid out for us," Lurie agreed, "but there's no reason why the nonhumans would then connect us with Wendy and Derek. If any of us have been abducted and tagged, then we're in no more and no greater risk than we were before you set this up."

Jeffery sipped her coffee and smiled at Wendy. "So, other than the space academy brain trust here thinking you to death, how's everyone feeling?"

"Scared," Wendy said.

"Angry," Steven said. "And, to be honest, Doctor, I'm very worried about Sarah."

Jeffery nodded. "I can understand that, Steven. I am too. How about you, Derek?"

Reese rubbed at his forehead. "With all respect to your friends, I don't think this is getting us anywhere. We've got to do something."

"Do something?" Zeifman repeated, drawing her eyebrows together. "Earl, you told me this was simply an informal role-playing symposium to set up a formal system for questioning people who report an abduction experience and seek out psychiatric help. I thought we were helping Dr. Jeffery *treat* her patients, not humor them."

Professor Lurie steepled his hands over his mouth and nose and nodded. "I agree with you, Doctor. But—I also agree with Margot."

Zeifman shook her head, then brushed some fallen curls from her eyes. "Uh-uh, Earl. You can't have it both ways. Either this is just a session like we had last year when we had that conference to develop cultural standards for life in an orbiting space colony—an interesting thought experiment and nothing more—or else you're . . . brain-damaged."

Wendy felt hurt and disappointed. "Dr. Zeifman, you mean you don't believe us? You don't believe what happened to me? To Derek?"

Zeifman shook her head. "Wendy, you're a sweet kid, but I guarantee you weren't abducted by aliens or nonhuman visitors or whatever you want to call them. It's just not so."

There was a bang as Steven swiped a stack of books off his cot and sat down on it. "What the hell are we doing here, then? What does it take to make you people believe us? What does it take to get you to help bring Sarah back?" Wendy had never thought her father could look so defeated.

"Proof, Steven," Zeifman said. "That's all anyone ever needs to take anything seriously."

"Oh, God," Steven moaned. "My business is on hold because I'm not allowed to have a telephone wire come in here. I've got a good friend back in New York in the hospital after fighting it out with the creatures, and I can't get any word on how he's doing. How much more serious do you want it to get?"

"Photographs would be a start," Zeifman said.

"We've *got* photographs," Fisher answered. "I took them."

"No, Merril," Zeifman corrected. "*You* don't have the photographs. An unknown government agency has the photographs. Are we ever going to see them, or is this the same agency that supposedly has had the bodies of a flying saucer crew on ice since 1947?"

"But we've *seen* them," Wendy said, filled with frustration. "I'm not lying! Give me a lie-detector test and I'll show you I'm not lying! That's proof!"

Lurie shook his head slowly. "Sorry, Wendy, but as I'm sure Margot can explain, a lie-detector test can only give an indication of whether or not the person being questioned believes his answers or not. It has nothing at all to do with what's true and what isn't true."

Zeifman sat back in her chair. "That's my point, Wendy. I can't argue with you about what you believe happened to you, but what you believe and what really happened can be two different things. Count on it."

Jeffery pulled a chair over to Zeifman and sat down across from her. "What would it take for you to believe that Wendy's nonhuman abductors are real? If we could get the photographs?"

Zeifman took a deep breath, considered the question, then shook her head. "Photographs can be faked. Especially if they've gone through any sort of enhancement process and are digitized. Not photos."

"How about one of the visitor's probes, then?" Jeffery tried. "Or something from their vehicles? An artifact of some kind?"

Another pause while Zeifman thought it through. "Not even that."

"Even if it was something that we couldn't duplicate? Something we had no idea of how to make?"

"One artifact, no matter how puzzling, wouldn't be enough to cause the kind of complete paradigm shift that acknowledging nonhuman intelligence would cause." Zeifman held up her hand to cut off Jeffery's protest. "If you show me a probe or an alien version of a Mickey Mouse watch that runs on solar power with an efficiency of, let's say, 80 percent, way more than we can manage right now, and maybe the metals in it have higher than earth-normal levels of iridium, and maybe it has, I don't know, complex monomolecular light guides that look like computer circuitry—you show me something like that and I'm still going to think that a clever undergraduate like Miles over there, raised on *Star Wars* and *E.T.*, has come up with a pretty good hoax. That's a lot simpler explanation than it being a product of nonhuman technology."

"Then what would it take?" Jeffery asked. "Carl Sagan making an announcement on television?"

"I know Carl," Zeifman said. "And he's a great guy. But if I saw him get on television and say that all these stories about aliens abducting our children were true, I'd just go, 'Poor, Carl. Brain damage.' "

Jeffery shook her head. "So you've just closed off your mind to the possibility. No matter how many sightings, no matter how many stories, no matter how many patients I get coming to me, desperately frightened by terrifying glimpses of memories that have been blocked, you will not even admit the possibility that some truth underlies it all. I find that sad, Doctor."

"Quantity of data is no substitute for quality, Doctor," Zeifman replied. Her tone was getting progressively more abrupt. "Of course, I will accept the *possibility* that there is some truth behind the stories. Why not? But I must also accept the cold, hard fact that I live in a world where little children see Santa Claus on Christmas Eve, where Catholic-school girls see the Virgin Mary on a hilltop, and where grown men and women see Elvis Presley in supermarkets and restaurants. Human beings have a long history of being able to see exactly what they want to see, Dr. Jeffery. And you can't deny that in addition to Santa and God and Elvis, there are a lot of us who would dearly love to see an alien spaceship."

"Would you like to see one?" Jeffery asked.

"What scientist wouldn't?" Zeifman said. "What a wonderful, thrilling thing that would be. And that's what it would take for me. The day you show me an alien spaceship, a huge mass of metal and machinery that couldn't possibly have been made in somebody's garage, the day you get one of those aliens with the big heads and big eyes to walk up to me and shake my hand and let Earl take a sample of its blood, that's the day I'll accept the data. But until then, the aliens are going to have to wait in line with Santa and Elvis." She shrugged. "Sorry."

In the silence that followed, Wendy felt herself become more and more furious. She couldn't believe the way Dr. Zeifman had just spoken, as if she, Wendy, were crazy, along with Derek and Merril and her father too. Wendy wanted to cry. And more than that, she suddenly realized, she wanted her mother. Because if what Zeifman said were true, that everything up to now had been some symptom of Wendy's deranged mind, then Wendy knew there was no other clue to her mother's disappearance. Sarah Gilmour was simply and forever gone. Without hope. And then Miles Hirschhorn spoke.

"Dr. Zeifman," the student began, ineffectually patting down his wiry hair with both hands, "are you serious about that?"

"About what, Miles?"

"About wanting to see a spaceship? An alien?"

Zeifman nodded. "Certainly. I think it would be very exciting. I think it would be exciting to work on Space Station, too. But I don't think either eventuality is very likely."

"Not likely," Miles agreed, "but you did say there was a possibility, didn't you?"

"Yesss," Zeifman said cautiously. "What's your point, Miles?"

"It seems that we might be the first people to be in a situation to conduct an experiment with UFOs. Not a thought experiment, but a real experiment. Nuts and bolts. Falsifiable."

Zeifman narrowed her eyes suspiciously. "And what would be the point of such an experiment?"

"To get you your spaceship," Miles said with an excited grin, "and Mr. Gilmour's wife."

Zeifman sighed. She had set the trap herself. "Go ahead, Miles. Tell me all about it."

And he did.

MONDAY, JULY 23, 16:30 PDT

"I hope I'm interrupting something," Roy Luck said as he swung open the door to Maria Perez's office.

Ed Gardiner stood up awkwardly from where he had been sitting on Maria's desk. Maria stepped back and turned to Luck. Gardiner's hand held hers for only an instant more, and then they were apart, nothing more than the professional co-workers they had been for years.

"You said you were going to wait for the doctor's report, Roy," Gardiner said, then watched as Luck made sure the door was closed behind him. He's in the basement of the FBI building, Gardiner thought, and he's still acting like enemies might be anywhere.

"Apparently there's some concern at the NRO," Luck said. "Tucker tells me they want to know what we're doing to track down the source of those . . . photographs. As Tucker says, we're under the gun, so to speak."

"I'm getting the feeling you're back to not trusting me again, Roy," Gardiner said. As if, he thought, I had ever believed you had changed.

Luck grinned, gesturing with empty hands. "Hey, Ed, I took

you out from surveillance, didn't I? You don't have one of my guys driving you around anymore, do you?"

Gardiner shook his head, knowing full well that Luck had simply substituted a more subtle form of surveillance. Gardiner had not been able to detect anyone following him for the past three days since the safe-house explosion. He had not discovered any hidden observers waiting for him in the shadows either at his house or at Maria's apartment. But that didn't mean that the watchers weren't there. Somehow or another, Gardiner knew, the OCI was still watching him.

"Fine," Luck said, taking Gardiner's silence for agreement. "What did you get out of the prisoner, Doctor?"

"Cy is not a prisoner," Gardiner said, not bothering to hide his indignation. He saw Luck and Perez exchange a quick glance, but couldn't read what had passed between them.

"Sorry," Luck said. "What additional details was Cy able to recall about Reese and the reporter?" He looked over at Gardiner. "Better?"

Perez sat down behind her desk and opened a red file folder. She tightened her mouth as she looked at Gardiner, then gave her report to Luck.

"Essentially, Cy had very little more to tell us," Perez said. "He confessed to harboring a deep fear of a bright light which he claims blinded him on the night Reese disappeared from the beach house. That's apparently why he puts foil on—"

"Does he remember getting out of the surveillance van that night?" Luck broke in.

"No," Perez said, checking her notes. "He only remembers sitting at the console with David. Then he was blinded by a bright light. Maybe a stun grenade? And when the light faded, he was in the ambulance. There's nothing in between for him to remember. He must have been right out of it the whole time."

"And Vincent wasn't," Luck said, shaking his head. "How about anything from the night Reese came to his apartment?"

"Again, he told us just about everything the first time he was questioned. I have no sense that he's trying to hide anything from us. However, with the drugs, he did recall that the reporter asked Reese if Reese knew about any safe houses in Mexico."

"What did Reese say?"

"That they'd talk about it when they left." Perez squinted at her notes. "Oh, and Cy said also that Reese knew about the bright light too. He knew about the foil." She shrugged.

"Mexico would be a bad bet," Luck said. "They'd be too conspicuous."

"Could be a transfer point," Gardiner suggested. "That's probably where the plane came from to pick up the computer parts. Could be that's how they're getting the explosives in."

Luck beamed at Gardiner. "Why thank you, Ed. I see you're beginning to take this seriously after all." He turned back to Perez. "That's it?"

"One other thing. Pretty bizarre."

"What's that?"

"Reese and the reporter were all set to leave. And then Cy says they came back, sat down, and watched television with him."

Luck looked at Gardiner, open for suggestions, then asked, "Waiting for the surveillance team to switch shifts?"

"Why?" Gardiner said. "They already knew that the surveillance team didn't know about the parking garage tunnels they used to get into the building."

"So what did they watch?" Luck asked.

"The 'Tonight Show,' " Perez read. "The first part only. Cy says that's why they watched. They seemed interested in the man who was the first on the show. Then they left."

"Who was it?"

"Charles Edward Starr," Perez answered. She saw Luck shrug. "We're checking to see if the bureau has any paper on him. And we've got a couple of agents running him down through the show."

"Sounds like a long shot," Luck said.

"That's all we got," Perez replied, then shut the red file folder. "Want me to type up a report?"

"No," Luck said. "Is that it?" He got up from his chair.

"Would you like to know how Cy is after being injected with all that crud?" Gardiner asked bitterly.

Luck shook his head. "If he's given us all he has to give, there's not much point to it." He reached for the door.

"You're a goddam bastard," Gardiner said.

Luck turned away from the open door and nodded his head. "Then I hope you're thankful that we're on the same side, Ed. Because if I'm a goddam bastard now, just think what I'd be doing to you if we weren't on the same side." He walked out of

Perez's office. "Please, get back to what you were doing." He made sure the door was shut behind him.

Perez got up from behind her desk. She took Gardiner's hand, looked into his eyes. Gardiner thought of their dancing, of those few times they had had when they didn't have to think. He held her to him, arms crushing her against his chest, trying to lose himself within her.

"What happens when you want the important things to change?" he asked her, burying his face in her hair.

"Some things don't change because you can't change them," Maria answered. "No matter how much you want to."

Gardiner closed his eyes, and in his mind, he danced with her then, taking them both away from everything and everyone that stood between them. And as they danced, he ignored Maria's tears, because he feared he knew the reason why she cried. And the reason why he was no longer being followed by one of Roy Luck's men.

14

TUESDAY, JULY 24, 10:40 PDT

For the first time in four days, Derek Reese didn't mind that the Tempest facility was not allowed any electricity other than what batteries could provide. He didn't mind that they depended on Margot Jeffery's coworkers for hot food and water so that gas and water pipes wouldn't connect the interior of the room to the outside world. And he was almost able to tolerate the relentless compulsion he battled to sweep Wendy into his arms and run off with her. But four more days, he thought, as he cleaned his disassembled Beretta on the green blanket on his low camp cot. Four more days and it would all be over, one way or another. Despite his first feelings of misgivings, Reese found he had come to like Miles Hirschhorn. The kid knew how important it was to take action. And that's what he was planning to do.

"Okay," Miles called out from beside the blackboard. "Now we fill in the details." He wrote a large figure 1 on the board. "First postulate?" he asked enthusiastically.

Rachel Zeifman sighed. She looked over to Professor Lurie, then to Dr. Jeffery. "I don't believe you talked me into this," she said.

"It's an experiment," Miles reminded her. "We can even write it up if we want to."

"All right," Zeifman said. "Postulate number one: The aliens want Wendy and Derek." Reese smiled at the look of embarrassment that came over the physicist.

"Therefore . . . ?" Miles prompted, making the appropriate symbol with three dots in the shape of a triangle.

"Therefore, the aliens will try to . . . abduct Wendy and Derek when they are removed from the Tempest shield and their transponders signal their location." Zeifman spoke quickly.

"So what can we do to prove that this postulate is false?" Miles asked, obviously enjoying his new role as professor.

"Remove Wendy and Derek from the Tempest shield on Saturday morning and observe them." Zeifman shook her head.

"Yep," Miles agreed, writing on the board. "Sounds like an interesting weekend to me."

"And if Wendy and Derek get picked up on *Monday* morning?" Zeifman asked warily. "After we've all gone home?"

"Then I'll agree with you 100 percent, Dr. Zeifman," Miles said. "If they are always only being picked up where there are no witnesses, then the abduction experience is only subjective and can't be considered worthy of scientific analysis."

"Hold on," Wendy said, and Reese felt a sudden spark rush through him at the unexpected sound of her voice. He had to put the gun barrel down and hold his hands together for a moment, to stop their trembling.

"Does this mean that after Monday we're on our own?" Wendy asked.

Zeifman smiled and nodded her head.

"If they're in as much of a panic to get you two as you've told us," Miles answered, "it won't take until Monday." He wrote a figure 2 on the board and beside it added "Observation Protocols." "Next?" he asked cheerfully.

Professor Lurie held up his hand. "To determine those, I presume we'll have to establish how we expect the aliens might manifest themselves. Do the aliens have to take Wendy and Derek away physically, or is there a chance that the aliens might be able to do something from a distance that would satisfy their needs just as well but without necessarily revealing themselves to us? That could make a difference in what we might expect to observe."

Merril Fisher, who Reese had thought was asleep on her cot, suddenly spoke out. "Of course the aliens need to physically take Wendy and Derek. There's some sort of breeding program going on. Abductees have seen crossbred babies."

"Spare me," Zeifman muttered.

"You know, I've been thinking about that part of the story," Lurie said, scratching at his beard. "And if these creatures *are* involved in crossbreeding experiments with human beings, then we certainly can't call them aliens."

"Of course not, because there's no such thing!" Zeifman said.

"Sorry, Miles," Lurie said, standing and walking over to the board. "And sorry to you too, Rachel, but I do think this has a bearing on what we might expect to see in the desert."

The professor took the chalk from Miles. "Now the way I see it, we've got three possibilities for the nature of the nonhumans involved in these abductions," he said. "The first, which I'm sure none of us is willing to accept, is that they are supernatural creatures, such as the dwarfs and fairies that Merril was telling us about yesterday. The very definition of the supernatural places it outside the bounds of anything that science could or should examine." He drew a quick diagram on the board and jotted in a few key words. "So, we put the supernatural hypotheses into its own little refuse bin along with ghosts, Uri Geller, and creationism."

Lurie pointed the chalk at Zeifman. "Next, we have the extraterrestrial hypothesis. Now, Rachel, I know all of your arguments against it. Enrico Fermi"—he smiled at Merril—"a physicist, of course, was the one who said that if there were extraterrestrials, then where are they? The premise being that since humans had developed such advanced technology in such a short length of time, then surely alien cultures in advance of ours by thousands, perhaps millions, of years would have at least sent interstellar probes out to our solar system."

"I hate that argument," Miles said.

The student looked around sheepishly. "No one can tell me that North Americans comprehend the ethical systems that make Middle East extremists drive car bombs into buildings or even why Japanese and American business styles are so different. And we're all human cultures! So how can North American scientists have the arrogance to sit around and claim that they know what the motives of advanced, completely alien cultures might be?

"With all deference to Fermi, maybe Charles Edward Starr was told a half-truth when he said they didn't want to talk to us yet until we had developed into something worth talking to. Or maybe in their mythologies, having five fingers is a sign of the devil and they think we're a race of demons. Or it's unlucky to land on planets with more than 50 percent of their surfaces covered in water, or on third planets, or—Their reasoning would be *alien*. By definition, we will not understand them, and it's wrong to presume that they will think as we do." Miles shrugged and sat down.

"Well," Lurie said to Zeifman with a smile, "so much for Fermi. But in any event, the problem with extraterrestrials is that the distances between the stars are so great that, in all likelihood, organic life forms could never survive any voyage of more than a few parsecs. Machines, yes, but living things, no."

"Even if they're extremely technologically advanced?" Fisher asked, still lying back on her cot with her hands behind her head. "You know, like if they had space-warp drive and could travel faster than the speed of light?"

"The speed of light is the ultimate speed limit," Zeifman said. "There is nothing in modern physics to suggest that there could possibly be any way to travel at or above that speed. No matter how advanced a technology you propose, it's an absolute barrier. Like absolute zero."

"You're not convincing me," Fisher said. "I bet we wouldn't be able to even comprehend a technology more than a few hundred years ahead of ours. What if it were a thousand years ahead? Or a million?"

"Then I think we're back to the supernatural," Lurie said with a laugh. "But technology isn't the point here, Merril. If we're going to consider that the nonhumans on board the craft we're discussing have come here to conduct crossbreeding experiments, then they absolutely *can't* be aliens."

"Why not?" Wendy asked.

"Well, if we accept that living hybrid babies have been born, then that implies that at some level human DNA is compatible with the abducting creatures' DNA. And if it's compatible, then they're not nonhuman. By definition, they have to be humans themselves. Or a closely related life form. At least some type of higher primate."

"I don't get it," Wendy said. "Why can't they just use advanced technology to mix alien genes with human genes?"

"It's like the speed of light, Wendy," Professor Lurie explained. "An absolute barrier. Life first appeared on earth about three and a half billion years ago, maybe even earlier. But, by at least that time, there were single-celled life-forms living here, and they passed on genetic information from one generation to the next with genes made from DNA. So, for three and a half billion years, life has been evolving on earth, and when we say evolving, we might just as well say that life has been adjusting to various *specific* conditions on the planet in order to keep reproducing successfully. When plant life started polluting earth's early atmosphere with poisonous oxygen, a whole new group of life-forms appeared that could breathe that oxygen. Every living thing on this planet is related to every other living thing. And with the exception of a few viruses and viroids and borderline things that may or may not be classified as living, DNA operates in them all."

"Couldn't there be DNA on other planets?" Wendy asked.

"There could be," Lurie said gracefully, "but there could be no possible way that extraterrestrial DNA would share any similarities with earth DNA. It's mathematically impossible."

"Why?"

"The DNA in our cells is the end result of those billions of years of evolutionary changes right here on earth. And most of those changes were forced upon life by random processes, like the End Cretaceous Event."

"End what?" Fisher asked.

"The Cretaceous is the last geological epoch during which the dinosaurs thrived," Lurie said. "We live in the Quaternary epoch. The End Cretaceous Event is the incident that brought the age of the dinosaurs to an end. Many scientists these days accept that about sixty-five million years ago, a massive extraterrestrial object hit the earth and set in motion a chain of environmental upheavals that led to the extinction of the dinosaurs over a few hundred or few thousand years, freeing ecological niches for the development of mammals. The DNA in our cells today has been shaped by that impact. It's shaped by all the end events—the great dyings in the past. Including at least one when up to 96 percent of the world's species might have been wiped out catastrophically.

"If *one* species of vertebrate hadn't survived a catastrophe more than six hundred million years ago, there might be no creatures with backbones on this planet today. If the End Cretaceous Event had never occurred—if the comet or asteroid or whatever had missed the planet by fifty miles or twenty minutes

—then there would probably still be dinosaurs on earth and mammals like us would exist only as ratlike predators. Even if every star in this galaxy had a life-bearing planet like earth, and even if all that life was based on DNA, and even if evolution on *one* of those planets did, after the course of billions of years cause to appear a bipedal species with intelligence that lent itself to technology, their genetic code would not, could not, reflect the random events that have affected the course of life on earth."

Miles looked over at Wendy. "Cats and dogs come from the same planet, they share a common ancestor, but they can't interbreed. How could interbreeding possibly take place between species that share no common ancestors? Not even a common planet?"

Fisher sat up on the side of her cot. "What if the aliens seeded us on earth? I remember hearing about that theory. Maybe they came by when the planet was formed and put the kind of life-forms they have on their planet on earth. So we *would* be related to them."

Lurie smiled patiently. "There are a great many theories about that, Merril, but the fact remains that there are no indications that at any time has one form of life on earth been supplanted by a chemically or otherwise startlingly different form of life. I'm not talking species here; I'm talking general organizational principles. There are no significant fossil gaps in that regard. That means that if earth has been seeded by extraterrestrials, the seeding had to have taken place billions of years ago with single-celled life-forms. That might give us an incredibly distant common ancestor, but we'd have no more chance of interbreeding with those aliens today than an amoeba could crossbreed with an elephant."

Steven stood up and walked over to the food desk. Reese saw that he had a haunted look on his face. "What you seem to be getting to is that these creatures are human. Pardon me, but that seems impossible. They don't look at all human."

Lurie shook his head. "What would you say is the way humans look, Steven? Do humans look seven feet tall, covered with black skin, like members of the Watusi in Africa? Or do humans look like Miles? Or like Innu? Or like you? Our species has a remarkable range of adaptation."

"No, no," Steven said. "These creatures have different eyes, three fingers instead of four, no lips, no nose, and . . . they even smell different."

"Time travelers?" Miles suggested. "A future version of humans?"

"Not much evolutionary pressure on us anymore to account for those kinds of changes," Lurie said thoughtfully.

"Genetic engineering?" Miles continued. "Artificially produced subspecies. Derek did say the different types had different functions. Maybe they were made that way for a particular purpose."

"Possible," Lurie agreed.

"What?" Steven blurted. "You people just spent twenty minutes trashing spaceships and alien creatures, and now you're all sitting there calmly discussing time travel? I don't believe it."

Zeifman turned to Steven, and Reese was surprised to see the physicist's smile. "At least there isn't anything in modern physics that rules out time travel, Steven," she said.

"You're kidding!" Fisher said. She stood up and walked over to sit by Zeifman. "A time machine?"

"About ten years ago Frank Tippler, an American mathematician, wrote up a description of one. Nobody's ever been able to come up with a solid reason for why it shouldn't work. Of course, it's impossible to build right now," Zeifman said happily. "But the theory fits in with space-time as Einstein described it and Gödel refined it."

"What would a time machine look like?" Fisher asked, eyes wide.

Zeifman laughed. "According to Tippler's calculations, it would be a cylinder about a hundred kilometers long, twenty kilometers across, rotating at approximately half the speed of light, and having a mass of . . . just a little more than our sun."

"Oh," Fisher said, more subdued.

"The theory being," Zeifman continued, "that a region of space-time distortion would be set up in the vicinity of the cylinder, so that if you traveled near it, your motion through space would be twisted into a motion through time. Sort of like rolling a ball bearing past a magnet. You impart momentum to the ball, making it roll forward in a straight line, but when it hits the magnetic field, it gets pulled aside, passes through a curved trajectory, and then when it leaves the influence of the magnetic field, it continues on, still in a straight line, but a different straight line."

"And that's possible?" Fisher asked. "That something could travel in time?"

"Let's put it this way," Zeifman said, "it doesn't appear to be *im*possible. And these days in physics, whatever isn't expressly forbidden is almost certain to exist. Of course, it's not the sort of thing we're going to have to worry about until we develop the technology to go around reshaping stars a few thousand years from now."

"Which is where you think those creatures might be from?" Fisher asked Lurie.

"Oh, I didn't say that, Merril. Miles did."

"But why would they be back here? Why crossbreeding?"

"To restore vigor to the stock," Miles said. "Maybe a couple of thousand years from now, humans will have genetically altered themselves into a slightly different form that leaves them open to a new type of plague or something and will want to try to correct their mistakes by coming back to the original source of their genes."

"Forget it, Miles," Zeifman said.

"Remember the Southern Leaf Blight Fungus," Miles said, waving a finger.

"What was that?" Fisher asked.

"That was a disease that stuck cornfields in 1970," Lurie explained. "Most domestic corn today comes from a uniform stock. Because there is little genetic diversity, uniform stocks are dangerously susceptible to disease. In a normal diversified population, the arrival of a new disease might result in a sizable death rate, but some members of the afflicted species will survive and their offspring will be immune. With no diversity, the entire species is at risk. That's how the Irish potato blight happened way back when too."

"How can *we* end up protecting future humans from a new kind of plague?" Fisher asked.

"Modern corn is constantly crossbred back to teosinte. That's the wild plant from which domestic corn developed. It has a natural immunity to three of the nastier viruses that threaten the domestic corn plant, so growers keep trying to transfer that immunity to plants that will then produce cobs just like the ones domestic corn plants produce."

"Teo-whatever doesn't produce cobs?"

Lurie shook his head. "That's one of the interesting things about domestic corn. It could never survive in the wild. The type of cob we have it produce would be useless for natural dispersion of seeds. It's an artificially maintained life-form."

"Gentlemen," Zeifman interrupted, "I'm out the door if you keep going on like this. Miles has an experiment to design."

"You know," Miles said, looking up to the ceiling for inspiration, "that premise fits the pattern of the abductions Merril told us about." He looked down and found a small scrap of chalk lying on the floor by the blackboard and hurriedly started writing.

"First, the creatures abduct huge numbers of humans. Starting with children because who's going to believe them when they say the bogeyman came into their room at night, right? That's when they take those preliminary scoops of skin and blood and identify the populations they want to work with." He wrote the word "populations" on the board, his chalk clicking in a rushing staccato. "Next, they establish their critical group." He wrote that term on the board above Wendy's, Sarah's, and Derek's names. "That's the target segment of related organisms which are genetically indistinguishable as far as their purposes are concerned."

"So what does that get us?" Fisher asked, fascinated.

Miles scrawled a final term. "The hybrid swarm," he said. "A continuous series of forms resulting from hybridization of two species followed by crossing and backcrossing subsequent generations." He underlined "hybrid" three times. "That gives you the babies that appear to be half-human, half-alien. The babies that look mostly human with some alien characteristics and the aliens that look more human than others." He smiled proudly. "You know, that pretty well accounts for all the different descriptions of babies that Merril said were in the books."

"Earth calling Miles," Zeifman interrupted. "Time travel is an interesting notion but raises all sorts of problems on its own. If I was going to try something like this—go back in time to collect genes—I'd head back at least another twenty thousand years and go after more primitive people."

"Why?"

"Because twenty thousand years ago, people weren't writing books about flying saucers, and reporters weren't sneaking around trying to take pictures of my time machine. If people started witnessing what was going on, which is what you're claiming is happening, then I run the certain risk of coming up against the grandfather paradox."

"What is the grandfather paradox?" Steven asked.

"Science Fiction 101," Zeifman muttered. "Here goes. I build a time machine. I go back in time fifty years. I kill my grandfather before he marries my grandmother. What happens?"

Steven shrugged.

Zeifman sighed. "My grandmother never gets married. My father is never born. Therefore, I'm never born. Therefore I can never build a time machine. Therefore I do not go back in time and kill my grandfather. Therefore he marries my grandmother. Et cetera, et cetera, until I'm born, build my machine, and go back in time and kill him, and it all starts all over again. Which time line is real? A paradox."

"What kind of paradox do the creatures after Wendy and Derek create?" Fisher asked.

"How about Charles Edward Starr?" Zeifman said. "He gets fried by a ray gun—killed by something from the future. If the soldier hadn't come back from the future and killed Starr, maybe Starr would have had children. Maybe his great-great-great-grandchild would have been President of the United States and kept the world out of a war or saved the life of a single hostage who would then have further descendants who would do lots of other important things. But by killing Starr now, hundreds of individuals might never be born, right up the time line. Maybe even one of the genetic engineers that designed the soldier in the first place. Or one of the scientists who built the time machine. *Anything* that a time traveler did in the past would cause paradoxes all along the way. Time travel is out and so am I."

"Please, Dr. Zeifman," Miles pleaded. "Ten more minutes."

"Can we stick to the experiment?"

"Professor Lurie?" Miles asked.

"Well, one last thought, then," the biologist said. "*If* the creatures are real, then they're *some* type of human. Or humans are some type of them. Otherwise, everything we know about genetics, biology, evolution, even chemistry, is a fraud."

"Earl, if you give me the choice as to which of the two possibilities is a fraud," Zeifman said, "I know which one I'd go for." She turned back to Miles at the blackboard. "It's Saturday morning and we're in the desert. Take it away."

Reese went back to his gun as Miles began outlining his plan, developing the fine points with everyone's help. Reese found he didn't care whether or not the creatures were humans or aliens or goblins. All he cared about was that they would never hurt Wendy again. And he knew, with deadly certainty, that he would soon see to exactly that.

He slapped the magazine into the Beretta's grip with a satisfying click. Whatever they were, the creatures could be killed. And with that thought, Reese felt the final barriers the creatures had set up in him crumble. He could think of them without apprehension. He could plan their destruction without fear.

And thinking of their death and destruction for the first time ever, Reese felt happy.

TUESDAY, JULY 24, 11:10 PDT

Maria Perez touched Cy North's shoulder gently and the man awoke with a scream.

"Shh," Perez said. "You're in the infirmary. You're fine. You're fine."

North looked blearily from Perez to Gardiner. Gardiner wondered how much more punishment North could take. But he had no choice. Luck had made that amply clear.

"How are you feeling, Cy?" Gardiner asked.

"Okay, I guess," North said, pushing himself up on the small bed to rest against the wall. "How did I do?" He rotated his head, bending his neck in all directions.

"Just fine," Perez said. "You only added a few inconsequential details that were left out from the first sessions."

"So you know I've been telling the truth?"

"That's all taken care of," Gardiner assured the man. "But there was one small detail that came up that we checked out—no fault of yours for forgetting it—and it might lead us to something important."

North tentatively touched his newly uncovered eye on its lid. "What detail?"

"Do you remember that the night Reese and the reporter came to your apartment they sat and watched television with you?" Perez asked.

North nodded slowly. "Vaguely," he said.

"With the . . . enhancers Dr. Perez gave you," Gardiner said, "you were able to remember that they were interested in a man called Charles Edward Starr."

"Never heard of him," North said.

"That's okay," Gardiner replied. "We were able to find out quite a bit about Mr. Starr. Seems he used to be a reporter for the *Wall Street Journal.* About fifteen years ago he started to investigate UFO sightings and seven years ago gave up his job to investigate them full-time. He's written six books about them."

"What's that got to do with Reese?" North asked.

"The day after Starr was on television, he got into a fight with a Steven Gilmour at a restaurant in town. Starr never went back to his hotel after that. He's disappeared."

"Who's Gilmour?"

"We tracked him down through Starr's publishers in New York. Gilmour runs a fairly big food-packaging business. Imports a lot of equipment from Italy. Apparently he'd been after Starr for a meeting or something. Left a lot of messages for him."

"Is there a connection?"

"An odd one," Gardiner said. "Gilmour, his ex-wife, and his daughter had just started some sort of psychological counseling with a Dr. Margot Jeffery of New York. And according to Starr's publishers, she had been in communication with Starr just before he came here."

"Anything else?"

"Starr got into a fight with Gilmour on Saturday night. The two of them, along with Gilmour's daughter, got kicked out of the restaurant. But the staff say all three of them got into a black van with an obscured license plate just a block away. Together. So that marks the disappearance of Starr. But on Friday night, the Pasadena safe house exploded, and according to the eyewitnesses who identified Reese and the reporter running away from the house just before it went up, Reese was carrying a teenage girl, and the second man has now been identified as Steven Gilmour."

"So Starr is the link to Reese and Gilmour?" North swung his feet over the edge of the bed and sat up.

"To Reese, Gilmour, *and* the doctor in New York," Gardiner confirmed. "AT&T shows that two hours after the house blew up, Dr. Jeffery received a collect call in New York from a phone booth in Pasadena. She made a flurry of calls after that, canceled her week's appointments. And on Monday came out to Los Angeles."

"Who'd she call?"

"A UCLA professor. Earl Lurie. Biologist."

"Any idea why?"

Gardiner looked over at Perez. "Is Cy okay, doctor? No aftereffects?"

Perez shook her head and smiled at North. "I only used minimal dosages. Cy didn't fight it."

"What's this about, Ed?" North asked.

"We think that the doctor and the professor and Gilmour are somehow tied up with Reese. We think they're all working together."

"For what?"

"You read the NRO report. What do you think?"

North nodded. "So you're telling me this because you want me to do something, right?"

"Roy Luck has received word that no one else can be cleared for this investigation until Reese is brought in. Or brought down." He left the question unspoken but could see that North read it in his eyes.

"So what are we supposed to do about it?" North asked, joining the team.

"Find Reese. Stop Reese. And everyone who's working with him," Gardiner said. "No matter what it takes."

"When?" North asked.

Gardiner held out his hand to shake North's.

"Now," he said.

15

WEDNESDAY, JULY 25, 09:10 PDT

Wendy walked in behind Reese when she was sure he was finished. He stood by the counter with its washbasin of water,
drying his hands on a paper towel. He looked up in surprise.
"No," he said. But she didn't believe him.

Wendy went to him and put her hands on his chest, pressing
into the soft density of his muscles. She slid her hands over
him. "We shouldn't," he said. She moved her arms around him.
"Not here," he said. She kissed him and he did not resist. He
couldn't resist. Any more than Wendy thought she could.

Wendy moved her tongue against his lips, let his tongue
move into her mouth. She drew back, nipping his bottom lip
with her teeth, pulling delicately. "We have to get out of here,"
she whispered.

"We will," he said, moving his head down to hers, his lips to
hers, drawing her back inside him.

She felt that she melted as he crushed her against him, that
she flowed over him, enwrapping him. "You make me ache for
you," she whispered. The pain of it was delicious.

Wendy found it hard to talk. Hard to breathe. She brought
her hand back to his chest, slid it slowly down over the taut
ripples of his stomach. She needed to feel him. The weight of
him. The force of him. And to make him feel her force.

Reese pushed her away. His cheeks were flushed. He breathed through his mouth. He looked as dizzy as she felt. He shook his head sadly.

"We can't," he said softly. "We're not alone."

"I don't care," Wendy whispered back, mouthing the words more than saying them.

"We'll be together soon," Reese said. "I promise." He stepped back to her and she raised her hands, but he clasped them together in his. "I love you," he said slowly, inches from her face.

Wendy felt that if he was not holding her then, she would collapse to the floor, her legs useless. "I love you," she said, feeling the power of those words as though she had never known their meaning before. She felt tears come to her eyes. "You are my heart," she whispered.

Reese nodded, his mouth a tight line of torment. He brushed his fingertips over Wendy's cheek and she felt her skin was painted with sunlight. He touched her lips and she tasted his fingertips, leaving them damp with her. He traced a line from her chin down her neck. Wendy closed her eyes, and her head arched back as his fingers moved lightly across her left breast teasingly above her tightened nipple, caressing the swell of her breast with his palm, then squeezing suddenly, sending arcs of sensation through her, cutting off her moan by covering her open mouth with his and kissing her as if time had stopped and all the world had no meaning.

And when she opened her eyes, he was gone. She heard his steady footsteps out in the main room and she was alone in the curtained-off corner with its washbasin and its mirror and its chemical toilet. She looked at herself in the mirror. The red flush of her face extended down her neck to disappear beneath the collar of her blouse. She held her hand to her breast, matching the outline of Reese's hand where the heat of it still burned against her. And she knew that that fire was more than just the calling out of two hearts. It was the force that drove life, from untold time in the shadowed past to this instant and beyond. And she knew she would not fight it.

Not just her heart, but every cell of her body cried out for Derek Reese. And she would have him.

It was twenty minutes before Wendy felt composed enough to step back out around the curtain. She instantly regretted doing so, because she saw her father was no longer sleeping—perhaps he hadn't been when she had gone in after Derek—and he glanced up at her from his desk with that horrible, empty look of sadness. She had to look away.

Derek was working at a large table Miles had brought in. There were boxes of equipment there, camera supplies and some fire fighters' breathing masks, and Reese was getting things assembled and organized for Saturday morning. Three more days, Wendy thought. That's when it will all be over. And that's when it would all begin.

Merril smiled at Wendy from her cot. She was sitting sideways on it, leaning back against the wall, reading a newspaper. Wendy went over to her.

"How are you holding up?" Merril said softly enough that she couldn't be heard over Steven's Randy Travis tape.

"Not so good," Wendy said, sitting down beside the reporter.

"It's sort of obvious," Merril said. "Same for Derek. And the same for your dad." She held Wendy's gaze. "It's probably not a good idea to go in there after him again." She looked over to the curtained corner. "One more minute and your dad would have been in there after you. Things are strained enough as it is."

Wendy felt another flush reach her face. "I know," she said, looking down at the floor where the Tempest mesh had been covered with an old piece of thin broadloom with a swirly brown-and-orange design. "Derek said the same thing."

"He's a pretty good fellow," Merril agreed. "He saved my life when the OCI or whoever broke into my house." She looked away. "I know what it's like to be in love."

"Beth, right?" Wendy asked gently.

Merril shrugged. "Smart kid," she said.

"So what does Beth do?" Wendy asked.

"Do you read comic books?"

Wendy shook her head. "Used to."

"Well, Beth draws them. Just loves it. All she ever wanted to do, and she's good at it. We should all be that lucky, hmm?"

"So who does she draw? Superman? Spider-Man?" Wendy smiled. "Wonder Woman?"

"I can't keep them all straight," Merril said. "But she used to draw something with a bunch of superheroes and Superman was one of them. She does a lot of those graphic novels now, where they adapt books into comics. She loves it. She's read all those things anyway. Loves science fiction. She'd be fascinated to hear what everyone was talking about yesterday."

"Where is she now?" Wendy asked and then immediately realized that she knew. "Oh, I forgot. The hospital."

Merril nodded glumly. "But she's okay. Reese and I saw one of the other FBI agents who was at my house that night. He told us she was okay. That they were just keeping her locked up to see if I'd call about her. But she's fine."

Wendy felt that Merril was telling her all that to convince herself, and not Wendy, that Beth was all right.

Wendy reached out and took Merril's hand. "I'm sorry," she said. "We shouldn't talk about her."

"No," Merril said, rubbing quickly at her eye. "It feels good to talk about her. I really do miss her. Like I guess you and your dad miss your mom. Parents, children, lovers. They're all special people, hmm?"

Wendy nodded. "Merril, this may seem like a stupid question, but . . . well, do you or Beth, like, have any children?"

"That's not a stupid question," Merril said. "No, we don't."

Wendy nodded again. "Then maybe this is the stupid one, but . . . do you want any?"

Merril laughed. "You sound like Beth," she said.

"Does Beth want children?"

"I take it you do?" Merril asked.

"Oh yes," Wendy said, nodding her head with great seriousness. "Someday. After I finish school. But definitely yes."

"Well, Beth would like a child too," Merril said with a sigh. "And I suppose I would too, if she really managed to talk me into it. But it's not as though all we have to do is stop using birth control." She laughed again.

"Um," Wendy said, wondering how to phrase the question properly, "aren't there, you know, clinics that you can go to, to get pregnant? I mean, like for women who don't have a husband. Or who don't like men?"

Merril looked serious for a moment, and Wendy was afraid she might even look a little mad. "It's not that we don't like men, Wendy. You musn't think of us that way. Men are fine. Most of them I guess. Some of them, at least." Merril shrugged, her face relaxed again. "It's just that, well, I've seen how you look at Derek. I know how you feel when you look at him. I feel that way about Beth. She feels that way about me. It's not a question of what we like or don't like. It's just the way we are."

Wendy thought she had just been read out, but at least Merril had done it in a nice way. "So, like, you could go to a clinic, right? If you really wanted a baby?"

"If we really wanted to," Merril agreed. She smiled. "Beth really wants to." She patted Wendy's hand. "It's amazing what some people will go through for children isn't it?"

"Yes, it is," Wendy said, feeling a sudden chill. And from Merril's shared look of surprise, she saw that the reporter felt it too.

It was all being done for the children.

Dr. Jeffery arrived at noon on Wednesday, and the moment she came through the wave baffle passageway Steven could see that something had gone wrong. His first thought was for Sarah.

"No," Jeffery said when he asked her. "Still no sign of her. But, uh, I did manage to find out about your friend Angel in New York."

Steven saw the message in her eyes. "Oh no," he said. "When? How?"

"The doctors didn't want to say much on the phone, I'm afraid. They asked me as many questions as I asked them. But apparently Angel died on Wednesday night. I'm truly sorry. I know how you feel."

Wendy came over to stand beside her father, comfort him. "Angel's dead?" she said in quiet disbelief. Steven put his arm around her.

"They wanted to know how I knew Angel," Jeffery continued. "They wanted to ask all sorts of questions about him. About his personal life."

"What about it?" Steven hated doctors with a passion. They forever kept information away from him, keeping him out of control. And they were doing it again now.

Jeffery sighed deeply. "They didn't come right out and say it, Steven, but between the lines and the significant pauses, I think they were suggesting Angel had died from complications of AIDS."

"No!" Steven said. That was impossible. "Angel doesn't do drugs. My God, he's been married for fifteen years. He hasn't had any surgery. He—"

"What complications, Margot?" Professor Lurie had come over from the table where he worked with Reese when he had heard the psychologist mention AIDS.

"That's what they weren't too clear on. And I couldn't get them to give me any more information. They said they'd discuss it with me if I would come in. In fact, they seemed quite interested to learn that I was a psychologist and they kept asking me if Angel had been in my care." She reached out to take Steven's hand. "Apparently he was quite delirious at the end. Talking about seeing little men with big eyes. And something big in the sky."

"This is your bodyguard?" Lurie asked. "The man you say shot one of the creatures up on your roof?"

"He wasn't a bodyguard," Steven said. He felt the big doors slamming shut inside him. Dividing him up. Those creatures were going to die. For Angel. For Sarah. For everything. His rage would be released. "Angel was a friend."

"But you said that he was hurt by them," Lurie continued. "That his hands were burned and that he was covered in a dark liquid similar to the one that Derek said came out of the one he shot. Is that correct?"

Steven nodded. He felt so helpless. What about Sarah?

Lurie turned to Jeffery. "Did the doctors give any sort of indication as to which AIDS complication it might have been?"

"They didn't call it AIDS. They just kept talking about how his immune system shut down or was overwhelmed. I got the impression they were talking about a massive infection. The doctors wanted to know if I had had any personal contact with Angel in the past ten days, if I knew of anyone else who might have. Apparently his whole family has been admitted to the hospital for observation."

"There's another bit of evidence to add to the pile," Lurie said.

"How is Angel's death evidence of anything except somewhere some doctor screwed up?" Steven said.

"Maybe it wasn't a doctor's fault," Lurie replied, trying to calm Steven. "It's just another piece of the puzzle that fits in with a great many of the other things Merril has been reading to us from the books on the subject. The creatures give the impression that it's not good for their victims to remain on board their craft for too long. Many abductees report being sick for days afterwards."

"Yes," Merril said, joining the group in the middle of the room, "but that could be a stress reaction. Or a reaction to the aerosol drugs they spray."

"But it could also be a reaction to bacteria or viruses or allergens that our bodies have no defense against. Remember how European smallpox decimated the native North Americans. It could be that when the creatures abduct humans, they must follow strict isolation procedures, both to protect us from contracting any of their future diseases and to protect themselves from contracting our ancient ones."

"But what the hell does that have to do with Angel dying?" Steven demanded. Wendy put her arm around him, put her hand on his shoulder. He felt a sudden wave of terror that the creatures were going to do something bad to her. He had to stop them.

"You said Angel burned his hands on his gun. They were covered with blisters. That means he lost the integrity of his skin covering—the first line of defense against infection. Then you said he was covered with a liquid that is most likely the creatures' blood. His immune system might have been overcome with a massive infusion of disease organisms against which he had no defense. No wonder his doctors might think he was battling AIDS." Lurie rubbed thoughtfully at his chin. "A good thing too, I suppose. If they handled him with standard AIDS-patient precautions, then there's a good chance that any of the infectious material in his body would be contained and not able to infect others." He turned to Reese, who had remained at the equipment table. "That might be something to keep in mind, Derek, if you insist on using that gun of yours against them. You must try not to get any of their blood or tissue on you or anyone else."

Reese smiled and pulled back the slide on his gun with a snap.

Miles arrived shortly after five, carrying a stack of newspapers and proudly showing off his vintage T-shirt: a Farrah Fawcett-Majors design more than ten years old, for which he claimed to have paid fifty dollars. But Miles didn't want to talk about T-shirts this time. He passed out the papers.

"What did I tell everyone?" Miles said happily. "They *are* desperate."

Steven took the paper, a Los Angeles *Herald*. The story Miles wanted him to read was on the bottom of page one. The headline read UFO COMEBACK?

"I know the guy who wrote this story!" Fisher said as she

paced across the room, reading her copy. "He's as straight as Howdy Doody. No way he believes this stuff."

"Unless it's real," Dr. Jeffery said, crinkling her paper as she turned to page two and the rest of the story.

"'The biggest UFO flap since the 1950s,'" Fisher read. "I love it."

"'All over the southwestern United States,'" Professor Lurie quoted. "'Unprecedented number of sightings . . . Air Force phone lines temporarily overloaded in New Mexico . . .'" He began to laugh.

"'*Claims that her family was taken aboard a UFO!*'" Fisher read at the top of her lungs. "'One of numerous such claims made in the past forty-eight hours . . . da da da da . . . experts connect it to this summer's science-fiction blockbuster movies and . . . unusually hot air masses causing—' Holy shit, listen to this: 'Leading UFO expert Charles Edward Starr is unable to comment. His publicist says that he's on vacation in California and has not been heard from since the weekend.' Jesus Murphy," Merril said. "It's really heating up."

"But why?" Wendy asked. "What are they doing?"

Miles came over to her and placed his hand on her shoulder as if he were knighting her. "They're looking for something they want, kid—you!"

"Derek?" Wendy said in a nervous voice, and Steven's heart ached to see her in such confusion, such fear. But his daughter went to Reese and not to him. He told himself it would all be over by the weekend. Saturday morning the last of the equipment would be in place, the observers would be gathered together, and they would head out into the desert to set the trap. Steven was going to enjoy that.

"Have you shown any of these to Dr. Zeifman?" Lurie asked Miles.

"Nope," Miles said. "I came straight here when I saw the headline. She said she'd be coming by after lunch anyway."

"Maybe you should go find her now," Lurie suggested to the student. "She might find it interesting, if only as an unusual coincidence." He smiled knowingly at Miles. "Why not go outside to the phone in the monitoring station and give her a call. Ask her to get down here as soon as she can."

"Good idea," Miles said. "I'd like to see her face when she reads it." He headed over to the wave baffle, bouncing jauntily. Steven watched the young man leave and found he loathed the people who could find enjoyment in their predicament. Didn't they understand how important this was? Didn't they know that he had lost his wife, his friend, and that he was on his way to losing his daughter? For a fleeting instant, Steven wondered if he should discuss these feelings with Dr. Jeffery. But then he thought he would feel much better if he could see Miles knocked flat on his ass.

Miles stumbled backward out of the wave baffle, took two faltering steps, then fell back to the floor. "What the hell!" he cried out as he hit, staring in shock at the figure who had appeared in the passageway.

Steven whirled to face the figure. He wanted to have Reese's gun in his hand. But the figure had one of his own, dark blue with a short, stubby barrel. And he leveled it at Derek Reese.

"Hello, Derek," the man in the entrance said evenly.

"Hello, Cy," Reese said. Without moving an inch, he added quickly, "Wendy, move away from me right now."

"But who—"

"Now!"

"I'm not looking to hurt anyone, Derek," the man said. "So why don't you keep your hands over your head and just move away from that table, all right?"

"Sure," Derek said, sliding his chair slowly back from the equipment table and keeping his hands cautiously raised. "I see you're looking better. Bright lights not bothering you anymore?"

The man laughed. "Look who's talking, man. You're living in a giant-size foil-wrapped room."

"What do you want, Cy?" Reese asked. Steven saw that he was trying to position himself near the far corner of the table. His gun was there, behind a video camera. Steven looked over at the man Reese called Cy. He didn't think Cy could see the gun on the table.

"Just you," Cy said.

"How about the rest of them?" Reese nodded to the others in the room. "Going to take them all in or just kill them right here? The way your friends tried that night at Merril's. Nearly got you that night too. Sure got David didn't they?"

"David sold out," Cy said. "Just like you."

"Who told you I sold out, Cy? Gardiner? Roy Luck?"

"Bigger than that," the man answered. "Move away from the table so I can see all of you."

Reese glanced at Steven, looked down at the gun on the table, the question in his eye: *Can I get it?*

"Move away now!" Cy ordered.

It would be so easy to do it, Steven thought. So easy to nod my head, have Reese go for the gun, have Cy shoot him, and then at least I would have my daughter back.

He looked at Reese. So easy to be back in control. But he couldn't do it. Reese deserved more. He shook his head: No. Reese stepped away from the table.

"What's going on here?" Rachel Zeifman said as she emerged from the passageway behind Cy.

The man spun, slashing his gun barrel against Zeifman's face. Wendy screamed. Steven crouched, ready to run to her. Reese had his gun in his hand. Zeifman collapsed to the floor. Cy wheeled back toward Reese. Reese fired.

Cy staggered backward into the entrance way. He returned the shot.

Merril pulled Lurie to the floor by her cot. Jeffery dove in beside them. Miles flattened and rolled over. Cy fired again. Sparks flew from the Tempest mesh on the ceiling.

"Down, Wendy!" Reese thundered. "Drop it, Cy! Drop it!"

Cy brought a second hand to his gun, trying to steady his aim.

"Drop—" Reese began, then fired again. The gun flew from Cy's hands, and he slumped against the first wall of the wave baffle.

"Steven! The gun!" Reese shouted. Then ran to Wendy. Took her in his arms. Steven ran for the entrance way. Merril was up and attending to Zeifman. Lurie and Miles slowly stood, faces showing their shock.

Steven retrieved Cy's gun. It was the first loaded one he had ever held, and he realized that he didn't know how to fire it. Somewhere, he knew, was something called a safety catch that he would have to switch off, but where?

Reese held his hand out to Steven. Steven put the gun in Reese's hand. Looked the man in his eyes.

"It was a tough call," Reese whispered. "Thanks." And with that, Steven knew that by giving Reese his life, he had lost his daughter forever. But some prices were too high to ever be paid, and despite the cost, Steven knew he had done the right thing.

Reese squatted beside Cy, examining the man's wounds with

Dr. Jeffery; evidently they weren't that serious. Reese lifted Cy two inches by his collar.

"Who sent you here?" Reese demanded. "How did you find us?"

"Gardiner sent me," North coughed. "The guy you saw on television at my place . . ."

"Starr?" Reese said. Immediately, everyone in the room stopped talking and moving, except for Zeifman, who still groaned, half-conscious.

"Yeah, yeah," North said weakly. Steven saw the man's shirt was spotted with blood. But Reese wasn't letting go. "Gilmour called him. The psychologist called him. We traced the psychologist's phone calls. We followed her here."

Steven felt a moment of relief. At least Cy wasn't in the same employ as Starr had been.

"What was the plan, Cy?" Reese asked. "How much back-up's out there?"

"Don't know," Cy answered. He was blinking as if he couldn't see anything. "Got to be small. They needed me because they couldn't bring in anyone else."

"Why not?"

"Too sensitive. Too secret. NRO report got it all figured out."

"NRO?" Reese repeated in amazement, though Steven didn't understand the significance of the letters. "What did they figure out?"

"Everything," Cy answered. "Put me down. I can't breathe." He began to cough again.

Reese settled the man back against the wall of the wave baffle passageway. Jeffery pulled at Cy's shirt. She looked concerned. The others had gathered around the entrance to hear what was going on. Fisher supported Zeifman, who had finally stopped moaning.

"From the beginning," Reese said, making sure the threat in his voice was not hidden, "tell me everything. Why was the NRO involved? Did they examine the photographs Merril took?"

Cy nodded his head.

"And did they recognize what they were photographs of?"

Cy nodded again.

Reese took a deep breath. He turned to the others. "So there's your answer," he told them. "The government *does* know all about them." He turned back to Cy. "What was the NRO's conclusion?"

"That you were picked up by a hovercraft—"

"What?" Reese said.

"Carbon fiber composite materials. Invisible to radar. Took you out to a ship."

"That's more like it," Reese said. "What kind of ship?"

"Trawler they thought."

"A trawler?"

"A Soviet trawler," Cy said. He peered at Reese. "You sold out, man. And they know it!"

"The NRO says I sold out to the *Soviets?"* Reese said. His mouth was open.

"Yeah. You let them smuggle out restricted technology. You help them smuggle in weapons for terrorists."

"What kind of weapons did they say I helped the Soviets smuggle in?" Reese spoke as though he were in shock.

"The stuff that blew up the safe house, for one thing," Cy said. "They haven't been able to figure that out yet." He moaned and clutched at his stomach.

"We'll get you to a hospital after just a few more questions. Did you see any of the photographs yourself?"

"Yes," Cy said. His voice sounded weaker.

"Did you see the thing that landed behind the beach house in those photographs?"

"Yes. Listen, you got to—"

"And what did it look like to you? Tell me, Cy. Tell me!"

Cy rocked his head back and forth. "It looked like a hover-craft, man. A *hovercraft."*

"How can you say that?"

"It wasn't a helicopter," Cy moaned. "It wasn't a water plane or a boat." He looked up to Reese, tried to grab his shirt with a blood-drenched hand. "What else could it be? *What else could it be?"*

Reese stood up. "They have the photographs in their hands," he said to Professor Lurie. "They've got the goddam photographic evidence in their hands, and they say it's the goddam Soviets. How many other photographs of them do you think they have in D.C.? How many file folders marked 'Soviet hovercraft'? 'Chinese blimps'?" He kicked at Cy's leg to make the wounded man open his eyes. "What did they say about the goddam guys who came out of the hovercraft, asshole? Did they say they were goddam Soviet *midgets?*"

Cy curled up to move away from another kick. "Yeah," he groaned. "Little guys to . . . to save fuel. Like they wanted to do with the astronauts once. They said they'd seen it all before. All before . . ."

"Do you *believe* this?" Reese said, stepping out of the wave baffle and back into the Tempest room. "Everyone in D.C. is like *her!*" He pointed to Dr. Zeifman.

"What's that supposed to mean?" Zeifman asked, one hand holding a towel to her bleeding lips.

"Lady, you wouldn't believe in flying saucers if one of them ran up and bit you on your goddam ass!"

"Derek!" Dr. Jeffery said. "You don't—"

"Don't you see what's happened?" Reese said, holding out his hand to them all. "Don't you understand? It's all been a joke! An accident!" He spun around and stormed across the room from them. "I've been hijacked by those goddam things since I was a kid. Wendy too. And how many others? Then one night they pick me up when I should be doing my job, and right away I'm a Soviet spy. None of this had to happen. Not David being killed. Not Beth being shot at. Not any of it."

Reese put his hand to his face. Wendy went to him and tried to hold him, but he pushed her back. When he took his hand away, his face was cold white with rage. "You were wrong, Merril," he said. "The goddam Martians didn't screw up. We did. We did. Because nobody looked up. Nobody even wanted to try and believe, just for a moment, that there might be something more going on than what they wanted to be going on. The same old tired shit." He reached out for Wendy. "I'm sorry, love. I'm sorry. But it's all been such a waste. And for what? What's going to happen now?"

For a moment, there was silence in the room. Steven looked at the man who held his daughter, the man his daughter held, and felt cast adrift. She had been passed from him to another. She was no longer a child. He was no longer a parent. He echoed Reese's question. What was going to happen now?

"Reese, Wendy, Steven, and Merril," Professor Lurie suddenly said in a voice of panic. "Quickly move into the wave baffle!"

The four looked up in puzzlement, but no one moved.

"Now!" Lurie cried. "Now!" He pointed over Reese's shoulder. "Look at it!" he shouted. "For God's sake, look!"

Steven turned to see what Lurie was indicating. His heart stopped.

By the far wall, a four-foot-by-four-foot section of the plywood ceiling was startlingly clear. A matching area of protective Tempest mesh hung down like an open skylight cover, its connectors severed by Cy's sparking bullets.

Their shield had fallen. The creatures now knew where they were.

And as Miles had said, this time they were desperate.

PART THREE

THE HYBRID SWARM

END QUATERNARY EVENT: T—34 DAYS

1

△△∠ ∠△△ △▽∠ ∠

"'I know a place where dreams are born,'" Sarah sang to her babies as she cuddled them. *"'And time is never planned . . .'"*

They cooed to her. Their tiny gray three-fingered hands reached out to grab her nose and lips with delight.

"'Just think of wond'rous things . . .'"

By the second incubator stall of the *kohanga reo,* an operator ran four drones. Each drone cuddled a single baby. Each drone held the baby in its arms, rubbed its head against the baby's face, and moved its mouth in exact phase with Sarah. All were bathed in the light that teaches. The lessons were going well.

"'And your heart will fly on wings . . .'"

The wide door spiraled open, and the one who stood beside her entered from the heaving, creaking corridor. The silent voice was urgent.

"But I don't want to go," Sarah answered out loud.

The one who stood beside her held out his slim hand to her. "That is something that I know, Sarah," he said. "But there are things to be done that others wish to stop us from doing. Things that will happen that others wish not to happen. We still struggle here."

A connection wearing a dress printed with leaves and flowers which Sarah could not identify waddled over to Sarah. The connection reached up her hands for Sarah's baby. But Sarah held the child closer, feeling the quick flutter of its tiny heart, full of newborn life. Behind her, the four drones perfectly mimed her refusal.

"It will not take long," the one who stood beside her said. "It is for your children that these things are to be done."

"My children?" Sarah asked. She looked down the long line of incubators. Other human mothers stood before them, cuddling their own sweet children, glowing in the light that teaches, accepting of their fate and their presence on board the *pa*.

"Your child," the one who stood beside her said. "Your last child." He inhaled to make a smile. "Time to gather up that last child. Then our work is almost finished."

"And then I can return here?" Sarah asked. The baby gurgled at her. Smiled at her with thin gray lips. Happy lips. Almost human.

"Yes," the one who stood beside her answered.

"And then I can go with you?"

"You are already with us, Sarah. More than you can know."

Sarah felt an incredible wave of relief wash through her, more intense and more real than anything she had ever experienced on the *pa* before. She *could* go with them and the other mothers. Her babies would never be lost again.

Sarah handed the child to the connection, carefully cradling its large head, which was still at the mercy of its still-undeveloped neck muscles. The connection held the child to her own chest just as Sarah had shown her. The silent voice whispered in Sarah's mind.

What shall his name be? the voice asked.

Sarah smiled at the newborn. He burbled and waved his tiny hands as she gently caressed the thin tufts of fine white hair scattered on his head.

"Peter," she said with a love that transformed them both. "His name shall be Peter. And he shall *fly*."

WEDNESDAY, JULY 25, 20:40 PDT

"What made him go ahead of us like that?" Roy Luck asked as he looked down on the body of Cy North, stretched out in the center of a room which was covered with layers of fine wire mesh over foil.

"What choice did he have?" Gardiner said, looking around the almost empty area. He walked cautiously to a curtain suspended from the ceiling, blocking off a corner of the room. He pulled it aside, his gun ready. A toilet, a washstand, a mirror, but nothing else.

"He was convinced you had already decided he was a traitor," Gardiner said as he returned to Luck. "That he had sold out like Vincent and Reese. The only way Cy could prove his innocence was to bring Reese in on his own. Otherwise, you'd make sure he'd be forced to resign. Or 'withdrawn.' At the very least." Gardiner slipped his gun back into the shoulder holster beneath his suit jacket. They weren't going to find anything more here.

Luck kept his own gun out and ready. "I didn't think North was that smart," he said. "I didn't think he knew what I had planned for him."

"What now?" Gardiner asked. "Do we print their pictures in the newspapers?" It was an insult.

Luck crossed the room and started digging through what few things had been left behind. He spread out four copies of that day's newspaper. "Looks like something interesting happened today," he said. "At least, something they were interested in."

Gardiner looked at the front-page stories. "Drought, heat wave, Congress promises action, riots in Johannesburg. Nothing new there. Maybe they use it as a code key. Are the stock-market listings still in it?"

Luck flipped through the papers. "The business sections are here," he said. "Nothing seems to be marked up."

"Could that be some sort of code?" Gardiner asked, pointing to the blackboard covered with cryptic scrawls in at least three different handwriting styles.

Luck stepped up to the board, reading it to himself. "'Populations . . . hybrid . . . swarm . . . goblins . . . aliens . . .

asthma inhalers . . . camera positions . . .' Hmm. We should get photos of this to cryptography. Could be important."

"David Vincent had asthma. He used an inhaler," Gardiner said.

"Maybe it was a recognition device for deep-cover moles." Luck shrugged and turned away from the board. He looked around the room. "It's not apparent what they were up to here, but with the amount of Tempest mesh they've got strung up, they must have had a sensitive computer operation going. Ties right in to what Reese was doing: smuggling restricted computer components to the Soviets. I don't think we have to look any further for the truth."

"Tucker should be here by now. Should we head back out?" Gardiner suggested. "Leave this place to forensics?"

Luck nodded, put his gun away, and stepped over Cy North's body, back to the wave baffle.

Gardiner paused for a moment, then went over to a stack of books by one of the cots. They were all by the missing writer, Charles Edward Starr. Each one about UFOs. He went back to the newspapers on one of the desks, remembering. In the bottom right-hand corner of the front page: UFO COMEBACK? On the blackboard: "aliens."

Gardiner folded the front section of the paper under his arm and stopped by North's body. Afraid of the bright light, he thought. He had a sudden flash of David Vincent, caught in the beam of the overhead helicopter's searchlight, screaming like a madman.

Like a madman, Gardiner thought. Like the kind of man who might believe in UFOs. He looked around the empty room a final time as though waiting for one more clue to magically appear, then hurried out after Luck. I shouldn't be thinking about things like this, he warned himself. Almost as if he had been given an order.

WEDNESDAY, JULY 25, 20:50 PDT

"He should be *back* here," Miles said as he bounced around in the rear of the Tempest van with the others. "They'll be able to *track* him up there."

"He's the best driver," Steven said. He wanted Miles to shut up. "He knows how to get away if there are cars following us."

"Following us where?" Miles said. He was shouting over the roar that filled the van as it careened and skidded, swerved and accelerated. Reese was driving like a maniac. "We'll never make it to Nevada this way. It'll be dark. We won't have enough observers."

"Will you *shut up*, Miles!" Professor Lurie said. He had wedged himself into a corner of the van between the counter and the forward jump seats. He was fumbling with a camera and a roll of film, trying to load it while everything bounced around him.

"Why don't we just go to the FBI and explain it to them?" Dr. Zeifman said. Her lips were swollen.

"The man who pistol-whipped you didn't look eager to hear an explanation, Doctor," Fisher said, bracing herself against the bench and bumping between Dr. Jeffery and Wendy. "He said the government had identified the UFO as a Soviet hovercraft. They don't need any other explanations than what they already have!"

The van lifted up on two wheels to take a corner. Wendy gasped with surprise. Steven reached over Merril to grab Wendy's hand. "It's going to be okay, kid. Derek knows what he's doing." He'd better, Steven added to himself. I don't anymore.

"The government conspiracy is still going on," Miles said bitterly. "After all these years."

"Forget it, Miles!" Zeifman said to him. "There is no government conspiracy. That was all a bunch of paranoid hooey so that the dimwits who believed in flying saucers could explain why they couldn't get any evidence."

"No," Miles said, raising his voice. "I'm sorry, Doctor, but you're wrong. The government *did* enter into a conspiracy. It's been documented. Papers were released under the Freedom of Information Act. While they were telling the public that there were no such things as UFOs and claiming that they no longer investigated them because there was nothing to investigate, they were actually conducting a serious covert inquiry."

"Why would they want to keep that a secret? Where's the conspiracy?"

"It was the 1950s. When the Air Force started getting reports of strange flying vehicles that could outperform pursuit jets and hide from radar, the government thought they might be Soviet spy planes. They couldn't afford to let the Soviets know that they weren't able to pick up those planes—if that's what they were. And they couldn't allow public disclosure of their search and detection techniques. So the Air Force said there were no UFOs in public, but in secret, it tried to find out everything about them. That's the process they kept from the public."

"What did they find out about them?" Zeifman demanded.

"They didn't find out *anything* about them," Miles said, "except that they weren't Soviet spy planes. And when the Air Force had concluded that, they didn't investigate anymore. That was the conspiracy. To keep hidden the fact that they thought the Soviets were making fools of them. And that's still what's happening to them today. They're still blaming everything on the Soviets. No wonder they won't talk about UFOs. The government has to keep everything secret so it doesn't appear weak. Jesus, I wonder how the Soviets explain them away? American spy planes?"

The van pulled suddenly to the left, thudded, and shook as it left a paved surface and hit a dirt track. They felt it slide sideways and almost spin out, vibrating crazily.

"Where's he taking us?" Wendy asked. "What's happening?"

The van shook as they heard and felt a splintering crash. Someone's voice shouted in the distance, but the van continued on, swerving constantly, its own horn blaring now.

"Some people have been taken right from their own cars," Wendy said, voice trembling with the vibration of the van's speeding wheels. "Isn't that what was in Mr. Starr's books?" Her voice became shrill. "Isn't that what they said happened to some people? That they came down and took their *whole car?*"

Merril put her arm around Wendy. "Shh, no. No. We're still on the ground. Reese is still driving."

The van shuddered, and they heard Reese shout something incoherent from the driver's compartment. Wendy screamed at the sound of his voice. The van shook, squealed to a stop, flew into reverse, then pulled forward again, sliding sideways on spinning tires.

Steven squeezed on Wendy's hand, trying to calm her. But this was worse than flying, leaving all responsibility in the hands of a pilot hidden away at the front of the plane.

The van charged on, tires slamming into potholes, getting

caught in ruts. Skidding and swerving until, with a bone-jarring locking of its brakes, it lurched to a sudden stop that threw the passengers from the bench to the floor.

The motor shut off. They heard the driver's door open, Reese's footsteps on gravel. The passengers moaned, tried to pick themselves up, collect their spilled equipment.

Wendy and Zeifman both gasped when the back door clanged. Steven reached for Wendy's hand again as the van's door opened suddenly. The stifling heat of the sealed compartment was replaced by a cool rush of night air. Air that smelled like oceans.

Reese stood before the open doorway, eyes wide with scarcely suppressed fear, a trickle of blood running from his nose. He moved away. Steven followed behind Wendy, stepped out, looked around. The sun had set, the sky was almost black, and he could hear the sound of the crashing surf in the distance. But he didn't know where he was.

Merril emerged. She looked once, then told them all.

"The beach house," she whispered. "This is where it all began."

WEDNESDAY, JULY 25, 21:10 PDT

The lift plate slowly ground forward from the side-door opening of Tucker Browne's van, bringing the man into the yellow glow of the parking lot's night-lights. Gardiner watched as the vehicle's bracing arms made indentations in the soft asphalt of the university parking lot, under the shifting weight of the man and his powered chair.

"Good evening, gentlemen," Browne said cheerfully. The lift plate did not descend, and Gardiner and Luck were forced to look up to Browne, like supplicants. "What results do you have for me?"

Gardiner let Luck answer. This was the OCI's operation now. It certainly wasn't the bureau's.

"North gave it away," Luck said.

"And did he also get away?" Browne asked.

"He's in the basement," Luck replied, pointing to the floodlit ramp leading down to the lower levels of the auxiliary psyche building. "Dead."

Browne tilted his head and coughed. "I suppose he was innocent, then." He smiled benignly at Gardiner. "Though I must say that the method he chose to convince us is like testing for witches. If they drown, they're innocent. If they float, hang them." He chuckled. Coughed again. "I trust you established where their next base shall be?"

"Gone," Luck said. "Completely. There's a blackboard down there with code words written all over it. They were living in a Tempest shield, so they're probably traveling with computers."

"To a transfer point?" Browne inquired.

"Possibly."

Browne puckered his lips in a tight smile. "Perhaps to a beach house in Malibu?"

"Why would he go back there?" Luck said. "He'd be crazy."

Browne nodded over his shoulder. "You've seen my Cobalt Halo communications equipment in here, haven't you, Roy?" Luck nodded. "Splendid for satellite transmissions. Secure patch-throughs to D.C. And superb, if a touch overpowered, for listening in to police radios." He leaned forward in his chair. "There appears to be a disturbance on a beach road in Malibu this evening. A van registered to UCLA smashed through the entrance barricade and made its way to a certain house which was the focus of an FBI investigation not two weeks ago."

"He'd be nuts," Luck said.

"He got away from that house once," Browne reminded them. "Perhaps he hopes to do it again."

"Insane," Luck snorted.

"Or a madman," Gardiner said quietly, tightening his grip on his folded-over newspaper.

Luck glanced at Gardiner but made no comment. He looked back up at Browne. "What's the situation at the beach house?" he asked.

"Under Special Agent in Charge Edmond Gardiner's authority," Browne said, "the road has been sealed off by a Special Tactics team with orders to hold back until the SAC himself can arrive and begin to negotiate the kidnapper's demand."

"Kidnappers?" Gardiner asked.

"Mr. Starr has been missing since the weekend. So has Steven Gilmour's wife. Derek Reese is obviously to blame, or so the press will conclude." Browne giggled like a child. "And we must remember that kidnapping is a capital crime, gentlemen. No effort must be spared, so to speak. No cost too high."

"And if the hovercraft arrives before we get there?" Gardiner asked.

"Then the Coast Guard helicopters on the scene will make sure it remains there," Browne said. "Shall we be off?"

Luck nodded. "I've got my car over there," he said.

"Very good, Roy," Browne said amiably. "And Ed, why don't you ride with me in my van? I'm sure you'd find it most entertaining. See you there, Roy."

Browne tapped the keypad angling up from the arm of his chair and the lift plate slowly slipped back into the van. When it was flush with the side of the vehicle and the support legs withdrew into their holds beside the wheel wells, Browne gestured magnanimously. "Please do come aboard," he said.

Gardiner put one hand inside the doorframe, stepped up, and pulled himself in, bending over to keep from brushing against the low padded roof. Behind Browne, a uniformed chauffeur pressed a control on a complex instrument panel and the side door puffed closed.

Browne smiled and motioned for Gardiner to turn around. "Perhaps you already know my coworkers," he said pleasantly.

Gardiner turned. Sitting at the back of the van on a plush, padded bench seat was Terry Chandler, still in a rumpled suit, the FBI agent who had sought employment elsewhere and who had been Browne's inside man during the events in the beach house. Beside him was Dr. Maria Perez.

The terrible thing, Gardiner thought as he stared at the two of them, is that I'm not surprised she's here. Someone had to have told Luck where Fisher's house was the night of the botched raid. He was only disappointed.

"Hello, Maria," Gardiner said as the van started up and slowly drove toward the parking lot exit.

Perez looked at him once, then turned her eyes to the carpeted floor, never to look up. And Gardiner thought how easy it would be for himself to be a madman too.

2

WEDNESDAY, JULY 25, 21:15 PDT

"Where are the police?" Professor Lurie said as he stumbled away from the Tempest van.

Reese steadied the biologist and guided him away from the others as they emerged.

"Sorry, Professor," Reese said as he saw he had marked the man's shirt with blood from his hands.

"Are you all right, Derek?" Dr. Jeffery asked. She passed him a wad of tissues pulled from a pocket in her windbreaker.

"Did that happen when we hit whatever it was we hit?" Wendy asked, taking the tissues from Reese and holding them to his nose.

"No," Reese said, trying to stay calm but firmly taking the tissues from Wendy and trying to wipe away the blood himself. "It just started to happen. Something's burning inside." He shook his head and sneezed.

Reese looked up to the sky. Almost as dark as the eyes in his nightmares. Stars shone. Watching. "Where are the inhalers?" he said. "Who brought them?"

Fisher scrambled back into the van and returned with a green Army surplus backpack with the name Miles painted across it in Day-Glo orange letters. She pulled an inhaler out of the pack and handed the canister to Reese.

"Everybody," Reese said. "Use them now." He looked up again.

"But what about the police?" Lurie insisted. "Why aren't they here?"

"The police aren't here because they've been told to stand off," Reese said, blasting the spray of cool medication into his open mouth and inhaling deeply. It felt like breathing snow. He coughed. Sneezed. A clot of blood burst from his nose.

"Here," Wendy said. "Better pack it. I get a lot of those too." She started rolling a small piece of tissue into a bullet-sized cylinder.

"Who tells the police what to do?" Lurie asked, amazed that such a thing should be possible.

"The FBI, for one," Fisher said, passing out the rest of the inhalers and showing the others how to use them. "And the OCI. Is that it, Reese? They want to come after us themselves?"

"That's it," Reese said. "They're probably going to hang back and wait for the"—he laughed—"hovercraft to sneak in from the trawler."

Reese looked at the cameras Miles held up, selected one with a telephoto lens, and gave it to Merril. "Take this one," he said. "Get back to where you were the night you took the first pictures."

"But that's too far away!" Fisher protested. "I want to be here."

"You were safe there before," Reese said. "Maybe you'll be outside their range again. Now go. Be a witness for us."

"No," Fisher said. She glared at Reese. "I won't leave you. I won't leave any of you."

Reese grabbed the woman by her shoulders. "Steven stays here because Sarah is up there somewhere. Wendy and I stay here because we have to face the things together. We'll have some of the others stay as decoys, just like Miles planned it for the desert. But you've been around them before. You were there when I shot one. They might want to pay us back. You have to go, Merril. For Beth."

Fisher took two deep breaths. She lunged at Reese and hugged him. "Rip out some lungs for me, Ace," she said, fighting back tears. Then she pushed herself away, hugged Wendy, looked her in the eyes. "Never forget what you feel when you look at him," she said it like a threat. *"Never!"*

"I won't," Wendy promised, bewildered. She fought back her

own tears. Wiped at her eyes. Her nose. Pulled back her hand. Reese saw blood on it. Wendy turned to Reese. "It's burning," she said. "I can feel it."

"Who's staying?" Fisher demanded. "Who are the decoys?"

"My idea," Miles said. "I'm staying."

"Since nothing's going to happen," Zeifman said, "I'll stay too."

"And me," Lurie said. "I've got to see them. I've got to know."

"Remember that they probably won't let you keep any memories of seeing them," Fisher said. "You're just to draw attention away from us."

"Part of me will know," Lurie said. "It'll be in there somewhere."

"Okay then," Fisher said. "Margot comes with me." She reached out to take Steven's hand. "Wendy will be okay," she whispered. "Your daughter's one of the special ones."

"I know," Steven said. "I know."

"Now go," Reese ordered. "Before they know you're here and see you hide."

Fisher and Jeffery jogged off past the beach house and down onto the beach. They were little more than dark smudges against a darker background by the time they disappeared behind the house, heading for a safe vantage point.

Reese used the inhaler again. Motioned to the others to do the same.

"But Starr said the dosage had been recalibrated, didn't he?" Wendy asked.

"The inhalers worked for Merril and me the night Starr found us," Reese said. "Maybe there's a limit to how much of the drug they can put into the air. Let's get into the house. Steven, bring the masks and the flashlights."

The police tape was gone, but a sheet of plywood had been nailed across the front door of the beach house. Reese clenched his fingers around one of the two-by-fours that held the plywood in place and pulled. The strain in his muscles felt invigorating. He was in action.

The metal nails shrieked against the wood and the two-by-four came free. Reese pried up a corner of the plywood, thrust his fingers behind it, pulled again. The whole covering came crashing down onto the wood of the deck.

They ran inside.

The beach house was dark. Reese fumbled for the light switches. The living-area lights still worked. Reese saw where a second sheet of plywood had been nailed up over the shattered floor-to-ceiling window that overlooked the rear deck and the ocean. But it wasn't a perfect seal. The house was filled with the roar of the ocean and the damp pungent smell of it. But the remaining windows reflected Reese and the others standing in the interior of the house and hid the sea from view.

"We're going to make it easy for them," Reese said. "Wendy, Steven, and I are going to go out on the beach behind the house where they landed last time. We'll be wearing gas masks and so will you three. But you'll stay up here in the house like you're trying to hide and sneak a picture of them when they come. Let's hope they take care of you but miss Merril down the beach like last time."

They gathered together in the empty house, helping each other adjust their fire fighter's breathing masks. Both Reese and Wendy had to use thick rolls of tissue to try and staunch the flow of blood from their nostrils. They kept sneezing and the tissue wasn't helping.

Reese led Lurie, Miles, and Zeifman—still disbelieving—to the kitchen. "If you keep this light off," he shouted through his mask, "then you can't be seen from the beach."

"Sure thing," Zeifman said caustically.

"How long do you think the FBI will keep the police away?" Lurie asked.

"At least for a few more hours," Reese said. "They'll try and repeat conditions as much as possible. The last time I got picked up here was between one-ten and one-forty in the morning. They'll wait at least that long. Maybe longer."

"Then what?" Miles asked.

"I don't think we're going to have to worry about that," Reese said. "Look!" He pointed out the kitchen window, toward the sea and the stars.

A dark shape was out there, slowly and methodically erasing the stars as it grew in the sky. A rippling pool of black. Coming closer.

"Let's go!" Reese shouted. He took Wendy's arm, half dragging her to the kitchen door, carrying his gun and his flashlight in one hand. He ran down the wooden steps, hit the sand, and ran forward to the water's edge. Steven's footsteps clattered down the stairs behind them.

"Do you see it?" Reese shouted. "Do you see it?"

The breaking waves were deafening. Star after star above them sparkled, shimmered, and then winked out. They were coming.

Reese turned suddenly to Steven. The man was transfixed by the apparition growing in the sky. Looming above them. A wave about to crash.

"Here," Reese said. "Take it!" He reached into his jacket pocket and passed over Cy's gun.

Steven looked at it questioningly, but Reese had no more time.

He drew Wendy near him, felt her arms go around him as they stood on the shoreline, between sea and earth, earth and sky, feeling the power of the ocean swirling around his legs, the power of the wind tearing at his clothes and hair, and the power of the thing in the sky as it descended, descended.

Reese waved his Beretta in the air. He screamed at them. Over the waves. Over the growing thunder and vibration that he knew he had heard a hundred times before. A thousand times before.

"Come and get me, you bastards!" he screamed to the stars. *"I'm ready for you! I'm reaaadyyy for youuu!"*

WEDNESDAY, JULY 25, 21:16 PDT

The man introduced himself as Special Agent Harry Dover of the FBI, but Gardiner had heard Luck use that name before and knew the man must be another one of the OCI's hidden soldiers.

Dover handed Gardiner a small radio transceiver. "Just clip it to your lapel like this," Dover began, but Gardiner pushed him away impatiently. "I've done this before," he said and connected the mike, the earphone, and the battery leads.

"Then you're all set," Dover said and led them to his car.

They arrived at a beach house with an open redwood deck swarming with FBI agents. "Go through this building to the beach," Dover told them. "Our guys are dug in about a hundred yards south. After that you're on your own except for the radio."

Luck and Gardiner arrived at the post on the beach a quarter of a mile down from the target beach house. Three agents crouched there with rifles and night-vision sniper scopes. Gardiner didn't recognize any of them.

"So far, nothing," one agent reported, sighting through the scope. He wore a black toque pulled down over his head and had covered his face with black greasepaint. "We've got a clear line of sight to the beach behind the target house, but there's no sign of anyone moving around yet."

Another agent, similarly equipped for night fighting, said, "When you head down the beach, keep at least four feet apart at all times so we can see that there are two of you when you reach the target. And try not to get between each other and us."

"What happens if one of us goes down?" Gardiner asked. The night fighters were kids, he thought. Kids playing guns.

"Then we have orders to eat their hearts, sir," the night fighter answered, his brilliant white teeth gleaming against his blackened face in the soft light from the windows of nearby beach houses.

Gardiner and Luck walked down the beach together, moving into darkness, four feet apart. Each man kept one hand free, holding a gun, while the other hand pressed the earphone into his ear, straining to hear all the reports over the pulsing roar of the waves.

"Angel One to Ground Zero," a thin voice crackled over the radio, the warble of helicopter blades behind it. "We have no rainbows at this time. Repeat, no rainbows. Over."

Angels Two and Three checked in. No one had any rainbows.

Just like the night Reese was taken, Gardiner thought. The Coast Guard radar hadn't spotted any rainbows that night, either.

Gardiner and Luck were eight houses away from their target when Gardiner saw a sudden sparkle of light from the corner of his eye. He dropped instantly to one knee, sighting his weapon toward his memory of the sparkle. Luck hit the sand beside him. The light had come from beneath an elevated deck on the house they had been about to pass.

"What is it?" Luck called over the ocean sounds.

"Reflection, maybe," Gardiner ventured. "Maybe a match." He got up and ran back twenty feet, then headed up to the houses and again advanced toward the elevated deck, slinking beside the back walls, gun held ready. Luck was under the deck when he arrived.

"Is this how you found them?" Gardiner asked as he stared at the two bodies slumped behind a stack of driftwood, fearful that Luck had killed them both.

"Relax," Luck said. He had been talking into his lapel microphone. "They're both still alive. And look at the one on her side." He played a tight flashlight beam on the body of a woman. Gardiner felt relief as he saw that she still breathed.

He squatted down beside her and gently pulled on her shoulder, rolling her from her side to her back. She had been lying on a camera with a telephoto lens. He could see that the camera back was open and the camera empty.

"Did you take the film?" Gardiner asked.

"That's just the way I found them, Ed. But take a look at her."

Gardiner studied the woman's face. Of course. It had taken a moment to recognize her because of the dark gout of blood that seeped from her nose, but he now saw the woman looked just like her pictures. It was the reporter Merril Fisher.

And then he saw something move in the shadows beside him.

WEDNESDAY, JULY 25, 21:20 PDT

Steven felt his entire body shake. Not with the thudding intensity of the surf but with the pulse of darkness. The same vibration that had shaken him the night he had run to the roof of his building to find Wendy safe, Angel dying, and Sarah gone. The same vibration that had . . .

It was happening again. He could deny it no longer.

Reese and Wendy stood five feet from him, and Steven could hear that Reese was yelling something into the night but couldn't make out the words. The waves, the wind, and the thing that descended were too overpowering.

It was happening again.

The wind picked up. A sudden gust pushed him off balance and he staggered. He steadied himself, glanced down the beach, eyes wide open, protected from the driving sand by the mask he wore. The lights of all the beach houses except for the one directly behind him had disappeared. Swallowed by darkness.

Steven hunched down, pushing against the howling wind, trying to turn back to Reese and Wendy. Now he could feel the vibration through the wet, packed sand beneath him. Something had touched down. But where?

A dark shape bumped against him. Steven wheeled and looked up into Reese's mask. The man screamed at him, but Steven could hear nothing and, in the almost absolute black of this night, could not see the words Reese's lips formed.

He felt Reese press something into his hand. A cylinder. A flashlight. Steven switched it on and shone the light up into Reese's face. They stood face to face, only inches apart, each looking over the other's shoulder. For an instant, Steven saw another flash of yellow light behind Reese. But it was only Wendy's face caught in her own flashlight's beam, floating in a swirling mass of flying sand. His daughter hunched over and took long, difficult steps to join them, struggling against the onslaught of the wind.

Steven looked back to Reese. Shone his flashlight up. Saw Reese's eyes behind his mask. Saw his face crimson with the blood that poured from his nose. "The gun," Reese mouthed. "The gun."

Steven held up Cy's weapon. Held it awkwardly. He just didn't know how to use it. Another light flashed behind Reese, blue this time, and Steven felt a concussion like lightning. He saw another flash of blue light on Reese's face and felt another blast of sound and fury against his own back. Reese's eyes widened as he saw something over Steven's shoulder. He brought up his gun and pulled Wendy to his side.

Wendy screamed, but there was no sound. Steven saw another flash behind Reese. A shape moved through the swirling sand. Reese fired at something over Steven's shoulder. Steven held up his gun to the shape that came toward him from behind Reese. The gun was hot, burning in his hand. He screamed and coughed on something thick and warm and liquid that burned down his throat, that splashed down his face from his nose. It tasted like blood.

The shape was closer. Not small. Not short. A soldier, he thought. Dear God, another soldier.

Steven tried to call to Reese, but even though he faced the man only two feet away, there was no hope of being heard. The storm had swallowed them like the blackness, like a living thing. Steven held up his gun. It was hot. The metal burned his flesh. He aimed the gun at the figure that determinedly approached. Another flash. Another thump. Reese's gun fired again. Steven pulled the scalding trigger. It wouldn't move. The safety, he cried to himself in frustration. I don't know where the safety is.

And then a hand reached out from the blizzard of sand and took the gun from him. A human hand. A hand that he recognized.

Two feet in front of him, smiling in the way that had won his heart so many years ago, was Sarah.

Steven felt the burning gun slip from his hand. He saw her reach up to his face.

And when his mask came off, the airborne drug hit him so fast that he did not even feel himself fall.

3

△△∠ ∠△△ △▽∠ △△∠

It was happening again . . .

Steven woke up. The house was quiet. He heard the scraping of the bushes outside his bedroom as their bare branches scratched against the window. He heard the far-off gentle snore of his father, coming from behind the closed door of his parents' bedroom around the corner. He heard a footstep in the hall.

Steven froze. The night fear building within him again. He wanted to run out of his bedroom, around the corner, and jump into his parents' bed for safety. But his father would be angry. His father would say, "You're six years old, Stevie. Act like a man. Don't give in to a little nightmare." But Steven knew this wasn't a nightmare. He heard another footstep in the hall. A cautious footstep. The kind he made when he tried to sneak up on a friend. The kind he made when he didn't want to be caught.

Another footstep.

Steven opened his eyes. His bedroom was so black that he could see swirls in the darkness. Bubbles and splotches of gray and black that mixed together like dirty paint. He turned his head slowly to his left to look down the hall, as black as his bedroom. All swirls and—

—something was there.

A little thing. A short thing. With two arms and two legs.

Steven pulled his blanket over his head. He heard his father snoring. He wanted to open his mouth and scream for help. But his father would be mad. His father would say, "Fight it, Stevie. Be a man."

Steven strained to hear all the sounds of the house he possibly could. The fan of the furnace. He heard it. A tap dripping in the bathroom. He heard it. That's all there is, he told himself. That's all I can hear except—

—another cautious, sneaking, tiny footstep in the hallway.

Steven inched back his blanket. Just enough for his nose and one eye. A picture in the splotchy blackness he told himself. That's all it is. He looked again and—

—something was closer.

A little bit bigger now. Longer arms. Longer legs. A chimpanzee, he thought. A chimpanzee is in my house. A chimpanzee with a circus-green vest and red pants and two six-guns strapped to his side like Roy Rogers.

Steven snapped the blankets back over his head. He was petrified. He knew he couldn't set foot from his bed. No matter what happened.

If it were a nightmare, he knew he could run. If it were a bad dream, he knew a light in the bathroom would take it away.

But there was something in the hallway that wasn't a nightmare, that wasn't a bad dream, that stepped forward one more time as quietly and as carefully as if it knew the biggest secret in the world.

Steven pulled back his blanket. Enough for one eye. Enough to see—

—it was in his doorway. Hunched over. Two arms and two legs and six-guns and all his favorite things thrown together as if it had been painted by the dirty night paint bubbling and swirling through his room.

Steven covered his face instantly. Nightmares didn't get closer. Bad dreams didn't creak the wood in the hallway so softly that Dad wouldn't wake up, that Mom wouldn't wake up, that no one would wake up except for Steven because Steven was the one that they wanted to wake up and Steven had to be a man and fight it. Fight it, Steven, he told himself. Six years old and he warred with himself. This can't be true. This can't be real. Call for Dad. Call for Mom. But he couldn't even open his mouth because *Shhhh,* said the voice. *This is a secret. Shhh,* said the voice. *No one must know. No one, ever. Now take down your blanket because we're in your room and it's time to go, so take down your blanket,* said the voice.

And Steven took down his blanket.

And the thing was there with its wrinkled face and big black chimpanzee eyes, and it was right by his bed and with its face so close to Steven that Steven could smell it and no matter what else—

—he couldn't scream.

Be a man.

It was a secret.

He was six years old.

It was happening again.

He felt cool hands on his forehead. Another voice spoke to him. One he could hear this time. That other voice spoke to him and told him it was going to be all right.

Steven got into a fight. He threw a punch. An eight-year-old's punch. But Billy McCauley did him one better and threw a rock, and it split his lip and Steven staggered home to his mother, bawling like a baby and she said, "Another nose-bleed?" But the blood came from Steven's bottom lip so his mother tried putting ice cubes on it and then had to call a taxi and go to the hospital and the doctor said, "Stitches."

They took Steven into a room and held him down on a wooden table. Then the doctor came in. The nurse came in. There was a bright light over Steven so they could see what they were doing.

And Steven shrieked. He knew his mother was there. He could hold her hand. And he knew they were just a doctor and just a nurse, but he screamed until his throat was raw because he suddenly remembered that the last time he had been held down on a table with a bright light over it in something like a hospital, the things that had bent down over him with their silver tools and sharp probes *had not even been people!*

"Don't let it happen again!" Steven cried to his mother. But she helped them hold him down.

For two years after it had happened again and the things that weren't people had bent over him like that, Steven got nose-bleeds every week, even when he hadn't put a finger near it. His mother had just come to say, "Another nosebleed?" and Steven never liked doctors again.

"Shh," said the voice. A cool cloth wiped his forehead. The roar of the sand was gone. The pulse of the darkness was gone. The hand was calming. Familiar. "Shh," said the voice. "It's going to be all right."

Steven peddled his tricycle to Bobby's house, but Bobby wasn't there and no one answered the doorbell, so Steven stood over his trike and pushed himself along the walk at the side of Bobby's house, waddling like a duck, and pushed open the gate and went into the backyard and not once did he think that he shouldn't be doing that. "Don't trespass," his father had told him. But Steven *knew* he had to go back there.

Then Steven sat on his trike and looked up at the big tree in Bobby's backyard. The sky was blue behind it. The leaves were green. The wind blew on them so they flickered light green and dark green like fish swimming in schools. Steven stared at those leaves. Saw nothing else but those leaves. Heard nothing else but the wind-rush rustle of those leaves. And realized that he was looking *down* on those leaves. Down down down from far away as he went up up up.

When he went home that afternoon and his mother said, "Where have you been? I was worried sick," Steven couldn't answer her. But he felt calmer and happier than he had ever felt as a child before. And thirty-three years later he still looked into trees, and the sound of rustling leaves still made him stop and try to remember—*Shhh, it's a secret.*

It had happened again.

Steven blinked. Opened his eyes. Saw a light that was dim and brown like sunlight in a deep cave. Something white descended on his face. Something white and cool. A cloth, he thought. I must be dirty.

The hands caressed his face. The voice told him he was fine. He thought he could remember that voice . . .

Steven ran through the park with his six-shooter in his hand. Rustlers behind every tree. So he ran into those trees, off the path. Deep into the woods for miles. And he came to a ranch house.

Steven stopped in the clearing and stared at the ranch house. He didn't know they still had things like that in New Jersey. He walked up to it. Tried to stare into the windows. What a great place this would be, he thought with excitement. It could be a fort for playing cowboys. It—

—the old guy on the porch with funny whiskers that covered almost all of his face invited him in.

Steven knew he shouldn't accept invitations from strangers. The rule had been drilled into him as thoroughly as the five-times table. But it seemed like a good idea, and he went inside and—

—the next thing he remembered, he was back in the woods. Alone. And he felt a thin trickle of blood run down from a scratch on the back of his knee.

Three weeks later, Steven couldn't find the ranch house anywhere. He couldn't find anyplace in the small park where he could walk for miles. So he put away his six-guns and decided he didn't like cowboys anymore. He wanted to play soldiers instead. Soldiers with machine guns and hand grenades and knives and radios you could use to call in air strikes. Because then you could really put up a fight when it happened again.

He cried himself to sleep for a month because he *knew* it would happen again. And in his dreams, his nightmares, he remembered what the old guy had looked like underneath his whiskers and what they had done to him in the ranch house.

Steven tried shifting his position. His body ached. He remembered Reese shouting at him for . . . what? And he remembered Wendy screaming. But at . . . what?

The hand caressed his face. The familiar hand. He reached for it. Held it in his.

"Wendy?" he asked.

"Shh," said the voice. "It's almost over."

This time they weren't playing games. He was in the basement watching "The Man from U.N.C.L.E." The television changed channels by itself. Steven knew enough to instantly look away. It was happening again.

"Turn back," the voice on the television said. "Turn back now, Steven."

"You can't make me," Steven said.

"We can make you sorry," the voice said.

"I don't care," Steven said, holding his hands over his eyes, twisting in his chair.

"We can make you look," the voice said.

"No you can't," Steven cried.

"Look at me!"

They were right. Steven had no choice. He looked.

The black eyes seemed to float out of the set, pulling a small gray face with them like taffy. "Time to go," the creature said. And Steven remembered the name he had been taught for that creature: an operator.

Steven went out to the backyard. They had put the portal in there. They told him to take off his clothes and sit in the portal. He did. The portal curved under him as if it had been scooped out of the soil. It felt cold. He waited.

Another type of creature, an engineer, came and put the transference device on his shoulder. Steven felt nothing as it cut into him. He just looked down into the liquid surface of the portal as it opened and he was transferred high over the trees and the houses below him as quickly as if he had fallen *up* a laundry chute.

They were busy that night. No time to lose. The main transfer bay was full. Other people sat there. Some with their eyes closed. Some with their eyes open. Some shaking with fear and screaming.

The drones moved around them, inserting the tracking beacons, removing the transference devices. Installing the ones needed for placement. Slights moved with slow, insectlike paces, lifting their long legs up too high, sliding forward too slowly. Connections sorted through clothing and other goods which some of the visitors had brought up in shopping bags. Engineers swarmed over a shiny 1963 green Buick which rested on an angle in the corner of the bay, studded with gleaming transference rings on its trunk and hood, filled with a silently screaming family. One of the engineers had removed the tire iron from the trunk and was twisting it around and around, trying to get it to work like a probe.

Steven didn't care about any of it. He was shut off. Compartmentalized. There was no more fear in him. It had been going on too long.

The drones came for him when it was finally his turn. They tapped his forehead with a probe and he straightened and floated. They guided him to a smaller bay. Medical this time.

Steven felt every tiny hand upon him. Pushing him along the invisible currents that ran through the place. Whatever the place was.

"Why don't you just leave me alone?" Steven said when he had been released from paralysis. "Why do you always come after me?"

The drones said nothing. They were busy. They strapped him to an examination table. They swung the bright light over him.

"Leave me alone!" Steven shouted. Not with fear but with anger. "I don't want to do this anymore!"

A connection came up to the table. She wore a cowboy outfit with tassels and fringes like Annie Oakley.

"I don't like cowboys anymore," Steven told her. "You're wasting your time."

The connection blinked, her huge black eyes sinking in and bulging out as her heavy lids swept down and then up. "What do you like?" she asked. "What can we get you that you would like?"

"I would like for you to leave me alone," Steven said.

The connection stared at him for a long time. Steven was used to them, but he couldn't take those eyes for long. He looked away. Two slights were standing by the open round door. They twisted their arms together, touching thumbs. "What are you staring at, bug eyes?" Steven sneered.

The slights jumped back. An engineer floated into the room. She touched her probe to his throat, and Steven was shocked to discover that he couldn't remember how to say anything. Anything. He moved his mouth, but nothing came out except for breaths of air.

"We have a thing to show you," the engineer said. She held up a gray metal box ten inches high and five inches by five inches at its base. The lower six inches were covered in ornate carvings or inscriptions which Steven couldn't understand. The upper four inches were smooth, the corners rounded.

"Look," the engineer said and slipped two fingers into an indentation that ran along one smooth side.

Steven stared at her. He wanted to know what it was. Why it was important.

"You will know how to use it when the time comes," the engineer said. She let go of the box and it floated in front of Steven, rotating so he could see all sides of it. The bottom was marked by a deeply etched circle inscribed with a cross that quartered it. "Remember," the engineer said and then picked the box out of the air and glided out of the examination room without moving her feet.

The operator who had brought Steven approached him. Behind him, two shorter drones walked in perfect step with his every movement.

"We have another thing to show you," the operator said. Then he bent over Steven, and Steven felt cold hands moving over his genitals.

Steven tried to pull back, but he was held in place. He tried to shout at the creature to leave him alone, but he didn't know how to speak, as though that part of his brain had been removed.

The creature stepped back. Steven looked down to his crotch. His penis was pinched in a clear glass clamp, and he felt himself become erect. He hated this. Of all the things they did to him, he hated this the most.

He closed his eyes, preparing for the shock that would course through him as they made him ejaculate. There was no pleasure involved. Only strain.

But nothing happened.

He heard the shuffle of drone feet entering the room and opened his eyes. They were bringing in another visitor. Another human. A girl.

Steven felt himself turn red. He had gotten used to being naked in front of these creatures. He had become resigned to the way they would handle his penis, sticking their machinery on him, making him come like a cow being milked. It was sickening to him, but he knew that he could only remember the details while he was with them. Once they had finished with him and let him go home, he would blessedly forget everything. That part of him shut down. That part of him kept isolated and apart. Until the next time.

Steven had come to accept their abuse as one of the prices paid for existence. But not to be like this in front of another person. Not to be bound like this. Humiliated like this. In front of a girl.

The operator adjusted his probe as the drones floated the girl in. Steven felt a momentary lessening of his embarrassment as he saw that the girl, too, was naked. His eyes were riveted to her dark brown patch of pubic hair. He had never seen that before. Not on a girl.

The operator held his probe over Steven's forehead, tapping directly into the implanted beacon. Steven's mind was instantly filled with the images of rustling leaves and sun-dappled shadows. He could smell the warmth of rich earth, a musky scent that burrowed deeply inside of him, snaking through him like a song he couldn't stop humming. I know what that is, Steven thought. I've smelled that before. He was flooded with intense feelings of calm and happiness. His body lost track of the bonds that held him to the table. His mind forgot the place in which he was confined. Instead, he exploded with sensation released by the subtlest scent of the leaves and the trees and the sun.

Steven moaned. He was rushing through the forest at a hundred miles an hour. The sun strobed past him. The leaves brushed by him. Every sense, every sensation feeding him, building him to a peak. His body thrummed like a struck cord. He felt himself expand. Felt himself grow. It was incredible. All-encompassing. He was building to a brink, a point from which there could be no turning back, a point at which he would outreach all the bonds upon him and explode out through the universe.

"Look," the engineer said.

Steven opened his eyes, rushing with the sensations of a thousand senses. The girl floated above him. Her own eyes wide, staring into his. And he saw the forest in those eyes. Saw she sped with him through the leaves and the sun and the warm earth. She opened her mouth. Moaned to him. He felt her join with him. It was her scent that filled him. Her presence that brought him this peace. Then the moment came and the top of his head was torn off as he felt himself exploding as if the universe had just then been created with his heart and his thoughts and his soul.

Then that universe contracted, reducing his heightened senses to nothing but memory. Steven felt his heart pounding, his body trembling. Felt the bonds that kept him to the table. Felt the pressure of the girl upon him. Around him.

He stared at her in shock. He had been inside her. She looked at him with the same mute expression of terror and wonder. And then he felt sick. The first time he had made love and it had to be like this. For them. He closed his eyes. Twisted his

head away from the girl. Felt her float off him, dragging him
with her for a moment and then letting him go.

He wanted to cry. He wanted to scream out his rage. But
they had cut his mind into little pieces. A little bit here and a
little bit there. The whole person broken down into parts that
could never talk to each other. Never share. Except when the
sun shone through leaves. Except when the wind rushed by.
Except when they came to him with the scent of warm earth
and deep forest and that scent made him whole.

"Remember," the engineer said. "So you will know what to
do when the time comes."

And when he had met her again, they had both known what
to do.

Steven stirred against the bed he lay in. He closed his eyes. He
saw that young girl's face floating in front of him. A face so
familiar to him now. A face—

"Sarah!" he cried. It had been Sarah.

"I'm here, Steven," Sarah said softly, sweetly. "Right here.
And everything's going to be fine."

Steven lifted himself up against the soft bed. He looked toward the sound of Sarah's voice and saw her there, standing
just on the edge of the room's portal depression.

"You're all right," Steven said.

"And so are you. They had to use a lot of the mist because of
your inhalers. But you'll be fine now. The fever's almost gone."

"The fever," Steven said, holding one hand to his forehead,
feeling the dampness of the cool cloth. "Thank you," he said.

Sarah smiled. But she shook her head. "It wasn't me," she
said.

Steven looked at her a moment, puzzled. Then realized she
was too far away to have touched him. Realized she looked at
something beyond him. He turned his head.

The creature was four feet tall. Its eyes as slanted as a demon
insect's, as black as Steven's fear. The creature's skin was gray
and shriveled and wrinkled around his swollen head. Yet it
wore a yellow sweatshirt, faded blue jeans, and a pair of children's blue Nikes.

The creature blinked its eyes slowly like a sunning lizard. It
held out a gray three-fingered hand, held a white washcloth in
it, dripping with cool water.

"Hello, Steven Gilmour," the creature said. "It is good to

meet with you again." The hanging flaps of skin around the creature's mouth crinkled grotesquely, making it appear to smile. "My name is John-John," the creature said.

And Steven Gilmour screamed.

4

△△∠ ∠△△ △∠∠ △

Gardiner awoke to the sound of screaming. He reached for his gun, but his holster was empty. He opened his eyes. Rubbed them, squinting as he saw that the light was wrong. Brown, it seemed. And the air was different too. Dry and hot and dusty like the desert at high noon.

He thought about that smell for a moment. It was familiar.

Gardiner sat up. The surface beneath him shifted slightly. As if in the hold of an ocean liner, he felt the steady vibration of engines, the slow heave and toss of stabilizers, the creaking and slow thumping of a superstructure fighting a storm.

He looked around. The source of the screaming was on the bunk beside his. Roy Luck. Hysterical.

Gardiner pushed himself to his feet, swayed unsteadily as the deck moved under him and the veins in his head throbbed. His mouth was filled with a metallic taste, something slimy. He spat it out.

"Roy," Gardiner said, leaning over the screaming man. "Get up!" he ordered. "Get up!"

He shook Luck by his shoulders. The man's head rocked back and forth on the bunk, eyes squeezed shut, wailing like an injured child. Gardiner grabbed Luck's head, held it firmly. Shouted at him. "You're all right, Roy! Wake up!"

Luck's eyes popped open and his screaming stopped. He stared at Gardiner as though he had never seen the man before.

"It's me, Roy. Ed Gardiner. We're okay."

Gardiner helped Luck sit up, steadying him against the sudden dips and rises of the deck. Luck looked around at the strange room, rounded and smooth, ribbed with curving support struts that arched up to the dim central light in the ceiling. A row of ten bunks ran through the room, lined up to point at the circular sealed door. The deck pitched.

"We're on the trawler," Luck whispered hoarsely. "The Soviets picked us up with Reese."

"I don't think so, Roy."

Luck grasped at Gardiner's arm, panic in his eyes. "We were under the wooden deck, right?"

"Yes," Gardiner agreed.

"They had already gotten the photographer, remember? Stolen her film. Don't you see? They were already there! We were expecting their hovercraft to come ashore again, but they had *already arrived!*"

"Then how did we get here, Roy?"

Luck grabbed at Gardiner's jacket. "They sent divers!" he said, full of desperation. "Don't you remember the divers? Under the deck? In the shadows?"

Gardiner remembered what had been in the shadows just before it had raised a glowing tube of light and the world had exploded into brilliant colors. "I don't think so, Roy," he said.

"They had to be divers," Luck moaned. "They *had* to be!" His head fell against Gardiner's chest, wracked with sobs.

Gardiner looked over Luck's heaving shoulders. Looked at the things that just now were peering over the tops of the bunks. Creatures with large black eyes and small gray faces. Just like the thing that had been under the deck.

"I don't think so," Gardiner repeated.

A creature slightly larger than the others came forward slowly. Gardiner watched its delicate motions in awe, the tentative movements of its small hands. A female, Gardiner decided, though had no sense of why he thought that.

"Is he finished?" the creature asked. Her lids flicked over her ebony eyes as quick as a snake's tongue.

"I think so," Gardiner said. He loosened his grip on Luck and the creature took a half step away.

"Do *you* want to yell?" she asked.

"No," Gardiner said.

"But you are the same as that one?" the creature asked, gesturing to Luck with her thumb. "He yelled."

"Not me," Gardiner said.

The creature remained silent while two smaller creatures in drab blue coveralls marched in step toward Luck and gently pulled him back from Gardiner's grip.

"I've been here before, haven't I?" Gardiner asked.

"Many have," the creature replied. She watched as the two smaller creatures busily laid Luck out straight on the bunk. One held a shoe-box-sized device of black metal over Luck's shoulder and wiggled it against the man, trying to clamp it onto his shoulder.

"May I stay?"

"No," the creature said.

"For a while?" Gardiner tried. "We could talk about why he yelled. Why I don't."

The two creatures who worked on Luck abruptly stopped. The female creature tilted her head at Gardiner. "Do you know why he yelled? Do you know why you do not want to?" She looked at Luck's rigid body. His eyes were wide open in terror, staring helplessly at the frozen arms of the little creatures poised above him.

"He is afraid of losing," Gardiner said.

"Are you not afraid of losing?"

"I have already lost." Gardiner smiled at the creature. "I have nothing more to lose. I have nothing more to fear."

The creature inhaled through the narrow slit of her mouth and twisted the loose skin around it into a misshapen reflection of Gardiner's smile. "Neither do we," she said. "You may stay, and we will talk of fear."

She looked back to the creatures over Luck, and they began to move again. The black device was attached to Luck's shoulder. One creature held a glowing shaft of metal over Luck's forehead. Touched it to the skin between his eyes. Gardiner blinked as a spark jumped between Luck and the rod. The smaller creatures withdrew.

"Please stand back," the female said to Gardiner. She stepped away from the bunk that held Luck. The two smaller creatures backed away beside her, step for step, elbow bend for elbow bend. Gardiner moved back in the opposite direction.

The floor beneath Luck's bunk turned to quicksilver. The

bunk began to smoothly sink into it, sending out ripples. Luck
bent his head up as the bunk slipped down into the liquid
metal. He opened his mouth in a high-pitched scream. Mindless. The sound of inescapable terror. He wrenched his head
around, stared at Gardiner. The sound he made grew. But
there was no reason to it. And there was no reason left in his
bulging eyes.

Gardiner smiled.

The floor parted and rushed over Luck's descending form.
Covered him with a small splash, rippled once, then he was
gone and the floor was smooth. A moment later, a smaller
section of the floor puddled and the black device popped up like
a cork out of water, jumping into the air. When it fell back, the
floor was solid again. The two smaller creatures walked over to
it, bent down, and retrieved it with flawless synchronization.

"What has happened to him?" Gardiner asked. Whatever it
was, he hoped it included awareness.

"He has been placed," the creature replied, "near where we
transferred him. Where there is water and land together. He
will be found."

Gardiner laughed and the creature jumped back.

"I'm sorry," Gardiner said hurriedly. "That was not a yell.
It was a sound of . . . happiness."

"Will you make that sound again?" the creature asked, and
Gardiner sensed apprehension in her wispy tone.

"It is not a sound of distress. I will try not to make it again."

The creature relaxed. The smaller creatures came back to life
and carried the black device to the round door.

"Tell me," Gardiner said to the female. "Will that man remember what has happened to him? Will he know he was here?
Tell others what he has seen?"

"All of the ones who have been here remember. All who
have been here know they have been here." The creature held
her left fist to her shoulder, elbow against her waist. She
reached across her chest with her right hand and used it to
cover her left. "It is just that they . . . don't have the words."

"Who doesn't?" Gardiner asked. "You or them?"

"Yes," the female replied. "It was us or them. You are very
wise. Please come with me, and I will bring you to a place to
stay. Things are to happen."

Gardiner was puzzled by the creature's reply, but before he
could ask another question, he felt a tingling sensation along

his spine like a thick electric liquid pouring up it. He fell back slowly until he was horizontal but not in contact with the floor. Then he felt the gentle pressure of two tiny pairs of hands, one against his legs, another against his shoulders, and as if riding the smoothest gurney ever made, he was pushed lightly to the door.

The door spun like a pinwheel, unwinding and disappearing from view in front of his feet. The dimly lit tunnel beyond resonated with the pounding and the shuddering of unseen waves. Gardiner floated out into that tunnel, but had no fear. His enemy had been utterly destroyed.

$$\triangle\triangle\diagup \diagup\triangle\triangle \diagup\diagup \triangle\diagup$$

John-John took Steven and Sarah to his room. It was a mess. The aftermath of an explosion in a shopping mall. Steven saw cardboard boxes filled with clumps of clothes, piles of opened suitcases, a set of Encyclopaedia Britannica strewn along part of the wide bench that ringed the walls, wooden packing crates, three empty glass demijohns with Crystal Springs labels, a small Mitsubishi television set rolling with static on top of a video recorder, a videocassette spilling yards of tangled brown tape, beer boxes, a stuffed Koko doll face down on a partially assembled child's bike, and that was only the top layer, the items he could see.

"What is this place?" Steven asked, lowering himself into something he assumed was a chair, tensing and relaxing his muscles, getting rid of the feeling he had had when John-John had floated him along the pulsating corridor. He couldn't decide which was worse, the sensation of moving through that shuddering corridor or the knowledge that he had passed through it innumerable times before.

John-John jumped up to sit on the top of a gray metal desk. The speed and ease with which he completed the movement made the hair on Steven's arms bristle. John-John might be dressed as a child, but he moved with an animal quickness, like nothing human.

"This is my collection," the creature announced. "My name is John-John."

"What kind of a collection is it?" Steven asked. He had to

keep telling himself that the thing that sat on the desk in front of him, swinging its feet in the empty air, was real, not just another stuffed toy thrown onto the heap.

John-John moved his hand to include the entire room. "These are my things."

"John-John is a connection."

Steven turned to see Sarah, sitting on a raised platform similar to the bunk he had woken on in the first room. She had pushed aside a collection of coiled wire, still with Underwriters Laboratory tags on it, to clear a place to sit.

"Connections are specialized," Sarah said. "They are the links between us and the ones who are not us. Some of us are assigned operators; some are assigned engineers or slights. But connections are the ones who tell each about the other. Connections try to understand."

"What are they?" Steven asked. His throat felt dry and raspy. "Where are we?"

"My name is John-John," the creature said. "This is the *pa.*"

"The *pa?*" Steven repeated. "Is this your ship?"

"Ships are for oceans. Ships are for space. Ships are for other things and other places. This is the *pa.*"

Steven looked at Sarah, but she shook her head. "I don't know. I've never seen a window. But it feels like we're moving, doesn't it?"

Steven felt the floor shift beneath his feet as a rolling rumble resonated in the room. "Where is Wendy?" he asked the creature.

"Still sleeping in her room," John-John said. "Less mass. The same mediator. She sleeps longer."

"Who is the mediator?" Steven asked.

"Mediator, mediator," John-John sang, touching his fingers to his nostril slits above the small gash of his mouth. "In the gases you breathe."

"They put something in the air," Sarah said. "To confuse people, make them less violent, less likely to have clear memories. A drug of some sort, I suppose. But they call it a mediator."

"No drugs of any sort," John-John chirped. "Drugs are outside. We want to keep you from having trouble with us, so we help you decide that you don't want any trouble so you can visit us. Whatever makes you do those things, you make." John-John patted his fist against his lower back. "In here. Inside. We give you mediators in the gases. They tell you how to make your decisions." He tilted his head. "Unless you keep them away." He acted out the use of an inhaler. "Then the mediators stay outside. Your body does nothing inside. You decide to make trouble. Things happen."

Steven didn't understand. He felt confused, gritty, and he didn't like to look into the creature's eyes. He turned to Sarah. "Do you know why we're here?"

"The babies," Sarah said. She smiled lovingly at him.

"Which babies? You mean"—he looked at John-John—"the hybrids?" Steven turned back to Sarah, saw her nod, and he trembled. Merril had been right. His stomach contorted and he wanted to be sick.

"Babies," John-John said. He nodded his head and he smiled.

Steven thought the imperfect expression grotesque. "W-why babies?" he asked. And what about Wendy? he suddenly thought in fear.

Wendy will be fine, Steven, said the silent voice in his head.

"Who said that?" Steven looked at John-John, who remained frozen with the sucked-in impression of a smile on his shriveled gray face.

Perhaps this will be a better way for us to talk, the voice said.

Steven peered at John-John's unmoving mouth. "Telepathy?" he asked.

Telepathy is a dream, the silent voice told him. *You are wearing your beacon. With it, we can locate you according to the schedule. With it, we can stimulate the speech and aural centers of your mind to create the illusion that you hear a voice.*

"I can understand you better this way," Steven said. John-John hadn't made a sound.

The devices that do these things use your words. When we speak aloud, we must use ours. It is more difficult.

"Why are you making hybrid children?" Steven asked.

John-John snapped open a desk drawer. He reached inside and drew out two small packages, one red and one blue. Steven watched with astonishment as John-John's miniature fingers deftly removed a white cylinder from the blue package. It was a cigarette. John-John lit it with a match from the red packet, then cupped both hands to hold the cigarette to his mouth, covering his nostrils at the same time.

"He's a connection," Sarah said. "They do everything we do, to try to understand us."

"But why the babies?" Steven felt dizzy. The room, the creature, the *pa*, were so unreal, the smell of the cigarette so familiar. It was disorienting. And what about Wendy?

We sense your question, the silent voice said. *Wendy is not of you and us. Wendy is the child of Sarah. The child of Steven. She is safe and sleeping.*

"When can I see her?"

When she is not sleeping.

"Why did you take her?"

We take many. We put them back.

Steven shook his head. "But you didn't put Wendy back. You kept her. You kept Sarah and Derek. Where's Derek? Where are the others?"

John-John stared out from the cloud of smoke that curled around him. He only inhaled and exhaled when his hands covered his face. The red point of the cigarette glowed with each intake of breath.

There are so many others that the question can't be answered. But Derek is sleeping. You may see him when he is not sleeping. The last time we took Wendy, we were unable to put her back according to the schedule—

"Why not?" Steven demanded.

We took Wendy. We took Derek. Others watched Derek, and one of them used a medication that sealed his lungs to the effects of our mediator. He came after us. He fired a weapon. Things happened. The schedule was disrupted. Wendy and Derek were returned late. But we did return them.

"But you didn't return my wife!" Steven said. "You're monsters! Kidnappers! I—" It was like falling into a pool of hot water. Steven felt his muscles go limp. Relaxation spread through him. Abruptly, in the midst of this madness, he felt . . . calm and happy. He had no desire to shout at John-John. Everything would be all right.

The devices that do these things can stimulate other parts of your mind also. Are you better now?

"Yes," Steven replied evenly. "I'm fine, thank you."

John-John held the burning cigarette away from him. He inhaled and exhaled rapidly, wheezing. He brought the cigarette back to his face. The tip glowed brightly.

Do you have other questions now?

"Yes," Steven said. None of his indignation remained, only intellectual curiosity. "Why are you doing this? How long have you been here? Where are—"

There are many questions. There are many answers. We have been here forever to learn what we must do. We have been here for fifty years to do what we must do. Your words are DNA/ genes/chromosomes.

"You want those things from us?"

John-John nodded, black eyes staring out from a veil of smoke. He threw the butt of the cigarette to the floor. It was extinguished the instant it hit.

"Why do you want those things?"

You have things in DNA/genes/chromosomes that we do not have. We take them from you, mix them with the things we have, the babies are stronger. Your words are "to strengthen the strain."

"No, no," Steven said. He turned to Sarah. "That can't be. Professor Lurie talked about that. There's no way those things' DNA can be compatible with ours." He turned back to John-John. "You have to be—*ah!*"

John-John was in front of him, no more than two feet away. Steven had not heard or sensed him move.

The things inside us are compatible.

"How can they be?" Steven asked. He pulled back as John-John stepped closer, touched him, pushed against his knees.

There is no need for that question. The devices that do this can read that you already know the answer.

"No," Steven whispered. He didn't want *that* to be the answer.

"Yes," John-John said aloud. He reached up his hands to his light-swallowing eyes. Put his fingers at their edges. Dug in.

Steven cringed as he heard the wet sucking sound of John-John's fingers in his eyes. Gasped as John-John pulled out his eyes—

—and held soft, black membranes in his small gray hands. Steven looked back to John-John's face. Into his eyes. They were huge, slanted. But they were black only in their centers, each center ringed by a wide circle of ribbed brown, floating in an expanse of yellow white, slickly wet, tinged by small black lines at the outer edges. Like tiny capillaries carrying black blood. Steven stared in shock as he saw the rings of brown expand into the centers of the eyes, reducing each black center to a pinpoint.

His pupils are contracting, Steven thought. Those eyes are large but they're just . . . ordinary eyes. "You . . . you're . . ."

"Human," John-John said. "As human as you."

5

△△∠ ∠△△ △∠△ △△∠

Wendy awoke on a soft bed of green grass. The sun shone on her, warm and golden. The breeze brought the fresh, cool scent of a stream and the sound of its water splashing over rocks in the distance.

She sat up from the grass, looking off to the horizon to the right. Nearby, willow trees waved long branches against the ground. Past them, rolling hills dark with more trees stretched away to be lost in a mist from which mountains arose. She looked to the left. Reese lay on the grass beside her.

"Derek?" she said in a whisper, as if she were in church and afraid to disturb the others. She reached out to him, touched his shoulder. He stirred. She leaned over him as his eyelids fluttered. She kissed him lightly and that is how he awoke.

"Where are we?" he asked as he stood up beside her.

"I don't know. All I remember is the storm . . . on the beach was it?"

Derek looked down at himself. For the first time Wendy noticed that neither of them wore their own clothes. Instead, they each were dressed in a white smock, light and fine like linen. She reached up and moved the fabric against her skin. She wore nothing beneath it.

"They took us again," Reese said, resignation and anger in his voice.

"But they've let us go," Wendy said. "Maybe they're finished with us."

Derek took Wendy's hand. "We can hope," he said. "But I doubt it." He looked around again. "See anything familiar?"

Wendy smiled. "Just you." She watched him as he scanned the surrounding landscape, admiring the strength of his features, the power of his eyes. She looked at that face and knew that he was the one with whom she was destined to spend her life. She had no choice and wanted none. Derek Reese filled her heart and her life and . . .

She put her hand on his chest, moved it over the fabric. He, too, wore nothing else.

"They don't look like mountains in California," Reese said. "Maybe Washington. Why did they put us down here?" He cupped his hands to his mouth and shouted, "Helloooo! Anyone therrre?"

Not even an echo. Only the breeze.

"I think that means we're alone," Wendy said. She moved against him. Felt every contour of him through the thin fabric. "I love you," she said.

Reese hugged her. She felt the contours of him change and push into her. She lifted her head to him, lips open. He watched the horizon.

"We're alone," she said. "They've let us go."

"It's not right," he said. "I don't like it."

"Do you like this?" she asked teasingly, brushing her hand against him.

Reese smiled, held her hand in place. "Yes," he said. "But not this place."

"I don't care. I want you now. While we're alone. While we have time."

She stared into his eyes. For one instant, she sensed, he might have looked away, talked her out of it as he had in the Tempest room. But he hesitated one moment too long and everything she felt for him was reflected in his eyes. Every need she had was echoed. He moved his arms around and under her, lifted her up to him.

She wrapped her legs around him, sighing as she felt him thrusting at her, into her, fabric against fabric. He squeezed her to him, and she felt his legs trembling, even as her own heart trembled. Tenderly he lowered her to the ground, and they used the robes as a blanket against the grass.

Long after, he stayed in her, never diminishing, and they made love again. And again. Then they lay beside each other on the robes, staring up into the blue sky and the wisps of clouds.

"I've never felt so happy," Wendy said, trailing her hand lightly over Reese's chest and stomach, lightly coated with the thin sheen of their sweat. "Never felt so peaceful."

"Neither have I," Reese said. But his tone was flat, no match for Wendy's emotions.

"Is there something wrong with feeling happy and peaceful?" she took his chin between her thumb and forefinger to cheerfully shake some sense into him.

"How do you feel about me?" Reese asked.

"I love you," Wendy said, and her heart was filled with that feeling as she said the words.

"But what do you think about me? My work? The things I do?"

"Is that important?" Wendy asked.

"Why do you love me?" Reese kept watching the sky.

"I've always loved you," Wendy said. She was puzzled by his mood. "I remember the first time I saw you, it was as though I had always known you. Known who you were and what you were like." Her voice lowered. "And what you would be like making love with me." She laughed, her mood mercurial. "Maybe we were lovers in a previous life."

Reese still didn't look at her. Instead, he held one arm straight above, with one finger pointing up, and closed one eye. Wendy shook her head as she saw his finger's shadow fall across his face. "What else do you remember about the first time you saw me?" he asked.

"Why, that I saw you . . . and knew that you were . . ." Wendy stopped, lost in thought.

"I can't remember either," Reese said.

The sun was warm on Wendy's body. But Reese's voice chilled her.

"I think that the first time we *could* possibly have met," Reese continued, "was when Merril and I hijacked Starr and took you and your father along for the ride."

Wendy frowned. "But I know I've known you much longer than that. And we've been . . . taken together . . . so many times." She stared at the shadow of his finger, which still fell across his eye.

"I know," Reese said softly. "I know that we've been taken together. And I think that the first time we met each other was *when* we were taken."

"I always, I don't know, thought you were a friend of my father's . . . my mother's . . . from . . . somewhere else." Wendy was feeling nervous. "What do you remember about the first time we met?"

"I don't remember where it was, but I remember the first time I saw you," Reese said. "It was as though I had always known you. Known who you were and what you were like and what you would be like making love with me. Maybe we were lovers in a previous life. It's word for word, Wendy. As if we had both studied the same script. Or had been taught the same script."

Wendy felt an unnerving anxiety grow in her. She sat up. Reese still didn't move, one finger still pointed to the sky. To the sun.

"What do you mean?" she demanded. "What are you saying?" She grabbed his upstretched arm. Pushed it aside. *"What are you doing?"*

Reese sat up. Shook his head at her. "How long have we been here?" he asked.

"I . . . an hour? Two hours? I don't know. What's going on?"

Reese squinted up at the sky. "The sun hasn't moved, Wendy. The sun is in the same place it was when we woke up here."

Wendy looked up at the sky. The sun was becoming obscured behind a growing wall of dark clouds. Her voice was quiet, nervous, a whisper. "What do you mean, Derek?"

Reese stood and picked up his robe. Wendy stared at him as the mountains in the distance were swallowed by the mist, while the willows dissolved and the forests faded. While the grass changed into a large circular mat of soft blue fabric and the sun became nothing more than a softly glowing brown crystal set in the topmost part of a curved ceiling, twenty feet above their heads.

"I mean they picked us up," Reese said as he pulled his robe over his head.

Wendy gasped and held her own robe to cover her nakedness

as the final remnants of the illusion broke down and the creatures appeared before them, surrounding them, filling every space on the wide bench that ran around the circular room they were in.

"But they haven't let us go," Reese said.

△△∠ ∠△△ △∠△ △△△

John-John held one tiny gray hand above his eyes to shield them from the dim overhead light. His enormous folds of gray eyelids half closed, and his bulging eyes withdrew, squinting.

We are compatible because we are the same, the silent voice said.

Steven dug his fingers into the chair. "But . . . but you told Starr that . . . you were from another world. Another planet."

John-John tilted his head from side to side. *We need help. We need helpers. The helpers need things to help them decide to help us. The devices that do things tell the helpers what they need to hear.* John-John put part of one soft black membrane into his mouth and held it there. He placed the other membrane over his right eye and with both hands slipped it into place, sliding the edges of it beneath his lids with delicate fingers.

Some are told we are Martians. Some are told we are fairies. Some are told we have universities on the moon. Some are told they have been taken to Venus. The devices tell them what they need to hear.

"And then no one will know the truth," Steven said. "So if some of the people remember being here and if they ever meet, each will tell a different story. And people will argue and fight and there will be nothing for them to agree about. And the rest of the world will say that they all can't be right, so that they all must be wrong." He shook his head. He smiled for an instant. "My word is 'disinformation.'"

We have a word that means the same. John-John replaced the membrane in his left eye, blinked several times, then looked around the room and up to the overhead light. Steven watched the creature's eyes move beneath the membranes and now that he knew what was behind them, he could see the faintest outlines of pupil and iris, the subtlest change in density between the center and the sides of each eye. The truth hidden behind darkness, seen only in shadows.

"What kind of humans are you, then? The first humans? Do you live on another planet? Are you coming back to visit us?"

John-John drew himself up to his full height of four feet. Steven got the impression that this was a pose signifying pride. "We are from earth," John-John said. And there *was* unmistakable dignity in his intonation.

"Where?" Steven asked. Immediately his mind filled with all the stories he had heard of holes in the North Pole. Underground tunnels, deep caverns, secret worlds.

"Wrong question," John-John said. He skittered around with unnatural speed, spinning like a top and returned to the same position in front of Steven. Steven jumped back in surprise. Pride he had understood, but this response had meant nothing.

"You should ask, 'When?' " John-John said.

Steven sat in confusion. When? he thought. Time travel?

Yes, said the voice in his mind. *To your frame of reference, we are from the future.*

"How . . . how far in the future?" Steven asked. The sense of calm and happiness was fading from him. He felt excitement and exhilaration and . . . fear.

Our measurements are different, the silent voice said and then added, *Further from you than you are from the first humans.*

Steven felt himself tremble with every breath. He looked at Sarah. She sat calmly. "Can you hear what he says to me?" he asked her.

Sarah smiled. "I know." Steven recognized the expression on her face, calm and happy.

Steven turned back to John-John. "But you don't look like us. You may be human, but you're . . . different. Aren't you?"

You do not look like us, yet you are human also, the silent voice said mind-to-mind. John-John smiled. Hideously, Steven thought.

"Why do you look different? How did you get to be different?"

John-John stood in the position of thought, his fist against his shoulder. Long seconds passed before there was a reply.

Our earth is different. We are different for it. The creature pointed to his eyes. *The light is different. Our eyes are different.*

He pointed to his nose. *The gases are different. The parts of us that interact with those gases are different.*

"How did the light and the air come to be different?" Steven didn't know much about the history of life on earth, but he did know that the dinosaurs had lived in a world where conditions were generally the same as they were now. The sun shone. The plants made oxygen. It rained and snowed. And that had been millions of years in the past. What could make it so different millions of years in the future?

"Things happened," John-John explained. *Many things,* the silent voice continued. *To the earth. To us. Some were done long before us. Your words for some things are genetic engineering.*

"People made themselves to be like you?" Steven asked in horror. "On purpose?"

For special purposes they were made to be like us. DNA/ genes/chromosomes were refined. Old things thrown away from them. New things added to them. Much of the DNA/genes/ chromosomes in you have been lost to us. Things that now we need. Much of the DNA/genes/chromosomes in you remains the same. You give us what we have lost.

"Why come back in time for it?" Steven asked. "Why not recreate it. Genetically . . . engineer it again?"

The things that are lost to us were billions of years in the making. The ways in which they were lost to us are also lost to us. We did not make ourselves to be this way. We do not have those among us who know how to recreate that which has been lost. But we do have those who know how to come back in time. We came back in time.

Steven closed his eyes, struggling to comprehend all that John-John was telling him. Each new answer opened a door to a thousand additional questions. He opened his eyes and jumped again. John-John was gone.

"John-John . . . ?" Steven called.

The creature appeared beside Steven, sliding into view without body movement. He held a copper rod in his hand.

"How do you move like that?" Steven asked.

Transference and placement, the voice said. *The two fundamental powers of existence. Beyond that, you have no words.*

"Is that what you used to come back here?" Steven looked around the room. "Is this . . . is this your time machine?"

"This is the *pa,*" John-John said, holding his hands above him and spinning once in a circle so quickly that he blurred before Steven's eyes. *Could you explain a computer to a Neanderthal?* the voice said, drawing on the half-formed image in Steven's mind. *The time machine remains where it was constructed. This is the part that does not remain where it was constructed. Listen to us.* John-John touched the probe to Steven's forehead.

A sense picture formed in Steven's mind, like a clear memory of something he had seen before. He saw a long channel cut through barren rock and lifeless soil, a channel curving with the shape of a world he had never seen. The bottom of the channel was liquid and shimmering. In his vision like a memory, he swept along that channel, flying above it. The walls of it rushed at him, then rushed apart. He gasped as he descended and kept descending. The channel was miles wide.

He flew above the surface as it rippled and swelled, silver and black, like a dissolving skin of something solid floating on a sea of mercury. He felt a rumbling in the rushing air as he flew. A black spot appeared on the horizon where the immense walls of the channel met at their vanishing point. Steven flew toward that spot.

It grew in his vision less rapidly than the walls rushed by him. The spot was something else that moved along the channel. But Steven gained on it.

He came closer and saw it was something artificial, as wide as the channel, miles wide, speeding over the liquid surface, inches above it, studded with lights and golden spires that glowed like the probes of the creatures. Steven gained on it. Flew over it.

The machine *curved* with the curvature of the channel, the curvature of the planet. *This planet is the earth,* said the voice. *You do not have the words for the size of this device.*

Still Steven flew over it, feeling it pulse with the power of . . . *transference* . . . seeing it shudder as it adjusted its structure to maintain the perfect separation between its lower surface and the rippling bottom of the channel, inch by inch, over its entire length, instantaneously.

How can it *do* that? Steven asked in wonder as he flew.

Placement, the voice said. *The fundamental powers of existence. You do not have the words for it.*

Steven approached the forward end of the device. A golden tower glowed there, taller than the machine was wide, blazing through the atmosphere at its upper reaches where the tower's speed was . . . *you do not have the words for it.*

Steven dove at the tower, felt himself twist and deform around it, shoot by it, ahead of the speeding device, looping through the channel and then flying back at the device as it hurtled relentlessly toward him.

It came at him. A blindly speeding mountain of . . . metal? *You do not have the words for it.* Closer it came, the edges of it passing from his field of vision. The golden tower disappearing above him as a fiery, sparking point of light as distant as a star.

Steven flew toward the rushing bottom edge. It was knife-sharp, speeding, slicing the air, drawing the shimmering molten surface of the channel up over it in a wave so thin it was . . . *you do not have the words for it.*

Steven flashed toward that leading edge. It filled his vision. The roar of it grew until his ears were deaf and the sound existed within his body, vibrating the air in his lungs, his muscles, his eyes, blurring all sight, all feeling, all sensations, until—

—he passed through—

Transference.

—the surface of the channel—

And there was *more* of it.

The device continued. The part he had already experienced was only a foothold, an anchor to a place and a time. But here beneath the surface was the time machine itself. Steven looked at it, felt it, tasted it, smelled it, tore through time with it, understood none of it.

You do not have the senses for it. You do not have the mind for it.

And he was through the surface again floating above . . . the *pa* . . . the probe, the knowing tip of the unknowable.

Steven flew at it, feeling relief. He could comprehend its length—three miles. He could comprehend its width—one mile. He could comprehend its hundred-story thickness.

It glowed with pinpricks of light, or it disappeared beneath a shield of blackness. It sent out other parts from itself, smaller tips of smaller probes, which scratched the surface of a world he *had* seen before. The earth, he thought. The earth he knew.

Steven flew at the device, wrapping clouds around itself, hiding between the pinpricks of stars, beneath oceans and deserts. Wherever it was not searched for, it was found. Steven flew at it, swerving around the probes that left it and returned. He plunged into it, speeding through the single dimly lit corridor that snaked throughout it, writhing with the shudders and strains of . . . *transference and placement* . . . the forces that held it in its place, anchored it to the future, stretched it through another time and place, to reach to Steven's here and now.

He slowed in a corridor. He passed through a door. He was in a room that looked like a shopping mall had exploded.

Steven opened his eyes. He found it hard to breathe, as though he had been struggling against a high wind. And he was drenched in sweat, rapidly evaporating in the room's dry air.

"This is the *pa*," John-John said.

He removed the probe. The lesson had ended.

"But you can't be from the future," Steven said. He wiped at his face, still trembling from the exhilaration of his vision, another series of induced stimuli to his mind.

How can we not be? the voice asked.

"Dr. Zeifman said there would be paradoxes. You'd split time lines. Set up impossible conflicts. Knowledge of the future would change the course of the past, which then changes the future."

Such things are true, the voice said. *Such things must be guarded against. Terrible things could happen if such things were not guarded against. Terrible things have happened when such things were not guarded against.*

"Then how can you be here? Having pictures taken? Having books written? Most of the people in the world already know something about you. Won't you change your future? I mean, your past? Your present?"

We are here, so we have not, the voice said. *Your words for it are "grandfather paradox." If you kill your grandfather before you are born, you will create a paradox. But what paradox would be created if you killed your grandfather's brother?*

Steven stared into the depths of John-John's eyes, seeing the blackness, the mystery of the membranes that covered them, knowing the truth that lay within them. "I don't understand," Steven said.

We use your words, the voice answered. *Your grandfather's brother travels on a ship which malfunctions. Your grandfather's brother is alone on an island, alone in the sea. For five years your grandfather's brother lives on that island. Then the island vol-*

cano erupts and your grandfather's brother is killed. John-John tilted his head, blinked his eyes. *What would the paradox be if you went back in time and killed your grandfather's brother when he arrived on the island, alone in the sea, never destined to interact with the rest of the world, leading to the future?*

Steven looked at Sarah. She smiled and did nothing. He looked at John-John. Couldn't read the expression of the non-human human face. "There would be no paradox," Steven said, shrugging. "If the man wasn't destined to have any impact on the future, no children, no important actions, then it would make no difference if he were killed the day he landed on the island or five years later when the volcano exploded." *So what?* he thought.

Exactly, the silent voice agreed. *If he is to have no impact on the future, then it would make no difference if he were killed. Or if he were taken to Venus. Or met with fairies. Or brought to the* pa *and remembered everything that happened to him here. No impact. No paradox. No difference.*

Once as a child, Steven had taken a shortcut through a ravine by walking along a train trestle. Halfway across the trestle, he had heard an approaching train's whistle. He felt the same way now.

Steven's eyes widened in terror. "But . . . most of the people in the world know something about you . . . ," he repeated in a raspy whisper.

No impact. No difference.

This was worse than the thing in his bedroom doorway. Worse than the old man with the whiskers, the eyes floating out of the television.

"You're saying that . . . most of the people in the world . . . will have no impact on the future?"

"This is the *pa,*" John-John said. "I am John-John. These are my things. You may know all these things that happen. You may remember all these things. It no longer matters." He spun in a circle. Looked at Steven. "No impact. No difference." He spun again and again. A whirlwind of gray and black. A whirlwind of eyes like the night.

"When?" Steven asked. His throat was dry. He heard the thunder of his heart, pounding in fear and in dread. "When does the . . . volcano erupt?"

And John-John gave Steven the book.

6

△△∠ ∠△△ △△∠ △

"And then what happened?" Dr. Lurie asked.

Reese paced back and forth in the circular room, eyes wild, pulling on his clothes, which the creatures had left for him. "They used their probes on us. Touched them to our foreheads. You stiffen out, float. I don't remember. I could hear Wendy scream. I couldn't move. Their hands were all over me, pushing me toward one of those disappearing doors. And then I woke up here."

Miles sat on the bench that circled the room, hunched over like a cowering dog in a cage, rocking and rocking against the trembling of the floor and the thunderous shudders that echoed around him. "And they floated you in here about ten minutes before you came out of it," he said. "Jesus. How do they do that? How do they do that?"

"Transference and placement they call it," Lurie said. Unlike Miles, the professor's face was flushed with excitement.

"How do you know what they call anything?" Reese asked tensely.

"I asked them," Lurie said. "When I came to in the receiving bay after blacking out in the kitchen in the beach house, there were at least five of them there. Two of them were quite talkative. I asked them questions and they answered." He smiled at

Reese. "They do everything by manipulating the forces of transference and placement."

"What are those?"

"I have no idea," Lurie said happily. "They told me I didn't have the words for it. Right now we think there's probably just one fundamental force in the universe that manifests itself as gravity, electromagnetism, and the nuclear forces. Maybe they operate on the assumption that there are two fundamental forces. Science has always changed with the times. No reason why it shouldn't keep changing in their time too." He shrugged as though it really made no difference to him.

"What do you mean, 'in their time'?" Reese asked, stopping his pacing and staring at the professor.

"Why, they're from the future," Lurie said plainly. He looked at Reese's glaring expression. "I asked them that too. They're very forthright little people. Quite human too. They're our descendants."

"But I thought . . . ," Reese shook his head, "I thought Dr. Zeifman said that was impossible."

Lurie looked over to the wider part of the room-circling bench that was presumed to be a bed. Reese looked too. Rachel Zeifman sat there, eyes wide and vacant. A tiny line of spittle drooled from her mouth.

"I don't think Rachel is saying much of anything right now," Lurie remarked.

"Did they say how they traveled in time?" Miles asked. He wrapped both arms over his head, moving with a start with each rumble, each creak of strain in the walls.

"Said I didn't have the words for it," Lurie explained.

"Did they say *why* they're here?" Reese asked, walking over to the scientist. "Did they say *what* they're doing with us? To us?" He grabbed Lurie by his shirt collar. "Did they say why they answered your questions when they haven't answered any of mine *for more than thirty goddam years?*"

Lurie tried pulling back from Reese, but the man was too strong, his rage too great.

"You should *know* what they're doing," Lurie said in a rush. "You're part of it. Wendy too. They're breeding present-day humans. Surveying the population with wide-ranging sampling techniques. Isolating the individuals in whom they're interested. Matching those individuals by pair-bonding them, then having selected offspring crossbreed with—"

Reese jerked up on Lurie's collar. "Pair-bonding? How?"

Lurie held both hands to his throat and started to cough. Reese let go and the professor stumbled to his knees. "They talk to us with the beacons that they put into our heads in the receiving room. The beacons can stimulate different cells of our brains. Make us hear words. Sense different things." He got up to his feet. "Don't you see, Derek? That's how they made you and Wendy think you were in the middle of a country field. Direct stimulation of your sensory inputs. Back in the Tempest room, when you and Wendy were talking about all your abduction memories, sight and sound confusion, as well as smell sensations, were all integral to them. Maybe the technique works better in this vessel than it does at a distance, so the illusions are better once you've been picked up, but the technique does explain a great deal."

"But how do they pair-bond us?"

Lurie still spoke rapidly, words falling over each other, cringing with each movement Reese made. "I'm not sure. But if they can stimulate the brain from a distance, maybe they abduct two people whose genes they want to concentrate in one individual and expose them to each other while stimulating their pleasure centers. They key the stimulus to scent clues or pheromones involving the most primitive parts of the brain so that the powerful pleasure memories will be triggered whenever the people are in each other's presence, sensing each other's scent. And then, when those two people meet back in the real world, they're overcome with the unremembered pleasure stimulus of meeting in this place, and they inevitably fall in love, have children—whatever these little people want them to do."

Reese wanted to tear down the walls with his bare hands. He wanted to rip the creatures' heads from their bodies. He—

—felt calm and peaceful.

Reese staggered backward as if the air had been knocked out of him.

"What's wrong?" Lurie asked but, judiciously, didn't approach the man.

"Nothing," Reese said calmly. "I feel fine. I wanted to . . . hit something. Damage somebody. And then, all of a sudden, I feel the way I did when I woke up in the field—the fake field—with Wendy. Happy. Not upset. Very peaceful."

"That's great," Lurie said excitedly. "That proves the point. You were getting wild, uncontrollable. They're only little beings and probably nervous about having giant humans go amok around them, so they have an automatic mechanism that senses your aggression, then fires off a series of impulses to alter your emotional state."

"Can nerve impulses alone make me feel this way?" Reese said. He felt just fine. Everything was going to be okay.

"I don't know for sure," Lurie said, relaxing as he saw Reese actually calming down. "Maybe when they have you up here, they give you all sorts of posthypnotic suggestions and then they can fire off just a single impulse to trigger the response to feel calm and peaceful." He walked over to Reese. "It's not important how they do it," he said. "What's important is that they *can* do it, and not by magic."

Reese looked up at the professor. He tried to remember the violent feelings he had had just a few seconds ago, but they were gone. "Is that why you look so happy?" Reese asked Lurie. "Are they stimulating your happiness circuits?"

Lurie laughed. "Believe me, Derek, my happiness circuits are being stimulated just by being here. This is *discovery*. This is the sublime moment of science. Seeing things and learning things that no one has ever seen or learned before."

"You have to write it up for it to be science," Miles said. He had curled up on his side on the bench, drawing his knees to his chest.

"Well, when they let me go, I intend to publish everything, my boy. I'll even get you and Rachel to help."

"What makes you think they're going to let you go, Professor?" Reese asked.

"Why, conditions have obviously changed," Lurie said. "I mean, this experience I'm having is like nothing any of the other abductees have reported. The little people are going out of their way to be helpful and answer all my questions. When they inserted the beacon in my nostril, they explained the entire procedure. There's no confusion to what's been happening to me, no rush. Maybe they've decided it's time to reveal themselves to us."

"But if they're from the future, Professor, then how can they reveal themselves to us without creating one of the paradoxes that Dr. Zeifman was talking about?"

"I don't know," Lurie said.

"Because you don't have the words for it?" Reese asked.

Lurie shook his head and grimaced. "Actually, I just plain forgot to ask."

$$\triangle\triangle\angle \quad \angle\triangle\triangle \quad \triangle\triangle\angle \quad \triangle$$

"Even in your time, you still use books?" Steven asked.

"We use transference and placement," John-John said. "You use books. You use this book." He tilted his head. "Please."

Steven ran his fingers over the cover of John-John's book. It was a foot tall, a foot wide, four inches thick. The cover felt and looked like heat-stressed copper, the pages were thick, yet the book weighed no more than a few ounces. Steven put one finger under the cover, lifted it open.

John-John took the book from him. Turned it back to front. "You use this book this way," he said.

Steven smiled. He opened what he would call the book's back cover. The first page held a familiar-looking symbol, a circle quartered by a cross. Beneath it were a series of nine small blue triangles arranged in groups of three. Each triangle was slightly different. Some shifted to the left, some to the right, some equilateral. A few of them were missing one side.

"Is this the book you showed to Betty Hill?" Steven asked, smiling, trembling. He held an object in his hands that would not be manufactured for millions of years.

We give the people the books they need. We give them trade routes between the stars. We give them visions from their gods. Whatever they need, that is what we give them.

Steven placed his palm on the circle. He looked at John-John. Dared those eyes. "Is this book what I need? Is this another lie?"

John-John looked away from Steven. Stepped back from him. Spoke aloud. "This book is what you need. But this book is not a lie." John-John held his fists against his left shoulder. "This book is what we all need. Though there are some on the *pa* who would not want you to look at it."

Steven turned the first page.

It was like looking through the window of a spaceship. The earth hung before him in space. He could see the sun glint from the Atlantic, the puffs of clouds, the mottled surface of green and brown. A fine tracing of North American city lights glittering from behind the terminator line dividing night from day.

"What is this?" Steven asked. The effect was stunning.

"The earth," John-John said.

"I know that," Steven said in annoyance. "I mean, how is this image formed? What is it?"

John-John stepped forward and peeked over the edge of the page to see what Steven saw. "It is a picture," the creature said.

Steven sighed. He could swear he could see the terminator creep across the surface of the planet. It was magnificent.

"And what are these?" Steven asked, pointing out another line of blue triangles that ran across the page. Twenty seven of them in groups of three this time.

"The image shows where," John-John said. "The words say when."

"Words," Steven repeated, shaking his head. He turned the second page.

More words. The symbols that crossed the page were incomprehensible to him. A blurred scratching of muddy yellow, orange, and blue angles, lines and dashes, difficult to resolve in the brown light of John-John's room.

"What do these say?" he asked.

"Turn the page," John-John said.

It was another window into space. This time even Steven could tell it was a dying world. A dead world. The land masses were brown and tan, the oceans green and purple, and what few clouds there were scattered near the poles were black. Steven stared in wonder at the image, watching as this world's terminator also slowly swept across its surface, bringing light and new details as he watched.

"Dear God," he said. The terminator swept over a land mass. The lines of it were wrong, but he recognized it. "That's . . . Africa?" he asked.

"That was Africa," John-John said. He touched the spine of the book.

The image speeded up. The terminator created the world with a swath of light.

"I see . . . Europe?" Steven whispered. "But where's England?"

John-John nodded. "Where is England?" he repeated.

The world turned. Something that might have been a child's

attempt to draw the outline of North America came into view. It held a new ocean at its center. It held nothing green.

Steven looked at the blue triangles. Meaningless.

"Is this what is to happen?" Steven asked, voice weak.

"This is what *has* happened," John-John said.

"War?" Steven asked. "Did we do this ourselves?"

"Not this time."

"Pollution? A comet?"

"Nothing you have imagined," John-John said gently.

"Can . . . can we stop it?"

What you see has already happened for us, Steven, the silent voice said. *If you could have stopped it, you would have stopped it, and we would not exist.*

Steven touched his hand to the surface of the picture. It felt soft and spongy like a bag of water. The dying earth spun beneath his fingers. He felt tears in his eyes and fought against them.

"I used to hear people talk about things like this," he said, voice choking. "I use to hear them say that this is why we needed a space program. We should have gotten off the planet."

"You should have gotten out of the system," John-John said. And Steven sensed bitterness in the comment.

"W-when will this happen?" Steven asked. He had never felt such helplessness. Not even when strapped to one of their examination tables.

"Soon," John-John said.

"And . . . and it's all destroyed?"

If it were all destroyed, then we would not be here, the voice spoke. *The DNA/genes/chromosomes pool will be depleted. But it will survive.*

"Most of the world," Steven whispered. "But not all of it."

Fewer than three hundred. They are the ones with whom we cannot interfere.

John-John shut the book in Steven's lap.

"And you're interfering with us," Steven sighed. "With Sarah and Wendy and me." The realization was his death notice. The end of his family. The end of all possible futures for his child and her children and forever.

John-John stepped back to Steven. He opened the book again. Showed him more pictures.

"What is this place?" Steven asked.

"The *marae,*" John-John said. *Your time is at an end,* the silent voice said. *Your line ends except for the DNA/genes/chromosomes we carry with us back to our present to strengthen the strain.*

John-John pointed one tiny gray finger at the pictures in the book. "The three hundred," he said. "My ancestors. The survivors from whom all human history and civilization will descend."

Steven looked at the pictures. They showed a town. A town of humans. A small town, judging by the buildings he saw. Recognizable ones. A church. A town hall. People in the streets. He saw horses pulling an old truck, so he knew the people struggled. But they lived. Had lived.

"These are the survivors?" Steven asked.

"This is the place that survived," John-John said. *Be happy that the children of your DNA/genes/chromosomes will find a new world to live in. Fields of grass and flowers to run through. Your line will continue, though you will not.*

"This is the place that survivors go," John-John said.

Steven met his large black eyes. Something was wrong. What John-John was saying and what the silent voice was saying seemed to be two different things.

"If I go there, will I survive?" Steven asked.

The future will be saved because of your children. They will find a paradise. Be happy.

"This is where the survivors were," John-John said.

Steven looked at the pictures in the book. He saw high cliffs on all sides, rounded by water erosion. He saw a narrow stretch of water. Small buildings with flat roofs that were banded in white, corrugated, and painted red. He looked closely at the truck pulled by horses, checking for all the details he could see. But there was no license plate and he didn't recognize the make.

Be calm and happy, the silent voice said. *Soon the world will be a different place. A place of hardship. Soon the world will be for the young. But your line will continue in the future. Your children will survive in the future.*

"The silent voice isn't your voice, is it?" Steven asked.

"The devices that do these things, do many things," John-John said.

"Are you telling me something different from what the voice tells me?"

"Am I?"

"I don't know what to do," Steven said. He trembled with confusion. Was it all to end or was John-John somehow telling him there was hope? A more immediate hope than genes being transferred through time?

John-John pointed to a picture of the town. Of the *marae.*

"Remember," the creature said, "so you will know what to do when the time comes."

Steven stared at the picture. It disappeared. John-John slapped the book shut, slipped it under his arm.

"Why have you shown me this?" Steven asked. "You've had me here before, kept me drugged or unconscious. Why keep me here awake now? Why are things different now? Why do you let me know about these things?"

"Because we made a mistake," John-John said. "This is my apology." He spun once, blurred. When he stopped, the book was gone. "Because I am a connection. My study of you is complete. I wish to see how you respond to the knowledge of your culture's destruction." He tapped his foot against the floor. "Because I have known you since before you were born. Since before I was born. Because some of this is true. Because none of this is true."

John-John tilted his head, his eyes unreadable. "Whatever makes it easier for you. That is what I tell you."

He spun again. The floor liquified beneath him. He was gone.

Steven shuddered. He tried to stand, but his legs were too weak. He turned to Sarah.

"We have to stop him. Stop them. Stop it," he said.

"We can't," Sarah said. Calm and happy.

"We have to at least try!"

"Why?" Sarah said. "Don't be fooled by John-John. He's not very good with the language, you know." She stood and went to him. "Don't you know the real reason why John-John told us all of this?"

Steven shook his head.

"No impact, no difference," Sarah said. "He told us all of this because we will never be able to tell anyone else. They're never letting us return home, Steven. They're taking us with them."

7

△△∠ ∠△△ ∠▽▽ △△

Wendy felt her face gently caressed with love. She opened her eyes.

"John-John?" she asked, disbelieving.

"Hello, Wendy," John-John said. He slowly took his hand away.

Wendy thought she should be screaming at this point. She thought she should be raging at them for what they had just done to her and Derek, for letting her do something like that while they all sat around and watched. But there was no fear in her. No anger. No humiliation. Nothing. "You're real," was all she could manage.

"You knew that," John-John said. "You always knew that."

Wendy nodded. "Yes," she said finally. "You were my friend."

"I am your friend still."

Wendy looked around the room she was in. Round and light brown and circled by a bench. Just like all the others she had been in dozens of times before. "Am *I* your friend?" she asked.

"You are more than my friend, Wendy." John-John shook his head and looked away. "More than my friend."

"Why are things so different now?" Wendy asked.

"How do you find them different?"

"I don't know. You . . . you wouldn't keep me here as long before. You never came after me like you did at my dad's apartment. I'd never seen soldiers before. It's like you aren't in control anymore. Things aren't going the way they should." She shrugged. "I don't know."

"The schedule has almost ended," John-John said. "I remember once you were mad at me because we took you when you were doing work for your school class. You said your work was late. You were out of time."

Wendy stopped smiling. "Is your work late, John-John? Is your work out of time?"

"Yes."

"Is there anything I can do to help?"

"You've done so much already." He smiled at her.

"You're getting better at doing that," Wendy said.

"I think I understand it now."

"A smile isn't supposed to be something you understand. It's something you feel."

"I only understand," John-John said. And Wendy heard the sadness in him.

John-John held out his hand to her, and she took it without hesitation. She remembered those hands playing with her in her sandbox, in the park. Showing her odd books, strange pictures. She remembered John-John's big black eyes as she patiently explained about Barbie and Ken. About her mother and father. About cars and school and just about everything in her life. She took his hand knowing that nothing bad could come of it. She looked in his eyes and saw the big warm eyes of a puppy. Friendly. Needing.

"I have something special to show you," John-John said.

"What?" Wendy asked.

"The *kohanga reo.*" John-John led her to the door, touched the black handle. The door unspun.

"What's the *kohanga reo?*"

"You will see."

They came to an intersection. A cadre of six drones appeared, marching like a drill team. Each carried a small gray plastic flight kennel with a sticker that said "Live Animals" in large red letters. Each kennel held kittens. Mewing, sleeping, purring kittens.

"Are you taking those with you?" Wendy asked, smiling at the kittens as the drones walked by, followed by their operator.

"Yes," John-John said. "Many things have been lost. Now many things will be found."

They came to a large door in the corridor, wider than it was tall. The symbol beside it was something Wendy had never seen before on the *pa*, but it looked Egyptian.

"The *kohanga reo*," John-John said, unspinning the door.

Wendy walked into the large room, blinking in the brighter light. "The babies!" she said with excitement. "I've never seen them before!"

She walked quickly to the first incubator machine in the long row. The babies were so small, so delicate. She smiled at them in their cylinders. Some slept. Some fussed. Some smiled back. Real smiles with real lips, however thin and unformed they were. No other creatures were in the room.

Then Wendy stood back from the incubator, turned to John-John. "I've heard my mother speak of these," she said. "Are . . . are any of them mine?"

"They are your brothers and your sisters, but none of them are yours alone," John-John said. "They were the first reason we came. We needed the things within cells that make us stronger, more . . ." He raised his hands in helplessness. "I do not have the words," he apologized.

Wendy touched her forehead. "Use the silent voice," she said.

"Your beacon has been removed."

Wendy felt a moment of shock. "But . . . how will you find me again? How will we talk?"

"We will not find you because we will not look for you. We will not talk because we will not see you again."

"You're leaving?" Wendy asked.

John-John nodded.

"Can I go with you?"

"Of all our visitors, you are the one who cannot."

"But you're taking the babies?"

"They are the first reason why we came."

Wendy looked at the tiny gray faces, stared down the row of incubators. There were hundreds of them. Perhaps thousands. She turned back to John-John.

"Was there another reason for you coming?" she asked.

"For the devices of the *pa*, no other reason." John-John said. "But for the others of us who work in shadows, our second purpose became to find you."

△△∠ ∠△△ ∠△△ △△△

Gardiner thought of the room as a lounge.

Instead of being circular, it was long, more like a half cylinder. Small round benches were arranged in it, more than one hundred in each direction from the central doors. Each bench had room for eight people. And each bench was full.

Gardiner saw men and women, boys and girls, black, white, Oriental, Middle Eastern, Native North American. Some wore suits from the streets of Los Angeles or New York. Others wore clothes or uniforms of different countries and cultures. Some wore little. Others had their furs and cold-weather clothing stacked beside them.

Yet for all their differences, the people were all the same. Each sat silently, staring into the distance waiting for his or her turn.

"Processing," the creature who had escorted Gardiner had called it. "Some will be staying. Some will be going home."

"Will I be staying?" Gardiner had asked.

"For a small length of time," the creature had said. "So we may talk of fear."

Gardiner had been floated to this room, had been guided to a bench, and had sat down. Then the creature had touched a probe to his forehead, and Gardiner had become more patient than he had ever remembered himself to be.

Time passed. Gardiner was in no hurry. Occasionally, small creatures in blue coveralls would glide by like puppets joined at the feet and arms. Some would carry black devices similar to the one they had attached to Roy Luck's shoulder.

Most of the groups of little ones would be accompanied by a larger creature, still only four to four and a half feet tall. The larger creatures reminded Gardiner of overseers.

Gardiner also saw taller creatures, more insectlike in their movements, slimmer, slighter than the others. Two had walked up to him as though gliding on skates. They had stood there for a long time, staring at him with their impenetrably black eyes. Gardiner had smiled. He remembered now. He had been here before. A long, long time ago.

After a while, some other people came to join Gardiner,

floated in by the smaller creatures. Gardiner turned his head as much as he was able against whatever force kept him seated to watch them be released from floating. A woman and three men. He was surprised to recognize one of them.

"Hello, Derek," Gardiner said.

Reese sat like an automaton beside Gardiner. He turned his head. Blinked in what Gardiner thought was surprise.

"Hello, Ed." Reese smiled. "Come here often?" he asked.

Gardiner wanted to laugh, but he couldn't. He felt numb. "Once," he answered. "When I was a kid. I always remembered a time just before Christmas when Santa's elves came into my room one night and took me to the North Pole to see their workshop. I think I was six. I thought it was a dream. How about you?"

"I started around six too, I think. But they kept coming back for me."

"Is that how you got out of the beach house?"

"Yes."

"And why you never called in for backup that night with the plane?"

"Yes."

It was a struggle, but Gardiner smiled again. "The OCI thought you had sold out to the Soviets. Thought the UFO that took you away was a . . . Soviet hovercraft."

Reese coughed. Gardiner watched as a peculiar expression came to the agent's face.

"I'm really trying to laugh right now," Reese gasped. "God, am I trying to laugh."

"I can see them down by the beach house now," Gardiner said, tears of laughter struggling to come to his own eyes. "Goddam Soviets. Goddam four-foot-tall Soviets with their bug eyes and their hovercraft did it . . . did it again."

Both men snorted.

"Who are the people with you?" Gardiner asked after the spasms of repressed laughter had eased.

"People who helped me," Reese said. He introduced Lurie, Miles, and Dr. Zeifman. "She hasn't had a lot to say since she got here. She was convinced they couldn't be real."

"Any idea what they are?" Gardiner asked.

"Time travelers from the future," Reese said. He snorted again. "Maybe, Soviet time travelers from the future."

"God, I wish I could laugh," Gardiner said.

"They *are* very militaristic," Professor Lurie interrupted. "Watch how they organize themselves. How they greet each other. There definitely seems to be a social hierarchy at work. Almost like a colony of army ants. Or like an army."

Gardiner glanced around as much of the long room as he could see. The marching columns of small creatures. The taller ones who seemed to somehow control them. Other creatures in darker coveralls wandering here and there with their large glowing metal probes. It *was* like the army the way they met each other, gave way, pointed at, or ignored each other. He looked at the milling action of the room and saw it in a new light. No longer the hopeless confusion of a train station, but the preparation activities of a military staging area.

"Why would an army travel in time?" Gardiner asked.

"They're breeding humans," Reese said bitterly.

"Why?"

Lurie answered. "To reintroduce lost genetic traits into the species of the future. Hmm. I wonder if there's been a war? If they're trying to repopulate?"

"Then why breed us? Why not just kidnap us to their time?" Reese asked.

"Dr. Zeifman's paradoxes," Lurie said. "They can take sex cells from us without affecting the time lines. But they can't take people. Or so I would imagine."

"Any idea what they're going to do with us?" Gardiner asked.

Six people floated by under the careful guidance of the small worker creatures. Each floating person had a black shoulder device in place.

"Looks like they're sending us home," Reese said.

"Too bad," Gardiner sighed. "There's not much left there for me."

Gardiner would not have thought it possible but an even stranger looking creature appeared before him. She was four feet tall and wore a business jacket, a narrow blue-pinstriped skirt, a white blouse, and a red string tie. She also wore an immense pair of glasses without lenses over her slanted black eyes. In the absence of ears, the glasses were held in place by a piece of yellow yarn.

"What branch of the military do you think this one's from, Professor?" Gardiner asked as the creature stared at him.

"I've been watching the ones in the odd outfits," Lurie said.

"They don't seem to fit into the hierarchy. I'd say they were civilian advisers."

Reese shook again, trying to laugh.

"Edmond Gardiner?" the female creature asked. "Derek Reese?"

Gardiner and Reese acknowledged her questioning tone.

"You are acquainted with each other?"

As soon as both had said yes, the female creature produced a probe, held it in front of Gardiner's face, and then thrust it up his right nostril.

It felt like she was pushing through the top of his head. He tried to twist away, but his head was immovable. Something clicked deep inside his nose. His sinuses burned behind his eyes. Something crunched. The creature pulled the probe from him, and it felt like a wire brush scraping the inside of his nose.

"Jesus—" he gasped as he felt blood pulsing over his mouth from his nose. The creature held the probe before him. At its tip was a tiny, silver cone, no bigger than a match head. "Remember so you will know what to do when the time comes," the creature said. Then she repeated the procedure on Reese and glided away between the other benches.

"What happened? What happened?" Lurie demanded.

"Our beacons were removed," Reese said. "God, that hurts."

"How will they be able to track you down?" Lurie asked.

"Maybe they don't want to anymore," Reese said, sniffing to try and stop the flow of blood. "Maybe they're finished with us."

"But they didn't take my beacon out," Lurie said. "And I saw them put them in Rachel and Miles when we came aboard."

"I—," Reese was cut off when one of the tall, slender creatures arrived—a slight. She was accompanied by a squat gray creature in a brown outfit. Four small worker creatures were in attendance too. They each carried a clear vial of liquid.

"Drink this," the squat creature said as the small worker held up the vial to Gardiner's face. But the worker didn't move the vial any closer than a few inches, while blocking the slight's line of sight. The drone trembled like a piece of equipment receiving conflicting orders.

From the corner of his eye, Gardiner saw that Reese was also presented with a vial but not made to drink. Yet he could hear Lurie choking and spitting as the liquid was poured down his

throat. For some reason, he and Reese were being prevented
from drinking. But why?

"That's terrible!" Lurie protested. "What is that . . .
that . . ."

He said nothing more.

The drones attached black devices to Reese, Miles, Lurie,
Zeifman, and Gardiner. Then they were floated.

Gardiner watched over his feet as the five of them joined a
bobbing line of floating people gliding slowly toward one end of
the room where a portion of the wall appeared to be a liquid
mirror. The people ahead floated into that mirror and were
swallowed as though they had penetrated a waterfall, and moments after each person's disappearance, a black shoulder device shot out of the wall to be caught by a drone.

"We're being sent somewhere," Gardiner shouted to Reese.

"Moscow!" Reese called back.

Then he slipped through the mirror and disappeared, and
Gardiner followed right behind, still struggling to laugh.

$$\triangle \triangle \diagup \quad \diagdown \triangle \triangle \quad \diagdown \triangle \triangle \quad \diagup$$

Reese hit the floor from a ten-foot drop. He felt a wrenching on
his right shoulder, then the placement device flew away from
him and disappeared.

He heard a crackling sound, looked up, and saw Gardiner
falling toward him from the middle of the air feetfirst. Reese
rolled out of the way just as Gardiner landed and twitched as
his own black placement device disengaged itself and flew
away, back through the hole in the air.

The hole disappeared. Gardiner sat up, rubbing his shoulder.
"Any idea where we are?"

"I don't know for—" The floor shuddered beneath them.
They heard the creak of the walls as the room shifted. "We're
still here," Reese said. He jumped to his feet.

This room was smaller than any of the others they had been
in. Its walls were straight, the ceiling flat with thin glowing
strips of copper-colored light running across it. And the floor
was rough. Reese looked at it, squatted, ran his fingers over it.
The floor was covered with raised symbols.

"They tell our story," a voice said from the corner of the

room. Thin and wispy. The voice of a creature. A future human.

Reese and Gardiner split up, approaching the dark corner from different sides.

"What is your story?" Reese said, peering into the darkness.

"The same as your story," the voice answered from another corner. Reese and Gardiner spun around. "We are the same as you, Edmond Gardiner. We are the same as you, Derek Reese. That is why we have kept you here."

"Come out into the light," Reese said.

"All right," the voice answered. From a third corner.

Reese and Gardiner faced it. Then they heard footsteps behind them, from the fourth corner.

This creature was a female and wore a soldier's uniform—U.S. Army. But it looked like a half-blind toymaker's version. The fabric was stiff, almost like cardboard. The color was too green, and instead of a name patch sewn above the top left breast pocket, the uniform had a metal plaque with three blue isosceles triangles. The only headgear the creature wore was helmet camouflage netting stretched over her enlarged skull.

"What the hell are you supposed to be?" Reese said. He was exhausted. One moment he wanted to scream in terror. The next moment, fall down with laughter and never get up. He felt he was ten years old and trapped in an endless Laff in the Dark.

"I am a connection," the creature said, batting her monstrous black eyes. "Your connection, Derek Reese. But you have never named me."

"My . . . connection?" Reese said. He approached her cautiously, staring into those endless eyes. And he recognized them. "You're the one . . ."

"Who brings you here," the creature completed. "Since you were a child."

"Why?"

"So you could meet Wendy."

"So you could steal children from us?" Reese felt indignation grow in him. Here was something he could blame. Something he could punish. He stepped back from her, expecting the sudden blast of calm and happiness.

"You are not to have children for the *pa*," the female replied. "The things in your cells are not needed in the future. You are to have a child with Wendy."

"What gives you the right to decide that?" Reese made a fist and felt no response of counteremotions.

"We did not decide it. It was already decided."

"By who?" He tensed his arm for a blow and felt no sudden urge to sit and be contemplative.

The connection blinked her eyes. "I do not know," she finally said. "It is a puzzling thing. We will have to ask John-John."

"John-John?" Reese repeated. "Wendy's John-John?"

"Yes," the female said. "John-John is Wendy's connection." She tilted her head accusingly at Reese. "Wendy gave him his name."

Gardiner stepped up to Reese. "Don't you people have names?" he asked.

"We are who we are," the connection said.

More confusion. Reese had had enough. He wanted to flatten her.

And nothing was stopping him.

"My beacon is gone," he said with sudden insight. "So you can't control my feelings anymore. You can't control my mind."

The connection spun in a circle, for an instant making it appear that she had melted and then reformed.

"The devices that do things cannot know where you are." She looked at Gardiner. "Or where you are." She twisted her tiny mouth into a smile. "You are not here."

"I could kill you right now," Reese said, enjoying his new power.

The connection shook her head. "You give me life, Derek Reese. Why would you kill that which you formed? So many years and so few words do I understand. Let us go now."

The creature walked past Reese without fear. She was within range of a sudden blow, a neck-shattering punch, but Reese made no move. The creature wasn't afraid of him. In some strange way, he felt she trusted him. He couldn't do it.

"Where do you want us to go?" Reese asked.

"Where you must go," the creature said, reaching out and unspinning the door. "Home."

The connection stepped out of the door into a larger room. Reese and Gardiner followed behind, moved their heads out through the door, checking back and forth.

"Isn't that where we were going with those other people in the processing room?" Gardiner asked.

The connection turned. The room was cavernous behind her, a dome hundreds of feet wide and high. And completely empty.

"If you had gone home that way," she said, "you would not have remembered. But your beacons are removed and the operators who fight for John-John against the devices that do things prevented the drones from making you drink the placement mediator. When you return you will know what to do."

"What will I do?" Reese asked.

The connection blinked her eyes. Reese sensed confusion.

"You will do what you did," the connection said. Then headed across the room. "John-John will explain more. John-John knows more."

"Why does John-John know so much?" Reese asked, following her across the subtly shifting floor.

"John-John is Wendy's connection," the creature said. "And John-John has been given a name."

8

△△∠ ∠△△ ∠△△ ∠

"Sarah, I'm going back. I want you to come with me."

"I can't leave my children, Steven. They need me here. The one who stands beside me wants me here."

Steven stopped digging through the baffling stacks of goods that John-John had called his collection. "Who's the one who stands beside you?"

"The one who's always been there for me," Sarah said patiently. "Since I was a little girl."

Steven's hands dropped to his sides. "They've been taking me since I was a child. You since you were a child. And now Wendy. We haven't had any control in our lives, have we? Everything's been set up for us."

"Destiny," Sarah said. She smiled. She always smiled here.

"But we have no choice, no control. They *mated* us, Sarah. Do you remember that? Here! On this . . . *pa* or whatever the hell it is. They brought me here when I was fifteen and they made us . . . make love. They linked us then, and when we finally met in real life, there was nothing we could do about it."

"Would you have wanted to do something about it?"

"I would have at least wanted to have the choice."

"We got divorced," Sarah said.

"But not until we had Wendy. And Wendy's the one they

wanted next." He slammed his fist on a GE freezer chest covered with a collection of magazines and newspapers from August 1984. "Think about it. Think how we were controlled. I mean, they cut off all my memories of being abducted but we never argued about Wendy. Never fought about visitation, schools, support. Everything we did for her we agreed upon. We never even had to discuss it. We didn't even want her to go to Dr. Jeffery."

"We knew what was best for our daughter," Sarah said.

"We were programmed, Sarah. Puppets on a string. Everything was laid out for us as if it was already history."

"To these people, Steven, it already is history."

"Then let's change it."

"You can't. You heard him. He's here, so it all happened. The disaster affects the earth. All except three hundred survivors in one small place perish. The survivors go on to rebuild the world. It's all history. You can't change it."

"At least I can make the effort, make the *choice* to try!" He went back to tearing through John-John's collection. Toys, appliances, clothes, books, comics, empty boxes of food, cartons of cigarettes, a small Honda electrical generator. What the hell was he doing with all this stuff?

Sarah sat back against the bed, feeling none of Steven's alarm or panic. "You never even made the choice to remember that these people had taken you, Steven. You think about that. Until you came here after the beach, you never even suspected you had been here. Your mind is shut up into little boxes, and all communications are down."

"They made me that way!"

"They found you that way. It's the way you've always been. Why think you'll change now?"

"Because now I have something to fight for," Steven said.

"There's no hope for the world, Steven. You saw the book."

"But there's hope for Wendy. We can find that place. Go to that place. We can survive!"

Sarah shut her eyes and rocked her head. "You don't understand how this was organized. John-John explained it so carefully. Since you're here and he's told you everything, you weren't one of the survivors. *Weren't.* It's already a fact."

"I don't care. I'm getting out of here and I'm taking Wendy with me." He found a hedge clipper. A stuffed hippopotamus. A starter set of Corelle dishware. He pictured John-John as an

insane pack rat. What in God's name had he left in exchange
for all these goods as he had slinked in and out of people's walls
and cupboards in the middle of the night?

Sarah walked over to him. Started opening boxes for him.
"You never were one to face facts, were you?" she said. "Want
to tell me what we're looking for?"

"Anything that can help," Steven said. "Guns, clubs, hand
grenades."

"How about this?" Sarah asked. She held up an old green
backpack with the name Miles written across it in Day-Glo
orange letters.

Steven snatched it from her. Dug into it.

"Bless the little bastard's heart," Steven said. "It's all here."
He pulled out two fire fighters' breathing masks. A handful of
asthma inhalers. And two guns, Reese's and North's.

"Now we have a chance at least," he said. Then looked into
Sarah's eyes. "You want to help?"

Sarah shrugged. She still hadn't lost her smile. "Everything
we do has been done. Nothing you will do is something that
hasn't happened."

"I refuse to accept it!"

"I knew you were going to say that," Sarah said. And she
laughed.

△△∠ ∠△△ ∠△△ △△△

The floor of the bucking corridor moved ceaselessly beneath
Reese and he stumbled as he ran. Gardiner, beside him, lurched
against the walls, dropped to his knees, kept running forward,
trying to keep up with the skittering connection in the imitation
army uniform.

They came to an intersection. The connection jumped to the
side wall of the corridor and hung there like a spider. Peered
out around the corner. Jumped down and scrambled back to
Reese.

"Engineers!" she said. "Go back! Go back!"

She loped ahead like a stampeding monkey. Gardiner tripped
and fell, ran forward on hands and knees as he struggled to find
the rhythm of the floor.

The connection squeaked at another intersection, turned, and ran back to them again.

"They know we are here!" she said excitedly.

"Who knows we're here?" Reese demanded. "Are we supposed to be hiding?"

"Yes, yes. That is why we took away your beacons. The devices that do things cannot find you now. But the engineers can see you. They know you did not go home. They know you are here."

"And we're not supposed to be here?" Gardiner asked.

"No to them but yes to us."

"Them or us," Gardiner repeated. "The one who was with me when I woke up here said something about that. There's some sort of fight going on here, isn't there?"

"Yes, yes," the connection said, rocking back and forth on her feet, looking both ways in the tunnel, checking both intersections.

"What kind of fight?" Reese asked. He wanted to grab his connection but was afraid of hurting her. He found it strange that he would think that way, but he was slowly remembering that he had known her for years, for decades.

"What kind of fight is there?" the connection replied.

"Is it a war?" Gardiner asked. "Are you soldiers?"

"The war is over," the connection said. "And soldiers are bigger." She looked at Reese, holding up her arms to him like a small child wanting to be carried. "Who do you fight better? Engineers or operators?"

"How many drones do the operators have?" Reese asked. The words were all there as soon as he needed them.

"Cadres of four," his connection said. "Three operators and their cadres."

"Engineers," Reese decided.

They ran for the first intersection. Reese's connection waved to Reese and Gardiner to stop, then hopped out into the intersection, shrieked, whirled, and ran away.

Six engineers chased after her. Three carried glowing coils of metal, two feet in diameter. The other three carried probes. Reese and Gardiner surprised them as they crossed the intersection.

The engineers carrying the coils released them, and the glowing metal floated up to the ceiling of the corridor and bounced along it. Reese took two of the creatures down with a body slam. He heard something snap like an old branch, and one of the engineers didn't move after he hit the floor. The second engineer tried to get up, and Reese swung his fist around in an arc that connected with the creature's head.

The head collapsed like a balloon full of liquid. Reese fell off balance, not expecting the weak resistance to his blow. He tried to regain his feet, but the hand he had used against the engineer was slippery and slid on the floor of the tunnel. He felt two hands grab his arm and pull him to his feet. He wheeled around to strike again. It was Gardiner.

"Their goddam heads are empty," Gardiner said breathlessly. His hands dripped with clear liquids and black liquids mixed together. Four bodies lay on the floor of the heaving tunnel. Three of them had only a glistening, deflated pouch of skin connected to their shoulders. The other two engineers in the group cowered against the undulating tunnel wall, holding their probes before them for protection.

"Go now!" Reese's connection shrieked.

Reese turned to look down the corridor he had run from. Three lines of drones slipped along the walls. Heading for them. Black eyes glistening, menacing, baleful.

Reese followed Gardiner running down the corridor after the connection. The floor jumped with a sudden blast of thunder, and Reese pitched forward. He rolled to his feet, slipped again. Looked behind him.

The drones were closing.

$$\triangle \triangle \angle \quad \angle \triangle \triangle \quad \triangle \triangledown \triangledown \quad \angle$$

"Which way now?" Steven demanded. He stopped in the middle of the intersection, rocking as if he stood on an air mattress.

Sarah pointed to the ankh symbol on the wall of one branching tunnel. "This way," she called out over the growling thunder of the *pa*. "John-John wanted to show Wendy the babies."

Steven ran beside her, the knapsack banging against his hip with each step. It was like running on a trampoline, he thought. A trampoline that was already in motion. Impossible to tell whether the next step would be onto a piece of the floor moving up, moving down, or jarringly stationary. And the motion seemed to be increasing in strength and in frequency.

They came to another intersection. Sarah pointed in the direction of the next ankh.

"Is it like this often?" Steven asked after pushing himself out from a wall and jumping forward again.

"I've never felt it this bad before," Sarah said, gasping for breath. "And the corridors are deserted."

They ran and bounced and stumbled and fell and ran some more. Steven spotted the ankh at the next intersection. Down that corridor, there was a wider door than was usual. It was also marked with an ankh.

"The *kohanga reo!*" Sarah shouted over a roll of thunder.

Down the corridor, something squealed, a sound that even Steven could recognize as being made by one of the creatures. And as being a sound of terror.

A little creature the size of John-John skidded around the far intersection corner, a hundred feet away. Steven dug into his knapsack for Reese's gun, the one Reese had taught him to use.

The creature tore at them. It wore a familiar green uniform. And then two more creatures appeared at the intersection. Also running. They were the size of soldiers. But they were humans: Reese and someone Steven didn't recognize.

"Derek!" Steven shouted as the uniformed creature slammed into the door and wrestled with its central black control.

"Run!" Reese shouted, legs pumping irregularly, trying to match the pulse of the floor beneath him.

Steven was frozen by confusion for one instant. Then he saw a stream of small malevolent creatures slip around the corridor walls, streaming after Reese and his companion.

Beside him, the large door spun open like an unwinding spring. The small creature who had opened it didn't let go of the control in time and spun around twice with it, squealing loudly before it dropped to the floor and scampered inside.

"Go!" Steven shouted to Sarah as bright light from the room beyond spilled in to the corridor.

Sarah rushed into the room. Steven moved the safety lever on the side of the gun until it clicked. He aimed at the small creature in the lead on the wall.

Reese passed him, charged into the room. His companion, an older man in a three-piece suit, dove in after him. Steven fired. The Beretta's recoil surprised him and he almost lost his grip. Down the corridor, the second creature in the sliding line flew from the wall with a sharp squeal and bounced against the far wall, motionless except for the corridor's own movement.

Steven fired again. The lead creature jerked, lost its grip on the wall, fell sideways, and bounced along the opposite wall. The other creatures slowed down. At the far intersection, Steven saw larger creatures peering around the corner. Steven fired once more without hitting anything that he intended. Then he ran inside the room as the door spiraled shut behind him.

"Daddy!" Wendy cried. Steven bent over with his hands on his knees, catching his breath. He looked up to see Wendy rush to him. He stood up and hugged her. "Derek," he heard her say softly. Felt her arms loosen around him. He let go. She went to Reese.

"This is wrong! Wrong! Wrong!" It was a creature's voice. Steven looked back to the closed door. It was John-John. He held a probe to the door control. A spark arced from one to the other, and the surface of the door control bubbled and turned green.

John-John turned back to Steven. "You have no beacon. You were supposed to stay hidden. The time is wrong. You have spoiled it—"

"Shut up, you little bastard!" Steven shouted. "I'm sick and tired of you! I'm through being jerked around by you. I want out of here and I want out now!" He aimed his gun at John-John.

Everyone else in the front of the *kohanga reo* was silent. In the lulls between the creaking and thunder of the *pa,* the mewing and crying of the babies could be heard.

"Don't, Daddy," Wendy said softly. "John-John is a friend."

"If he's a friend," Steven said, gun never wavering, "he's going to send us home."

"That is what I want to do. That is what I need to do. That is what I did."

"No more goddam games!" Steven shouted. "Speak so I can understand you!"

Reese stepped up beside Steven. "Is that the only gun you have?" he asked gently.

"I've got North's in the knapsack," Steven said, not taking his eyes off John-John.

"Why don't you let me cover him?" Reese suggested. "I've got a bit more experience."

Steven took a deep breath, glanced at Reese, looked back at John-John, then handed the gun over.

"But I want to go home," Steven said.

"You will," John-John replied. "But now you have made it so difficult. Before you were a secret. Easy to place you from the *pa*. Now they know you are here. They know you know. The devices that do things will not let you go."

"Is that who you're fighting?" Reese asked. He didn't hold the gun as threateningly as Steven had. "The devices that do things tell you what to do?"

"They tell us nothing," John-John said. "We tell them; they do. Some of us tell them one thing though. Others tell them another. That is the fight. Which shall we do."

"And the devices that do things listen to the others and not to you?"

"We are only connections," John-John explained. "We know things the others do not know. The others can do things that we cannot do."

"What do the others want to do with us?" Reese asked.

"Make you not remember what to do when the time comes."

"Why?"

John-John looked at Reese's connection. He held out his hand to her. She looked nervously at Steven, then at Reese's gun, then scampered to take John-John's hand. They entwined their short arms, touched thumbs, faced Reese's gun together.

Reese looked at his gun, almost sheepish, then stuck it into his belt. "I'm sorry," he said.

"What are you doing?" Steven demanded. "How can you trust them?"

"It's okay," Reese said. "They want the same thing we do. Right, John-John? Tell us what you want to do with us."

"Send you home so you can choose to recall this time. So you will know what to do when the time comes."

Reese looked at Steven. "Satisfied?"

"I hate them," Steven said. "I hate what they've done."

Reese turned back to John-John. "Are you responsible for what has been done to Steven? To Sarah? To Wendy and me?"

"There are many things I do not have the words for, Derek," John-John said. "All this I serve." He waved his free hand around the *kohanga reo*. "All this is right and must be done for us . . . for me . . . for her"—he looked at Reese's connection—"to go home too. But Steven, Sarah, Wendy, you . . . I serve alone."

"We weren't part of the grand plan?" Steven asked. "We weren't supposed to be part of all this?"

John-John shook his head. "You were not to be part of the schedule. It was okay to add you, okay to add Sarah. But not Reese. Not Wendy."

"For God's sake, why?" Steven asked.

"I do not have the words," John-John said. But he said it too quickly for Steven to believe him.

"Why aren't they trying to break down the door?" Reese asked before Steven could continue.

"They are just drones and operators," Reese's connection replied. "They are waiting for the soldiers."

"Can the soldiers break down the doors?" Reese asked.

"They do not have to," John-John said. "They are soldiers."

"Remember the safe house in Pasadena?" Steven said. "It dissolved like the floors around here."

"The soldiers won't do anything bad to us while we're here," Sarah said. "No one wants to hurt the babies."

"That is true," John-John agreed. "But we cannot stay here. You must be placed."

"We're going home!" Steven said, correcting John-John's statement.

"That's what he means," Reese said. "You are *transferred* to the *pa*. But you are *placed* home. Right?"

John-John looked at Reese, looked at his connection, looked back. "I understand your words but not your meaning," he said. "But you will go home. You have gone home. But to go home, first we must go to the main portal."

"What's the main portal?" Steven asked.

"I do not understand the question. The main portal is the portal that is the main portal. What question can there be?"

Reese held up his hand to Steven. "Where is the main portal? How do we get to it?"

"I do not know," John-John said. "The devices that do things know all the portals. If we go through one, they will know and transfer us elsewhere. Only at the main portal can you be placed without their knowledge."

"Sounds like a manual override," Reese said, looking at the closed door. "How long do we have before the soldiers get here?"

"I do not know why they are not here yet," John-John said.

"I told you," Sarah said. "No one wants to do anything to harm the babies."

"Would they just leave us here?" Steven asked.

"They did not. They will not. It is a problem for the devices that do things. They do not deal efficiently with paradox."

Steven walked over to the first incubator, looked inside. Sarah joined him.

"Aren't they beautiful?" she asked.

Steven stared at the rows of little beings in their cylinders. "They're obscene," he said.

"You only say that because you don't understand. They are the most precious thing on the *pa*. They are the reason for the *pa*."

Steven watched as the tiny hands groped the air while the tiny mouths made crying sounds. Some of the pale gray babies nursed from thin tubes that snaked from the side of their cylinders. Steven walked back to Reese, smiling.

"What if we were each to take a baby, hold on to one when we went through the portal? Could the computers, or the devices that control the portals, separate us from the babies? Or would they have to let us go where we wanted to?"

John-John and Reese's connection looked at each other. Steven had the feeling they were communicating somehow.

"We cannot harm the babies," John-John said. "Neither can the devices that do things. We shall go through the portal with them to the main portal. But they shall remain there. And they shall not be harmed."

"John-John, you can't," Sarah said. Her smile was finally gone.

"They must go home. They must go to the main portal. There are no other answers."

John-John and Reese's connection ran over to the incubators and began moving their hands over control surfaces. Steven could hear the hiss of gases escaping, the clicks of locks and seals disengaging.

Sarah ran to join the two creatures, pleading with them to stop. But Steven saw that John-John and the other didn't listen to Sarah. They didn't even try to argue with her.

"Do you think that might be John-John's . . . girlfriend or something?" Wendy asked.

" 'Or something' is right," Gardiner said.

Wendy smiled, her hand in Reese's. "What's her name?"

"I don't know," Reese said. "I don't think she has one. I don't think any of them do."

"John-John has a name."

"But you gave him that one. His friend is my connection, but I guess I never gave her one. John-John seems to have something special. At least his friend thinks so."

John-John and Reese's connection opened an incubator and carried cylinders to Wendy and Steven. Reese and Gardiner returned with the connections to the incubator and received theirs. Then Sarah and the two creatures had one each and the incubator was sealed again.

John-John stood by the wall-mounted feeding portal, cradling the cylinder in his arm. "Follow me," the creature said. "You must not stop to look. You must not harm the babies. I will take you to a device that I can work alone without the devices that do things. I will use that device, and the main portal will place you."

"This is wrong, John-John," Sarah said. There were tears in her eyes as she looked down at the wee one in her arms.

"It is right, Sarah. But I do not have the words for it." John-John looked over them all, stopped at Wendy, drew his mouth into a smile. "I remember a game you taught me," he said, then turned back to the control panel of the portal and rubbed his fingers across it as though trying to remove dirt.

The wall shimmered.

"On your mark," John-John recited. "Get set. Go!" And the wall swallowed him like a living mirror.

9

△△∠ ∠△△ △▽∠ △∠

For an instant, Steven felt he was back in his vision of the time machine. As he passed through the portal, he could sense the structure of the *pa* around him, see his path through it as the portal mechanism tunneled him from one place to another. He clutched the cylinder to his chest, felt himself pass into the baby and out again, feeling the confusion and the fear of its infant mind, passing on the determination and the resolve of his adult intellect. And when he emerged from the portal, an infinitely long instant later, the baby no longer cried and Steven felt the childlike wonder of discovery that was fueled by confusion.

But in the chaos of the main portal room, the new feelings and knowledge were lost.

It was hell. It was madness. His mind could not contain it.

"This way!" John-John called to him. He stood across from the *kohanga reo* arrival portal, carefully wrapping his cylinder in his arms.

Steven could scarcely hear the creature over the crashing roar, the ear-numbing rumbling of the air around him. It was like falling through a thundercloud. Being torn apart by sound itself.

He felt two tiny hands upon him. The creature in the uniform pushed him toward John-John. Steven went to him. They were on a ledge. He looked over its railing, into the rampaging frenzy of the two fundamental forces of existence.

He couldn't see the far side of the room. It was a cavern. Mist shrouded it, blazing with shafts of lights from the hundreds of craft that tore through it, shrieking through the air, spinning madly, swerving around each other like an aerial avalanche.

The flying craft screamed overhead. They rumbled in the distance. Twisted through the air and dove straight down to an ocean of roiling silver. Steven could see the flying things hit that surface, then deform as they flattened so thin that . . . he knew he didn't have the words for it.

Other sections of the portal erupted in thick circular swells as a returning craft pierced it, reassembling themselves from two-dimensional smears. And with each disappearance, each reformation, the air shook with the the thunder, the soul-quaking fury of—he knew them now, experienced them now—transference and placement.

This was the source of the *pa*'s quaking and shuddering. No matter how good the devices that did things were, they could not completely dampen the forces at work here. Those energies bled through the *pa,* twisting it, tearing at it, making it fight back. A fight, Steven realized, that was almost at an end.

He turned away. The others were with him. Gardiner's mouth hung open. Wendy huddled over her cylinder, eyes fixed on the floor. Reese tore himself away from the whirlwind of sensation before him and fixed his eyes on the wall behind. And gently but insistently, John-John and his friend moved Steven and the others along.

They entered a sheltered ramp that angled down. "What were they?" Steven asked. His voice sounded like it belonged to someone else. It had no strength behind it, no feeling that it was something Steven had made.

"Our scoutships," John-John shouted to him as they ran along. "Our UFOs, our beamships, our trading vessels from Zeta Reticuli. That is how we pick you up for transference. That is how we sample and track."

"But they're all different!"

"So those that see them will never agree and the secret is kept." John-John turned to check the progress of the others. "We must hurry!" Steven ran.

The ramp opened out onto a wide surface that ended at the shore of the gleaming silver sea of the main portal, as shiny and as mutable as the surface of the miles-wide channel that curved with the curvature of the earth and that would not be built for millions of years. Its edge was in constant motion, ebbing and flowing as solid changed to liquid changed to solid again, as if at the edge of the effect, the portal's boundaries were uncertain, undefined.

John-John ran from the end of the ramp to a disk-shaped structure that was one hundred feet across and rested on the hard surface of the main portal, well back from its shifting edge. Steven and the others ran after him. A gale-force wind blew from the surface of the portal like a rising storm.

"We must leave the babies here," John-John said, resting his cylinder carefully in an indentation in the surface of the disk. "They must not be harmed."

"How far do we have to go without them?" Steven yelled, reluctant to give up their shields. "What about the soldiers?"

"Just to the edge," John-John said. "To the edge of the main portal, and then you go home!"

Reese put his cylinder down. Wendy put hers beside it. Then Reese's connection and Gardiner laid theirs beside the others. Only Sarah hesitated.

"The babies must not be harmed," John-John said. "They must be left here."

"I know," Sarah said, eyes wild. "I can't leave them."

"Mother!" Wendy shouted over the raging wind. "You have to! You have to come with us!"

"They're my family," Sarah said. She hugged the cylinder. Steven saw tiny gray hands waving within. "I'm their mother."

"But we're your family! You're my mother!"

Sarah smiled sadly. "Not anymore," she said. She reached out a hand to Wendy, ran it through the girl's blowing hair. "You're not a child any longer. And if you're not a child, how can I be your mother?"

"But I love you," Wendy said, tears streaking her face in the wind.

"We must hurry," John-John said. "The soldiers! The soldiers!"

"I love you too," Sarah answered her daughter. "I always will. Now go, if you're sure that's what you're supposed to do."

"It is! It is!" John-John shrieked. "Hurry! Hurry!"

Steven faltered as the others stepped away from the sheltered disk, the babies, and Sarah. He held out her hand to her. "Please come," he said.

She shook her head. "This is what I'm supposed to do. They don't know how to take care of babies. They weren't made to have babies. They don't know how to love babies. I'm needed here."

"You're needed at home," Steven pleaded.

"The only ones needed at home are the three hundred survivors. No one else makes a difference. Now go. Try. If that's what you need to do. This is what I need to do." Sarah sat down beside the cylinders, lifted one into her lap. "I'll be fine," she said.

"You'll be alone!"

"No, I won't. There are a lot of babies. There will be a lot of us to care for them." She smiled down at her babies. "Do what you have to do, Steven. Do what you already have done, millions of years ago."

Steven cried senselessly in anguish, then turned and ran after John-John. The wind of transference and placement howled after him.

John-John and the other connection scampered like charging chimpanzees. They headed for a small angled platform shaped like a giant crystal of black quartz, rising ten feet out of the hard surface of the main portal. Beside it, around it, the surface flickered from solid to liquid and back again, right at the fringe of the effect.

John-John was fifty feet away from the structure when its near side shimmered, turning silver.

John-John tumbled as he came to a halt. Reese's connection stumbled against him. Steven stopped, reached into his knapsack, took out his gun.

A soldier emerged from the new portal opened in the side of the crystal, his glowing blue probe streaming white exhaust that whipped away in the bellowing wind. And even from that distance, his almost vertical eyes could be seen to be tracking them. He stepped to the side, bringing his probe to his shoulder. A second leg slipped out of the portal beside him.

Reese waited beside Steven, his own gun in his hand. Gardiner was weaponless but stood with them. Reese kept Wendy behind him.

"Where do we have to go?" Steven asked John-John.

"To the top. Where the controls are."

"How many soldiers will there be?" Reese asked.

A second soldier stood beside the first. A third began to appear.

"As many as they need," John-John said.

Reese dropped to his knee. Gripped his gun in both hands. "Their suits are bulletproof," he said to Steven. "Aim for their weapons."

Reese fired. The explosion was like a pop against the howl of the wind. He hit nothing.

"Damn wind," Reese said. "We'll have to split up and run for them to get closer. Confuse their fire. Wendy! Stay behind me."

"No!" John-John yelled. "Wendy must go first."

"What?"

"Wendy must go first. They all know Wendy. They will not harm her. Please, Derek! Please, Wendy! Go first to the platform."

"Why?" Reese shouted again. There were five soldiers by the platform now, and the side of it still shimmered. "Why is Wendy so special?"

"I don't have the words for it," John-John screamed. He pushed at Wendy. "Go first! Go first!"

Wendy looked at John-John in confusion. Then Reese and Steven.

"Do it," Reese said. He turned to John-John. "And if they hurt her, I'll kill you."

"If they hurt her, it will not be necessary," John-John said. He fell in behind Wendy, and the others followed, walking toward the steaming probes of the soldiers.

Steven walked at the end of the line. Wendy walked forward quickly, urged on by John-John with words Steven couldn't hear. But it was working. The soldiers lowered their probes, raised them, half lowered them again. He could see them turn their immense eyes to each other, questioning each other. Wendy in the lead was a problem for them. But why?

The soldiers began to fan out.

"Everyone touch her!" John-John screamed, waving Steven and Gardiner up from the rear. They clustered behind Wendy. Steven and John-John held her right arm. Reese and Gardiner her left. Reese's connection walked beside Wendy, her fingers hooked into a belt loop on Wendy's jeans. They were twenty feet from the platform.

The soldiers hesitated again. An operator's head emerged from the portal in the side of the platform, looking around.

"Stop that one!" John-John shouted.

Reese took aim and fired, and the operator's head exploded. The soldiers froze in place.

"Run!" John-John shouted. *"Run!"*

He tore ahead of the others, reached the platform, leaped up the stairs to the control panel.

Steven stared at the motionless soldiers. Like drones, he realized. And their operator was dead! He ran for the platform with the others.

John-John crouched by a low panel on the top of the platform. Steven could see no obvious switches or controls on it, but John-John ran his hands over it as though trying to dig his way through it. The uniformed connection hung over the railing around the fifteen-foot-square platform, peering into the pulsing of the portal's edge. John-John yelled, "Now?" and she yelled, "No!"

Steven checked the soldiers. They were still frozen without an operator. Could they get another operator? Steven wondered. He tried to remember what had happened at the safe house when Reese had shot one. Had the drones come back to life? He couldn't recall.

John-John and Reese's connection began shouting at each other in words Steven couldn't understand. He looked away from them to the center of the main portal, still writhing with the comings and goings of hundreds of flying ships. It's a wonder everyone hasn't seen one at sometime, Steven thought. Then Gardiner screamed.

Steven wheeled. A soldier advanced up the stairs and there was no time to gather around Wendy for protection. Reese ran to the top of the stairs as the soldier raised his probe. Reese fired. Sparks erupted from the probe and it clattered to the stairs. The soldier reached down for it. His waist pleated in two directions.

Reese jumped on him. The soldier bent his arm backward and swung it around Reese's head, grabbing his throat. Steven moved back and forth at the top of the stairs, trying to get a clear shot. Reese groaned. Wendy screamed. Gardiner jumped for the soldier. Steven saw Reese bring his gun around to the soldier's neck, push the barrel into the gap between the helmet and the gray and silver jumpsuit that blazed with the light of a captured sun.

The soldier's head flew away from his body as his neck disintegrated. Gardiner pulled the still grasping hand from Reese's neck. Reese fell back onto the stairs, rubbing his neck, gasping for breath, and Wendy ran to him.

Another soldier advanced, raising his probe. Steven fired at the soldier. But the bullets were absorbed by the soldier's suit with no result.

Wendy struggled to pull Reese up the stairs. Gardiner reached down, picked up the fallen soldier's probe. He aimed it at the approaching soldier.

The approaching soldier paused. Swung his own probe around toward Gardiner.

Gardiner looked at the control panel on the side of the probe.

"Not that way!" John-John cried.

Gardiner smiled. He howled in victory. He pressed something on the probe.

Steven felt the heat of the blue flame that flared around Gardiner and crackled down the stairs to engulf the approaching soldier. It was like a lightning strike.

The blue glare faded and Steven struggled to see past the yellow lines etched into his vision from the brilliance of the energy bolt. He could see just enough to know that Gardiner was no longer there.

"Not that way," John-John said.

"It is here!" Reese's connection called from the edge of the platform. "John-John! It is here!"

John-John ran back to the control panel. Dug away at it again. "Go to the edge!" he shouted. "Get ready! Get ready!"

Wendy and Steven stood behind Reese's connection as she leaned from the railing.

"What are we supposed to do?" Steven asked her.

"Go through when John-John connects the portal with your home," she said. "He must do this without the devices that do things. It is difficult."

"Now?" John-John called.

"Soon!" the connection answered. She pointed urgently at the rippling edge of the portal at the bottom of the raised platform. "Do you see? Do you see the connection forming?"

Steven leaned over and saw only black reflections. Then

John-John was at his side. "You must jump through that when I call out."

"Where will it take us?" Steven asked.

"It will place you home. You must go home. You have gone home. Jump when I say!"

Reese's gun popped into the wind again. Steven looked back toward the stairs. There was nothing there. But Reese was firing at the center of the platform. A second, smaller portal had opened in its floor.

Steven ran beside Reese. He fired at the creature emerging from the portal in the platform floor. It wore a round helmet with a wide brim stepped in raised concentric circles. Reese's bullets did nothing to it. Steven's gun clicked. He threw it at the creature, and the impact at least jarred the thing's head, made it slip back a few inches.

"Now!" John-John screamed.

"Derek! Come on!" Wendy shouted, pulling on his arm.

The muzzle of a soldier's probe appeared in the portal.

Reese ran forward and kicked at it. The muzzle slammed to the side of the portal in the platform floor and stuck there, becoming intermixed in the solid material surrounding it. The contact point began to sputter and smoke with the release of some sort of energy.

"Go through with Wendy," Reese said to Steven. "I'll follow after she's safely through."

"But I want to go with you!" Wendy said.

"I don't want them shooting you in the back," Reese said. "Now get out of here. Do what John-John says."

Steven took Wendy's hand in his. She didn't resist. "I love you," she called to Reese.

"What choice do we have?" he said and he turned from her. Kicked again at something coming through the floor.

"To the edge," John-John said, pulling on Steven's arm. "To the edge and jump."

Steven and Wendy climbed up on the railing. Steven reached down to John-John, grabbed the creature's neck. "Where's the *marae?*" he demanded. "Where do the survivors go?"

"I don't have the words," John-John choked out. "You must jump!"

Reese screamed. Steven looked away from John-John to see Reese fall to the floor. A mechanical claw gripped his leg like a giant's hand. It pulled him toward the smaller portal in the center of the floor.

Reese's connection sprang from the railing and attached herself to Reese's right arm, pulling back with all her strength, but making no difference. Reese slid toward the opening.

"Derek!" Wendy screamed. She tried to pull away from Steven but his hand was like iron. He wasn't going to lose her too.

Reese's legs disappeared into the portal. He flipped around on his stomach, clawing at the unyielding black surface of the platform. His connection pulled against him, slipped forward with him. Her legs passed through the surface beside him.

Wendy's scream was inarticulate. She writhed against her father. John-John started to go to Reese and his connection, now sliding down to their waists. But he turned and pushed at Steven and Wendy. "Jump now!" he said. "The link will not hold without the devices that do things."

"Nooo!" Wendy screamed, as loud and as mad as the wind. She reached out her hands to Reese.

"Go!" Reese bellowed. His face contorted in agony. The edge of the portal connecting with his chest began to glow and sputter. Smoke rose from the contact point, streaming away in the wind. His connection shrieked like a tortured cat, wrapping herself around his arm. Burrowing her face into his neck. Sliding down with him. Dying with him.

Steven trembled on the brink of the railing. Reese looked up to him from the brink of death. Their eyes met.

There was understanding.

Reese's chest erupted in flames. His face dissolved as light ate it from within. His connection was consumed at his side.

Steven grabbed John-John. The little creature squealed and kicked and struggled as Steven lifted him over the railing by his neck. Wendy's screams were the screams of all the ships that rose and fell before them. The scream of the one fundamental force of existence that was above all others.

"Let's go find those words you need," Steven spat at John-John. And with Wendy in one arm, John-John in the other, Steven hurled himself from the railing.

And they were placed.

10

SUNDAY, JULY 29, 15:47 PDT

Wendy swirled out from the portal, intermixed with all the ships that left, all the beings they contained, and her father, and John-John. And she was blind to them.

She fell through the *pa*. Saw her progress through its devices. Saw herself focused and gathered, shaped and transported. Saw herself— She knew the word was "placed," but she didn't comprehend it.

She touched her mother as she fell. Saw her with her children. Sensed the other women with her. The other mothers. For just the instant of the fall, the *pa* was open to her. All was open to her. Yet in it, she could not find what had been Reese. And so she was blind and her heart was numb and the secrets of the *pa* passed before her unheeded.

The ground slammed into her and knocked her breath away. She saw Reese's face consumed by light. She didn't struggle to draw in another breath. Why?

She heard her father grunt as he landed beside her. She didn't open her eyes. She saw smoking flesh. She saw death. What more was there to see?

She heard a small thud, a small rustle, as John-John joined her. She lay still, refusing to acknowledge him. He had been her friend, and she had led Derek to be swallowed by something black and mechanical and so hideous that she would never have a friend again. Never have anything again. She longed for a portal that had no other opening. The moment of transition, then oblivion. That would be enough for her.

John-John cried beside her. Cried like a baby.

"What's wrong with you?" Steven snapped at the creature harshly, angrily, full of hate but a hate that was nothing like Wendy's. She had seen her lover's flesh consumed from within. That was the nature of her hate. Her father knew nothing.

"You did not let me go to Reese's connection," John-John sobbed.

"You couldn't have done anything," Steven said. Wendy heard him stand up. Brush at his clothes.

"It would have been enough to go to her," John-John moaned.

"What would that have accomplished?" Her father was cold, brutal. But not cold and brutal enough for Wendy.

"You don't understand," John-John whispered. "I couldn't even call out to her."

Wendy listened to her connection.

"Why not?" her father asked. But didn't care whatever the answer might be.

"Because . . . ," John-John sobbed, and for a moment he couldn't speak. And when he did, it was mournful in a way that Wendy had not heard before. "Because she did not even have a name . . ." His wail was like the wail of all lost lovers. The cry of those caught in the final portal. Wendy recognized it. She opened her eyes.

She took the hand of her friend.

SUNDAY, JULY 29, 20:10 PDT

"How long do we have?" Steven asked John-John. They had found a road and a sign about an hour after landing. They were in Topanga Canyon with less than an hour to go before sunset.

"Until when?" John-John said. He trudged along the rough dirt path with them, well back from the road, holding Wendy's hand.

"Until they come for us."

"How can they come for us? You have no beacons."

"Why were our beacons removed?"

John-John kicked dirt ahead of him on the path. "So they could not come for you."

"Why is it important that they wouldn't be able to come for us?"

"Because they didn't come for you," John-John sighed. Then quickly added, "I do not have the words for it."

Steven walked along in silence for a few minutes. He could tell by the way her feet scuffed the dirt and the way that her head hung that Wendy was near collapse. He couldn't be sure about John-John, but the creature walked so slowly, with such dejection, that he seemed incapable of escape.

"Do you have a beacon?" he asked John-John.

"Why would I need one? Where would I go?" John-John said softly. "My duty is to the *pa*. How can I leave? My life is with the *pa*. How can I live?"

"You're doing all right now," Steven said, watching the sky turn deep blue above them.

"No matter how quickly it happens, Steven, death takes time."

"It doesn't have to," Steven said. "You can tell me where the *marae* is. Where the survivors will be."

"The *marae* is the *marae*," John-John said sullenly. "I do not know where it is. I am not an engineer. I am not a slight. I am only a connection."

"When will the disaster hit?" Steven asked. He hadn't considered this. He thought John-John was being obtuse on the *pa*. He had never really considered that the creature might not know anything more than what he had already told Steven.

"Soon," John-John said, shuffling his feet and shrugging with his one free hand.

"And do you know what it will be?" Steven asked. He stepped quickly ahead on the path to stand before John-John.

John-John stopped, confronted by Steven. He looked up at Wendy. "In my school we were taught many things. We were taught transference and placement. We were taught duty to the *pa*. We were taught that the disaster that struck the earth was something you had not imagined. We were not taught what that something was." He turned to Steven. "You should have thrown a slight through the portal. But you threw only a connection."

John-John let go of Wendy's hand, stepped back on the path,

and spun like a dervish, kicking up a small billow of dust in the last light of day. When he stopped, he lifted his arms to the darkening landscape around him—scrub grass, stunted trees, blowing dust, all to be laid waste by something unimagined. "My name is John-John," the creature shouted to the darkness and the pale stars of twilight, darkness and stars reflected in his own nighteyes. "My name is John-John," he whispered as the landscape faded around them. "My name is John-John, and these are my things."

WEDNESDAY, AUGUST 1, 04:10 PDT

Steven opened his eyes from a nightmare. He looked around the motel room. The nightmare was real.

It had taken two days, but he had managed to get his secretary in New York to wire him fifteen thousand dollars in two transactions using the blank, signed draft forms he kept in his office safe. Then he had told her to cash in her private shares and take a vacation. A long vacation. Penny had been concerned about Steven, worried that he had been in some trouble because of the FBI agents who had been around asking about him and Sarah. And the people from public health who had been asking about Angel. But Steven had told her how to use one of the blank draft forms to take a five-thousand-dollar bonus for herself and not to worry, because he'd be back in a month to straighten things out.

A month is what John-John had figured was left. He said it would be obvious in the last two weeks. He said he had been taught that many people had guessed what was to happen in the last two weeks. Steven read four papers every day. Except for the largest numbers of UFO sightings in modern history and a disturbing national increase in missing women, no one was predicting global disaster. Yet.

Steven's face had shown up in the papers four days after the escape from the *pa*. John-John had explained that there were a lot of people such as Starr in the world. People who would help the *pa*. Since the devices that did things couldn't locate Steven without a beacon, they were using local resources. Steven was wanted for the kidnapping and suspected murder of his wife and daughter. That was to make sure that Steven would disappear into police custody the instant he might try to go public and announce John-John to the world. The ones left in the *pa* could take no chances that any of the three hundred survivors would hear that story. John-John said they had been very strict about paradoxes, that they 'had seen what paradoxes could do. But those discussions were difficult because, John-John claimed, he didn't have the words for it.

Steven sat up on the side of the bed. Wendy was lying on her bed, staring across the room at John-John, sleeping wrapped up in extra blankets on the sofa.

"How's he doing?" Steven asked quietly.

"Not eating," Wendy said.

"Nothing tempt him?"

"He thought the oranges tasted good, but he threw them up too. Got little blisters around his mouth."

"No luck describing tastes? Or any of the food on the *pa?*"

"It was just food, he said. It came from the *pa*. Sometimes it was orange. He just keeps repeating that he's not a slight. There're a lot of things he doesn't know."

Steven sighed. The little creature wasn't going to last much longer. He liked to smoke. He said it cut down on the burning things in the gases he had to breathe. And he kept his fluid intake up with distilled water. But so far they had found nothing John-John liked to eat that wouldn't make him throw up or make his skin break out in blisters. And his eye membranes had to be washed every two hours or a green film began to grow on them. Steven thought it might have something to do with the humidity. The air on the *pa* had been bone-dry. Desert-dry.

Not that staying alive was going to be worth anything in a month or so. Unless they could find the *marae*.

"Did you know he's seen dinosaurs?" Wendy said as Steven straightened his bed.

"Dinosaurs?"

"When they were coming back for the first time," Wendy said. "It was difficult to aim. Hard to control how far back they would go. So the first time they jumped back, he said there was nothing on the earth. No life, nothing. Then they tried again and it was too late. So they kept overshooting and under-shooting."

"Focusing," Steven said.

"Yeah, like that. And anyway, once the *pa* came out and there were dinosaurs all over the earth."

"Did he know what kind?"

"They don't have names for them. Not needed on the *pa*, he said." She smiled, keeping her eyes on John-John's peacefully sleeping form. "But he said they were big. His eyes got so wide when he talked about them. Big, big, he said. Bigger than the *pa*." She laughed softly. "He's like a kid, you know. Those big eyes, big head, little hands and feet."

Steven watched the rapid rise and fall of John-John's small breaths. "Did he ever say how old he was?"

Wendy shook her head. "They don't have birthdays on the *pa*. Or else they're not born. It was something else he didn't have words for. I asked if he had parents and he said he had a mother. But he wouldn't say anything more."

"Did he always live on the *pa*? Never on earth?"

Wendy looked at her father, narrowed her eyes with concern. "You know, I get the feeling that in his time, no one lives on the earth."

"Do they live someplace else. In the moon? On Mars?"

"All he talks about is the *pa*. The first and last *pa*. Then he uses a lot of words I don't understand." Wendy lay back and closed her eyes. John-John moaned a bit in his sleep, kicked his feet once, then rolled over. Steven saw with surprise that his thumb was in his mouth, and beneath the flaps of skin that were his lips, John-John sucked it.

Steven headed for the shower as John-John moaned again. He will wake up from his nightmare too, Steven thought. And he will find that the nightmare is real.

SUNDAY, AUGUST 12, 03:00 PDT

Two weeks after the escape from the *pa*, John-John was delirious. His skin had stretched tightly over his bones. The black membranes buckled across his shrunken eyes. He moaned in an unknown language. His own, Steven guessed. And he couldn't even keep water down.

Wendy had him wrapped up on her bed. She sat beside him, wiping his forehead with a cool cloth, trying to drip some water from it into his puckered and cracked mouth.

Steven sat, watching his daughter and the creature. The

blinds were drawn and the only light in the motel room came from the half-opened bathroom door.

"I cannot feel the portals!" John-John suddenly cried. "The *pa* is hit!"

"Shh," Wendy said. "You're not on the *pa*. You're on earth."

"Wendy?"

"That's right. I'm Wendy."

John-John sighed with relief. "My name is John-John. I have a name." He tried to blink his eyes, but his lids were dry and stuck on his protective membranes. "Take them off," John-John whined, fluttering his fingers over his eyes.

"Will you be able to see if I do?" Wendy asked. "It won't hurt you, will it?"

"I want to see you," John-John said. "To look at Wendy and not just your picture."

Wendy delicately lifted the membranes from John-John's eyes. He could blink again and squinted at her. He raised a hand to her face, stroked her cheek, drew in his lips in a broken smile. "Wendy," he sighed.

"Where did you see a picture of me?" Wendy asked.

"In the book."

"Which book?" Wendy talked to him as she would talk to a child, and he responded in kind.

"The book of the disaster."

Steven sat forward. "The book with the picture of the *marae?*" he asked.

"Yes," John-John said.

"What was Wendy's picture doing in there?"

"Shh," John-John said. "It's a secret." He held Wendy's hand. "We are not on the *pa?*"

"No," Wendy said. "We escaped. You helped us escape."

"Good," John-John said. "You were supposed to escape." He cried out wordlessly. "Derek was supposed to escape."

"Why, John-John? Why were we supposed to escape?"

John-John smiled. "Because you did escape." He closed his eyes and slept.

MONDAY, AUGUST 13, 02:27 PDT

They both sat beside him when John-John awoke for the last time.

"I am sorry I don't know more, Steven. I am sorry I am just a connection. I wish I could tell you more about your time. About the future."

"That's all right," Steven said gently. "What things can you tell me?"

"What things do you want to know?"

Steven shrugged. John-John's voice was like the dying whisper of a still, slow wind. There could not be much breath left in him. "What's the future like? What are your cities like? Your restaurants? Movies?"

John-John nodded silently to each question. He held Steven's hand. Steven continued. Trying to hide how much he wanted to cry for the little creature. The little boy.

"And do you live in golden cities? Do you live in space? Travel to other planets?" John-John nodded. "And do you live without sickness? Do you live without crime? Have you finished with pollution?" John-John nodded. Weakly. Slowly. "And do you travel between the stars?" John-John nodded. "Is there intelligent life on other worlds?"

John-John's eyes popped open. He looked at Steven. With his real eyes. His human eyes.

"Not anymore," John-John wheezed. He forced his parched lip flaps into a smile. "Not anymore," he whispered. "We won."

The tears came to Steven's eyes then. He saw the vision of the time machine. The device that curved with the curvature of a world that was stark and void and without life. *This planet is earth*, the silent voice had told him. Stark and void and without life.

And John-John had won. Won what? Against what?

At what price had the *pa* had to reach through time to re-populate a planet?

They weren't made to have babies. They don't know how to love babies, Sarah had said.

Because they were not supposed to. They were drones and engineers and operators and slights and connections. Each genetically engineered for a specific purpose. Each with a specific function. And not one of those functions was to reproduce.

Steven felt hot tears roll down his cheeks. He squeezed John-John's hand in his.

"You're all soldiers, aren't you, John-John? You're an army. And you went to battle. And you won. And there was nothing left when you came home, was there?"

John-John smiled. Wendy reached across and took John-John's other hand.

"You have no fear, no love, no emotions except what you learn from us, because it wasn't built in, was it? Wasn't necessary for the war you fought. Wasn't necessary for the *pa.*"

"The *pa,*" John-John breathed like the breath of salvation. "We won."

They held his hands. His breathing slowed. His eyelids fluttered. Time stopped, and Steven did not know, did not care, how long he sat there and held the man's hand.

"Wendy?" John-John said in a painfully dry whisper.

"Yes, John-John?" She held his cold, still hand to her lips.

"I do not want to die . . ."

"I don't want you to die either."

John-John opened his eyes. Looked at her.

". . . because . . . I have not even been born yet . . ."

Steven felt the passage of life through John-John's hand.

And for the first time in his life, Steven Gilmour did not try to control his feelings or his tears.

We won.

11

FRIDAY, AUGUST 17, 16:30 PDT

Merril Fisher walked into Beth's studio. The stool by the drafting table was empty. But the crutches were still there.

"Jesus H. Christ," Merril said. She walked over to the balcony railing. "Beth! Are you down there?"

She heard Beth call back from downstairs. "She's not supposed to be wandering around like that," Merril mumbled and headed down the stairs.

She walked into the kitchen. It still smelled like fresh paint and window caulking. The FBI had been very nice about apologizing and fixing all the damage that had been done. Merril still couldn't get over how David and Cy had been Russian moles all this time. Too bad she had gotten banged up when they had tried to take her hostage and get out of the country. Oh well, she thought. The nice FBI doctor—Perez was her name—had said that her memories might come back in the future. She said they usually did. Eventually. Given enough time. And for some reason, Merril Fisher felt she had more than enough time.

Beth wasn't in the kitchen.

"Elizabeth!" Merril shouted. "Where are you hiding, kid?"

"Darkroom!" Beth answered.

Merril walked through the living room, shuddered when she looked out into the small deck where those bastards had shot

Beth, then came around to the small powder room that Beth had turned into a darkroom.

"What's this all about?" Merril asked as she saw Beth balancing on a kitchen chair, reaching up through the open fan vent hole. "A sudden urge to wear your grandmother's jewelry?"

"Hold on," Beth said. "Just a minute. And for God's sake, don't turn on the light!"

"Don't worry, kid," Merril said as she leaned against the doorframe. "I won't try electrocuting you until the doctors say the bullet wounds are healed. Then you're on your own."

Beth stood on her tiptoes and reached her arm all the way into the vent hole. "There it is," she said. "I thought I remembered."

"Remembered what?" Merril asked. "I thought the reason they let you out early was because you were in such a hurry to finish that graphic novel whozits. You haven't touched it."

Beth pulled a box out of the hiding hole and reached down for the back of the chair to steady herself. "Can't get through to New York," she said. "That big satellite breakdown has really fouled up everything. And the phone company says all the ground lines are jammed because of it. I'll try Roger at his home tonight. See about a deadline extension."

"What do you need an extension for?" Merril asked.

Beth stepped down from the chair. "I don't know," she said. She looked at the box in her hand.

So did Merril. "That's not our jewelry box."

"I know," Beth said.

Beth walked into the living room. Sat down on the sectional couch and put the box on the coffee table. It was made of a peculiar gray metal and was about ten inches high and five inches by five inches at its base. The lower six inches were covered with some sort of intricate design. Maybe a type of inscription. The upper four inches were smooth, with rounded corners and had a thin indentation on one smooth side.

"How long have you had that up there?" Merril asked.

Beth shrugged. "I've had it longer than I've known you. Funny. I keep carrying it around from place to place, hiding it, and then it's almost as if I forget about it until it's time to move again. Or now."

"Where'd you get it?"

"Somebody gave it to me," Beth said.

"Who?"

"I—You know, this is really stupid, but . . . do you remember me telling you about Mr. Whites?"

"The guy you thought lived in your closet when you were a kid?" Merril asked. She laughed. "You're going to tell me Mr. Whites gave you that box?"

Beth chewed on her bottom lip. "I told you it was stupid. I know it can't be true. But that's what I seem to remember." She laughed. But not as long or as strongly as Merril had.

They sat in silence for a while. Until neither of them felt like laughing at all.

"So what are you supposed to do with it?" Merril asked. It bothered her, but she thought she had once seen something like it.

"That's what I'm trying to remember," Beth said. "I know I *am* supposed to do something with it.

"But only when the time comes," Merril said oddly. She looked at Beth. "Right?"

Beth nodded. "Right."

More silence. "You think the time has come, kid?"

"I think so," Beth said. Her hand trembled as she reached out to the box. She slipped two fingers into the indentation on the smooth side. She slid her fingers along it. Something felt warm in there.

"Oh my," Merril said.

"Wow," Beth said.

The wall across from the couch began to shimmer like a pool of molten silver.

They stared at the glistening spot as it grew to cover the wall. Part of it spread beneath a framed Rob Vanderhorst print. The picture slid down the wall, hit the floor, then fell against the wall and kept going, disappearing into the silver.

"My, my, my," Merril said with a small smile. "That cost five hundred dollars."

Beth looked at her. She grinned, almost looked embarrassed about something. "I think maybe the time has come, partner."

"So do I."

"Any idea what this is all about?" Beth asked as she stood up and walked around the coffee table.

"Not the faintest," Merril said, smiling even more as she walked around to stand beside Beth.

"Think we're going to find out?" Beth asked.

"Real soon," Merril answered.

They stepped up to the shimmering wall, watching their reflections twist and flow in it.

"You know," Beth said. "I've got this real strong feeling that —Well, I'm glad we both like kids."

Merril laughed. "I was just talking about that with someone, you know. But I can't remember who." She shook her head. Reached over, took Beth's hand.

"I guess we're supposed to go now." Beth took a deep breath. Squeezed Merril's hand.

"Flame on," Merril said.

The time had come.

They stepped through the portal.

MONDAY, AUGUST 20, 10:00 PDT

"I think this is it," Steven said. He looked over at Wendy. She brushed her hair in the mirror over the dresser. It was odd to see her in short black hair. But it was odd to see himself with a beard and moustache. Their pictures had stayed in the papers off and on for a few days after John-John had died. Now, it seemed, the newspapers had other things to run.

Wendy held one lock of hair away from her head and stuck her tongue out. Then she turned to her father. "What is it?"

"Two things," Steven said. "Everyone's talking about how the UFO flap faded out faster than it started. Nobody has reported any sightings like they had a few weeks ago for at least five days. 'Almost as though they've gone back where they came from,' this paper says." Steven pointed at the Los Angeles *Herald.*

"What's the second thing?"

"The American Museum of Natural History was robbed on the weekend."

"What did they take?"

"Fossil bones," Steven said. "Early humans. Hall of Paleontology. Reports say that at least fifteen paleontological exhibits in North America were cleaned out in the past two days."

Wendy held her father's eyes. "I guess they figure no one will be needing them anymore."

"I guess not too many museums are going to make it through

the next few weeks. Early human bones must be rare in the future."

Wendy walked over to a small chair by the door of their new motel room. They had left California after taking John-John's body out into the middle of a small lake, weighting it down with rocks, and letting it slip beneath the water under the stars.

"I guess this is it, then," she said. "It's all about to start. The end of things, I mean."

Steven closed the newspapers and left them with the dictionary and the folded-open travel brochures. He had traced some of the words that John-John had used. He had found pictures of small houses with red corrugated roofs and white frames, just like the ones in the book of the disaster. If the airports would just stay open for another two days, he knew where to look for the *marae*. The meeting place. He got up and went over to his daughter.

"Daddy," Wendy said softly, holding his hand but not looking at him. "I'm pregnant."

"Reese," Steven said. Not a question. Not an accusation. Only a statement of fact. An accepted, expected, statement of fact.

Wendy nodded.

Steven smiled. "You know, if you had told me something like that a month ago, I think I would have fainted."

Wendy still didn't look up. She seemed like such a little girl right now, Steven thought, curled up in her chair.

"But you're not upset now?" she asked.

Steven sat down on the arm of the chair. He held both of Wendy's hands.

"It was very important to John-John that you both were to escape from the *pa*," Steven said. "This means that a part of him did."

"But what should I do, Daddy?"

"First of all, look at me," Steven said. She did, and he hugged her with all the love that he had to give her. "What you should do is to keep your baby and have your baby and love your baby so it will grow up and have babies of its own."

"But . . . but how can I? John-John said . . . John-John said that everything was coming to an end."

Steven looked into his daughter's eyes. "For us maybe. That's one way to look at it. But for John-John . . . for John-John, this is when everything begins."

"I don't understand," Wendy said. "I don't understand so much of this. John-John is dead."

Steven shook his head and placed his hand softly on his daughter's stomach, trying to feel the power that grew there, the life that would live forever.

"No, he's not, baby," Steven said softly, with pride and with love. "He hasn't even been born."

DARGAVILLE,
NEW ZEALAND

END QUATERNARY EVENT: T—17h 24min

They traveled only in the early morning now and in the late afternoon and at night. Whether even those times were still safe, Steven wasn't sure because the Daihatsu camper's radio had picked up nothing but static since the night they had rented it in Christchurch. Even the news in the local papers was days late, even older with the breakdown of satellite communications, and could give them no help. Some of the smaller papers still carried stories of the sightings in North America.

Steven drove slowly along the smoothly finished two-lane highway that ran along the western bank of the Wairoa. The steep cliffs to the left were softly rounded, splotched with the green of small tenacious plants. But the towering kauri trees, as tall as any redwood, were yellow-leaved or barren, unable to resist the day's combined onslaught of ultraviolet and whatever else it was that streaked through the air like a shimmering curtain of incandescent dust. It was not just the sun that attacked them.

"You should have gotten out of the system," John-John had said. But the local papers gave no clues about what fell upon them now. Steven drove north in the shadows of the tall cliffs.

The road came to a sweeping curve to the west. The town was half a mile ahead, across the water. Steven pulled off to the left, stepped out of the camper, brought the binoculars to his eyes.

"Is that it?" Wendy asked. She was subdued, in discomfort. Sleeping during the day, her morning sickness came in the late afternoon now.

Steven scanned the town in the compressed perspective of the binoculars. The corrugated tin roofs painted bright red were there as they had been in the brochures and travel books—a traditional New Zealand style. The spire of the church was familiar, along with the building he thought was the town hall and the river that flowed past. All had been in John-John's book. He thought. He prayed. Dargaville. Population of thirty-five thousand of which fewer than one percent would survive. It could only be a matter of days now. Perhaps even hours.

"I think so," Steven said. There could be no other option if it weren't. Only in one place would there be survivors.

Someone approached on a small red Vespa. He was a Maori, tall, his skin rich brown, his dark hair long and parted in the middle.

The Maori smiled as he rolled to a stop beside the camper.

"Do you like the look of our little town?" he asked. His dark eyes sparkled. Steven wondered where this man's genes would be a million years from then.

"I think so," Steven said.

"Have you been here before?" the man asked. He turned to watch the last direct rays of sun capture the brilliant white of the buildings behind him, across the water.

Steven shook his head. "No," he said.

The Maori turned back to Steven. "Have you seen it before, then?"

"I think so," Steven said. "In a . . . book."

"Like looking through a window, those books are, wouldn't you say?"

"Very much so," Steven agreed.

The man smiled at Wendy in the passenger seat. He held out his hand to Steven. "You've come to the right place. This is the *marae* you're looking for. My name is Bob," he said. "Welcome."

Steven shook his hand, feeling the relief flood through himself. "My name is Steven," he said. "And this is my daughter—"

"Wendy," the man said with a smile. "I've seen her picture in the book. We've been expecting you."

TUESDAY, AUGUST 28, 22:20 NZT

Wendy was surprised that when they finally arrived and met the others who had gathered there, no one knew why it was to be Dargaville. That New Zealand was important to the future, everyone agreed. The Maori tongue still existed in some form among John-John and his people. Dargaville was the *marae*, the meeting place of the survivors to be. The babies had been kept in the *kohanga reo*, the nursery school of the Maori, where they and the drones had been taught by the light that teaches.

And no one knew why, but all were frightened to guess, why their craft, their base, and the place to which the future humans had owed their allegiance and their lives, was the *pa*.

The fort.

A handful of the survivors-to-be talked about it that night when they had gathered in the Kauri House Lodge. "They were soldiers," Steven said. "Not just the tall ones with the guns, but all of them. Specially bred for a single purpose. No reproductive organs. That worked, at least. Brains that functioned with only an outermost layer for intellect, none of the deeper structures of emotion."

"Small to save resources."

"Locked into place in the bodies of children, never to grow old."

"And they won their war, and there was no one to come home to," Steven said.

"So they came back for us," an Oriental woman said.

"Some of us," another man added.

"Some of us," Steven agreed. "To repopulate their world. To give their victory meaning. Taking the people whom the time line wouldn't miss. The genes that had not survived."

"And while they were here," a young pregnant woman in a flowered dress said in a voice of wonder, "they looked for their ancestors."

"Who wouldn't?" Wendy said. She held her hands over her stomach, straining for the day she would feel Reese quicken there.

"And my connection," said the woman, "told me that they couldn't find all of them. They didn't exist. Wouldn't exist."

"Unless," said a black man with a Brooklyn accent, "they created them."

"Wouldn't that be a paradox?" Steven asked.

"This is their past," the young woman said, cupping her hands over a swollen belly which Wendy regarded in awe. *That will happen to me*, she thought. "It had already happened," the woman continued. "If they *didn't* make it happen, that would have been the paradox."

"According to John-John and the other connections," Wendy said, understanding.

"But not according to the devices that do things," Steven said. "That was what the connections fought against. They knew they had to create a paradox to avoid a paradox. The devices didn't understand."

"Do we understand?" Wendy asked the survivors-to-be.

The Oriental woman smiled at her, cuddled a sleeping child in her lap. "In a few days," she said softly, not to wake it, "one way or another, we will."

TUESDAY, AUGUST 28, 23:55 NZT

Wendy walked out along a narrow path behind the hotel. There was a small park away from the streetlights, and she sat down on a bench there, wrapped her arms around herself, and stared up at the shifting red and green of the blazing aurora australis. Everyone said they had never seen it so close or so brilliant. The Maori said things were going to happen.

Steven joined her. Sat beside her. Watched the night with her in silence.

A dark figure walked up to them. It was Bob.

"I was told to give this to you," he said and held out his hand to Wendy. "Your connection, John-John, wanted you to have it."

Wendy took the object from him. Despite the darkness, as soon as she touched it she knew what it was.

Cool and small and so precious. Physical memories to be passed from one hand to another. Her grandfather's watch, taken from the Tiffany box in her bedroom, thousands of miles away.

"How . . . ?" she asked.

Bob shrugged. "Transference and placement? I do not have the words for it," he laughed. "I became very sick of that phrase."

"Why was Wendy's picture in the book?" Steven asked. "Why didn't John-John show it to me?"

Bob sat down on the bench beside them, stared up at the shimmering night sky, the mysteries in the darkness behind the light.

"To avoid paradox, I suppose. You had to come here because you chose to come here. Not because he made you come."

"A fine line," Steven said, the aurora painting his face as it suddenly flared with a brilliance that made him close his eyes.

Wendy squinted at the display and wondered what the dawn would be like. What had happened on the other side of the world just now.

"He was confused," Bob said. "Just a child doing the best that he could." He leaned forward and turned to Wendy. "There was a woman in Africa a half million years ago, and of all the hundreds of people that must have lived at her time, hers is the only line that has survived to our present. All of us in this world—me, you, the people back in the hotel—we are all her descendants. There is a living legacy from that woman's cells that lives in us all.

"For John-John's people, you are that woman, Wendy. Our children will survive; they will struggle and join and have children of their own. But millions of years from now, when the people who live then look into their own cells, they will find a part of you in everyone. That is why your picture was in their book, alone among all others. You are their mother, Wendy. They are all your children."

Wendy squeezed the watch in her hand. "Couldn't they have helped us more?" she asked. "Couldn't they have given us more?"

"What more do we need, Wendy? They have given us what we have always had. All we can ever ask for. All there ever need be—hope."

Wendy looked back to the sky. She held her father's hand. Held her grandfather's watch as he had held it, as her father had held it, as her children would hold it. All her children.

The stars burned through the aurora. Something hid among them even now, she knew. *Is there intelligent life on other worlds?* her father had asked. *Not anymore*, her child had answered. *We won.*

Something hid there. But her children would be victorious. Her children would live with hope.

Wendy Gilmour held her father's hand. Held her grandfather's memory. Held the new life within her. The unbroken cord that bound them all.

And the stars held no mysteries for her.

And the night was dark no longer.

And for the first time in a long time, she was not afraid.

ABOUT THE AUTHOR

Garfield Reeves-Stevens is a Canadian writer whose previous novels are *Bloodshift, Dreamland,* and *Children of the Shroud.* With his wife Judith, he is coauthor of the *Science Around Me* series of textbooks for children and of the novel *Star Trek: Memory Prime.* They live in Los Angeles.

Nighteyes took our fascination with UFOs to its ultimate. Now Garfield Reeves-Stevens turns his talents to a *new* suspense thriller set on the cutting edge of science—in the bizarre, chaotic world of subatomic particles and elemental energies.

What little we understand of quantum physics assures us of one thing: that whoever first penetrates the secret of the quantum will harness power undreamed of. The invisible bonds within every atom are laden with energy—energy that can supply our needs for all time . . . or destroy us utterly.

The main character of QUANTUM KILL is brilliant physicist Anthony Cross, the youngest Nobel Prize-winner ever. He is the first scientist with an *intuitive* grasp of quantum physics—the bewildering world where cause and effect break down, matter and energy are created from nothing, and the outcome of experiments depends on whether or not an observer is present.

But the brilliant scientist is also a brutal serial killer. For Anthony Cross has discovered that the transition between life and death fuels his thought processes—that only by committing a savage murder can he gain the inspiration to extend his knowledge. He needs just one more breakthrough, and the power of the quantum will be his. . . .

Here is an excerpt from QUANTUM KILL, coming later this year from Garfield Reeves-Stevens.

Anthony Cross stepped out of his shower, through his bathroom, and into his office, leaving dark footsteps in the light gray carpet. The windows that looked onto his private terrace and the ocean were covered with matching gray vertical blinds. It was still night outside, but the SHARP facility knew no time constraints. Every hour of every day, it served its master.

Cross folded a thick white towel around his waist and used the smaller towel around his shoulders to dry his hair. He felt awake and alive and inspired. "How long?" he asked enthusiastically.

Rich Daystrom looked up from the four pages of notes and drawings arranged on Cross's desk and rubbed at his eyes, still half-closed and full of sleep. His usually rich black skin had taken on a chalky undertone. Cross recognized it as exhaustion, something he had seen in most of the workers at the facility from time to time. But Daystrom was young and the infirmary by the main entrance had doses of B12 and smelling salts, even amphetamines if they became necessary to meet a deadline, so Cross didn't worry about pushing the man. Besides, he was a programmer. He had a cot in his office. He was used to it.

Daystrom glanced at the notes again: ballpoint pen, scrawled down so rapidly that it seemed only the first half of each word or string of numbers had been inscribed before the next had begun. "I could breadboard it in a day or so—"

"How many hours?" Cross asked. "We've got the D-RAMS in stock. I checked. How many hours to put it together?"

Daystrom frowned at the diagrams. "Eight, maybe ten."

"But . . . ?" Cross prompted, hearing the unspoken word in Daystrom's answer. Why couldn't anyone here ever have a simple conversation, give a simple answer?

"Well first," Daystrom answered, tapping out his points with one of the many pens from his stuffed breast pocket, "I could simulate this chip array on the Cray in about half that time. And second, it won't work."

Cross's mouth tightened. Daystrom's eyes widened.

"Sorry, Dr. Cross, that came out the wrong way," he said rapidly, holding his hands up in apology. "I meant to say I'm not quite sure exactly what this array is supposed to accomplish."

"It's all there on the diagrams," Cross said icily.

"Right, right," Daystrom said in defeat. He looked back at the half-formed sketches, talking himself through some understanding of what Cross's concept was. "It's a timing array, I can see that. An elegant one, too. Very efficient layout. Cascaded parallel processors, each level subdividing the internal clock signal of the one above it."

"So what's the problem, Rich?" Cross leaned across his desk, supporting himself on tented fingers. His nails were perfectly clean now, even arcs of pure white at each tip, contrasting starkly with the black leather surface of the desk. Other than the four sheets of paper, a high-intensity lamp, and a scattering of perfect hemispheres of liquid dripping from Cross's wet hair, there was nothing on the desk. There was little Cross needed for His Work that could be left out in view for strangers.

"I don't have a problem with it, Doc, it's just that at about the fourth level of subdivision of the time signal here, I believe these specs exceed the operational capabilities of the computer chips we have in stores. Or, uh . . ."

"Go on."

"Or the capabilities of any chip currently being manufactured," Daystrom concluded, looking away.

Cross laughed and the programmer jumped.

"Is that all it is, Rich? Boy oh boy, I thought I had gone and done something dumb the way you were moping over those plans." Cross made up his mind to fire Daystrom as head of computer operations as soon as Covington could locate a replacement. SHARP needed people with vision. People who could see beyond.

Cross came around the desk and stood beside Daystrom. "Look at page three, Rich. Second diagram."

Daystrom ran his finger along it. "Oh yeah, the offset. I think I'm going to have to work around this somehow because it will probably set up interference across this band here and—"

Cross successfully fought to control his rage, displayed no outside evidence. "Rich, it's supposed to create interference. That's why the alternating levels are offset. Each chip will double the resolution of the timing signal from the one above."

Daystrom was hesitant. "Well, yeah, in theory the math will work out. You'll keep doubling the sensitivity and all. But really, Dr. Cross, these chips can't operate faster than a certain megahertz. I can wire them up this way, have them feed signals to each other this way, but it'll be like blowing up a photograph past the resolution of the grain. By this level here, when the operational capabilities of the chips are exceeded, you'll just be generating noise."

Cross took a deep breath. "Rich, the operating

capabilities of these chips are determined from testing averages, aren't they?" Daystrom nodded. "And that means some chips operate at a slightly lower efficiency, and some at a slightly higher efficiency—"

"Yeah, but the burned-in software determines the precise clock rate of each chip. That's an industry standard."

Cross stepped back from the desk, afraid to remain within arms' reach of the programmer. There were limits, after all, to what even SHARP's master could get away with.

"This is an *advanced* research facility, Rich. We're not interested in 'standard' here. We're interested in going beyond the standard. We're interested in exceeding *everything* that's gone before. Isn't that right, Rich?"

"Well, yes, sir, but—" Rich began to turn around to look at Cross.

"Stay where you are, Rich." Cross's words were a command. He couldn't let Daystrom see him this way, see what was crawling to the surface. The man was being an obstinate fool. A moron. A mindless nigger shit cocksucking— "Look at the diagrams, Rich. Carefully, carefully. And understand them. Understand that I wouldn't ask you to do anything foolish with your time. . . ." Clouds of blood erupted before Cross's vision. He saw the scalpel enter the cat's stomach, the fur and skin and muscle layers peeling back as the creature screeched and struggled against the wire, spraying blood, joining the pattern, caught in the transition. "You are a valuable member of the team here, Rich." He saw the blood spurt from Daystrom's eyes as his fingers gouged into them, teaching the interfering apefaced shitsucker his lesson, *the* lesson of all time. "And I think that you'll see if you just wire everything up the way I . . . suggest there, then the type of signal the array will produce will be fairly obvious and guess what, Rich, that's exactly the kind of signal I want it to produce." Cross added a small happy chuckle, tasting the flesh of the programmer in his vision, seeing the copper twist and bind and . . .

"But you won't get any sort of coherent signal at all," Daystrom protested.

The programmer turned his head a fraction of an inch and heard Cross make a sound like a small, high-pitched groan. Fortunately, there was something in that sound alone that stopped Daystrom from turning all the way around. He turned back to look at the diagrams.

With a sigh, Cross said, "The diagrams, Rich, please just look at the diagrams. And believe me when I say that of all the billions of offsets and timing interference signals that array will produce each second, on average, *on average*, Rich, one or two of them will succeed. One or two absolutely precise timing signals every couple of seconds of operation, Rich, that's all I need. On average."

"Well, okay," Daystrom said. "I can see how this might work like that—"

Cross sighed, so deeply, so gratefully. "Oh, thank you, Rich. Thank you for saying that. Now will you build it for me?" The decision had already been made as far as Cross was concerned. One more provocation on Daystrom's part and he would be taken apart and laid out like a grandfather clock, each shining well-oiled part and gear in precise alignment, skin stretched out over spikes and hooks and—

"Oh, I can build it for you, Doc. I don't have any problem with that."

Cross sighed and stepped back to the desk. "I'm glad

to hear you say that, Rich. For a few seconds there, you made me feel as if I were asking you to do something insane."

"Oh, not you, Dr. Cross."

"No, Rich. Not me."

A large white paw reached up past the side of the table, landed on the bloody mass of Cassie Riley's face, then slowly started to drag it over the edge. At the last second, Detective Nogura placed a finger on the photo and kept it from slipping off to the floor. The paw stayed in place for a moment, then two pointed black ears and a spray of thick white eyebrow whiskers appeared above the table, followed by two curious green eyes.

Nogura smiled evilly. "Boo!"

The cat's ears flattened and it hit the kitchen floor with a thud that rattled dishes on the counter. Duvall turned away from her coffeemaker by the sink. "What was all that about?"

Nogura settled back in his chair, going eye to eye with the black-and-white cat as it glared at him from under the dining room table in the next room. "Your cat wants to get involved in police work."

Duvall laughed, pouring fresh coffee into two mugs. "My cat wants to lick the emulsion on those photographs."

Nogura thought it was funny. "That would be a hard one to explain to the DA. 'What are these marks on the evidence, Detective?' 'Cat spit, ma'am.' "

Duvall laughed again as she returned to the table that was covered with the paperwork and photographs generated by the murders of Cassie Riley and Amanda Frost, the sometime hooker found in unit eight. Duvall cleared two spaces to put down the mugs she carried.

The silence after the laughter lasted a few seconds too long.

"Nuke . . ."

"Yeah, I know. 'Thank you for sharing this with me.'"

"Catch fire, Nuke."

Nogura smiled. "That was my second guess." Then his expression became unreadable, the expression detectives practised for use during interrogations, when they couldn't risk giving up any information to their prisoners, however subtle. "I've been thinking, though, maybe we should be partners. I don't think Erhlenmeyer would mind putting it through."

Duval was puzzled. "What about Ernie?" Nuke Nogura and his vacationing partner, Ernie Burton, had been partners for more than a year. They had a good record with a solid conviction rate and Duvall hadn't heard any talk about trouble.

"Ernie's bored. Wants to get into Narcotics." Nogura reached for his coffee mug. "He watches too much television. They assign anyone to you yet?"

Duvall shook her head, arranging the photos of the two bodies side by side, matching content and angles. Seen quickly, the two sets of photographs might be mistaken as being images of the same victim. "I gave up asking about a new partner two months ago. Guess Erhlenmeyer won't do anything more about it until I'm back on duty."

Nogura cleared away some typewritten forms, giving Duvall extra room for her comparison of the photographs. "Heard you turned down a couple that he offered."

"It wasn't like that," Duvall said. Though it had been. But what else could she say? That the department had wanted to pair her with one or the other of two detectives who had reps for getting "involved" with their female partners? Erhlenmeyer had stopped both assignments when she had informally indicated she might feel incompatible with either choice. As far as Erhlenmeyer was concerned, the longer Duvall went without a partner, the harder hit her arrest record would be and the more oppressive her caseload would become. So what?

"So, what about it?" Nogura asked, breaking her out of her reverie. "You and me?"

Duvall considered the proposition. Nogura didn't carry around any stories of colossal screw-ups. Definitely good in a fight. And though Duvall was sorry she had to make it part of her overall judgment, Nogura did have his girlfriend's photo prominently displayed in his office. Maybe he'd be safe.

"What's taking so long?" Nogura protested her silence. "I mean, look at this stuff here," he gestured to the table and the grotesque material upon it. "We're practically partners on this one, aren't we? Even if I am on my own time." He played a final card. "I could've got into a shitpot of trouble if Seabrook or Erhlenmeyer had caught me taking this stuff."

"I know, Nuke. And I appreciate it."

Nogura shook his head in frustration. "Yeah, I'll try you again when you're back from Hawaii. Maybe you'll be in a better mood."

Duvall decided it was time to say it out loud, the decision she had made driving home from the motel last night. The decision she hadn't been able to tell to Jesse when he had called this morning. With this new case, even if it wasn't official, the panic of the empty days had fled, and so had her need for reconcilement.

"I'm not going to Hawaii, Nuke." Saying it had made it real and she felt better.

"Why not?" But Nogura read the answer in her eyes. "Because of this?"

Duvall nodded, more determined than ever. "You just spent the last hour going over this stuff, too. What would you do?"

"Go to Seabrook. Tell him what you think's going on." Nogura was actually angry.

"And what if he's part of it?" There, that had made that element of her suspicions real, too.

Nogura's mouth opened, closed, opened again. "*Joe*! Taking evidence from the scene? Not his style. Forget it."

Duvall dug through the photos again. "Nobody's taking evidence from the scene, Nuke. That's what makes all of this so bad. Somebody's taking it *after* it's tagged and bagged. See here?" She pointed to photo 27 from the Riley kitchen.

"Yeah, yeah," Nuke conceded. "The surgical gloves you say you saw."

"Did see. And they were rolled up in this mess of bloody pads."

"I know. And the pads are in an evidence bag."

"And the gloves aren't. Somebody opened the bag up, pulled out the gloves, sealed it up again. After everything was admitted into custody."

Nogura sighed. "I thought this sort of conspiracy shit went out in the seventies."

"I'm not saying it has to be a conspiracy, Nuke. Could just be one guy paying off a mob connection or something. Who knows? But even if it is one guy, that guy . . . or woman . . . is a cop. Has to be, to have access to evidence."

Nogura pushed aside the Riley photos and pointed to the gridded placement shots from the motel room.

"But you can't say that anything's missing from these shots of the second murder, can you? Seabrook had all sorts of close-ups done. Sort of like he listened to what you said about the gloves and made sure it couldn't happen again. If it had happened in the first place. Seabrook's covering every angle. If he's guilty, why's he being so careful?"

"Throw us off track?" Duvall was reaching and she knew it.

Nogura knew it, too. "Try again, Katherine."

"Okay, but look at the evidence list from the motel room. Compare it to the list from the Riley apartment." She pushed both out in front of Nogura. The Riley list was longer.

"Yeah, so?"

"Yeah, so," Duvall said, running her fingers along both lists, reading them upside down though she already knew what each said. "At the Riley apartment, we found scalpels, a half-used roll of adhesive tape, the empty box the gauze pads came from, surgical scissors and . . . these brain probe things, a jar of surgical sealant. Even a squeeze bottle to hose down the blood. You get it? These are the killer's tools. Throwaway stuff. Probably untraceable. But in the motel room, we got none of it except for some gauze pads. Somebody had already gone in and cleaned it up."

Nogura wasn't impressed. "Sorry, Kate. We've seen that kind of thing before. In the Riley apartment, the killer got spooked. Had to leave before he could clean up. But in the motel, he had time and was able to take everything with him."

Duvall's words started coming faster as she felt her excitement build. The details all fit if only Nogura would open his eyes. She pulled out other forms, spread them over the staring emptied heads of Riley and Frost. "Look at the time of death versus time of the anonymous calls for both women. At least four hours' difference. The killer had the same amount of time in each place. In fact, the four-hour delay before calling in a tip might be part of his pattern. Maybe he lives four hours away from the areas where the murders were committed. Maybe—"

Nogura reached across the table and took Duvall's hands to stop her from digging out even more forms and sheets and photos. "Pull back, Kate. You're jumping too far ahead. Stay with what we can know." He let go and sat back again.

Duvall nodded. She sat back and took a deep breath. Maybe it was time to go all the way.

"How do you draw the line?" she asked. "When you're making a conclusion. Combining two facts to make a supposition. How do you know the difference between a . . . logical inference and a . . . leap of faith?"

"Why do you think that there's a difference?" Nogura slumped in his chair, resting his chin in his hand.

"If the facts are correct, then the inference is usually right. The other can be wrong."

"A good detective's leap of faith *is* a logical inference. Experience makes the difference." He smiled at her, wary. "This shit is too philosophical for cops, Kate. What're you getting at?"

"What we know," Duvall answered enigmatically, then decided it was time.

Nogura looked thoughtful, finding the meaning behind her words. "You mean that you know something that isn't in these reports? Not like the gloves, but something definite?"

Duvall smiled as she nodded. Maybe he'd end up being her partner after all. "Do you remember the name Charis Neale in all of this?" She gestured to the material on the table.

Nogura closed his eyes and his face returned to a neutral expression. "Riley's boss, right? Showed up at the apartment the night of the murder." He opened his eyes again. "It's in Seabrook's first report and then there was a follow-up interview at her place of business."

Duvall heard the tension creeping into her own voice, despite herself. "So, was it a coincidence that Neale showed up at Riley's apartment that night?"

Nogura's sudden change of expression showed he could see she was building to something but that he didn't know what. "Seabrook put in his report that Riley had missed a few days at work and that Neale was coming by to fire her. Sounds sort of reasonable, doesn't it?"

"Sure," Duvall agreed. "Now why do you suppose Neale was outside the motel last night when Amanda Frost's body was found?"

Nogura frowned. "Are you serious?"

"Right across the street from the driveway entrance. I got a perfect picture of her right here." Duvall tapped a finger at the side of her head. The legendary eye.

"Did you tell anyone?" The wary look came back to Nogura's face.

"Seabrook had already shut me out and . . . right then . . . I didn't know how far I could push anything." She settled back in her chair. Everything was on the table now.

"What do you know about Neale?" Now Nogura took Duvall seriously. He looked worried.

"She was at both scenes. She was Riley's boss. That's it."

"Where was it they worked?" Nogura started flipping through the forms, looking for Charis Neale's interview record.

"Some company out by Pepperdine in Malibu," Duvall said. "A research company. Science stuff."

Nogura didn't look up, still digging. "The Hughes aerospace set-up?" he suggested.

"No." Duvall stared up at the ceiling, trying to call up the name of the place Neale worked.

"Here it is," Nogura said, pulling out the pale pink interview report with Neale's name on the top. He skimmed through it. "Not Hughes, Shannon Industries." He rolled his eyes. "Big difference. The Shannon Facility for Advanced Research in Physics. Yawn."

"SHARP," Duvall said suddenly, remembering at last.

*　　*　　*

It is time for Anthony Cross to kill again. Don't miss QUANTUM KILL, the gripping voyage into brilliance and madness by Garfield Reeves-Stevens.

"There is no question in my mind that **When Gravity Fails** was the best science fiction novel of its year. There is no question in my mind that **A Fire in the Sun** is even better."

—Mike Resnick, author of **Ivory**

The Masterworks of
George Alec Effinger
WHEN GRAVITY FAILS

A finalist for the Hugo and Nebula Awards for Best Novel of 1987. Ghetto boss Friedlander Bey hires street hustler Marid Audran to stop a madman. But first Audran must undergo the most sophisticated of surgical implants in order to carry out his job: to stalk—and stop—this killer, whose bootlegged personality implants give him the powers of every psychopath since the beginning of time.

"A terrific story—fast, cool, clever, beautifully written, absolutely authoritative. A kind of cyberpunk Raymond Chandler book with dashes of Roger Zelazny, Ian Fleming and Scheherazade—but altogether original . . . I loved it."

—Robert Silverberg

A FIRE IN THE SUN

Marid Audran finds himself on the other side of the law as a policeman, hunting for the power behind brutal killings and rising chaos erupting in the Budayeen, power that may well be stemming from Abu Adil, the only man in the Budayeen whose influence rivals that of Friedlander Bey.

"Effinger's prose is terse, direct, vivid and often laced with an enchanting sense of humor."
—*The Providence Sunday Journal*

On sale now wherever Bantam Spectra books are sold.

And coming in July, 1990:
The Exile Kiss

**A Doubleday Foundation Hardcover
and Trade Paperback**

Astronaut Edward Gibson has traveled 34.5 million miles in space. With his stunning debut novel he returns to space and takes his readers along for the ride. . . .

REACH
Edward Gibson

"[Reach] fascinates not only with its futuristic space-adventure plot but with its authoritative, fully enthralling evocation of what space travel is really like. An inspiring achievement."

—*Kirkus Reviews*

Edward Gibson brings to his extraordinary novel of outer space a vision that could only have been created by one who has experienced space's vast, quiet darkness. It is the story of *Wayfarer Two*, a space expedition launched in search of its predecessor, *Wayfarer One*, mysteriously lost beyond the edge of the solar system. Once they arrive at their destination, mission head Jake Ryder and his crew encounter a power that is overwhelming, terrifying in its immensity, a power beyond anything humanity had ever conceived of before.

"Ed Gibson was an astronaut with the Right Stuff. It's apparent that as an author he still has the Right Stuff. In most books I've read the astronauts think and talk like Hollywood actors. Not so here. It's a pleasure to find characters who think and act like real astronauts."

—Alan Bean, *Apollo 12* and *Skylab 2* astronaut

On sale now wherever Bantam Spectra Books are sold

PHILIP JOSÉ FARMER'S

THE DUNGEON

☐ 27346 **BLACK TOWER:**
Dungeon #1 *Richard Lupoff* $3.95

☐ 27640 **THE DARK ABYSS:**
Dungeon #2 *Bruce Coville* $3.95

☐ 27958 **VALLEY OF THUNDER:**
Dungeon #3 *Charles de Lint* $3.95

☐ 28185 **THE LAKE OF FIRE:**
Dungeon #4 *Robin Bailey* $3.95

☐ 28338 **THE HIDDEN CITY:**
Dungeon #5 *Charles de Lint* $3.95

Look for them at your bookstore or use this page to order: